Madison Keith Ghost Stories
Fatal Cut
Shallow Water
Unholy Child

ALSO BY CATHRYN GRANT

MADISON KEITH GHOST STORIES VOLUME ONE

CATHRYN GRANT

ABOUT MADISON KEITH

Both the living and the dead like to reveal their secrets to Madison. As the administrative assistant in the basement office of a suburban church, she gets plenty of opportunity to hear from both. Through it all, Madison offers up a steady stream of opinions on everything from the subject of religion and ghosts to finding a soul mate.

MADISON KEITH GHOST STORY COLLECTIONS

VOLUME 1
   Fatal Cut, Shallow Water, Unholy Child

VOLUME 2
   Stone Cold, Deadly Streets, Lonely Ghosts

VOLUME 3
   Last Chance, Eaten Alive, Empty Home

VOLUME 4
   Ugly Truth, Beloved Ghosts

FATAL CUT

A Suburban Noir Ghost Story

By
Cathryn Grant

Published by D2C Perspectives

CHAPTER 1

*T*HE FIRST TIME I walked into the office of Central Avenue Church, I knew they needed me as much as I needed them. What I didn't know was that I would find a dead body within six weeks, but by the time that happened, I already loved my job. I wasn't inclined to look for another just because of one corpse surrounded by a large, bright red lake of blood, behind the fellowship hall. Actually, the moment I found that body, I knew who had killed the guy, but I wasn't sure the police would see it that way, being all caught up in forensics and proper procedure as they are. Procedures always seem to obscure things, in my view.

I don't mean to sound cold, calling it a corpse, calling him a corpse. But I'm just saying it like it is. After all, once that person you cared about is gone, that's all it is – a corpse. They're off somewhere else. Who knows where that place actually is, physically speaking, but they surely aren't in that body anymore.

Working in a church might not have been the best career move in one sense because it's a small, claustrophobic world, especially after working for a global corporation. There's no room for advancement, and there's only slightly more opportunity to meet people, especially guys, which is something I think about, but try not to obsess over. When it happens, it happens. But I wanted to be in a job where I felt needed, and I knew the minute I talked to Pastor Joe that they needed me. I'm not the kind of girl anyone would ever expect to see working in a church, but even though I don't look like eye candy, maybe it doesn't matter. Churches probably aren't looking for that sort of image like corporations are. The reason you might not expect to find someone like me in a church office is because I have my various tattoos, all more or less discreet, and my cascade of hoops down each earlobe, that you don't typically see on church-goers. At least not on suburban church-goers. Growing up, I never went to church. My mom worshipped the earth and raised me all vegan and whatnot, and my dad just loved my mom and said, whatever you think is best, sweetie.

Even though Pastor Joe said right away that he wanted to hire me, the youth minister did not like me from the start. I could tell from the way she folded her lips together as she considered the tattoo peeking out of my sleeve.

I know you're thinking about that corpse, and I'll get back to that eventually, but I wanted to introduce myself. I have a name that's no name – Madison Keith. My first name is after a city where I've never lived, in a state where I've never been. My last name is a guy's first name, and since you can't tell by my name that I'm female, sometimes solicitors and other strangers call me Keith. I was born on January 31st, under the sign of Aquarius, which means I'm outgoing and amiable. Aquarians are also considered eccentric at times. We can live on many mental levels, which is why I'm so intuitive. Apparently, all that might be changing now that they've discovered the thirteenth sign of the Zodiac. How unlucky is that? Anyway, at twenty-seven, I already know who I am and what my sign is, and I'm not changing it for anyone.

There's so much to tell here, I'm not really sure where to start. You probably want to hear about the corpse, but I also should tell you how I came to be working in a church and how I kind of knew how the corpse got there before the police even arrived on the scene. And you need to know a little about me to understand how I might grasp the inside scoop on something like that. I promise not to tell you my whole life story, not yet. Only the details you need, in order to understand how I knew the reason why a man's life had ended with murder.

I've always been able to see things other people can't. Don't take that in a mystical sense, that I have second sight or that I work with crystal balls and Ouija boards and cards and talk to the dead. Except that bit about talking to the dead. I don't talk to them in any real way, like someone who conducts a séance, but I do have a way of seeing into people's souls and their minds, and I know what they're feeling. In the end, that can kind of seem like talking to the dead, because you know what was in their soul before they left.

Seeing what other people can't comes from a lot of things in my background. My mother, for one thing. And growing up by myself. I was an only child. I was homeschooled. I lived in an old cottage built in the 1920s that was pure white inside and out, with pale green trim around the windows and doors. My parents kept it freshly painted. They liked things empty, and so my bedroom had nothing but a bed and a tiny writing desk with thin legs from an antique store. There was an old chair that my mother let me paint glossy purple. I had a bookcase in my closet and a little shelf over my bed. That's it. We grew organic vegetables and didn't eat meat and didn't have a TV or a computer. Are you already seeing how I might look at the world differently from most females my age? Also, I talk a lot. I'm very chatty, and I don't censor much of what I say, I just let what's in my head spill out, and that makes people feel as if they can also say whatever is on their minds.

When I finally went to real classrooms in high school, I wasn't used to being around many kids my age. We'd had some neighbor kids, but they were in school during the day and in sports after that, so I was alone most of the time until I was a teenager. It's not like I looked different on the outside. I wore jeans or skirts, and shrunken t-shirts like the other girls. I had long hair, I still do. Lots of them wore makeup and I didn't, but otherwise, I fit in if you saw us standing on the front lawn of the school on a spring afternoon with the sun warming the tops of our heads, making us happy to be alive. But when they started talking, oh boy. I couldn't keep up with their comments about TV shows and music and movies and stuff I never heard of. So I listened. I restrained my chatty self and let them talk. It was pleasant, really. Their words flowed over my face the same way the air flowed over our skin during May.

Once in a while, I would be alone with one of the girls at my school and I would be my normal self. I would talk on about our garden and the book I was reading and how I liked the big, sweeping lawn at the front of our high school. How impressed I was with the school's stately appearance – columns and fifteen steps up to front doors that were twenty feet high or more. The other girl, whoever she was at the time, would then start talking. She would tell me I was different, and that I wasn't absorbed with the same things as the other girls. And then she would tell me what she was thinking – that she hadn't liked this particular movie, or didn't understand why everyone thought that band was so good. And soon I realized that what people said in a group situation was not always what they really thought.

I also see things that other people miss because I meditate. When you meditate, your mind gets quiet and thoughts that you didn't know were out there in the ether can float into your head. I don't know where they come from, of course, who knows where any thoughts come from. But I think when you get your brain to quiet down from the constant chattering that goes on day after day, week after week, year after year, the mind gets cleared out. It's the same as my parents' cleared-out house. When your brain is all clogged up with what you're going to do this afternoon, and what you have to pick up at the store, and maybe you have a headache a little bit, and you're kind of tired and wondering if you can go to bed early tonight, and you're thinking about how that guy cut you off when you were patiently waiting for a parking spot, and how you're pissed off that you had to pay taxes instead of getting a refund last year and that better not happen this year, you can see how it kind of clogs you up. I see things most people don't because I take some time every day to clear out all the junk and let in the fresh air. When I explained that concept to the one and only boyfriend I had in my life, he said, "That must be why you're such an airhead." That was the end of that.

Before I came to Central Avenue Church, I was working at a Silicon Valley high-tech company. It was a good job and paid quite well, but I felt like I never saw the light of day. My cubicle was on an interior hallway, and the only time I glimpsed the outside was when I went into my boss's office which had windows on two walls, or walked past a window on my way to the restroom. At lunchtime, I would go outside to a bench near the fountain that spilled into a round pool with a dark blue tiled bottom. I listened to the steadily splashing water and felt the quietness of the grass and the palm trees, but I didn't like being locked up in that building the rest of the day. And I do mean locked up. You couldn't go from one building to another without passing your badge through a device to unlock the door. A uniformed guard sat in every lobby and security trucks patrolled the parking lots. I know it's a scary world out there – shootings, and maybe they were worried about people walking in and seeing all their PowerPoint slides that outlined their plans for the next three years, but still.

I started looking on monster.com for jobs and I found this one. Very twenty-first century for this church to be using the internet to find an administrative assistant. That impressed me right away. Even though I didn't grow up with a computer, I have one now. I like computers and I love going on the internet. I like all the things you can find out. I have a laptop, a Mac, so I can go outside and enjoy the sunshine while I keep in touch with the whole world right in front of my eyes. It's amazing.

Pastor Joe sent me email when he read my resume, and asked me to come in for an interview. It was early April and pouring rain, so I wore a soft, pale gray dress and an almost matching gray sweater and black tights and boots. I left my hair down so I wouldn't call attention to my seven earrings in the right ear and four in my left. I shouldn't have been concerned. Pastor Joe is a cool guy. He met me at the door of the office wearing jeans and a pullover sweater. His hair is black, and he has a mustache and a goatee and doesn't look at all like a preacher. To me, he looked more like a card shark. Not that I've ever met one, but that was my first thought.

During the interview, it became quite clear how much they needed me. Joe seemed like a guy who wanted to unburden himself. He told me a lot of things he probably shouldn't have, like how people come in for counseling and they might be cheating on their spouses, or stealing from their employers, or gambling, or using drugs on the sly. One or two might even be considering helping an elderly mother-in-law die – euthanasia, not murder – even though that kind of help is frowned on by the church. These people are desperate for Pastor Joe to tell them they're not bad people. He mentioned it's hard because he has to keep all this stuff to himself. He can't tell his wife the secrets that are spilled out behind the closed door of his office. It would be a breach of professional ethics. He said when he was in school, training to be a preacher, no one mentioned that part – the unending weight of all those secrets. He's learned to live with it, but he can't have a member of the church sitting in that office, watching this stream of people and their secrets and their burdens progress in and out the doors, and then have them spreading gossip all over the place. "Churches are hotbeds of gossip," he said.

"Isn't gossip considered a sin or something?" I smiled so he wouldn't think I was judging them.

He laughed, but it sounded almost a little bitter. "You're right, but it's the hardest thing for people to avoid. Juicy secrets about others are the lifeblood of some people. You could think of them as emotional vampires."

I nodded, not really sure where he was going with this.

We were sitting in his office. Bookshelves covered three entire walls, from the thin brown carpet up to the off-white ceiling. They were crammed full of books from his high school years, college, and when he was studying at the seminary in New York state. I asked whether he had any books at home. He said the study in his house looked more or less the same as this office. The desk was pine, stained a funny pale yellow color. It consumed the whole corner of the room. He sat behind it with his chair pushed back and his ankle balanced on his knee. The light was dim which made his hair and his beard look darker, ominous. It almost scared me, being alone in that room with him, silence in the outer office because it was a Monday and no one was anywhere around a church on a Monday.

It was supposed to be his day off, but he came in for this interview because he was so anxious to get someone hired. Showing your cards like that, telling the candidate that you're desperate, didn't seem like a smart move to me, but he didn't seem to be aware of how that might come across, which made the slightly scared feeling fade to almost nothing. He was actually a little naïve. At the time, I thought I could see how that might happen, spending most of your life hanging around a church, not noticing the realities of society. How wrong I was about that. After a while, observing the goings on at that church, I realized all the realities of the world were lined up in the pews every Sunday.

He said he'd only been at this church two years. The youth minister had only been there for ten months. Before that, he'd been at a church in New York for seventeen years. He showed me pictures of his four daughters. Looking at all their long, nearly black hair, just like his, and their dark blue eyes, just like his, the ominous feeling completely disappeared. I realized it wasn't something scary at all that I was feeling, but the burden of all those secrets. Years and years of people telling him things they wouldn't tell another soul, hoping he would ease their loneliness, shifting their guilt onto him. That was a lot for one person to carry.

In one corner near a window was a brown plaid sofa and in

front of the desk was a stiff, tan armchair, where I sat. I wondered if all those people coming in with their soul-searing problems and crimes sat in this chair, or on the sofa. He mentioned these crimes repeatedly. I started to wonder what kind of people belonged to this church.

"Why did you quit your last job?" he said. "That's very impulsive, quitting before you have something else lined up."

I tucked my hair behind my ear, forgetting, for a moment, my string of earrings. But he didn't look like he even noticed. "I felt trapped. Locked inside all the time."

"Then why are you looking for a desk job?"

I rested my fingertips on my dress, rubbing it softly, hoping he didn't notice, didn't think I was weird, rubbing my legs. But it helped me think, so I could explain myself clearly. "I like organizing things, and I want to feel like I'm necessary. At TDP I felt like a tiny wire in a computer closet full of machines and cords and plugs and blinking boxes. Half the people I worked with were on the other side of the country, or around the world. I only knew them in email and on the phone. I hate that. After a while, you feel like your life isn't even real, that it's just messages and voices without any flesh and blood people."

He nodded at me and his eyes got wider as if I'd surprised him.

While he was nodding, I considered what my options had been at TDP. In all likelihood, it was only a matter of time before I lost my job anyway. They were always laying people off, delivering flattened white boxes that the ex-employees had to construct to carry out their stuff. Rejected children toddling off to their nice cars, probably worrying about how they would make the payments without those lucrative salaries. That's why I always lived cheaply and saved everything I could. People are dispensable to large companies. Over the few years I worked there, lots of my admin friends got laid off. The company figured managers could book their own conference rooms, do their own expense reports. Having an administrative assistant was a luxury that was increasingly reserved for the guys, and the occasional gal, near the very top of the pyramid.

"Everyone here is very much flesh and blood," said Joe. "There isn't a lot of email. Parishioners will email information for the newsletter each month, but that's about it."

I smiled. It was perfect for me. I was sure he would see, if he hadn't already, that I was exactly what Central Avenue Church required – someone who liked people and wasn't trying to get ahead or take control, but simply wanted to do a good job. Someone who might loosen things up. Since Joe seemed like a somewhat tightly wound guy, I figured the rest of the members might take their cue from him. Trying to be good all the time can be quite exhausting. That might be why he had that crease at the center of his forehead and a tight look around his lower eyelids.

I leaned back and rested my elbows on the chair arms and crossed my legs. I swung my foot and waited for more questions. For several minutes the room was nearly silent. The fluorescent light hummed like a mosquito, and outside I heard raindrops plopping off the overhang, landing on the leaves of the ivy that surrounded the offices and grew up the side of the hill. The church is an odd design, with the sanctuary slightly above street level and this whole basement area with a few separate rooms – the reception area and Joe's office at the front, a conference room, and two other offices built off the sides – and a huge empty space in between. It's not a complete basement, there are windows on two sides, but it's below ground level so you look out at a small incline, and all you can see of people walking past are their feet and lower legs. That's what made the room dim – not only the weak lights, but being more or less below ground like that.

Pastor Joe must have made his decision during those silent moments, because he started outlining more about the job. The hours were shorter than normal, just thirty-five hours a week. After working close to fifty hours a week in my high-tech job, thirty-five hours sounded heavenly, if you don't mind the lame pun. My job, he actually said that, *Your job will include* ... Then he went on to list the various duties – answering the phone and taking messages for him when he was out visiting the elderly and the sick, giving information about activities at the church, as well as taking messages for the youth minister who was mainly responsible for keeping the teenagers entertained and off the streets. He actually said that too – *off the streets.*

They didn't want members of the church or random people in the community who called for help, getting voice mail unless it was after hours. People should get a warm, human voice, even if all they wanted was to find out what time church services were on Sundays. Joe said I'd be surprised at how often non-members contacted the church, not just about services, but desperate to talk to a spiritual person. I guess there are a lot of people in the world who want someone to tell them what to do. And if that person has the trappings of God around them, so much the better.

The responsibilities also included typing up the Sunday flyers listing the worship service agenda and prayer requests and editing the monthly newsletter. I also had some social responsibilities like making visitors feel comfortable, providing coffee, and helping with luncheons for the elderly.

Was it dishonest of me not to let him see that I have all those earrings, as well as vines tattooed around my ankles and down my left arm, and a thread of ladybugs across the back of my neck? I don't think so. He said he wanted someone who wasn't part of the group, and I certainly fit that bill. It wasn't as if I had a pierced lip or had dyed my hair purple. Over time, he never even seemed to notice my bodily decorations. The youth minister sure did though.

While I sat there, he phoned the youth minister, Kate, and said he wanted her to come into the office because he'd found someone he wanted to hire. She said it was her day off. I could hear her voice, kind of screechy, as he held the receiver out from his ear a bit. He informed her that I was a "perfect fit". That made me smile. She said he should have set it up ahead of time and it sounded like he'd already made up his mind anyway, so what difference did it make whether she met me that day?

He hung up the phone and offered me the job. The salary he quoted was much less than I'd been making, but I'd expected that. Quality of life is better than money. I don't want to be one of those people who wakes up when I'm fifty years old and realize I've spent my whole life in a building, my whole life staring at a computer screen, my whole life at work. There's this beautiful world full of trees and blue sky and rain and birds and perfect moments, like licking a mint chocolate chip ice cream cone, and watching people wander around the outdoor mall, not there to shop, but just to enjoy the benches and plants and warm air and the sounds of other human beings and feel connected to the rest of their community, even if they don't actually speak to each other as they pass by.

I didn't meet Pastor Kate until Thursday of that week, the first day I started working at the church. She was only the first of many of strange encounters I had in this new world – encounters with the living, the dead, and those in-between.

CHAPTER 2

*W*HEN I ARRIVED at eight-thirty on Thursday, April 14, for my first day in the new job, Pastor Joe's white and black Miata wasn't in the gravel parking strip at the front of the church. There was one car – a champagne colored Camry. I parked my Beetle a few feet away, grabbed my satchel that had my sandwich for lunch and my orange metal water bottle and hopped out of the car.

I trotted up the stairs from the front parking strip to the church grounds, then down the stairs to the offices. The rain from a few days earlier had moved on, and the sky was clear blue, but it was still chilly. The office door was unlocked, so I assumed the Camry belonged to Kate. Inside, it smelled like coffee and the furnace rumbled, although there wasn't much evidence of heat yet. I stashed my bag and saw that the computer on my desk was already turned on, and recently, because the screensaver wasn't activated. A blank spreadsheet was open as if it was waiting for me to start working.

After I filled one of the mugs that was on the shelf below the coffee maker, I went through the door into the basement area. It was a large room that reminded me of a roller skating rink, although the ceiling was lower than you'd expect for a room of that size. There were two offices, one to my left that was unoccupied, and one across the hall with the lights on. To my right was a conference room and at the far end was another door that led to the restrooms. Pastor Joe had shown it all to me after my interview, but I was struck again by the seemingly unplanned layout. The church had been built in the fifties, and they were afraid of nuclear attacks back then, although I suppose we still should be, it just doesn't seem to be top of mind anymore. Now we worry about planes getting blown up or the economy collapsing. They built a basement under the church, even though it wasn't a real basement. Maybe they wanted some kind of bomb shelter but they didn't have the will to follow through with that.

I walked across the open area. My heels echoed through the room and I wished I'd turned on the lights. Even though light spilled out of Kate's office, the place was still quite dark. The furnace was still blowing which made me feel as if I was in some kind of factory, cold and dark and full of subterranean rumbling. I shivered and stopped. I blew on my coffee and took a sip. Even though it was still too hot, it comforted me to have that strong, earthy-smelling liquid touch the end of my tongue. I started walking again and stopped in Pastor Kate's doorway.

The office looked like a child's playroom. Kate had her back to the door, so I had a moment to glance around the office. Posters of baby animals with Bible verses printed across the bottom edges covered the walls. Like Pastor Joe's office, there were floor to ceiling bookcases, although only two walls were lined with shelves, and between the shelves on the wall facing me, was a sliding glass door opening out to the ivy-covered incline. The shelves were full of books, but between the books were craft supplies – bottles of paint, jars containing brushes, a plastic bag full of modeling clay. A tambourine had a small section of its own.

Kate spun her chair around and half stood. "You scared me," she said.

Her voice was too loud and my instinct was to step back.

Instead, I walked into the office. "You must be Kate." I held out my left hand since the coffee mug was in my right. "I'm Madison."

"That room is big and dark and you should announce yourself instead of sneaking up on me."

I shifted the mug to my left hand. It warmed those fingers like it had my right hand. I blew on the surface of the coffee. "I figured you knew I was coming because the outside door was unlocked."

She settled down in her chair and tilted it back. She had short blonde hair that looked almost white under the fluorescent lights, a head that was somewhat too small for her very curvy body, and fleshy shoulders that looked plump even through her cable-knit sweater. She wore jeans and clogs with wooden soles and lots of dark brown eyeshadow, mascara, liquid foundation, and creamy blush which stood out quite sharply against that pale hair. It was all artfully done, but still quite startling.

She must have realized her greeting sounded rude because now she tried to smile, but it was too late, and the smile looked tired and not very genuine, so maybe she shouldn't have bothered.

"Why don't you sit down and we can get to know each other. Unless Joe already gave you work you need to get started on right away."

"He gave me a few things, but there's plenty of time." I sat in the chair facing her desk.

"His work is always the first priority."

"Sure."

"Joe seemed quite anxious to hire you. Why don't you tell me about your background. I read your resume."

I sipped more coffee while I tried to think about how I should answer. Was she really thinking she was going to interview me after I already had the job? Or was she awkward and didn't know how to have a casual conversation? I decided to give her the benefit of the doubt, despite her harsh welcome. After all, most people don't intend to be rude or abrupt, they just don't think about how they sound.

As if she'd read my mind, she gave the smile another shot, and this time it looked real. "Why do you want to work in a church?"

"I want to go home at the end of the day and feel like my job matters. At TDP, I felt like part of a machine. If I didn't show up for work, another admin would step in and set up meetings, do the expense reports, and all those other things, and it wouldn't make any difference whether or not I ever came back. To be honest, most of the people in the group I worked for acted as if I was some kind of robot. They only wanted to get information from me, they didn't really think of me as a human being. After a while, I felt like I didn't exist."

Kate looked down at her hands. She spread her fingers and stared at her palms as if she was trying to understand the direction of her own life. Without looking up, she said, "But why do you want to work in a church?"

"Are you interviewing me? Because I already have the job," I said.

"I know that. I'm curious."

"Why not work in a church?"

Kate turned her chair and looked out the window, although what she saw out there, I can't say. The view was ivy, nothing more. "This is a place for God's work, and you seem more interested in how *you* feel."

"Oh, I didn't get the impression that matters to Pastor Joe. He didn't say anything about God. Although, I'm a very spiritual person, although I think it's against the law to ask me about that."

"I didn't ask. I was talking about God."

"I meditate. And I think everyone is part of God. Even animals. If you've had a pet, you know they have souls." I didn't tell her I could sense people's thoughts, even after they're dead. No matter how that's worded, it sounds like I'm saying I can read their minds, or that I'm into weird psychic stuff. It's not reading their minds, knowing every phrase of specific thought, it's a sense of knowing what they're thinking about. Maybe more than reading minds, I read their hearts. I know how they're feeling. That's not meant to be arrogant, I'm just explaining how it is.

"We don't believe in animism here. What I meant about God's work doesn't always have to do with the spiritual realm, however you perceive that, which is a bit off-base, I must say. What I'm talking about is caring for people in tangible ways so they can know God cares for them."

I nodded. "Sure. Although I think I'm supposed to focus on doing administrative work."

"Of course," said Kate. "But part of that job is talking to people who have problems. Sometimes very big problems. And it's greeting people with sensitivity."

"I'm very sensitive."

"For example, one member's daughter was murdered four or five years ago. She's still grieving. And last summer her husband suddenly passed away. A stroke. A young man to have a stroke, he was only forty-two."

"How sad." My throat tightened. I didn't know what to say, and I wasn't sure I could speak.

"Are you prepared to meet people like that? There might be times when they're waiting to see Joe, that they'll end up talking to you. They can be very raw."

"Okay."

"Can you handle that? Can you keep your thoughts and opinions to yourself and just listen? Without trying to do the Pastor's job? You sound like a very opinionated person."

"I am. But I told you, I'm also very sensitive. Very." That was my own hint to myself that I was more sensitive than she'd ever imagined. It was far too subtle for her to pick up on, but it made me feel like the conversation was back in my control.

Kate smiled and I wasn't sure how to interpret her expression, but I was pretty sure it was a smile of disbelief.

I stood and lifted the mug to my mouth and slurped some coffee, which was now a more bearable temperature. The movement made my sleeve ride up my arm, and I could feel her eyes burning into the tip of my vine tattoo. Her smile kind of sagged like it was sliding down her chin and dripping off her jaw.

"I better get to work," I said. "Maybe we can have lunch together soon and you can tell me more about what you expect. What Joe expects."

She smiled again, with less vigor this time. "I have no idea what Joe expects."

As I walked back through the basement room, my heels tapped so loudly it felt like someone was walking around in my head. I wondered how this was going to work out. Kate and Joe clearly weren't on the same page in terms of who they wanted running the office. Was she this snippy and pompous with Joe, or had she reserved that attitude for me? It wasn't like I was hired to teach religious classes or that anyone who came into the office would care one bit what I believed.

Behind my desk was a large window with the drapes pulled closed. I opened them to let in more light, then re-filled my mug. The mug was white with a gold crown on it. I wasn't sure if that crown was supposed to be about God, or if the cup had been a freebie at a Vegas casino. It could have gone either way.

CHAPTER 3

*M*Y STOMACH WAS GROWLING by eleven-thirty, so I grabbed my sandwich and water bottle and went outside and up the stairs. I walked around the church grounds looking for a place to eat. Kate had gone out at eleven, saying she would be back about three or so. It was a little cold, but I had my wool coat with me which would keep my butt warm if I could find a place to sit.

Twelve rose bushes, the kind that are like small trees, lined one side of the path that led from the top of the stairs to the other two buildings. A few of the houses that I'd passed on the way to work had rose bushes, and one of my neighbors had a few in pots on her deck. All of them were covered with blooms – fifteen or twenty, at least – but the church shrubs only had three or four tightly closed buds on each rose tree, the rest were the pods with a few wilted petals hanging sadly to the side, which the gardener was snipping off. It struck me that he was a little late in pruning them since nearly all the petals were gone.

I shoved my sandwich back into my bag and stopped a few feet from where the gardener was working. After spending all morning alone in the office, I was feeling somewhat batty from talking only to myself. Kate hadn't come out of her office until she left. Apparently, Pastor Joe wouldn't be in until the afternoon.

"Hi," I said. "I'm Madison."

The gardener straightened slowly, stiff from bending over even that little bit. He looked about seventy years old, with longish, curly gray hair, and very blue eyes. The kind of eyes that look like they come from another world, pale and yet not so washed out that they made him look crazy, but really clear. He pulled off one of his gloves and shook my hand.

"I'm the new administrative assistant."

"Fred."

"Nice to meet you, Fred. Isn't it cold working out here?"

"Needs to be done." He squatted and scooped up the dead blossoms out of the dirt bowls around the shrubs and tossed them into a plastic trashcan that stood on the path. "But it is chilly, the coldest April I remember in a long time."

"Do you take a lunch break, Fred? I wouldn't mind some company."

"Nah. My wife lets me come home. She heats up soup for us. It's easier than packing it and transporting it here. But I could use a smoke." He stood and looked at me again. "You probably don't like smoke. Kate says it stinks up the place, and I should keep my dirty habit at home. If the kids see me, I'm setting a bad example. She thinks I shouldn't be allowed to smoke anywhere on the property. Do you mind?" He walked over to the building that was a wing of classrooms and stopped near the open door to a large closet where the garden tools were stored.

His question was like a punch in my gut. I've been trying to quit smoking for three years now. Everyone at TDP hated that I smoked. Hardly any of them did, maybe one percent of the employees, maybe less. It was as if they worked in such dust-free, climate-controlled buildings, they couldn't contaminate themselves with tobacco or ash or even sulfur on their fingertips from matches. They were a really clean bunch of people.

I was down to three cigarettes a day. I rationed them – one with my morning coffee while I sat on the back deck of my condo, one after work, and one right before bedtime. It was working quite well, but I couldn't yet bring myself to cut further. The thought of a cigarette right now was enticing, because, after all, that's part of what makes a person start smoking to begin with. It's the whole social atmosphere, that sense you get of relaxing, slowing down your brain and your hands. Drifting, smoke flowing into your lungs and out again, floating up into the sky. The companionship of doing it with someone else is beyond compare. Even if you're not talking, just standing there watching the end of the cigarette glow, tasting the smoke, blowing it out in long, smooth streams, and feeling that rhythmic connection with another person. I'm sure it's why indigenous people smoked peace pipes. It helps break down the walls between people. Especially nowadays when smokers are shunned. We're like the village outcasts they used to have back in the middle ages, or the eighteen hundreds, or whenever. Shut out of buildings, locked into narrow corridors. Smokers freeze when the others are tucked inside a warm building; or sweat when others are enjoying the air conditioning. Passersby give us dirty looks, downright mean, snarly looks. Some even cluck their tongues in disgust or go into these exaggerated, fake coughing fits. It's quite funny, but also can be a little bit hurtful. No one wants to be shunned, even if they know they should stop what they're doing. Sometimes there are too many good reasons to keep on doing what you're doing, even when it's harmful.

"Can I have one?" I said.

"A cigarette?"

"Yes."

"You smoke? A young kid like you? It's not good for you."

I laughed, and he laughed too, until he started coughing. "Sure, hon." He pulled the pack, a red and white Marlboro box, out of his pocket. He opened the top and let two pure white sticks, soft skin like linen, slide out as if one had my name on it. He handed it to me and lit both of them with matches instead of a lighter. I liked him for that – the matches, not the act of lighting my cigarette.

After three slow puffs, he leaned against the corner of the building. "If Pastor Kate sees us, she'll harp at me that I'm corrupting you."

"I can't be corrupted."

"Because you already are?" said Fred.

If he wasn't so old, I would have thought he was flirting with me. This is what I love about old people. It's like they turn back into themselves, no longer caring what people think, just relaxed and going with the flow, like they're kids again. Maybe that's why kids and old people tend to get along. Not all of them, but quite a few. It's all the people in the middle who are kind of messed up. "I don't believe in corruption," I said.

"How's that work? What about right and wrong?"

"Is corruption the same as right and wrong? I don't know. But I don't think anyone can be corrupt. That makes it sound like there are bad people and I don't think there are."

"There most certainly are," said Fred.

"Even though people might joke about it, like enticing someone to drink or smoke or whatever. You can't really change another person," I said. "And no one's bad, even if they make mistakes."

"I wasn't just talking about smoking. What about stealing? Cheating? Hurting kids? Murder?"

"Usually there's a reason."

"So you think it's okay if someone sells drugs and kids end up dying from using?"

"I didn't say everything is okay. But it's a long way from not okay to corrupt. There's always a reason and it's often a pretty good one."

"Like what?"

"I don't know. Maybe someone can't find a job."

"What they sell hurts other people," said Fred. "A lot." Even though there was still quite a bit left, he dropped his cigarette on the ground. He stomped on it so hard, twisting his boot back and forth, it looked like he was killing a tarantula.

I guess we weren't connecting through the common bond of smoke after all. I wished he could understand, or that I could explain better. I just don't think anyone is all bad. That would mean they were born bad, and how can that be? When has anyone ever seen a tiny, soft, doe-eyed baby with perfect fingers and toes and tiny fingernails and thought, *that person inside those clear eyes, staring around at the world, is bad.* It doesn't make sense. "I'm not explaining it very well," I said. "I only know there's almost always a reason people do things. Not almost. There always is."

"You're wrong," he said. "When you know someone who's been corrupted, you might view it a little differently."

"I don't think so," I said.

"Do Pastor Joe and Pastor Kate know about this belief system of yours?"

I took one last puff and dropped my cigarette and twisted my toe on it to put it out. I bent down and picked up both cigarettes.

"You can drop those back down," said Fred. "I'll sweep them up."

I no longer felt hungry, so I decided I'd eat my sandwich for an afternoon snack. I didn't want to walk away and leave Fred annoyed after our first meeting.

"You're a strange one," he said.

"I guess I am."

"Have time for one more?"

One more would make me close to doubling what I was allowing myself. Five cigarettes in one day, heading in the wrong direction. I supposed I could skip my after work one, but I had been waiting weeks to psych myself up to take that step. I wasn't ready to do it right on the spur of the moment like this. Still, I didn't want to leave Fred, not having completed our conversation. Maybe I could make it more clear what I meant about corruption. Although it wouldn't be the first time someone failed to understand what I was saying or agree with my point of view.

He handed me a fresh smoke and the matches. I lit my cigarette. The sun was getting brighter and the dampness on the pavement was disappearing, leaving it gray and chalky-looking.

Fred stuffed the matches in the pocket of his jeans and walked across to the rose bushes. He put his cigarette between his teeth and waved his arm across the top of the first rose bush. "Doesn't this look strange to you?"

"What's strange? They look very healthy. You must take good care of them. Although you'd think there would be more roses at this time of year."

He nodded. He sucked on his cigarette then pulled it out of his mouth. "Someone is cutting them. Snipping off the blossoms. I found six partially opened buds lying on the ground today."

"Maybe someone took the others for table decorations." I walked over to where he was standing. Now that I was closer, I could see they must have been covered with blooms because there were quite a lot of stems that showed they'd been recently cut. The empty stems were mangled at the top as if they'd been chewed by an animal. The pods Fred had trimmed were clipped smooth.

"Why would they leave half of them on the ground? And some of the petals are torn off the pods."

"Then what do you think happened?"

"There are kids that hang out here at night. Smoking pot. I found the stub of a joint more than once." He nodded his head toward the back of the property. There was a small grove of pine trees with a concrete bench nestled in the middle. "They sit back there."

"And you think they're cutting the roses? Why would they do that?"

He shrugged. "Pure malice. Corrupt. See what I mean?"

I wasn't sure about that. "If kids come here to smoke pot, I don't think they'd bring pruning shears with them."

"There's no other explanation," he said.

I was pretty confident there had to be another explanation.

"I didn't just find the ends of their joints. I was here at night once. The roses needed to be sprayed, and I'd forgotten to do it before the sun was overhead, so I came back at night. I saw them hanging around back there."

I dropped my cigarette on the ground and stomped it out. I was getting light-headed and didn't want to go back to work feeling sick. "Did you see them cut the roses?"

He shook his head. "I know it's them. Two guys and a girl. It was the girl."

"How do you know that?"

"She loves the roses."

"Do you know her?"

"Not really."

"Then how ..."

"It's a shame to see them damaged, cut off for no reason, left on the ground. And they belong to the church."

"Did you tell Pastor Joe?"

"I told Kate. She wasn't really concerned. She thinks I'm a crazy old guy who reads too much into things."

"Are you?"

He laughed. "Most people wouldn't ask that question."

"Well are you?"

He straightened his back and adjusted his jacket on his thin shoulders. "I am not. And Kate should have been worried about who these people are. If a bunch of partiers gets too comfortable here, who knows what might happen."

"I'm sure she's happy that you're looking out for the place. Maybe you should tell Pastor Joe too."

"Kate came close to laughing in my face. Told me I'm seeing things." He shoved his hands in his pockets and looked down. He nudged my cigarette butt with the toe of his boot.

"I better get back to work," I said.

"Sure." He tried to smile, but it looked more like a sneer. I don't think he meant it for me. He was thinking about his concerns being ignored. It wasn't good for an old guy like him to be here alone at night. I wondered who the kids were, if they were from Kate's youth group, maybe just kids sneaking out to party. Or maybe no one at all.

CHAPTER 4

$\mathcal{B}$Y THREE O'CLOCK that day I was beginning to wonder if Pastor Joe was ever going to show up. How long could hospital visits take? But then, what did I know about ministers and their schedules and sick people? Not much. Nothing, actually.

At three-thirty the phone rang. The first call all day. It was Joe telling me that someone had given birth and the baby was having trouble breathing so he'd be spending the rest of the afternoon with the family. He'd see me the next day to go over my work. He didn't even ask whether I'd met Kate. I suppose fear for the baby made him forget all about that kind of trivial detail, although he still seemed concerned that it was my first day and didn't want me to feel as if I was getting ignored by my boss. I assured him I didn't feel ignored. Kate had returned earlier when I was in the bathroom. When I walked past her office, she was on the phone and didn't look up as I went by.

A few minutes after I finished talking to Joe, I was eating my sandwich when Kate appeared in the doorway. She'd slipped off her clogs. Her stocking feet hadn't caused even the whisper of a footstep as she walked across that expanse of linoleum, the hard tiles from the fifties, not the fluffy flexible stuff they have today. I shivered a little. I almost wondered if she was sneaking up on me, walking quietly on purpose, thinking she would catch me doing something I shouldn't be doing. But what, exactly, would that be, in a church office? Surfing the web for porn? I don't think so. Digging through the cabinets for missed cash from the offering plates?

"Why are you eating now? Didn't you take a lunch break?" She stepped back out through the doorway and waved her hand. "It smells like smoke. Was Fred in here?"

I took a bite of my tomato and cheese sandwich and enjoyed the yummy goodness of soft mozzarella and the sweet, juicy tomato. It worked, because Kate didn't ask more about the smell of smoke, and took my non-answer to be logistics over eating rather than rudeness. I think.

"Have you met Fred?" said Kate.

"Yes. He's a nice guy. He seems to love the garden."

She laughed. "He thinks it's an extension of his backyard. He's too territorial."

"Why do you say that?"

"The way he fusses over the roses, acts like they belong to him. Has a fit if anyone wants to cut some and put them in a vase for a lunch or potluck supper."

I took another bite of my sandwich and chewed slowly so I wouldn't have to respond.

"He imagines things. He might be getting too old to handle this much property. It's a lot of work for one guy. We should probably think about hiring a service, although that's pricy."

"He seems like he's in good shape for his age."

Kate leaned against the door frame. She ran her finger along her chin as if she was checking to be sure her makeup was properly blended against her skin. "He thinks people hang around at night, smoking pot. He thinks we should have police patrols and hidden cameras."

"Really?"

"He hasn't said that, but he hints around about it. Worrying about the roses getting damaged." She walked into the office and settled on one of the armchairs facing my desk. There were two of them, with a table in between. A wood carving of a baby seal sat on the table. Kate stroked the seal's back. "I think he's getting paranoid. His wife chases him out of the house to putter around here six days a week, and I don't know if she even notices how he is."

I couldn't tell if Kate was being cruel or if she was really concerned. The way she was holding and rubbing that baby seal seemed quite tender, but the impression she left me with earlier that morning was not one of tenderness or concern for anyone. That morning she'd struck me as a person too caught up in her own head, her own agenda, whatever that might be.

"He seemed fine to me. Worried about people loitering, that's all. There do seem to be a lot of missing roses. You can't call that paranoid."

"The cameras are too much. He needs to relax. No one's deliberately destroying or stealing roses. And if they are, it isn't his responsibility."

I wondered what she was getting at. Why was she suddenly so friendly, sitting here talking to me? Maybe she got lonely, back there on the other side of that dark room, all by herself. When she had events with the children's groups or the teenagers, it was probably fine, but maybe she wanted adult conversation. If Pastor Joe was out like this a lot, it must be weird being in this empty, underground building by herself, with a church sanctuary hanging over her head.

"What kind of things do you work on?" I said. I laid the rest of my sandwich on the plastic it had been wrapped in. "Pastor Joe told me some, but he didn't give very many details."

"He probably doesn't know the details." Her voice was sharp, louder than it had been and she put the seal back on the table.

"Why don't you tell me?"

She ran through a whole list of things – day camps in the

summer, junior high bowling teams, high school basketball games, arts and crafts classes, and even a book club for teenaged girls. They were thinking about maybe starting after-school daycare.

While she talked, the hard lines alongside her nose seemed to smooth out into the rest of her skin. Her voice sounded almost melodic, instead of reminding me of aluminum cans being crushed, as it had earlier.

"Would you run the daycare all by yourself? Or hire more people?" I knew the answer but wanted to keep her talking, wanted her to be this nice, energized, interesting Kate, not the woman I'd met earlier who acted as if she preferred a clone of herself managing the church office. Not the woman who had such a harsh attitude toward a nice old man who did an awesome job keeping the church gardens looking like a park.

"It would be great to make it free, or nearly free," she said. "Help people out. That's what we're here for. But if there were more than four or five kids, we'd have to hire staff."

I finished the last of my sandwich, wadded up the plastic wrap, and stuffed it in the trash can under my desk. I opened my water bottle and took a long swallow. "Back to Fred," I said. "You don't think he'll come here at night, do you? That could be dangerous. Depending on who's hanging around out there."

"Why would he come here at night?"

"He was here once before at night and he saw them. He just didn't speak to them. If you don't take his concerns seriously, he might do something risky."

Kate stood. "Don't start butting in on your first day. You don't know any of these people or anything about the situation."

I almost fell off my chair, which isn't hard to do with the smallish seat and the wheels that spin wildly in whatever direction they choose. Where had that come from? I thought we were having a nice conversation and now she acted like I didn't even belong here. Like asking a simple question to help an old guy who was obviously worried was none of my business? What the hell?

"I'm not saying I know anything about the *situation*. I'm just telling you that Fred is upset. He might be old, but he's full of fire. I can see him coming here at night. He's sure they're cutting the roses, and I don't want to see him get beaten up or something."

"Don't worry about it."

"What if he decides to confront them?"

"Confront who? We don't even know there's anyone hanging around. Because he thinks he saw some kids smoking pot? He doesn't wear his glasses when he works in the garden. It's not even definite that he saw anything at all."

Why was she getting so hot about it? I felt like she thought I was prying and all I wanted to do was make sure Fred was safe. I didn't get this woman at all, and I sure didn't understand why she was so hostile. You'd think I was trying to tell her how to do her job or give her advice on romantic matters. I looked at her hand. No ring. From the thin line on one side of her lips, she looked to be about forty. Maybe she was one of those women feeling like her life was slipping through her fingers, and she wasn't sure she would get what she wanted. Not every woman has to be married, and maybe she had a boyfriend or a girlfriend, how would I know. It's just that disappointment seemed to be oozing out of her skin like sweat in August, and no matter how much she tried to plug up one leak, the sourness seeped up in another spot she hadn't been paying attention to.

I don't mean to stereotype Kate or make it sound as if she's some caricature of a spinster, like that kind of woman even exists anymore. This is the twenty-first century. I'm single, and I love it. But I know that at some point I want to meet my soul mate, and after that, I'll want to settle down and get all nested, probably have babies, although I don't think about that too much, it seems so huge. Most people want someone, and I couldn't believe Kate was any different. And I've noticed that when people don't have someone, or they're no longer pleased with the one they did get, if the person didn't measure up to what they thought they expected, they can get really snarly. *Really* snarly. They act as if nothing's right with the world and they want everyone else to be as frustrated and lonely as they are. This sounds really backwards, like I'm some gal from the 1800s who thinks a woman needs a man. It's not that a woman does, it's that if she wants one and doesn't have one, or even if she wants another woman and can't admit that, then she's just not happy. I suppose it all comes down to not getting what we want. It's not only about love or companionship, but being deprived of what we want. All of us can get quite snarly when we're deprived. I know I can.

I decided to end the conversation. I wasn't interested in swallowing her BS that I was inserting myself where I didn't belong. All I did was express a simple concern for a man who gave all his energy to keep her church looking beautiful. "Well Fred's concerned," I said. "And I think it's disrespectful not to listen to him and I hope nothing happens."

"Don't be an alarmist," said Kate. "Besides, the whole reason Joe hired you is to be an outsider and not get yourself involved in issues here, so stay out of it."

I smiled. Grinned, really.

She glared at me, not sure what to make of my smile, probably wondering if she'd over-stepped a bit and now she'd made me want to poke my nose in more since she'd over-reacted. Did she see that? She had to be aware that she sounded both completely heartless toward an old man that she was supposed to love as a fellow member of the human race – at least that's what her church would advise – but she was also sounding somewhat careless. You don't ignore threats to your property and write it off as an old man's over-attachment to his job and his poor eyesight.

"I'm glad you agree with me," she said.

I kept smiling, but now I was really confused. Clearly, Kate saw only what she wanted, and not arguing must mean, in her world, that I agreed I'd been an alarmist and that Fred was blind.

CHAPTER 5

*T*HE NEXT TIME I SAW Fred, the weather was that kind of soft sunny type that makes you love the spring, and especially love the spring in the San Francisco Bay Area because it's so pleasant it's almost like summer, but still comfortable. The air is fresh and clean-smelling, not that smoggy dry odor you get in July and August.

I was wearing my favorite boots that reach just above my ankles, made of soft leather that collapses down and leaves plenty of room for me to tuck in my jeans. By now I knew that Joe and Kate wore very casual clothes most of the time – jeans and sweaters. At the same time, I still looked professional in my jeans because I topped them with a really nice red tunic with cap sleeves so I wouldn't be too hot later in the day, and matching red earrings shaped like hooks. I was almost the same color as the petals on the rose bushes that lined the path from the sanctuary to the other buildings.

Fred stood near the roses where the path splits off in two directions, one branch leading to the fellowship hall and the building with the classrooms, and the other to the small grove of trees and the concrete bench designed for contemplation.

A woman I'd never seen before, which wasn't surprising since I'd only met four or five church members at this point, stood about ten feet away from Fred. She had pure white hair wound up into an elaborate bun at the base of her skull. The bun was so large, full of twists and turns, I was sure her hair went well past the middle of her back. It was that silky white, like the fur of a cat, that makes you want to stroke its softness. Maybe all white hair is that way, it's gray hair that you think will be stiff and wiry, although it isn't always. Of course, that made me want to stroke Fred's hair, just to get a comparison to see if I was right about the texture, but I shook off that weird thought.

The woman was very slender, her body like a dancer's. She wore a short-ish coffee-colored skirt and a white top and a tight-fitting jacket that matched the skirt. Her heels were about three inches high and she had long red fingernails. Despite the pure white hair, she looked like she was only in her early forties. She leaned slightly toward Fred, talking in a way that the movement of her lips contorted the skin around her nose and forehead. Fred glared right back at her. He said something, and she stomped her foot like a two-year-old. I walked closer, extremely curious to know what was going on, and worried that Fred might have a stroke or something, his face was so dark with blood it was almost purple. I could hear their voices biting at each other, and I worried both of them might drop from a stroke right there, and I'd be left with two writhing bodies on my hands, or two dead bodies, for all I knew.

The woman was almost shouting at him now. "Don't make excuses. It's your responsibility."

"I'm not making excuses, and I'm damn tired of you blaming everything on me."

I stopped. Neither one of them appeared to notice I was there, much less listening to their argument.

"These are prize-winning caliber. They're meant to be a tribute. People from the community drive past and admire them. You should be thinking of them as a way to attract new members. If we don't get more contributions coming in here, you won't have a job."

"I'm not here for the money."

Fred was almost shouting now. I stepped closer, only about four feet away. The woman turned. Her whole face twitched as if she hadn't noticed me at all and I'd crept up and whispered, *Boo.*

"Can I help you, Miss?"

I stuck out my hand. "I'm Madison."

She stepped back. I let my arm fall to my side.

"What can I do for you, Mattiss?"

"Madison."

"What?"

"My name is Madison. I don't need anything, I wanted to introduce myself."

She stared at me. Well, she sort of stared at me. She didn't seem to really see me, but looked through my eyes, right through my head and out to some place far past me. It was such a strong feeling that I almost turned to see what she was looking at.

"I'm the new administrative assistant."

She nodded but didn't smile.

"You sound so upset. What's wrong?" I said.

The woman ran her fingers down the bone of her forearm, then tugged at the cuff of her jacket. She tried again to smile. "I'm Jan Waverly. Thank you for your interest, but we don't need any help."

"I wasn't offering to help with anything. I was concerned." I turned toward Fred. "Are you okay?"

"She's blaming me for the damage." He gestured toward the ground.

I looked down. Red petals were scattered across the weed-free soil, like fat puddles of blood. I looked closer and saw that the seed pods from about half of the few remaining roses had shreds of torn petals stuck to them. The petals on the ground hadn't fallen in the normal cycle of a blossom fading and dropping its petals, they'd been torn off like skin ripped off a piece of chicken.

"It's those people who hang around here at night. Smoking dope."

"No one hangs around here. Not now. No one is smoking anything, except you and those filthy cigarettes."

I shivered slightly at this. Guilt over my own smoking, maybe? Or the sheer force of the venom in her tone? I almost expected her to start hissing.

"Well I didn't steal all the blooms, and I didn't tear up those petals. I think it's those kids."

Jan lurched toward him. "You're imagining things."

"I saw them."

She grabbed the front of his shirt and twisted it. "You didn't see anything."

He pried her fingers off his shirt and pushed her. "Leave me alone. I'm doing the best I can. I might be old, but I'm not blind. I saw those two boys. And the girl. Druggies. Losers. Frying their brains."

Jan raised her hand. Her fingernail polish glittered in the sunlight. She slapped his cheek.

"Why'd you do that?" I shouted.

Fred didn't get mad. He clicked his tongue against the back of his teeth, turned, and stomped off toward the large closet where the garden tools were stored.

Jean shouted after him. "Come back here!"

"Why did you hit him?" I was almost crying.

"He's a lazy old man. I donated these roses to the church, and I pay to have them properly cared for. And now they're destroyed."

She looked like she was about to cry herself. I think my mouth was hanging open because she clenched her jaw like she thought it might force my mouth closed. You know, that thing where you do something hoping the other person will mimic you? Like when they have mustard on their lips and you lick your own, thinking they'll do the same.

"There's no reason to hit him. And he's not lazy."

"What do you know? You're new here and you know nothing about the history of this situation."

"Why don't you tell me."

She stepped back suddenly, apparently surprised that I didn't shut my mouth and scuttle off to my underground cave. Her heel slipped off the concrete into the dirt area and she stumbled. She grabbed at the bush and of course, wound up with a fist full of thorns. Surprisingly, she didn't cry out or whimper. She simply opened her palm, displaying bright red lines running across her pale skin. "Look what you did."

"I'm sorry you hurt yourself."

She took my meaning. She lifted her palm to her face and lapped at the scratches, like a dog licking its wound. Then she let her arm fall to her side, not seeming to care whether she streaked blood across that beautiful silk skirt.

"You should put some ointment on that," I said.

"It's nothing. I'll look after it in a minute."

She stepped back onto the concrete and took a deep breath, obviously preparing to tell me something important.

"These roses are a memorial. When my ..." her shoulders began to shake. Her whole body trembled and then she drew herself up, stiff and suddenly motionless. "Before my husband passed on to join our daughter in paradise, he wanted to make sure no one ever forgot her. She loved roses from the time she was a toddler. David was teaching her to care for ours when she ..." Jan took another long, deep breath. Her voice got hard, loud. "He had already set aside money so we could donate all of this. I advised that we should have an expert hired to tend them properly, but no. Fred thought he knew it all and he could take care of them just fine. But he acts as if they're *his*! And I know he's cutting off all the blooms, and now he's tearing them just to hurt me." She was shouting again.

I'm not often at a loss for words, but I really didn't know what to say. If she didn't look so upset, I'd have laughed. Not at her loss, but at her twisted view. I actually started to and had to bite my lip to stop myself. It sounded to me as if she thought the roses belonged to her. Why was everyone so damn upset about Fred taking personal pride in his work? She and Kate seemed to be somewhat unglued over the fact that he behaved as if the garden belonged to him. Well, surely he didn't think he actually owned any of this. He cared about keeping it nice, that's all. Since when was that a bad thing? "I'm sure he doesn't think they're actually his."

"You'd never know it from the way he behaves. He complained because I cut three small blossoms to take home for my dining room table."

Twice in five minutes, I didn't know what to say. Who was being territorial here? She thought because she paid for the roses, she got to cut them and take them home?

"You cut the church roses and take them to your house?"

She looked genuinely surprised. "I bought them."

"But they belong to the church."

"In one sense."

"What do you mean, *in one sense?* You gave them to the church as a memorial. For your daughter. You just told me that."

"You're a very argumentative girl. Does Pastor Joe know that?"

I shrugged. I was probably stepping way over my boundaries. But I was still upset. She slapped him! And why hadn't he done anything about that? I suppose it was none of my business, but how could I say nothing? This woman was batshit crazy, acting as if she could donate roses but still retain full ownership. Where did she get off thinking she could control the church property? And Fred, for that matter. Did she really think Fred destroyed the roses he cared so much about? It made no sense and she clearly wasn't thinking logically, so I felt sort of compelled to point that out to her, whether I was supposed to be an impartial office assistant or not. "If Fred acts like the roses are his, why would he destroy them like this?" I pointed my toe at one of the torn petals.

"To hurt me."

"I think you're a little over-emotional about these roses." I put my hand on her arm. "Don't get upset. I'm not trying to be cruel, but you're taking your grief out on Fred. You're acting as if your daughter's soul is living in the roses."

She yanked her arm away from my fingers. "That's ridiculous. My daughter has been gone for five years. She's singing praises in heaven. They both are."

"Yes. I didn't mean she's actually in the roses. I think you're putting all your grief into this situation, and they're not really related. Fred loves these roses, and he's taking care of them exactly like you wanted."

"Half the blossoms are gone. Rose bushes at this time of year should be covered with blooms."

"But he didn't do that. He wouldn't."

"Someone did," she said. She folded her arms and turned. As she walked along the path, her heels tapped on the concrete.

I thought she'd turn and shout back over her shoulder that I should mind my own business, or that I didn't understand, or that I didn't really know Fred. But she didn't do any of that. She just walked away. Even though I was angry at her for the way she treated Fred, and her rudeness to me, underneath it all I could feel something else – utter, endless pain. She dismissed me, but I was right. She really had poured everything she had left, which wasn't much, into those roses. Maybe her loud voice and her attitude that she could do as she pleased were how she tried to keep her pain under control. She disappeared around the front of the church, but I still felt her presence around the rose bushes, all her pain and rage and hopeless effort to get back what she'd lost. I bent over as tears pressed hard against the backs of my eyeballs. For a few seconds, it was difficult to breathe.

A moment later, as if he'd been listening and knew Jan was gone, Fred popped out of the storage room. He waved at me but didn't come back over to where I was standing.

I stood there, not knowing what to do. A torn piece of petal drifted across the toe of my boot. The other petals moved slightly in the dirt beneath the shrubs, even though I couldn't feel the breeze that was shifting them around. My arms got cold, so there must have been a breeze, I was just to numb to feel it.

CHAPTER 6

$\mathcal{A}$FTER THAT, I DECIDED to really insert myself where I didn't belong. It seemed odd that Fred was so insistent that kids were hanging around at night, smoking pot and tearing up roses, while Kate and Jan were adamant that he was seeing things. Was Fred delusional? Maybe there was some history that I wasn't aware of. Whatever was going on, I'm a very curious person. In fact, I don't think it's overstating to say I'm consumed with curiosity. If something doesn't add up, I have to know more. I would come by at night to observe for myself.

Spring weather can be uncertain, so I brought gloves and a knit hat that my mother made for me when I was twelve, but it still fits. The hat is goofy. It's purple with a long braid of yarn that dangles down my back. I have no idea why I wanted it so badly, but she was knitting the hat with a tassel in the pattern and I begged her to change it to a braid. I was a weird kid. I guess I still am a little weird, but in a good way. If someone can't appreciate my weirdness, then that's okay with me. I can't be anyone different from who I am.

There was no way of knowing what time these kids might show up. It had to be well into the evening, after the traffic around the neighborhood had evaporated to nothing, so I figured ten or eleven o'clock at the earliest. I didn't want to ask Fed what time he'd been there at night because I didn't want him to know what I was up to. I was prepared to wait for awhile. I had a thermos of hot chocolate and a plastic bag full of extremely fat green grapes, and some roasted peanuts, to satisfy the salty craving that was sure to come as I got tired of sitting in the dark. Reading a magazine or a book was out of the question, and I wasn't sure I wanted to listen to my iPod. If they hung out by the back fence and I had plugs in my ears, there was a chance of missing them entirely. But the thought of sitting there in a little alcove on the church steps, tucked around near the double doors with nothing to do for potentially two or three hours, maybe more, was somewhat intimidating. The more I thought about what I could do to occupy the time, the more I had to discard every single idea. There was nothing to do but sit.

So, I decided to view it as a lengthy meditation session. I've meditated for an hour before, but let me tell you, it's rough going. That's a long time to sit still with nothing to entertain you but your breath. The awareness that you can't stop your crazy mind from introducing thoughts for more than fifteen seconds at a time is quite humbling. It goes like this – take a breath, let it out slowly, take a breath and suddenly my mind says, *my back itches*, or *I need to water my orchid*. Then it's off and running to a whole bunch of other stuff. After a bit of these random, pointless thoughts, I suddenly wake up to what's happening inside my head. Then I have to gently carry my mind back to noticing my breathing.

Sitting alone in the dark for a few hours might be interesting. I was somewhat scared. Not of who I might run into, but of my own impatience. I suppose having snacks while I faced this three-hour meditation experiment was kind of cheating, but I think any kind of spiritual endeavor goes much better if a person is realistic and practical.

Underneath my yoga pants, I wore tights so I would be as warm as possible. I brought a thick wool blanket and a pillow. Three hours on concrete is a long time. Of course, maybe I would be lucky and they'd show up ten minutes after I hunkered down, and then all my prep would be for nothing. Still, better to be safe than sorry, as they say. I wore a fleece jacket that goes past my hips and my goofy hat, and lace-up ankle-high boots, and a turtleneck shirt and a scarf. There was a chance I would be too warm.

The sky was clear, dotted with stars glittering like they wanted to say "Hi", making me feel the world is a welcoming place. The moon was about three-quarters full. I left my car down the street, parked in front of a house that had no lights on. The front yard was surrounded by shrubs that were taller than I am. There are no sidewalks in this area, just hard-packed dirt and gravel that serves as a sidewalk, so it's easy to park without the car hanging out into the street.

It was five minutes to ten when I got out of the car. The grapes and peanuts and thermos were all in a canvas bag that dangled from my right arm, and I had the blanket and pillow tucked under my left. The most worrisome thing was whether I would have time to settle into my alcove before anyone saw me.

The street was deserted as I walked the half block to the church, passing four houses. All but one were as dark as the house where I'd parked. The soles of my boots crunched on the gravel. Once I hit the concrete path, my feet whispered on the ground as I hurried past the rose trees and up the steps to the sanctuary doors. I slid myself into the space behind the half wall that would help keep me warm, spread out my blanket and put the pillow on top. I settled down with my legs crossed at the shins, and felt quite cozy because the blanket and pillow had absorbed some warm air from the car heater.

With my hands tucked into my pockets, I straightened my back, closed my eyes and took a long, slow breath. I hoped I was up for this, but more than that, I hoped that if these kids actually existed, they would show up soon. Preferably tonight.

I have no idea what time it was when I heard something like voices, but not. It was disembodied, a male and female voice floating

46

among the tops of the trees. The sound drifted over me as if it was part of my dream and I realized I'd fallen asleep. Then the sound stopped and I wasn't sure I'd heard anything at all. The pressure of my crossed legs and the cold that was seeping through the blanket had caused my left foot to go numb. As I uncrossed my ankles, my foot throbbed and tingled like glass shards stabbing at my skin. I wanted to stand. Sitting in the corner, although they had no idea I was there, had no way of seeing me, made me feel vulnerable. But I couldn't walk without that fuzzy pain shooting up my leg. I moved onto my knees and then stood, but kept the pressure off my left foot so the blood could return slowly.

After a few minutes, my foot was functioning again. I folded the blanket into a bundle and shoved it and the pillow and my bag of food into the corner so I wouldn't be encumbered in case they threatened me and I had to run. I could always come back to get my supplies the next day.

I stepped out of my hiding place onto the church steps and tried to peer through the darkness. A single light was attached to the overhang in front of the sanctuary doors. Those small garden pathway lights were placed along where the rose trees were planted, but they were too dim to reveal much. I waited for my eyes to adjust, although it only took a moment or two since the moon was bright, and there's that constant glow of ambient light across the sky. It's never completely dark when you're around a large metropolitan or suburban area. All those lights, all gathering together and reaching into the atmosphere as if they want to erase the idea of darkness altogether.

Slowly, pausing with both feet on each step, I made my way down. My eyes had adapted enough that I could see two forms standing in the grove of trees. The one I assumed was a girl because she was significantly shorter than the other figure, although they were so shadowy it was hard to tell, had a joint pinched between her fingers. At least I think it was a joint, that's how she held it. I sniffed and thought I smelled pot, but wasn't quite sure. The guy bent over and brushed debris off the concrete bench. He stepped back and the girl sat down, glided to one side, and he sat next to her. He put his arm around her waist, and she held the joint out to her left and leaned her head against the hollow of his shoulder.

Seeing them leaning into each other forced me to pause on the bottom step. The absolute tenderness of it buckled my knees. Her head was almost swallowed by the bulk of his shoulder, and she looked so collapsed into him, as if he were her sanctuary, as if nothing else mattered but his arm holding her close to his side, not the cold night air, or the chance of getting caught smoking pot, or the hard surface of the ancient-looking bench. For several long minutes, far too long, I wanted to be where she was, sitting under that protective arm, drifting in a haze of altered brain cells, warm and forgetful of the entire world.

I'm not sure how long I stood watching them. All desire to confront them, to defend Fred's territory, dissolved into vapor and then evaporated. Clearly, they weren't up to anything harmful, at least not harmful to the church or the roses. As I watched the smoke rise in the cold air, almost a solid form of its own, the boy stood. The girl handed him the joint, soundlessly and willingly, as if they'd followed this routine countless times before. He sucked on the scrap of paper and weed, then held the smoke inside for longer than I thought possible. When he exhaled, he wasn't gasping for air, but calmly letting the smoke slide out between his lips. He took a second hit and turned toward the sanctuary steps where I stood, but didn't appear to notice I was there. Was it that dark? Did he have poor vision or was he in such a fog of dope he couldn't recognize anything unfamiliar in his surroundings?

After all my preparations, all that waiting, falling asleep in the cold, worrying about Fred, I suddenly didn't want him to see me. I wanted him to finish the joint and return to sitting near the girl. I wanted to leave them alone to their thoughts and their holding on to each other. I'd been looking for something sinister, but now I felt like a voyeur. As much as their affection made me feel happy and teary-eyed, I didn't want to watch any more.

If I moved, he might notice me. I took a slow breath and waited, but he continued to stare in my direction, not seeing. There was no sound of traffic this late. Only in the suburbs does all movement, all outside activity fade into nothing late at night. The streets are deserted and the houses dark and there's not a human soul anywhere. In some ways, it's scarier than a large city, where people are always moving about, stores still open, a mixture of business and residential in a self-contained neighborhood. Here, you could go for blocks and see nothing but an occasional cat skulking along the sidewalk, wondering where everyone had gone, daring to stroll across the street without fear of a car.

It was another ten or fifteen minutes before the boy finally turned. He dropped the stub of the joint on the ground, shoved it around with his toe and crossed his arms, leaning back slightly, then further back, until I thought he might fall over, especially with all that THC swimming in his veins. He still didn't speak, and he and the girl now seemed almost oblivious to each other's presence. And both of them didn't notice me. All three of us were in our own piece of atmosphere, disconnected from the others, silent and alone.

I moved back up the steps. Literally. I walked backwards, one step at a time, feeling around for the edge of each one with my heel. I sidled over to the alcove and waited. I was more tired than I thought possible. I wanted to go home and sleep, and now I wondered why I'd even come here. What had I intended to say to them? For all the attention I'd paid to my creature comforts, I had no plan for the actual encounter. I'm not a big planner, not down to the details, but I usually have some vague idea of what I'm going to do. Or maybe I'd had a plan and it drifted away in my sleep.

The couple hadn't moved. I almost wondered whether they were breathing, they were so still, like statues carved in the moonlight that was now diffused behind some high, wispy clouds. I closed my eyes, trying to think what to do. It was only for a few seconds, I think. When I looked again, the couple was gone. I picked up my stuff, walked past the roses, down the stairs to the parking strip, and along the footpath to my car. I'd come here to help Fred, thinking, if I'm honest, that I could vindicate him in some way. But as I left, I wanted the couple to return, to sit undisturbed on the bench forever.

CHAPTER 7

*W*HEN I WOKE the next morning, it all felt like a dream. My bag of food sat on the kitchen counter, a few grapes missing from the bunch. The blanket and pillow were in the passenger seat of my car. So it must have happened, right? The evening before lingered with that confusing, real but not, quality. The memory of the silence was so intense it echoed inside my head. The couple moving slowly as if they were underwater, then nearly immobile as the guy stared at me without seeing, and then sat down again, his form spilling over the woman's. Neither one had given a hint they'd seen me. Maybe the guy was simply defiant, daring me to object to the pot smoking. Or, he wasn't there at all, nothing but the figment of a cold, half-sleepy, sluggish brain that didn't like seeing my smoking buddy agitated about the damage to his garden.

As I drove to work, the taste of the cigarette I'd smoked with my morning coffee while I tried to put the events of the previous night into focus lingered on my tongue. I realized I hadn't had my bedtime cigarette the night before. That meant I was allowed an extra today. On the other hand, wasn't I trying to quit? Shouldn't I look at the missed smoke break as a sign that I was ready to cut back even more? Yet, as I drove, the more I thought about it, the more I wanted one with the cup of coffee I'd pour once I got into the office.

What a weakling I am. Maybe I don't even really want to quit. And on one level, I don't. I like the pulling away from the world that smoking offers, the chance to be alone with my thoughts most of the time, to not be *doing* anything else, to just be. That's what I strive for when I meditate, but somehow smoking is a shortcut to that state of mind. Of course, it could also be a shortcut to death, so there is that to think about.

The office was dark. I turned on the lights, cleaned out the coffee dregs from the day before, and made a fresh pot. By the time it brewed, I hadn't shaken the thoughts of premature death. You know how sometimes a thought drifts past and other times, that same thought rises up and your brain grabs onto it like a crocodile snapping at raw meat? The mind gets a grip and won't let the thought move on, until you begin to think it was planted there, or that it's a message of some kind. You start feeling as if you know it means something more than the endless stream of reflection and analysis and worry and fear and wanting. It takes on a life of its own and turns into something tangible. As my mind circled around death, it got that thick, solid feeling so I wondered if I was getting a hint of my own death from smoking cigarettes. Or someone else's. Thinking about death helped me sip my coffee and ignore the lingering whisper that I wanted a few puffs of nicotine.

I turned on the computer and worked while I drank two more cups of coffee. During those morning hours, Joe came in, made some phone calls, then left for hospital visits. Kate arrived as he was going out the door. By then, I was jittery from too much coffee, too fast, and still feeling sleepy at the same time. I envied their schedules. There had been a high school youth group meeting the night before, a casual support group led by one of the kids to help other kids organize music and photos on their iPhones. When Kate or Joe had evening events, they took their time about arriving at the office the following day.

Kate greeted me, ignored my offer of a cup of coffee, and darted through the door into the basement area. Her clogs thumped on the floor as she walked to her office. I didn't see her again all morning.

At lunchtime, I ate my sandwich quickly. I turned off the coffee pot, which had less than an inch of liquid left in it and was stinking up the place with its burning odor. I hadn't even noticed the smell until I was eating the last few bites of my sandwich. I went upstairs and walked toward the grove of trees to check out the situation that had been festering at the back of my mind all morning. The sense of unreality was nagging at me so much by now that I nearly wondered if I hadn't even been there myself, not to mention whether two shadowy people had been there. Nothing seemed real. Were they kids lingering after the iPhone class? Had Kate been there still, and seen them herself? It had been after ten, and the class went from 7:30 to 8:30, so I didn't think anyone was still around, but I had never checked the back parking lot.

The air was damp and cold, the sky a blank, white ceiling of fog. Fred was nowhere around, although the door to the storage room was open, so I figured he must be working somewhere. I walked to the end of the path and stepped onto the strip of grass that ran past the education wing, then faded off under the pine and eucalyptus trees into dirt and ground cover – bits of wood and fallen needles and leaves.

I stopped at the concrete bench where the couple had been seated. It was swept clean of dirt and tree droppings, so that fit with my memory. I kicked at the stuff on the ground, stabbed my toe at a cluster of dried weeds, their roots still firmly clinging to the soil, but no sign of life in the brown, crunchy stalks and seed pods above ground. So far, no stub of the joint I'd seen them drop. It was possible a bird or squirrel had grabbed it, smelling something sweet and thinking it might have potential for nest lining.

The air wasn't as cold over here, with the trees to block a bit of the chill that pressed down as hard as it could on a day like this. It seemed as if the sky wanted everyone to stay inside, to give the earth a break.

I sat on the bench and closed my eyes, trying to remember what the couple looked like. Nothing came. It had been so dark, they wore dark clothes, the boy had on a baseball cap, I think, and the girl had a hood over her hair. There was nothing to identify them. If I did see them again, I might recognize the way her body melted into his, but that was it. And how distinctive is that?

I stood and walked to the fence that ran along the back of the property. One board was missing, and the one next to it was angled slightly. I pushed on the angled board and it moved like a swinging door. Easy enough to make room for anyone to fit through. I could see where someone had nailed smaller boards to hold it in place and they'd been pried away. The small pieces of wood were grayed, so they'd been there for awhile. On the other side of the fence was a vacant lot and next to that, a very tall, very new looking fence surrounding a house. At the back edge of the vacant lot was a row of thick, tree-height junipers, and I could faintly see another fence behind those. The front of the lot opened onto the street that ran perpendicular to Woodcrest, which is the street that the church faces on to. Easy enough for anyone to wander through the lot and into the grove of trees on the church grounds.

As I walked toward the path and the backs of the buildings, I kicked at the ground, still looking for that joint stub. I sat down again and moved to the same spot I remembered the couple occupying. A few feet away was a flat piece of Styrofoam from a cup or one of those earth-unfriendly takeout boxes. I stretched my leg toward it and flipped it over with my toe. Nothing.

I stood, picked up the Styrofoam, and walked back to the storage room. The door was still open, but no Fred. Then I caught a whiff of smoke. I walked past the closed doors of the classrooms, four in all, and out toward the vast expanse of blacktop, missing the traditional white lines, but serving as a parking lot. I'd driven by on a Sunday once. Everyone had managed to park compact cars,

SUVs, and trucks into tidy rows and sections despite the lack of guidance. I suppose we're programmed to follow the conventions of our culture, even when the lines are blurred, or missing completely.

Fred stood near the end of the building. Judging by the pile of butts near his foot, he'd been there for awhile.

"Hi," I said.

He nodded and blew out a puff of smoke. He held out the pack of cigarettes. Since he didn't say anything, I figured the only way he'd talk to me would be if we smoked companionably through at least one cigarette. I pulled one out of the pack and he lit it for me. I'm not going to die yet, there's still time to quit. Besides, look at Fred. He was fit enough to care for two acres of property all by himself.

He finished his cigarette, dropped it into the pile and lit another. After two puffs, he cleared his throat. "Did you see more roses were snipped off?"

I shook my head.

"I picked them up. I guess you didn't notice there are only two or three buds left on each bush."

I hadn't even looked at the roses. All my attention was focused on the grove at the back, wondering whether I'd find evidence of the couple I'd seen. Part of me wanted to go back there with a rake and comb through every pine needle and chip of bark. I wouldn't stop until I found that joint. But what would that accomplish? "When did it happen?"

"Sometime last night."

"That can't be, I was here last night."

His hand stopped with his cigarette half way to his lips. He turned. "Why?"

"I wanted to see if anyone was damaging the roses. Jan thinks you did it. To hurt her. Why would she think that?"

"What did you see? What time were you here?" He dropped his half-finished cigarette on the ground but didn't stomp it out. It burned slowly, a thin wisp of smoke rising as if it wanted to hang on to the hem of his jeans.

I pressed my toe on the cigarette. When I looked back at his face, his eyes were glassy.

"I got here around ten, and I think I left around 12:30."

"Did you see anything?" His voice was hoarse as if he wanted to cough again and was holding it back. Or maybe he was going to start crying.

"What's wrong?"

"Last night was the anniversary."

"Of what?"

"Jan's daughter was killed right back there. Shot," said Fred.

He pointed at the grove of trees. Most of the area was blocked by the building, but I could see that was the area he was referring to.

"Oh, that's terrible." The words caught in my throat, tearing at the tender skin.

"Five years ago. April 28th."

"What happened?"

"She was a druggie. Something went wrong with her supplier, he'd given her some freebies, I guess. He pulled a gun and she tried to grab it. He shot her."

"She grabbed a gun?"

"She was a very aggressive girl."

I didn't know what to say. It explained the pain I felt emanating from Jan, from the tightness in her face, to her absolute obsession with the roses.

"They used to smoke back there all the time. Almost every night."

"Who's they? Were there more of them? Is that who I saw?"

"Their spirits."

"What?"

"You saw their spirits. They've been here before."

"Ghosts?"

He nodded.

"There was a couple."

"Her boyfriend. Lover, I suppose."

"Do you believe in ghosts?" I said. I wasn't sure what I thought about the subject. It's not impossible, but they were so real. And yet, not.

"I think people who had a violent death might linger. Their spirits want to put things back how they were."

I'm quite open to a lot. We're all so consumed with what we can see and touch and hear and taste. We get so caught up in our own heads, we miss a lot. I can believe there's a parallel realm. Maybe more than one.

"It doesn't matter what I believe," said Fred. "I've seen them. From time to time. On the third anniversary."

"Has anyone else seen this?" It wasn't that I didn't believe him. It was possible. I do believe people who die are somewhere close by, but we can't see them. That's easy to believe. A parallel realm, as I said. Where else would they be? Floating in the sky? Standing in the same room makes as much sense as that. But what I'd seen was so ... real. Their forms. On the other hand, it was strange how they didn't make any sound after that first hint of voices that had woken me from my drifting, not-really-meditating state. And strange that they didn't seem to be aware of my presence. Now that I thought about it, there was a lot of strangeness. The feeling I'd had when I woke up, that none of it had really happened.

Fred chuckled. "I'm not crazy. Do you think I'd tell people I'm seeing ghosts? They'd fire me. They don't go in for that kind of thing at this church."

"You told me you saw them."

"You're different. Besides, you experienced it first-hand."

"I don't know what I saw. I fell asleep. It was ... I can't describe it."

"That's what they do to you. They shift the whole atmosphere around you."

"So Pastor Joe and Kate don't know about this?"

"They know Jan's daughter was killed. But neither one of them worked here when it happened."

"Has Jan seen … anything?"

He kicked at his half-smoked cigarette, shoving it closer to the rest of the butts. "How would I know."

"You talk to her."

"No. She talks to me. Makes accusations."

"What kind of accusations?"

"I gotta get back to work. Anyhoo, I'm glad you saw them. I don't feel like a crazy old man anymore."

"What should I do?"

"There's nothing to be done. You probably don't want to come back at night."

"Do you think ghosts are cutting the roses? Can ghosts do such a thing?"

"I don't know anything about ghosts. Only what I saw. But if they can walk around the property, smoke pot, who knows what they can do." He picked up the dustpan propped against the side of the building and started to sweep up our discarded cigarettes and ashes. I took one final puff, dropped my cigarette on the ground, and stomped it out so he could scoop that up too.

"Was the boy killed too?"

Fred's hand shook. The dustpan tilted forward and most of the butts and the ash cascaded over the edge. Ash flew around and clung to my clothes, and Fred's as well. "Not that night," he said.

His voice was so low I almost didn't hear him. He stared at the pile of ash and cigarettes, but made no move to scoop them up again.

"Are you ok? Can I help you with that?"

"I guess they're here to stay. I'm an old man, maybe I'll be joining them soon."

"I don't think of you as an old man. You're my smoking buddy." I hoped my voice didn't sound fake, because I really meant it. I liked him, and I felt like we were friends. I hadn't thought much about his age at all until he brought it up. "How old are you?"

"Seventy-nine."

That caught me off guard. He really was in very good shape. "Have you always been a smoker?"

He pulled out his pack of cigarettes, removed one and lit it. "A pack a day since I was seventeen. A pack a day, a beer a day, a fried egg a day. None of it ever hurt me. Moderation in all things."

"I agree completely," I said.

"That girl was a creep, as bad as any thug."

"How do you know that?"

"I just know."

"Did you talk to them other times? When they were alive?"

"She got her claws into my son." His voice was so quiet again, I wasn't sure I'd heard correctly.

"What do you mean?"

"Corrupted him.

"How did she do that?"

"It goes back to our conversation a while ago. About corruption. She was a bad seed, and she got him mixed up with that drug dealer."

Wait. Now I was confused. "The boy smoking pot is your son?"

"Was. He's dead now."

I put my hand on his arm, then moved it up and wrapped my arm around his shoulders. Fred looked at the ground. The cigarette, only loosely held between his lips, slipped out and fell on top of his shoe. I nudged it away with my toe.

"I'm so sorry," I said.

After a minute, I let go of his shoulders. Tears filled my eyes, more than I'd seen in Fred's a few minutes earlier. I felt the ache in my chest, the pain of his grief seeping through his jacket and into my arm, winding its way to my heart and carving out a big opening that made me feel that no matter how much air I sucked in, it couldn't take away that hollow feeling. "Was your son shot too?"

"No. Beaten to death. He was living on the streets in Santa Cruz. I didn't find out until he'd been dead four days."

"Oh!" I started sobbing hard.

"She corrupted him. Got him into drugs, introduced him to that guy. And when they owed him money. When he came here with a gun and threatened them, the girl laughed at him and grabbed it. He shot her. My son was never the same after that."

I nodded. I was still a little confused, but I didn't really want to try sorting it out. There was too much, too much sadness, falling down on me like a heavy blanket, making it difficult to breathe or move my limbs.

"Later, my son killed the guy. Stabbed him. That's why they came and beat him up. But he wasn't like that. He wasn't a killer. She did that to him."

"They loved each other."

Fred turned and spat at the ground where the concrete joined the blacktop of the parking lot.

I touched his shoulder lightly. "I know they did. If those were their spirits. I could feel it, the way they held each other, I've never seen anything like it."

He bent down and scooped up the cigarette butts. Together, we walked to the storage room. He emptied the dustpan into the trash, and I said goodbye and walked to the stairs leading to my underground office, not sure at all what I was feeling. My mind was blank and white like the sky.

CHAPTER 8

A FEW DAYS AFTER THAT, Jan Waverly came into the office and said she wanted to talk to the Pastor. I told her he was out at the nursing home, but due back in half an hour. She plopped herself down in one of the armchairs and said she'd wait. Her hair wasn't twisted up and folded into a bun like the last time I'd seen her, but was loose, flowing well past her shoulders. It made her look older, and yet it also made her look like she didn't quite belong in this world. It was so startling white against her black scoop-necked shirt. She wore a black skirt that draped across her feet when she was seated.

For about ten minutes I worked on the church bulletin. It was giving me problems – the layout wasn't working as well as usual because they were having a special service that weekend, and there were all kinds of additions to the usual agenda. It looked crammed no matter how I arranged it. As I started to tweak the font size again, Jan spoke and I nearly jumped out of my chair.

"It's awfully quiet in here. Why don't you put on some music?"

"I like the quiet."

"It's nerve-wracking. Just sitting here. No sound but the keys clacking. And you breathing too loud."

I smiled so my words wouldn't sound too harsh. "You could go walk around in the garden while you're waiting."

"No."

Apparently, *she* wasn't worried about her words sounding harsh. I smiled again and turned back to the computer.

"That garden gives me no pleasure anymore. He's ruined it."

I didn't have to ask who she was talking about.

"He's cutting off all the blossoms. I can't believe he'd go so far as to tear them into pieces. It's like he wants to shred my heart. I wrote an essay about that. Getting your heart torn to shreds. Pastor Joe was going to put it in the monthly newsletter. Then he didn't. He said he would help me get it printed in the newspaper, but he didn't do that either. After he read it, he said I needed time to heal. I'll never heal."

I didn't know what to say. This was way out of my league. Was this what it was going to be like? When Joe listed "making people feel welcome" as one of my responsibilities, he didn't mention they'd be raw and ranting with grief. It sounded like Kate had a better sense of that reality. I had no idea what I was supposed to do now. I gave her a smallish smile to show her I couldn't even imagine her pain.

"We should have a professional caring for those roses. Not some Godless old man."

"He loves those roses as if they were his own," I said.

She glared at me. I smiled, even though my cheeks were starting to feel stiff from all this needless, programmed smiling. "Can I pour you a cup of coffee?" It was probably a mistake to ask because she sounded wound up enough already. Caffeine was the last thing she needed, but she settled back in her chair and snapped her head forward. I suppose that was her interpretation of a nod.

When I handed her the mug, she thanked me.

"Roses are a symbol of love. Red roses. I could have had white because my daughter was so pure. Ellie. Elinore after her great-grandmother, but we called her Ellie from the day she was born. Pure. Innocent. God's little flower."

I folded my hands in my lap. Clearly, I wouldn't be completing the preparation of the bulletin until Joe returned and Jan was safely closed up in his office.

"That's what I wrote about. Roses are love, the blood of life and love. Like the blood I poured out when I gave birth. Children aren't supposed to die before their parents. It turns the whole universe upside down. Red is for love, romantic love, they say, but red roses are the most beautiful of all. Other colors seem like pale imitations next to a dark *Firefighter* rose."

I saw Joe's shadow pass the window. I let out a long sigh. I hadn't realized I was holding my breath, terrified she would start crying, or worse, wailing like a lost soul. The pain that bled out of every pore of her skin was like a perfume, filling the room, making it difficult to breathe, making the silence oppressive. Maybe that's why she wanted the radio turned on. Silence is pleasant for me because I'm not grieving. For Jan, silence was terrible and eternal.

The door opened and Joe stepped into the office. "Jan," he said.

It didn't matter that I'd only known him a few weeks. Anyone could have read the tiredness in his voice when he saw her waiting.

Jan stood. "I need to talk."

He nodded and unlocked his office door. He held it open for her and she walked past him. I heard her purse fall to the floor with a thud. Joe nodded at me and went inside. Now, I wanted music. I popped open a web browser and went to *Pandora*. It couldn't be too loud, too un-churchy. I'd never listened to music while I worked before, but I needed something to lift the mood in that office. I went to my alternative station, but before I could get something playing, Kate appeared in the doorway. She walked past my desk and stopped to pour herself some coffee. This time, she was warm-and-friendly Kate. I was beginning to think the woman had a split personality or was some kind of Jekyll-Hyde character. Or is that the same thing?

She stood there, holding her coffee, not drinking. She ended up chatting the whole time Jan was in the pastor's office. If I didn't think it sounded paranoid, even in my own head, I'd have thought she heard Joe's door close and didn't want me listening to anything that might leak out through the gap under the door. She decided to stand there, making noise so I couldn't eavesdrop. These people were certainly worried about their confidences. For a group of upstanding church-goers, they seemed to have more undercurrents than I would have expected. Or maybe I'm a little paranoid. Either way, she shouldn't have worried. I was planning to listen to my music. I still felt that thick, heavy silence behind the sound of Kate's voice.

When Joe's door opened, Kate put her other hand around her coffee mug to hold it steady, turned and walked through the door into that dark, empty multi-purpose room. Her footsteps were quick and determined, all the way across that empty expanse until she reached her office.

Jan's face was bright red. She gave me a quick glance, a very suspicious-looking glance, as if she, too, thought I'd been listening. Okay. I'm nosey, but why were they all assuming I was trying to listen? Was it somehow evident in my eyes, the way I looked at them? Or were they projecting their own curiosity onto me since I was an outsider? Besides, she'd already told me about her daughter. And her husband. Was there some secret she was telling the pastor? Not likely. Maybe she wanted her grief to be private, although she hadn't acted that way earlier, or when I'd spoken to her in the garden that time. I directed my eyes back to my computer screen, hit print so I could see how the bulletin looked on actual paper. I turned my chair so I could lift the pages off the printer when they shot out. I set the printed copy on my desk. The layout wasn't too bad. I'd proofread it and then shrink the font for the prayer requests down one more size.

The door slammed behind Jan when she left. Pastor Joe plopped himself onto one of the armchairs. I could see how these chairs might quickly turn me into the welcoming committee. I hadn't recognized that fact when he told me I'd be both administrative assistant and receptionist, keeping on top of all that office stuff, but also keeping visitors entertained, or perhaps keeping them from going over the edge before the pastor was ready to meet with them. Jan sure looked like she'd gone over the edge with her blood-red face, the color seeping all the way down her neck and across her collarbone.

"Well, I think I soothed her feelings. For now."

His voice was loud, resonating through the small office. He seemed proud of his skills in shepherding one of his lambs into a serene pasture. I wondered how long it would last.

"She sure looked upset," I said.

"She's distraught over the damage to the roses. She thinks Fred is 'conjuring up' some kids hanging around at night. I'm worried about her. She's been through more than most people can handle."

I pushed the bulletin to one side. Proofreading would have to wait a bit. I was confused. Wasn't it a breach of his ethics to talk to me about what a church member said in private? What about all those secrets and the gossip he was so concerned about? Or was he assuming I wouldn't gossip because I wasn't part of their church family, as he liked to call it?

"Her daughter was shot right here at the church," said Joe. "About five years ago. It was some drug-related activity, and the man who shot her was killed, so Jan never had any closure. Not that punishment of the killer eases the grief. But the wound does stay open without that."

"Fred told me about it," I said.

Joe lifted his eyebrows. He opened his mouth as if he was going to ask more about Fred, but then he didn't.

"It's so sad." Again, I felt that stabbing in my heart. For both Fred and Jan. Such boundless, constant grief. How did you live out your life when there was a crater that big right in the center of it?

"She wants me to fire Fred." He stretched out his legs and

balanced the heel of his left foot on the toe of his right. He stared at his feet as if this trick was going to help him figure out what he should do. "Maybe she's right about Fred. He's too old to care for this much property by himself. Maybe he's imagining things."

"That's not fair," I said.

"It's not right that someone would damage such beautiful flowers. Especially when they have so much meaning to her. That makes it much worse."

I wasn't sure about that. Destruction is destruction. And anyone vicious enough to tear rose petals into shreds was already disturbed. And unless it was the spirits, it was unlikely they knew there was a deeper meaning to the roses, that they were a memorial. I wanted to argue, but I didn't really want to tell him about the other things Fred told me. About the spirits. Then they'd definitely think Fred was losing it. And I couldn't back him up by telling about my evening adventure. I couldn't think how I would explain it to Pastor Joe. He'd immediately ask why I'd risked my safety like that, followed quickly by puzzlement over why the heck I went to all that trouble and didn't even try to speak to them. Whoever they were. Or whatever. No, it was better to keep that to myself. "Destroying anything is terrible," I said. "Tearing flower petals? It's not like Fred can be here 24-7 to guard them."

"That's why she thinks he's the one tearing them up."

"Why? Why would he do that? Have you talked to him?"

He unbalanced his feet and straightened himself in the chair. "Not yet. I need to mull it over. I'm only thinking out loud, reviewing what she said."

"Oh."

"Something ..."

He was quiet for so long I wondered if he realized he'd started a sentence.

"Something-what?" I said, finally.

He stared at me as if I was leaving half-finished sentences out there. He stood.

"What were you going to say?" I leaned on my desk, staring at him.

He looked suddenly disoriented, as if he'd disappeared, or didn't realize he was standing in the church office, that I was sitting five feet away, or that he'd even been talking to me.

"No. Nothing. There's something ... I need to think."

He went into his office and closed the door. That in itself was unusual because he never closed the door except when someone was in there seeking guidance. It seemed to me it would be quite difficult to write a sermon without private space where you could concentrate, but he seemed to be fine with it, always open for interruptions. I guess if he really wanted to be alone, needed to think deeper thoughts without intrusion, he would go to his home office. Although at home, his four daughters were fluttering around.

It was difficult to concentrate on proofreading the bulletin after that. I had to read it three times. My thoughts kept wandering away, and I'd realize I was six or seven lines down and hadn't even checked for those typos that sneak in because they're real words that the spelling checker doesn't catch.

My mind drifted from Jan's essay to her irrational insistence that Fred was tearing the flowers to shreds, to Joe's lack of recognition that accusing Fred of such a thing made no sense. I deliberately did not think about the spirits, ghosts, whatever you want to call them. I preferred to let them remain hidden, a powerful emotion living beyond the grave, but not entities that were interested in, or even capable of, plucking rose petals off a blossom and tearing them into shreds like secret notes that had been passed between lovers back when there was no texting or IM available to communicate your passionate thoughts.

CHAPTER 9

*T*HIS MIGHT SOUND insane, but I became so obsessed with who was tearing up those rose petals, I started up a nightly vigil. Whether spirits of deceased children strolled around church property in the dark, looking for true love, or whether living teenagers were smoking pot and taking a break to shred rose petals, I pushed my fears aside because my curiosity is stronger than my fear.

Every night at nine-forty I left my condo carrying my thick blanket. I abandoned the pillow idea so I could be more efficient instead of lugging an entire campsite full of stuff. The evenings had turned mild, so it wasn't such a problem with the concrete feeling like a sheet of ice. I abandoned my snacks too and brought only the thermos of hot chocolate.

From ten at night until two in the morning, I sat in the alcove. I sipped chocolate and let my mind drift. I thought about Fred and how sad his life must be, to have his only son taken away so brutally. His feelings had become part of me as if I'd sucked them in along with his exhaled cigarette smoke. I studied the outline of the rose bushes and kept my focus on that dark area under the trees that stretched to the back fence. For thirteen days, I never saw anyone.

On the final night I sat there, when I'd already told myself it was the last night, I saw them. I didn't see them arrive, so perhaps I'd dozed off for a minute, even though I still held the cap of the thermos in my hand. It hadn't tipped over and dribbled hot chocolate, so I couldn't have done more than close my eyes for a second, half a second, an extended blink.

They were seated on the bench. The girl leaned into the guy like that first time I saw them. Once again, I felt the warmth of wanting what they had, a longing so intense it made my heart cramp. I had to lean forward over my crossed ankles. I poured out the rest of the hot chocolate into a dark puddle on the concrete and screwed the cap on the thermos. I set it on the blanket. This time, I didn't hesitate walking down the steps and along the path toward the grove of trees. I had to get a closer look. They certainly weren't paying any attention to the roses, and gave no hint they planned to drift that direction and start tearing the few remaining blooms. I wasn't completely sure they were teenagers. They had an ageless quality to them that I can't explain – the way the girl let her whole body fall into the guy seemed like an adult woman, old and weighed down by life, yet at the same time so freshly in love, like a young girl.

I don't know what happened, if I looked away, if the path twisted more sharply than I'd realized and for a moment the area where they sat was blocked by the corner of the building, but when I arrived at the spot where the path dissolved into the lawn, I looked at the bench and it was empty. At first, I thought I was confused. I jogged along the branch of the path that edged the strip of grass. I was sure they must still be on the church side of the fence, they couldn't have moved that quickly. But they had. They were gone.

Somehow, I knew they weren't shredding the roses. I was also pretty sure they were visiting from another realm. Then I saw something else.

I'd walked back to my blanket and sat down to drink one last cup of chocolate and try to think about what I'd seen, to make sure I truly believed they were spirits. That this was Jan's daughter, coming back to find her lover. I swallowed the last of the chocolate, licked my lips, and replaced the cap. When I stood to fold my blanket, I turned my back to the pathway. I put the thermos at the center of the blanket that was already folded in quarters. Then I folded it two more times so the thermos was snugly inside. I picked it up and turned and saw what at first looked like a caricature of a ghost. Immediately after that thought, I realized it was Jan, with her long white hair glistening in the half moon that shone without the dilution of any clouds. She wore a long white nightgown that dragged on the concrete. Through the thin fabric of the gown, I could see she was even more slender than I'd realized before. The shape of her body was visible, and I could tell she wasn't wearing anything but that gown. Her feet were bare. I knew she lived only three houses away from the church, but still, walking at night in bare feet must have been painful and cold.

In her right hand was a very large pair of sewing shears. Slowly the blades parted, and she pressed the center joint up close to the petals of one of the rosebuds that had finally started to open. With a squeeze of her hand, the sheers snapped closed. The top pieces of the petals fell on her hands and must have floated to the ground because she kicked her foot like she was shaking something off. She moved the scissors to the stem, gripped what was left of the bloom, and gnawed at the stem right below the little leafy part that sticks out around the base of the flower. Although the shears looked deadly, they weren't the right tool for the job, and she was having some trouble cutting the thick stem. She gave up gnawing at it and let the scissors fall to the ground. I was surprised they didn't stab her in the top of her foot. She pulled off a petal and tore it down the center. Then she tore those pieces. She held her hands out at arms' length and let the torn petals fall at her feet as well.

I clutched my folded blanket close to my ribs and walked to the edge of the steps.

Jan bent down and picked up the sheers. She took one handle in each hand and started attacking the stem again. Holding them like that prevented her from getting the force she needed, but it took her quite a few minutes to recognize that fact. Finally, she switched the shears back to one hand, grabbed the mangled bloom in her left hand and worked at the stem until she chewed off the top.

I wondered if she'd sense my presence at some point, feel me looking at her. That's how I am. There's a crawly feeling that runs across my scalp when someone is observing me. I've always wondered what that is, the knowing that their eyes are on you. Is it some type of energy coming out of their brains, the fact that their thoughts are focused on you? I don't know if that happens to everyone, but it sure does to me. I know when I'm being watched. Apparently, Jan didn't, because she moved to the next bloom and began the process again, first snipping off the tops of the petals, plucking some loose and tearing them to shreds, then sawing off the bloom with an inch or two of the stem.

A breeze started moving among the trees and grew until even the tops of the rose bushes responded. Jan's nightgown plastered itself against her legs, but she didn't shiver. It wasn't cold, exactly, but she seemed to feel nothing, not the chilled concrete or the breeze or even the hem of her gown tickling the tops of her feet. She was single-mindedly focused on destroying every remaining bloom on the twelve rose bushes. It was too late to stop her from that activity, but I didn't want to stand on the steps all night. I was tired. I'd found the answer to one question – Fred wasn't crazy and he wasn't slacking off on his responsibilities, and the roses weren't being destroyed by ghosts or teenagers from the church. I suppose that's a lot of answers to one question, but now the question was, should I sneak past her and leave her alone with whatever demons she was battling? Or should I demand to know why she was blaming Fred for her own craziness?

I walked down the steps, not taking any care to quiet my footsteps. I thought she'd hear the soles of my boots tapping each step, but she was still oblivious to my presence. As I approached, she moved along to the next rose bush. Her hair flowed around her shoulders, so smooth it looked like melted wax running onto her nightgown. Another breeze passed through, strong enough to make me shiver, so sudden it made me picture the ghostly couple. Was it them, walking past? Or was I shaking because I could sense Jan's grief in the harsh snapping of her scissors, the lack of care for her bare feet, the complete absence of concern over how little her night-gown hid from a casual observer, even in the dark? Hard at work, hacking at the top edges of the petals with her scissors, Jan didn't appear to shiver or even notice her hair blowing across her cheek, a few strands clinging to her lips.

The breeze died and I stepped closer. Was she walking in her sleep? It seemed like too much activity for that, but what do I know about sleepwalking, or sleep gardening, for that matter? It's possible people do more than wander aimlessly when they sleepwalk. Perhaps they garden, or make a sandwich, or comb their hair. If I spoke, I might frighten her, or wake her and really screw her up. Touching her would probably be even worse. I debated about turning and walking across the front grass area and down the slope to the street. She might not even notice I was there. I stood watching for several more minutes.

Suddenly, she was finished. All but one of the blooms and their torn petals were scattered in the dirt under the rose bushes. Jan turned, and as if she'd known I was there the entire time, said, "There, that's done."

I decided on an open-ended question, to try to assess the state of things – sleep-walking versus deliberate destruction of something she claimed to adore to the point of near-worship. I also decided not to point out that she actually wasn't done. A single bud remained on the bush closest to the wing of classrooms. It was darker at that end of the path. She must not have seen it. "What are you doing?" I said.

"Killing them."

"The roses?"

"There's no beauty left in the world."

"Well, there certainly isn't any beauty in this rose garden. You've destroyed it all. I thought you loved them. I thought they were a memorial to your daughter."

"My daughter is dead."

I nodded.

"I don't want to love anyone ever again. It's too painful."

"You loved your daughter when she was alive. Was that painful?"

"I still do."

"Of course," I said. "Why are you cutting off all the blooms? Did you cut the others?"

"Yes." She sighed.

Her words were senseless enough that I decided she must be sleepwalking. Yet her eyes were open, they seemed to be looking at me, they moved rather than freezing in a steady stare. She blinked from time to time. Nothing had the appearance of sleep except the near-nonsense of what she was saying.

"The roses are too beautiful. I never should have given them. Fred is so proud of them and he has no right. They don't belong to him."

"He's trying to please you, to do a good job." Half of that was a lie, but in some ways maybe not. He certainly didn't want her to accuse him of not looking after them.

"Ha!" She clutched the shears to her chest and turned. Without noticing the sharp pebbles, tracked up from the parking strip, she walked quickly, half-running, to the set of stairs that led down to the street. She didn't bother to steady herself with the handrail, but jiggered down the steps, across the gravel strip, again not exhibiting any outward evidence of pain. She walked along the dirt path and disappeared from my view behind a large oak tree that hung over part of the street.

I should have stopped her. Should have called someone to help. She hadn't been carrying anything but those large silver shears. Had she left her house unlocked? Was she safe in there alone? I know I should have called the pastor, maybe even the police, but what had she really done? What would I say? *Jan was here in her nightgown, tearing up rose petals?*

When I walked back to my car, all of the nearby houses were dark except Jan's. She was in the center of her living room with the curtains pulled open. She looked fine, standing as if she might be staring at the TV, drinking something out of a teacup. I didn't see the flicker of a TV, but she looked okay. There was no sign of the scissors.

CHAPTER 10

*T*HE NEXT DAY was Monday, May 16th. One of my Monday duties was re-counting the contributions from the offering plates the day before, as a double-check on the church deacons who counted the money on Sunday afternoons. I'm sure they loved that, having their accuracy doubted, but it was an extra safeguard. Everyone makes mistakes.

By ten, I'd counted the cash, totaled the checks, bagged it all for the bank deposit, answered one phone call asking about prices for weddings held at the church, and downed three cups of coffee. I needed some fresh air and a quick walk up the stairs and around the property to get the jitters out of my hands and the kinks out of my neck and back. I think the whole world is going to go into early rigor mortis, the way everyone sits frozen in front of computers all day long and some people, for half the night. I know I said I love the internet, love computers, but still, human beings weren't designed to sit in tiny chairs all day with shoulders hunched up, fingers tapping, and jumping around from website to website.

Before I took the first step up the stairs, I looked up and saw Jan. She'd planted herself on the path near the last rose bush. Her hair was wrapped up in that fancy bun, and she wore black slacks and a long black silky jacket thing. One arm was folded tight across her ribs. In her right hand, she held those wicked shears I'd seen the night before. I put one foot on the first step but didn't move forward. The conversation last night, only a few hours ago, had been confusing. I wondered if she remembered we'd run into each other, because I still wasn't sure if she'd been awake or asleep or in some other state of mind I hadn't yet considered.

She lowered her hand and slowly opened the shears. She squeezed them around the last remaining rosebud, leaving just an inch or two of the stem. She slammed them closed, and this time, rather than having to gnaw at the thick stem, the infant blossom was cut loose and fell to the ground.

I saw Fred walking along the side of the fellowship hall. Maybe he was afraid of what he'd seen at night, but he wasn't afraid of Jan. He strolled toward her with his usual loping stride, not in a hurry, and not trying to hide his presence as if he was sneaking up on her.

It didn't matter. When Jan saw him, she shrieked and dropped her scissors into the dirt.

I took a few steps up. They glared at each other like two vultures, so I didn't think they'd notice me and I definitely wanted to hear every word of their conversation.

"What are you doing, Jan?" Despite his scruffy look, Fred's voice was even-toned. While he waited for her answer, he slipped his hands into his pockets. It looked like he'd lowered his hackles somewhat. He knew he had the upper hand.

"I have a right to cut them."

"The stem is too short."

"I want to put it in a bud vase."

"Did you destroy the others?" said Fred.

She bent down and picked up her giant yellow purse and the shears, but didn't touch the rosebud lying in the dirt. The way she started to move away from him, it seemed that she'd forgotten why she was even there, didn't recall what she'd been doing when he startled her. "It reminds me. David called Ellie his rose, you know."

"Why do you have to take these? What happened to your own rose garden?"

"They died. They always die. Everything in my life dies."

Fred winced as if she'd stabbed the shears into his stomach.

"Why couldn't you take a few cuttings. Why did you have to destroy them?"

"Because you act like they belong to you. And they don't. They're mine. And I don't want you touching them after what your son did to Ellie."

Fred said something I couldn't hear. I crept up a few more steps, but I was still far enough down that they couldn't see me without walking over to the top of the stairs.

"He was weak." Jan whimpered. "A weak, grubby boy. He didn't even love her."

"He was just a kid."

"He left her to die all alone."

"He didn't know."

"He knew."

"I see them." Fred picked up the rosebud and held it out to her. "They come by. They linger. And he did love her, Madison saw them."

"You can't see them." She backed away from the offered rosebud as if it was a flame.

Fred's hand remained steady, holding the bud. "I see their spirits."

"No. You don't. You're only saying that to hurt me. As if your son didn't already rip out my heart. Now you have to tell me this?" Suddenly, Jan threw her head back and laughed like she was watching the funniest thing she'd ever seen. "You're lying. They're in paradise. You didn't see anything, if you did, they were demons. Good people don't return." She continued laughing in a loud, unbroken stream that was more like a shriek. Her throat was long and white. It looked like it belonged to a bird the way the shrieking laugh vibrated inside, making the skin bulge. She laughed longer than you would consider normal. She kept laughing and laughing and then she was screaming and the scream slowly transformed into a howl. "You never should have said that to me. That you saw them. You keep doing more and more to torment me. I want you to leave me alone!" she screamed. "I want you out of here."

Fred stood with one arm dangling at his side, still holding the rosebud in his other hand. When she lowered her head and was finally silent, he stuck the short stem into her twisted, knotted hair. They stared at each other, once again reminding me of birds, both of them with their feathers spread out like spikes, reading the other, waiting to start pecking. I feel sad to say this now, but I had a feeling that Jan would win. She would peck Fred to death.

Fred was longing for his son, seeing ghosts that comforted him. Maybe seeing the ghosts let him know that his son had found some happiness in life before it exploded in a violent death – a death that was dismissed as insignificant by most people – another drug addict who ate up his own life with his desire to get high, to feel good. Even though the ghosts scared him a little, even though he didn't really want them around, he saw their love, the way they melted into each other. He didn't want them around because maybe he was ready to let go.

Aside from that maniacal laugh, Jan was the kind who grieved in anger. She didn't simply ache for the loss of her daughter, she was furious that grief had happened to her as if it had singled her out. She thought she had some special right to do whatever she pleased with those roses because she'd paid for them. She not only thought she owned the roses, she owned her daughter's memory, and I bet she thought she owned her daughter when she was alive. After all, she'd contributed cells, and a womb, and had given birth, and done countless other things for her child. Some people turn that into thinking the child belongs to them in some tangible way. When her daughter died, Jan took it personally. A great big assault from the universe, taking away what belonged to her. The rage inside that woman was visible from the roots of her pure white hair to the tips of the cherry red claws on the ends of her fingers.

They remained motionless, staring for so long that my feet ached and my back started to get stiff. There was something so intimate in the way they looked at each other, I almost felt as if I was spying on a couple making love. I know that sounds ridiculous. They hated each other. Why would I think of lovers? But that's what I thought. There was something naked in the way they looked at each other. Jan's pure rage that she hid from everyone else, but allowed Fred to see in all its ugliness. On Fred's side, all his grief was blatant in his expressionless face, reflecting the flatness of his life without his son.

They stood there with all that heat between them. They almost seemed to glow with a dark, black aura that blended at the edges into a murky red, pulling them into a single entity of grief and rage and all the sorrow of life.

After a while, Fred turned and walked to the tool room. He disappeared inside. A moment later, Jan went to the steps that led to the parking strip. As she thumped her feet on each step, the rosebud jiggled in her bun. Then it fell out, but she didn't notice, if she'd even noticed it was there to begin with. She walked across the gravel and turned toward her house.

I wanted a cigarette in the worst way.

CHAPTER 11

I NEVER WENT to find Fred that day. I wish I had. Every single time I smoke a cigarette on church property now, I think of him. But that day, I thought maybe he needed to recover from his encounter with Jan. I didn't mention any of it to Joe – not the ghosts or Jan in her nightgown cutting roses or the intimate, vicious encounter between Jan and Fred. It was a crazy week, with two church members passing away on the same day and a teenaged girl in the hospital for dialysis, and Joe trying to be supportive of the girl's parents during her treatments. Kate was gone for five days at a convention. I was so busy with phone calls regarding the two funerals, I never made it outside for a break to talk to Fred or have a smoke.

The following Monday when I went out for a smoking break, hoping to see him, I found his body. I didn't think for a single second that he'd died of a stroke or a heart attack or any other age-related problem. That's because an enormous pair of sewing shears protruded from his neck and that big pool of blood I mentioned early on. A lot of blood. I don't need to describe that. The enormous scissors and the wound in his neck made me puke and lose all desire for either lunch or a cigarette. It almost made me wonder if I'd never want another cigarette as long as I lived. It might be the cure for smoking. Right away I felt guilty for analyzing my addiction to cigarettes, my lack of self-control, and for thinking about myself at all when I was staring at a bloodied body, the body of a man I had started to think of as my friend. Now he was gone. Suddenly I felt very friendless in this church full of people.

Then I cried.

Of course, I knew they were Jan's scissors. It wasn't any deduction on my part. She's not the only woman in the world with enormous sewing shears, but it doesn't take a genius to add up the scissors she used to destroy the roses and her rage at Fred's son for leaving her daughter to die alone.

I covered Fred with my sweater, so at least his face and shoulders weren't exposed, staring up at the sky, so vulnerable like that. It was like he was lying in his bed, but out here where squirrels could run across his body, or people would walk by and stare at him, and he couldn't do anything to regain his dignity.

I ran down the stairs, flung open the office door, grabbed the receiver, and dialed 9-1-1. The operator was patient, and that helped me stay calm, but I was crying even harder at this point. My hands were wet, as the tears ran down my face and got on the phone receiver and then made my fingers slip around the slick black plastic. It felt slimy, and that made me think of all that blood covering Fred's chest, and pooling under the white shirt he wore every day to work.

As soon as the operator assured me some detectives were on the way, I called Joe and told him about Fred. He said he'd call Kate and would be right there.

I went outside and started back up the stairs, walking slowly. I stopped halfway up and made myself take a deep breath, then slowly release it, then another. That helped somewhat, but my heart still thumped about five extra beats a second. I wondered if it was going to burst out of my chest, and I don't think it was just from the exertion of running. At the top of the stairs, I looked toward the front parking strip. It was more out of habit than expecting to see anyone there. The entire property was deserted. Even the birds were quiet. There was no breeze. It's a strange feeling to be the only human life, to know you're the only one breathing, the only one moving about, the only mind thinking and running through its normal cycle of activity. Tears swam around my eyes, and I desperately wanted to walk around the corner of the building, to look away from Fred's body, but I felt I owed it to him not to look away. To be with him while his spirit wandered over that line we all know is there but can't conceive of until we cross it. I sat next to him, near his feet. I reached into his shirt pocket and pulled out his pack of cigarettes, removed one, and lit it with the book of matches he kept tucked inside the box. Our last smoke together.

THE CIGARETTE WAS gone by the time the police arrived. I'd even had time to stand up, get the pins and needles out of my ankles and carry the cigarette butt to the trash can, lick my fingers to moisten the end of the butt and drop it into the can with the grass clippings. It didn't occur to me until I slid the pack back into his pocket that I'd touched his body and this was a crime scene that I'd now managed to contaminate.

There were two detectives, a woman and man. The woman was about fifty and the man was young, probably my age, although he was trying so hard to act strong and in control, he seemed younger, like a little kid playing cops. He kept his shoulders back. His shirt, pressed with those creases that run down the center of the sleeve, fit him perfectly so I could see that he lifted weights, that his shoulders and upper arms were muscular, but not all bulked out, making the fabric as tight as a sausage casing, like some guys do. Neither one of us smiled when he said he was Officer Brad Holcomb, and asked my name. I could tell we would have smiled if we weren't standing next to Fred's body.

Asking my name was the last thing he was allowed to do. From there, Detective Karen Palmer took over. She pestered me with so many questions, I was exhausted by the time Joe and Kate walking past the roses, headed in our direction. Most of her questions were about time – when did I arrive at the church, what did I do first, how long did that take, what time did I find Fred, how long did I wait before I called 9-1-1? When she asked if I'd touched anything, I hesitated. The pause was long enough that it became my answer.

"What did you touch?" she said.

"I took his cigarettes out of his pocket."

A smirk might have flickered across Officer Holcomb's face, but I couldn't be sure. Detective Palmer sighed.

A van pulled into the parking lot. Right after the van was a white sedan. A woman got out of the van, poked at her cell phone, then walked to where we were standing. She introduced herself as the medical examiner. That made me want to start crying again.

Kate and Joe slowed their pace, in lock-step with each other as they drew closer. They stopped right at my side. "I'm the pastor, and this is our youth minister." Joe put his hand on Kate's shoulder. "What happened here?"

Detective Palmer held her hand up. "One minute." She looked at me. "What did you do after you took out the pack of cigarettes?"

I looked Detective Palmer in the eyes. "I smoked one. Then I put the pack back in his pocket."

"You shouldn't have touched anything."

"Well I wasn't exactly thinking straight," I said. "All I could think about was losing my friend, and I wanted to have one last cigarette with him."

"You considered Mr. Tolly your friend?"

I nodded.

"How long have you known him?"

"Since I started working here. About a month ago. We took cigarette breaks together."

"You smoke?" said Officer Holcomb.

I nodded again.

Detective Palmer looked at him, and he took a step back, then took a few more steps back toward the building so the medical examiner could get close to the body.

"Come with me." Detective Palmer walked down the corridor and Joe, Kate, and I followed her like a line of ducks.

She asked Joe and Kate a bunch of questions. A lot of those were also about time, what time Fred usually came to work, what time they came to work, what time was it when I'd called to tell them about Fred? Joe explained their Mondays off, then Kate interrupted to mention people hanging around, smoking pot. Maybe selling drugs.

"He was really worried about those kids using the garden for a party spot," said Joe. "Kate mentioned he had some kind of confrontation with them."

The detective went off on that line of thought – who'd seen them, how often were they around? Her eyes darted back and forth from Kate to Joe as she fired questions and they tried to answer – had *they* ever seen anyone? Was there any property damage? Did anyone know who they were? How old were they, how many of them were there? Of course, Joe and Kate staggered through most of the questions, unable to provide any information because they'd ignored the whole thing.

Finally, I couldn't stand it anymore. They were directing her down an imaginary path, a path where only ghosts walked, as far as I knew. Kate made it sound as if they'd believed Fred all along. It wasn't right. Kate dismissed his concerns, almost ridiculed him. Joe had acted like he agreed with Jan's opinion that Fred had "conjured up" the kids smoking pot. Now, all of a sudden, they were going to act as if they'd believed him from the start? I was about to jump in when the detective said, "Did anyone report this?"

"No," said Kate. "Like we said, there wasn't any damage and it didn't seem to be a huge problem. I guess now we see that was the wrong ..."

Joe interrupted. "To be honest, we wondered if Fred was imagining it. He's old. Was old – seventy-nine."

The detective nodded. Obviously, she could tell that from looking at Fred's body. I had to give Joe credit because his cheeks were a little pink. At least he recognized he'd been dismissive of Fred, hadn't bothered to ask about his concerns, maybe hadn't treated him with much respect.

"Fred talked about these kids, but no one ever saw them and there was no trash left around, no graffiti, so we didn't do anything," said Joe. "I see now that we were wrong."

"Whoever Fred saw has nothing to do with this." I didn't think it would help the conversation, or the investigation, to introduce the ghosts of Fred's son and Jan's daughter. "You should ask Jan Waverly a few questions," I said.

"Madison," said Joe.

"What?"

"Jan would never … she's a sensitive woman. She isn't capable of doing something like this."

Kate nodded, eager to punctuate Joe's opinion. "Jan was so supportive of the work we're doing with teenagers. A really good person. Caring."

"There wasn't anyone lurking around who stabbed Fred," I said. "The partiers are ghosts." I looked at their faces. "You can laugh all you want, but that's what Fred saw. There were no physical people hanging around here."

"How do you know there weren't any kids partying back there?" said Kate.

"I came here every night for two weeks. I never saw anyone. At least no one that was still flesh and blood." I shivered when I said that because it made me picture Fred with all his blood seeping out onto the pavement. "So maybe there were kids smoking pot here at one time, but you're not going to find a gang of teenagers that killed him."

"It's much too early for a conclusion," said Detective Palmer.

"Tell me more about Ms. Waverly, but let's try to avoid any discussion of ghosts."

"Jan was obsessed with those roses. She thought they carried the soul of her daughter. She was hacking them off, tearing the petals, sometimes taking them home." I paused for a breath. "She blames Fred's son for her daughter's death. She thought he should have protected Ellie. He ran away when Ellie was shot."

Joe put his hand over his face and bent his head forward. I suppose he felt guilty that he didn't know the full story. Kate stared at me. She didn't blink for almost a minute. Finally she spoke. "The boy was Fred's son?"

"They blame each other. Fred thought Ellie corrupted his son, getting him into drugs. Jan thinks if Fred's son acted like a man, Ellie wouldn't have died." I choked when I said that last part. I would miss my smoking buddy. I reassured myself that it had seemed like Fred was ready to let go, just not in the way I thought. He didn't deserve to die like this. No one does.

Joe folded his arms across his chest. "When I read that essay she wrote ... she wanted it in the newsletter. It sounded like it was written by a lunatic."

Out here in the light, I noticed a few gray hairs in his jet-black beard that I hadn't seen before. "When Fred told Jan he saw the ghosts, their spirits, whatever, she lost it. She was laughing and shrieking and moaning. It was horrible."

"I kept thinking it was grief, more than most people could bear," said Joe. "But then I wondered if it was something more. Madness. I don't know, I'm not always equipped. I'm here for spiritual counseling. I don't always know where the line is. I should have ..." said Joe.

"We all should have," I said. I told them about seeing Jan in her nightgown, tearing the roses, walking around in the cold as if she felt nothing.

. . .

LIFE AROUND THE CHURCH got back to normal, although I didn't know yet what normal was. There wouldn't be any more dead bodies, I was sure of that.

The roses grew fresh buds, lots of them. I pruned them until they hired a new gardener. I'm not sure if Joe or Kate noticed I was taking care of the pruning, but it made me feel like I was still connected to Fred. Every day at lunchtime I'd unlock his storage room door, get out the pruning scissors, and snip off the blooms that were loose and floppy, their petals turning to that fabric-like texture. I dropped them into a bucket and carried them to the grove of trees. I scattered the petals on the ground and threw away the stems. After that was done, I stood at the edge of the back parking lot and smoked two cigarettes. My addiction was headed in the wrong direction because now I was up to five a day. Smoking calmed me, and I knew that once I stopped missing the man who poured his whole life into the church gardens, I would cut back again. It startled me how lonely I was without the presence of an old guy I'd known for only a few weeks. And for now, the sting of smoke in my throat mirrored the sting in my heart.

I settled nicely into my job. Kate was friendlier to me, although she still had a bit of that Jekyll-Hyde thing going on. Maybe she decided I was valuable after all, since I could see people for who they really are. That Fred was a wonderful human being, and she had misjudged him. Or maybe she only thought I'd be useful if there were other strange things going on, with the living or the dead.

SHALLOW WATER

A Suburban Noir Ghost Story

By
Cathryn Grant

Published by D2C Perspectives

CHAPTER 1

*I*T WAS THE first time that the annual retreat for Central Avenue Church included the discovery of a dead body. Of course, I had to be the person who found her floating near the rocks. Not that there wouldn't have been a murder if I wasn't there, but why did it have to be me to see her, as if I have some kind of corpse radar?

The retreat takes place every fall in Half Moon Bay, California. The town is an eclectic blend of suburban streets and clusters of beach cottages, interspersed with homes that could rightly be called palatial. The exclusive Ritz Carlton Hotel sits on one side of the bay, near the golf course. The Beach House, which is like a stately old home, is at the center of the half-moon shape, and the Oceano Spa faces the Ritz. All along the coast, there are amazing restaurants, lots of good sandy beaches, and a bit of surfing for those who aren't yet ready to venture further up Highway One to Mavericks Beach where the experts ride the waves.

When the annual retreat rolled around, I'd been working for Pastor Joe and Pastor Kate for almost six months. They insisted I needed to attend the retreat to make sure the schedule stayed on track, manage the logistics, and take care of any other behind-the-scenes details that might come up. This proves an administrative assistant is always needed, even when she's not a member of the church, and not involved in most of their activities. This meant I had lots of free time to walk along the shore and find dead bodies.

The retreat has two purposes. One is to plan the calendar of events for the coming year to make sure there aren't any conflicts, such as a Friday night slumber party for pre-teen girls followed by a Saturday morning senior breakfast. The second purpose is to give people a quiet place and some definite time away from their normal lives so they can consider their own plans and the state of their spiritual affairs.

Once everyone knew I'd found a woman's body in the shallow water near the breakwater that protects the harbor, I'm sure that shone a different light on their spiritual contemplation.

The Beach House is a pretty great place for contemplation. Nearly all of the rooms look out over the bay. The designer was brilliant – the rooms are a split-level style. There's a sitting area with a fireplace, table and chairs, and a kitchenette. The sleeping part of the room is three steps up from the sitting area with a low wall dividing the two areas. You can sit up in bed in the morning and see the ocean. How clever is that? When I walked into that room, I thought I could easily live there instead of at my condo back in Silicon Valley. What else could I need? Even after I find the soul mate I hope to meet one day, there would be plenty of room for a couple that enjoys a lot of togetherness.

Everyone arrived on Thursday afternoon for the extended weekend. The next morning I previewed the conference room to make sure there were enough chairs and that the tables were arranged for the food that would be brought in for lunch. I carried in boxes of folders that contained all the information I'd put together to provide an overview of potential community projects that would be voted on for the year. Once everything was ready, I walked outside to the patio that looks out across the sand dunes and onto the smooth water of the harbor between the breakwater and the docks cluttered with sailboats and fishing vessels.

I followed the walkway that goes between the hot tub and the small swimming pool and went down the steps to the path that winds for several miles along the coast.

There are ropes blocking the dunes for the coastal vegetation protection project, so I walked along the path to the area where the vegetation ends, and it opens up onto small sand dunes. I stepped out of my flip flops and onto the sand. I crossed the beach and walked to the edge of the water. Large waves can't make it into this protected area, so the waves are small, like the tiny curls at the edge of a lake, lapping at your toes and ankles.

I walked along the water line, letting the cold water slide over the tops of my feet. The Pacific Ocean is rarely more than sixty degrees in the central and northern coast, so it basically feels like someone pouring a glass of ice water on your feet, although after a while your skin gets numb and you don't really notice it.

Ten or fifteen fishermen stood along the rock finger that's the breakwater. Most of them were in groups of two or three people. They held their poles or tucked them between the rocks. Behind them, five-gallon plastic paint containers held the rockfish and lingcod they'd caught that day. Some of them were clearly casual weekend fishermen, but other groups were families with children who had less complex equipment, making me think rockfish might be keeping the family fed.

I walked along the shore to the breakwater and climbed up, taking long steps from rock to rock, pausing on each one to be sure my wet feet didn't fly out from under me and send me slipping between the boulders. I thought about how lucky I was to have a job that allowed me to climb on rocks at the edge of the ocean rather than being trapped in a climate controlled building like I was at my previous job. At Central Avenue Church, even though one of my responsibilities is answering the phones, I have the freedom to go outside whenever I want. I can even forward the church line to my cell phone so that I can sit in the garden for an hour, checking the monthly newsletter for typos and answering phone calls, giving information out, and taking messages for Pastor Joe and Pastor Kate. And now look at me. Feeling the spray of the ocean, listening to the gulls, and watching the waves crash against the rocks on the opposite side of the breakwater – and I was getting paid. Not a lot, but enough to live on, and save some.

There's a sign at the area that leads on to the breakwater, warning people not to walk on it. The sign says tsunami waves can come without warning, that you're risking your safety, that even non-tsunami waves can spring out of nowhere and whisk you off to sea. Everyone ignores those signs. Tourists walk all the way out to the tip where there's a fog horn. Hopefully, the boats listen better than the people. But then, I wasn't paying attention to the warning either. It was too much fun, feeling as if I could walk out to the center of the bay. Besides, the waves didn't look that large, which makes you wonder if the warning sign is just there as a CYA for the state of California, or whoever would get sued if someone was washed away.

The breakwater extends about four or five hundred feet into the bay, and I walked halfway out where there were fewer people, and I could really feel as if I was alone with the ocean. I sat on one of the rocks and brought my knees up in an inverted V to help me keep my balance. I set my flip flops next to me and closed my eyes. The air was cooler out here, but I didn't mind. I sat that way for a few minutes, letting my mind drift, not thinking anything, half-meditating which I like to do in a more disciplined way every day, but it's also very nourishing when I can do it out in nature, away from my regular routine.

After a while, I opened my eyes and saw that two windsurfers had set up in the area between the breakwater and the docks. They were zipping along like skateboarders, zig-zagging past each other. I stood because my butt ached from pressing against the rock. I walked as far as I could along the face of the rock where it went below the surface of the water. I looked down. A piece of blue-gray fabric, hard to see because it was almost the same color as the water, floated below me. Part of it clung to the rock. I watched it fill with air so it looked like a fabric balloon and then deflate as a small wave washed over it.

From the corner of my eye, I saw one of the windsurfer's sails go down, bright yellow and orange floating on top of the water. The guy paddled his board toward shore, dragging the sail behind him like a dead fish.

I looked down again and saw the fabric had pulled away from the rock. At the edge was something milky white. I squatted so I could see better because I had an extremely creepy feeling it was a foot. Part of me wanted to throw up, it looked like the white that spills out of an egg when it's boiling and the shell cracks. There was a tiny chunk missing. Another part of me wanted to scream, but I'm not a screamer. I often feel like I should scream or shout or do something crazy to draw attention to what I'm thinking, but I never seem to be able to do that. I think about screaming and it stops there.

Then I started to wonder if I was imagining things. It was a piece of clothing that had been washed off the beach or the rocks, and the white thing was a fish. It couldn't be a foot. But it was.

I stood and backed up the rocks, looking around to see who else was nearby. A few yards away was a man with two small boys and a woman holding a baby. The man and the older boy held fishing poles. The younger boy was poking a stick in their bucket of fish. I didn't think it was a good idea to solicit their help because I didn't think the kids needed to see this. If it really was a foot. Which of course it was, but my mind was still trying to adjust to that. And then there was the question of whether there was anything more than a leg attached to the foot. I looked back down. The toes had broken the surface of the water. They were painted pale pink, so I couldn't spend any more time trying to convince myself it wasn't a human foot floating in the bay.

I looked past the family. There was a man fishing by himself. He wore waders and a white tee shirt and a baseball cap that said Ritz Carlton, and he had a long, uncombed brown beard. He was struggling to reel in something. I walked in his direction, trying to figure out what I was going to say, although I suppose that should be obvious.

"Excuse me," I said.

"Hang on, Miss. I have my hands full."

I waited, and couldn't help wondering if he would regret not telling me to go away altogether.

It seemed to take far too long. I kept glancing behind me, but because of the slope of the rocks, I could no longer see the foot or the fabric, and I half-worried it had sunk to the bottom and he'd think I was crazy and that I'd have to jump in and drag it up to the surface to get him to help. I suppose I should have walked back and gone to get someone official, have the hotel clerk call the police or coast guard, but I felt I couldn't leave, that she, or the part of her I'd seen, would wash out to sea and she'd be lost if I left her for that long.

Finally, the fisherman had his catch flopping on the wet rock. I looked away while he pried the hook out of the poor thing's mouth. He dropped the fish into his bucket and looked up. "What's the trouble?"

"Hi," I said. "I'm Madison Keith. I'm staying back there." I waved my arm toward the hotel. "I saw a foot, a body, I think, floating in the water over there.

He wrapped his fingers around his beard, ran them down to the tip, and twisted the end slightly. "A foot?"

"Come look."

He glanced down at his fishing pole and bucket.

"I'm not sure what to do," I said.

He looked at me. "Are you high?"

I shook my head. I took off my sunglasses so he could see my eyes were clear and white, not all dazed and loopy-looking. "What's your name?" I said.

"Pete."

"Please come look, Pete. I can go call someone, but I don't want it to float away."

"It could be a mannequin," said Pete. "I found a plastic arm once."

"I don't think so."

He stuck his pole between some rocks and picked up a big knife that was lying on top of his tackle box. He followed me to the other side of the breakwater. With a much more sure-footed approach than I had, he climbed down as close as he could to the edge of the water. He squatted and leaned out. He poked the tip of the knife at the fabric and lifted it above the surface of the water. I could tell it was heavy, that it wanted to pull him down because he had to lean back slightly to resist the tug of wet cloth and the surf. The fabric formed a tent-like structure. He stabbed the knife further and nearly lost his balance, but the fabric pulled back from the skin it had been clinging too, and there were two feet and legs. Then, as if the corpse wanted to ease my mind, I saw blonde hair, very long blonde hair, swaying like kelp an inch or so beneath the surface. I was extremely relieved that this wasn't chunks from a human body drifting past.

The knife started to slide out of Pete's grasp. He looked as surprised as I felt. He stumbled back and sat down hard on the rocks. He grunted and wiped the knife blade on his waders, but it didn't really dry off on the rubber.

Hair floated everywhere, covering the face, which I was thankful for.

Pete stood. "We need to call the coast guard."

I nodded.

"Do you want to do that? I'll stay here and make sure she doesn't float away."

I felt a little queasy, thinking about how he was going to "make sure" of that, but I pushed it out of my head.

"Go into the hotel." He jerked his head toward the Beach House. "The person at the desk can help you."

It wasn't necessary for him to spell that out for me, I knew how to get help, but he was as unnerved as I was, so I'm sure he wasn't trying to be insulting. Talking about what to do helped shift my mind from the woman floating in the water to something a little less gruesome. Even if it only shifted a fraction of an inch.

I walked as quickly as I could across the rocks. When I reached the end of the rocks, even though I was barefooted, I jogged back to the coastal path.

After that, everything was a blur of activity that further removed my mind from the reality of a woman's death. Except for when they pulled her out of the water, although I only saw that from a distance because they made everyone move off the breakwater and two guys walked out there with a stretcher. It was gruesome, watching them pull her out of the water. When they returned with her body, she was completely covered. Not that covering her made it less horrifying. By this time, Pastor Joe, his wife Cindee, and Pastor Kate, and a few others from the church had joined me, and they'd figured out the worst news of all, if there can be anything worse than a woman drowned in the bay. She was a member of the church – Lorraine Jarvis – a good friend of Cindee's. No one had any idea how she'd ended up dead.

Pastor Joe felt we should cancel the retreat, but Pastor Kate and the church deacons said we'd spent too much money that couldn't be recouped. Then Joe thought he should drive Cindee back home. She said she wouldn't feel any better at home without him, she'd rather stay, but it would be nice to get away from the scene for an hour or so. Two sheriffs talked to each of us, asking when we'd last seen her. They asked about her family. Cindee told them Lorraine didn't have any children and her husband was traveling on business. That ruled him out, which always seems to be the first choice when a woman is dead. A sad commentary on the world that the man a woman loves the most is the odds-on favorite for her killer.

Of course, they couldn't be sure she'd been killed. There wasn't any blood, and it seemed as if she'd simply drowned, although the water on that side of the breakwater is only a few feet deep for quite a ways out. Of course, you can drown in inches of water, but normally you don't.

Cindee kept saying she wanted to get out of there, and the third time she asked me to go with her. Until that point, I hadn't spent any extended time with her. We'd chatted when she stopped by the office to say *hi* to her husband. She had asked me a lot about my background. My childhood was somewhat unusual because I'm an only child and I was home-schooled until I was fifteen. I grew up spending a lot of time playing outdoors by myself. Joe had mentioned it to her, and she seemed quite intrigued by that. She'd shown me photographs of her daughters. She'd mentioned that she liked to paint, and once she brought a few of her paintings. They were mostly images in acrylic of people shown from the back, looking shadowy and blurred, almost as if their forms were dissolving. They were quite interesting, and I was looking forward to seeing more of her paintings, hearing about her philosophy some day.

Cindee suggested we could drive up the coast a mile or so to a small restaurant and have a glass of wine. Her eyes were red, but she looked more angry than sad, so I was definitely interested in hearing what she might have to say.

CHAPTER 2

INDEE DROVE JOE'S MIATA, which is the car they'd brought to Half Moon Bay for the weekend, obviously planning on a drive along the coast with the top down at some point. Right now, putting the top down somehow seemed inappropriate, so we pulled out onto Highway One going north, all closed up inside the tiny car, with the windows cracked open so we could breathe. It was strange to think about breathing because that made me think of Lorraine Jarvis, what it would be like to no longer have access to air, but gasping for it anyway, and having water flow into your nostrils and down your throat and filling up your lungs like a hot water bottle.

About three miles from where we were staying, past the bay itself, was a road that wound through a woodsy area. It was filled with overgrown plants and pine trees. Pale moss hung from the branches, which made me think more of a swamp than the Pacific Ocean. There were quite a few small cottages that had been there forever and some newer, much larger homes. Out at the end of the curving, narrow road was a restaurant that had been built in the early part of the twentieth century. It's called the Moss Beach Distillery and sits perched on a cliff that drops to a small beach about 200 feet below. The building is adobe with a tile roof and lots of windows looking out over the cliff to the ocean. You can't see the Half Moon Bay harbor or any of the big hotels, so it feels very secluded, almost as if we were stepping back in time to the day when prohibition made it a perfect place for bringing illegal liquor to shore. It proves that people will figure out a way around any regulations that hamper their fun.

Cindee suggested we sit at the bar. There was a couple at the end nearest the windows, turned so they could look out at the water, huddled close together, making me think they were on a romantic getaway. Cindee and I sat at the opposite end.

The bartender was cute. I noticed that right away. It's not that I'm anxious to find a guy, I want to take my time, I'm only twenty-seven, and I don't feel that urge to settle down just because lots of people my age do. I want a lot from marriage. A soul mate, to be exact. I don't want to be in a relationship where we'd rather be with our girl and guy friends than together. I want someone who doesn't want to change one single thing about me, and someone who wants to listen to what I have to say. And I have a lot to say. I'm willing to wait for that. But I definitely notice when a cute guy crosses my path. It seems a little creepy to go off on this rant about what I want in marriage the minute I see a good-looking guy behind a bar. It's just that one thought leads to another.

This guy was about my age, over six feet tall, with dark, almost black hair pulled into the smallest stub of a ponytail I'd ever seen. He wore a white t-shirt that looked like he'd taken it off the shelf at the store and pulled it over his head. It looked quite nice next to that dark hair. His eyes were brown, with long lashes and he had dark stubble on his face, which I always like and I have no idea why. Maybe I do know why – it makes guys look like they just woke up, which is very endearing.

He ran a cloth over the counter, although it already looked polished to me.

"What can I get you?"

I was glad he didn't call us ladies or gals or some other lame thing, trying to be all polite and charming, because it never comes across charming, it sounds stupid. No woman nowadays considers herself a lady, and gal might work for some, but it always makes me think of a rodeo.

"What kind of white wine do you have?" said Cindee.

He named off the varieties, and she chose a Sauvignon Blanc from New Zealand called *Infamous Goose*. That name was almost enough to make me want a glass.

He looked at me.

"Water."

Cindee poked my arm. I suppose it was cheap of me since he was waiting on us. But it's really the only thing I like to drink. That, and coffee. Everything else seems pointless. I'd rather eat a piece of candy than drink a sugary glass of liquid, and alcohol tastes like it belongs inside a car engine, no matter how much you dress it up with syrup and fruit and ice. Wine tastes sour and makes me even more thirsty, so why drink something and get thirstier as you go?

"I'll have iced coffee. Do you have real cream?"

They did, which was a pleasant surprise since many places don't.

"And water."

He grinned. He knew all I really wanted was the water, despite asking about the real cream.

After he put out little napkins and set our drinks precisely in the center, he strolled to the other end of the bar to check on the couple. Very considerate of him, I thought, making sure he wasn't hovering around so we could start our conversation.

Cindee took a sip of her wine. She set her elbow on the bar. She stared at the liquid then moved her hand slightly so the wine swirled up the side of the glass. "The minute I heard you found a woman's body in the water, I knew it was Lorraine," she said.

"How did you know that?"

"I've always thought she would die."

"Why?"

"Her husband is a monster. He says cruel things to her, tells her she's ugly. He calls her a moron and makes her do degrading things. She was scared to death of him, and even though he never hit her or did anything that you'd consider physical abuse, I always felt he was holding it back and eventually, when he did touch her, that would be it."

I sipped my coffee. The glass was wet, the ice melting fast under the heat of the coffee. I wiped it with the little napkin the bartender had provided. I glanced at the end of the bar and saw he was still talking to the couple. That surprised me as they'd seemed quite into each other and not really open to outside conversation, but they were staring at him, and the tone of their voices sounded as if they were asking questions. They were definitely interested in whatever it was he had to say.

"He's supposedly in Chicago," said Cindee. "But I bet he got some rich friend to fly him here."

"Who's in Chicago?"

"Stop drooling over the bartender," said Cindee. Her lips looked weak as if she had to strain to lift them into even the hint of a smile.

"I'm not."

"You are." She tried again to smile, but tears filled her eyes so fast it reminded me of water spilling out of the tray around the bottom of a plant when you put in too much and it suddenly overflows the dish, even though you thought it was soaking into the dirt all along.

Cindee has beautiful eyes. They're green, like mine, but more muted, and her lashes are dark brown. She has perfect eyebrows in a natural arch that doesn't require waxing and threading and plucking.

"I know he found a way to sneak out here, even though he said he was in Chicago. You saw that little airport we passed?"

I nodded.

"She was going to leave him, but it took her a long time to get the courage to even think in those terms. She had the idea that any marriage can be salvaged, if you just work hard enough."

"So you really think he killed her? She didn't slip and lose her balance?"

"I hate even hearing people talk about marriage being *work*," said Cindee. "Why does it have to be *work*?"

I nodded again. I know nothing about marriage. Well, I guess I know what I observed from my parents and a few friends. Marriage is like an iceberg. When I'm married, I'll find out what it's really like to live with someone day in and day out and try to agree on what kind of life you want, and stay with that person until you die. Then I'll know more than that small icy tip, but right now, I have no idea if it's work or it's easy, or it varies depending on who you marry. And who *you* are, for that matter. I have to admit, the idea of working to get along and be happy every day sounds exhausting, but maybe they don't mean work in the same sense I'm thinking of it.

"The sheriff said it was implausible, but I know it was him," said Cindee.

"With cell phones, who ever really knows where anyone is," I said.

Cindee sipped her wine. "That's true."

It fascinates me, thinking about smartphones and the disembodied state of the human race. Someone can be sitting on the beach and you think they're in the office, because that's where they're supposed to be. As long as they have high-quality headphones that block out the background noise, a person can pretend to be anywhere on earth. I ought to know, people at the high-tech company where I used to work did that all the time. They even let me in on it – *Oh, don't tell my manager, I'm running out to do some errands, but I'll have my cell.* It's a portable office in your pocket, easy to work all the time or never really work at all, depending on what kind of person you are. Although there was the guy that got busted when a rooster crowed when he was trying to make a point during a conference call.

From the corner of my eye, I saw that the conversation at the end of the bar was winding down. The bartender stepped back and walked toward us.

"How are you two doing?" he said.

"Fine." Cindee sipped her wine.

It was starting to seem like a nervous tick, her tiny sips, like a hummingbird sticking its beak into a feeder and drinking, but you don't really notice the level of the liquid going down at all.

"Are you from around here?" said the bartender.

"Silicon Valley," I said. "I'm Madison, this is Cindee."

He smiled. "Larry. But everyone calls me JD."

"JD?" I said.

"For Jack Daniels."

Cindee gave him a tiny smile. "We're here for a church retreat," she said.

"At least we were supposed to be here for that. A woman from the church drowned," I said.

"I heard about that," said JD.

"Really?" said Cindee. "Madison only found her body about two hours ago."

"You found her?"

I shivered and goose bumps appeared on my arms, running along the vine tattoo that's on my left arm. "I'd kind of like to forget about it right now," I said. "She looked pretty horrible, and it was so awful seeing someone under the water like that, it almost seems like it didn't really happen."

JD crossed his arms. "That's how it is whenever a person sees something out of the ordinary. We get the same reaction from people who see the Blue Lady."

Cindee shifted on her chair. She did that sippy thing with her wine again. She crossed her legs and turned a bit so she was facing me, but no matter how much she wiggled around, I wasn't going to stop talking to JD. He was so cute, I couldn't take my eyes off him, and he had a nice voice too. The whole point of coming here had been to get away, so why not talk to a stranger, get a slightly different perspective on things. I suppose that wasn't very considerate of me, since she wanted to talk about her friend, and I was thinking about a guy, and ignoring her obvious signals, but he wouldn't stand there forever, and I didn't see the harm in talking to him for a few minutes, especially after that little teaser. He dropped that comment in there so quickly, I knew he wanted to change the conversation away from the woman I found floating in the bay. I took the bait. "Who's the Blue Lady?" I said.

He reached under the bar and whipped out two sheets of paper and handed one to me and one to Cindee. There was a small photograph of the restaurant, and a pencil sketch of a woman superimposed over two columns of text. The woman wore a long, fitted dress and a big hat tied down with a scarf. I read while JD turned and opened the fridge behind the bar. He pulled out the *Infamous Goose* and topped off Cindee's glass.

"I don't want any more," said Cindee.

"It's on the house."

"Thanks. But no more after this. I have to drive," she said.

The sheet of paper told the story of a woman who used to come to The Distillery during the early 1930s. She was having an affair with the man who played the piano in the bar. During his breaks, and after the restaurant closed for the night, they walked along the beach below. One night her estranged husband showed up and got in a fight with the piano player. The next day, the young woman, wearing a beautiful blue dress, was found dead on the beach. She'd been stabbed. Some thought it was her husband, known as a man who tended toward violence. No one ever saw the husband again. The piano player continued to entertain, and the Blue Lady began to haunt The Distillery. She walks along the cliffs outside the windows, searching for her lover. She plays little games by moving objects inside the bar and restaurant, and pinching men who work in the kitchen.

I set the sheet of paper on the bar. Cindee was still reading. I looked at JD. His eyes met mine directly and we stared at each other for several seconds until I felt, more than actually saw, Cindee look up from the sheet of paper.

"People are imagining things," said Cindee. "It's a PR gimmick." She pushed the paper across the bar.

JD ignored her gesture. A standoff over a sheet of paper. Cindee wouldn't touch it again because it would demonstrate doubt, and JD wasn't going to pick it up until he cleaned, lest he admit defeat. Although what he'd be defeated at, I couldn't imagine. He grinned, still looking at me. After a minute, I glanced out the open door that faced the ocean. It was a pristine day with a spotless blue sky. Gulls hovered over the water on a light breeze. The door to the back patio area was open and the TVs were turned off. The only sound was the faint roar of the ocean at the base of the cliff. When I could breathe normally, I turned back to face him. "Have you seen her?"

"Don't encourage him," said Cindee. She took a long swallow of wine, followed quickly by another.

It looked as though I would be driving her car back to the Beach House. She thought I was flirting, but I wasn't. After several encounters with the spirits of a murdered girl and her dead boyfriend in the garden of Central Avenue Church the spring before, I was very open to the idea of ghosts. *Open to suggestion* was what Pastor Joe called it. Based on Cindee's reaction, she and Joe appeared to be in alignment with their view of ghosts. I wasn't so sure. Actually, that's not true. I was sure. I know I saw that couple in the church garden, holding each other, giving off a feeling of love that was more powerful than anything I'd experienced from a couple that was still living.

"I only saw her form twice," said JD. "But I've been the butt of her jokes several times."

"How long have you worked here?" I said.

"Six years."

"Do your customers ever see her, or does she only show herself to the people who work here?"

"Stop," said Cindee.

"You don't believe in ghosts?" said JD.

"No. People conjure them up when they're grieving. It comforts them to imagine their loved ones are still in some kind of tangible form."

I turned toward the open doors. The couple seated at the end of the bar stared at us, clearly interested in our conversation. JD must have been telling them about the ghost. It must be his habit to shake up tourists or new customers with a ghost story. It was certainly more interesting than talking about the weather or football or baseball. I wondered if he really believed she existed or if he did it as a conversation piece, to size up what kind of person he was talking to. Did people order more drinks if they believed in ghosts, or if they were non-believers? If you went with Cindee's theory that the believers received comfort from their ghostly encounters, then the non-believers probably needed more alcohol.

As if to prove my point to myself, Cindee picked up her glass and took a big gulp of wine. This was followed by a few quick sips. She set her glass toward JD's side of the bar. "I will have another glass."

JD opened the fridge to get the bottle of *Infamous Goose*, and Cindee turned so quickly to face me, she started to slip off her chair and had to catch herself by shoving her elbow against the bar. She steadied herself then rubbed her elbow. "I suppose Lorraine probably slipped and fell. Although you wonder how she could drown when the water is only a few feet deep right there," said Cindee.

"Maybe she was walking out near the foghorn and her body drifted back closer to shore after she died."

"Maybe," said Cindee.

JD put the wine glass on a fresh napkin. He also set a new napkin in front of me.

I sucked a piece of ice out of my coffee and rolled it around in my mouth. I wanted to find out more about the Blue Lady, about what JD really thought of her, what it had been like, seeing a ghost. I suppose I wanted to compare it to my experience. It wasn't that I doubted what I'd seen in the garden, twice, but after

Fred, the church gardener, was murdered, I had no one to talk to about it – to try to make sense of the whole idea of people coming back after they've died, or hanging around, or whatever it is. Whether they're all around us and only a few of them are visible once in a while. I chewed up the ice cube so I'd be able to speak clearly.

"It's hard to believe it was an accident. Do people frequently slide off the rocks and hit their heads?" Cindee's voice was a whisper.

I think she was talking to herself. She didn't really want JD joining the conversation, and I suppose it was somewhat dense of him to not read her signals. On the other hand, my signals were quite different and perhaps quite a bit stronger.

"People get washed off the rocks all the time," he said. "Even on a calm day. They don't realize how a larger than average wave can come out of nowhere."

Cindee nodded but didn't look at him. She stared into her wine glass. If she thought her coldness would send him away, she was mistaken.

"Do you record every sighting of the Blue Lady?" I said.

Cindee looked at me, a mixture of hurt and irritation.

I know my question was dull and way out of context. Cindee wanted to verbalize her shock, that feeling that you should have done something, even if it's completely outside the realm of possibility that you *could* do anything to prevent someone from dying. I wonder why we feel that way? Is it with all death or only the unexpected ones? But I didn't care if I appeared to be flirting and not being very compassionate to her. Besides JD being so damn cute and having that soul-searing tenor voice that enticed me to keep talking to him, I really wanted to know more about this ghost.

"Some locals have a listing of every incident. I don't know every recorded encounter, but I've kept track of all the sightings since I started working here."

"Tell us about when you saw her." I pushed my coffee to the side.

JD picked up the glass without asking if I was finished. He set it under the counter and poured fresh water for me.

"The first time ..."

"You look out at a blue sky over a blue ocean and think you see the shadow of a woman dressed in blue?" said Cindee. Her face had kind of sagged and her eyes looked vague, the pupils large in the dim light of the bar. She stared at him without blinking. It was clear she had no interest in hearing about the ghost sightings at The Distillery.

"I really want to hear this," I said. "After what happened to me at the church, you know?"

She shrugged and picked up her wine.

"Actually," said JD, "The first time I saw her was in the main dining room, so the sky and ocean didn't play into it." He grinned and it softened his words so it didn't sound like he was arguing with her, but I don't think she noticed.

"For the first two years I worked here, I was looking for her every day. There are so many stories going around and the place is known for our ghost. Well, also for our good food and a well-stocked bar."

Shelves of liquor bottles lined the wall behind him – gold and brown and clear liquid, some with dark sides so you couldn't see the color. I had no idea what any of it was or what kinds of drinks they went into. Since I don't drink alcohol and my parents never drank, and I didn't have a lot of relatives in my life, I don't have any close experience with drinkers. I have friends from high school and my old job who drink beer or wine, but that's mostly for dinners or parties. I've probably sat in a bar about three times in my entire twenty-seven years. I don't think that makes me naïve, as some people have said, it just isn't part of my experience. I know more about smoking pot than I do about alcohol, but that's a whole other story.

"After the first two years I settled down," said JD. "I decided I wasn't the kind of guy who sees ghosts. In fact ..." He looked at

Cindee, but she refused to let her eyes meet his. "I mostly thought it was only people who are open to suggestion. Gullible types who were so bought into the legend that they thought they saw a bluish figure. And then it fed on itself, people thinking they heard or saw unusual phenomenon. The light over the ocean can do amazing things. And some of the other stories, the check folders falling over, sounds, lights going off, there are other ways to explain those events."

The couple at the end of the bar stood. JD strolled over and pulled their credit card and the receipt out of the glass where he'd kept their running tab.

"I can't believe we're listening to this," said Cindee. "It's a story. A bunch of people seeing what they've been told to expect."

"He said he used to think the same thing, but he doesn't any more."

"Of course not, he came to expect it too," said Cindee.

"Then think of it as a story, something to take our minds off Lorraine."

"Talking about dead women re-appearing is not taking my mind off Lorraine."

I put my hand on her arm.

JD set the couple's dirty glasses on the counter behind him. "Do you want to hear all of this? Maybe you two came here to talk."

"We can talk later," I said. "I want to hear all of it."

JD looked at Cindee. She was staring into her glass. He uncorked the bottle and gave her another splash.

"You would expect to see a ghost at night, so that's why it caught me off guard. I was opening on a Tuesday morning. It was sunny, one of those stellar days at the ocean, the sky clear with a dark gray layer of fog hugging the horizon. Not the kind of atmosphere where you'd expect to see a ghost. I was in the main dining room looking out the window because the day was so incredible. I turned to go into the bar and she was standing in the center of the room. It seemed like time stopped, like I wasn't breathing."

Hearing him tell it made me feel like I couldn't breathe either. I put my hand on my water glass but didn't think I had the strength to pick it up. My fingers refused to grip the glass, and the moisture made it seem impossible to hold anyway. My heart started to beat faster, and I could feel my blood pulsing through every vein in my body. Picturing the Blue Lady standing in the dining room made me remember how it was seeing the couple in the church garden, that overwhelming silence, the sense that time wasn't moving.

JD looked at me. "Are you okay?"

"Not really, but keep going."

"She looked exactly as everyone described, although the past few years there have been stories of her appearing in different clothes, when I saw her she was wearing a long blue dress with a big hat, looking very much like she was going out for a ride in a classic roadster."

"Except it wouldn't be classic for her," I said.

JD laughed. "I didn't know what to do. I didn't want to scare her away, and somehow I knew I couldn't talk to her. I couldn't even tell if she saw me. I wasn't sure where she was looking. I didn't move and neither did she. Because of the feeling that time had stopped, I can't say if it was two minutes or ten. Then she disappeared. I can't explain how that happened, if she faded gradually, or she was there one minute and not there the next."

"So you think because you weren't expecting it, because it was morning and that's not a time people normally see ghosts, that proves it was real?" said Cindee. "It couldn't possibly be that you'd heard people talk about it and looked at that drawing for two years and when your mind was off it, all those subconscious memories materialized. You were staring out at the ocean, your vision was probably blurred from the glare, you turned and looked at an empty dining room and thought you saw blue."

JD looked sad. I didn't even know the guy, so it wasn't as if I was familiar with his expressions, but I knew. His eyes had this expanded quality as if he was trying to peer right inside Cindee's head. His mouth was partially open. Not in shock or irritation, more as if there were words that weren't quite making their way out. He ran his hand over the top of his head and stopped at his ponytail, tugging it slightly. "The thing about that kind of experience is that it changes you. It doesn't matter whether or not anyone believes what I saw, or if they think I'm nuts, imagining things, or a story-teller. It happened, and it really doesn't matter one way or the other if anyone believes it." He smiled.

Cindee slid off her chair. She picked up her purse from where it was looped over the back. She reached inside and pulled out two twenties and set them on the counter. JD picked up the bills and turned to the cash register. Cindee grabbed her wine glass and gulped down the rest of it. "We should get back," she said.

JD turned and held out her change. Cindee waved her hand. "Keep it."

I slid off the stool and took a few quick sips of my water. We weren't going to get to hear about his other sighting, or anything about how it changed his perspective, which I was extremely interested in knowing. I wasn't sure if Cindee didn't like me being so friendly with a bartender or if she didn't like ghosts or if it was simply that she was upset about Lorraine. Somehow, it seemed like it was about more than her friend.

In the car, Cindee said, "I'm sorry if I was rude. I don't believe in ghosts."

"That's okay," I said. "You're upset."

"Although," said Cindee, "the story of the woman who was murdered did make me hope that maybe Lorraine was having an affair, and if she was, good for her. That would make me happy, knowing she died feeling loved."

The rest of the way back to the Beach House, Cindee talked about the horror of imagining her friend filled with water, her body nibbled at by fish, all her hopes washed away. While Cindee curled up in the passenger seat and talked, I drove and thought about the Blue Lady.

CHAPTER 3

*O*RIGINALLY, I'D ARRANGED a dinner for everyone at Sam's Chowder House, the restaurant right next door to the Beach House, but because of the drowning, and the detectives asking questions, it was decided to move the group dinner to Saturday night. The investigators had found one of Lorraine's shoes wedged by a solitary boulder near the shore, which led them to believe she hadn't wandered out to the end of the breakwater by herself and been grabbed by an aggressive wave. They thought she might have had a tussle, most likely on the rocks, and fallen and hit her head. She had a broken fingernail and a bruise on her temple. They also found a wine glass on the shore, but the word was that could mean something or nothing. Most things you find on a beach don't have an easily identified source, although the fact that it wasn't broken made it more likely it had fallen there recently and that it came from someplace nearby.

Pastor Joe and Cindee left for dinner in the Miata. Cindee looked like she'd been crying again. She leaned on Joe's shoulder all the way to the car. They headed south on Highway One, so I guessed they were going to one of the restaurants in downtown Half Moon Bay. The Beach House is more like a B&B with a continental breakfast, and wine and appetizers late in the day, but they don't have a restaurant. You have to go out to eat, unless you bring your own food and plan to cook, but it's not set up for major meal preparation.

I stood on the tiny balcony outside my room and watched Pastor Kate and a few others walk along the path, headed toward Sam's. No one thought to invite me, but that's not surprising. Pastor Joe wanted the administrative assistant to be an outsider. When he interviewed me, he said he was specifically looking for a candidate who wasn't a member of the church. Quite a lot of people visit the pastor in his office to talk about their problems, almost like he's a professional therapist, and he doesn't like them feeling that someone they sit next to on Sunday morning will know they're anxious about lying or their finances, or having trouble in their marriage or with unruly children. He was very clear about that, not wanting an assistant who would be tempted to gossip. When the administrative assistant sees all these comings and goings, and then sees those same people at church events, things have a way of unintentionally slipping out. Of course, that's not the only reason he hired me, but it was a consideration. He also hired me because I had great credentials from my short-lived career in the high-tech industry.

Not being invited to dinner was fine by me. There was only one thing I wanted to do, and I wanted to do it by myself. I waited until about six-fifteen, so I could be pretty sure I wouldn't run into someone in the hallway or the lobby, and they'd accidentally invite me to dinner in such a way that I couldn't get out of it. I closed the door to my balcony, leaving a small crack so the ocean air could still get inside.

I walked to the center of the hall and took the main stairs down to the lobby. I waved at the desk clerk and went outside. A strong breeze had sprung up, brought in by the fog. The flags on the pole near the entrance to the parking lot flapped erratically like bats coming to life at dusk. My Beetle was parked at the end near the swimming pool. I heard a little kid shrieking in the pool and a dad telling him or her to use an indoor voice. It was cold for swimming, but little kids never seem fazed by that. They see a pool and want to go in. Adults can't get past the cold to have fun in the water. I wonder if kids have something in their brains that allows sheer fun to shut off any discomfort. When I see kids playing, I mostly think about when I was their age, and how eighty percent of the time, I was playing by myself. I didn't do a lot of shrieking.

The drive to The Distillery was quick, and it wasn't until I started looking for a parking spot that I thought JD might not have as much time to stand around and tell ghost stories as he had earlier in the afternoon. There were several people standing on the bluff, looking out at the ocean. The sky still had a glow, even though the sun was below the horizon. The waves were easy to see because of the way the rising moon made the water glow and the foam was bright against the blackness of the water. It's so soothing to stand and watch the waves follow each other to shore, one after the other, over and over again until you feel as if your breath is moving with the same lifting and breaking. Of course, the people standing there might have been pretending to look at the ocean but truthfully hoping to see the Blue Lady. They wouldn't want to admit they were standing at the edge of the Pacific Ocean waiting to see a ghost float past.

Inside, two couples and a group of four women waited in the tiny alcove for a table. I could see the bar area from where I stood inside the door, and it looked crowded, but not overflowing. There was one empty seat at the bar and several empty tables. The question was still, would JD have time to talk? I realized I should have come later after things quieted down. It was probably their peak time. And a Friday night.

Some people don't like to eat by themselves in public. I don't know if they're self-conscious, worrying that other diners will think no one wants to eat with them, or if they don't enjoy their own company. I like thinking about the taste of my food, considering each bite. I don't even need the TV, snapping images at my eyeballs like someone flicking a wet towel at the back of your legs. I'm happy to eat and let my mind wander. I don't need a companion, like a prop that proves to a bunch of strangers that I'm somehow legitimate.

JD noticed me right away. He grinned, set the wine bottle he was holding on the counter, pulled out a glass, and filled it with ice and water. He placed it in front of the empty seat. If he was this good at remembering drinks that other patrons ordered, I imagined he did quite well in the tip department. That, plus his stories of personal encounters with the Blue Lady. I hoped that was part of his regular routine, and even if I couldn't talk to him alone, I could at least hear the re-telling of the first time he met her and get the scoop on the second meeting as well.

It was nice of him to serve up the water right away without me having to ask, but with all these people, it would have been rather selfish to take a seat and not spend any money. "Can I eat dinner at the bar?"

"You sure can." He set a menu on the bar and went back to pouring wine.

There were so many things that looked good, I had a hard time deciding between crab cakes, clam chowder, or crab and avocado quesadillas. Finally, I settled on fish tacos, which JD said were really good. I was suddenly starving. The iced coffee late in the afternoon had sent enough caffeine into me that it got my stomach grumbling.

I watched him move from person to person. He didn't act like he was in a hurry, rushing the drink preparation, even though he didn't ever seem to stop. It was fun watching him mix cocktails, splashing the alcohol out of the spouts, adding ice and the finishing touches like salt or sugar around the rim, olives on a plastic stick, or a thin shaving of lime peel. I couldn't figure out how he managed to pour the alcohol out of that metal spout and stop it with the right amount without measuring. I'd have to ask him about that later. After I asked about the Blue Lady.

The first taco was gone before he stopped and asked if I wanted more water.

When I nodded, he filled my glass and said, "Where's your friend?"

"She went to dinner with her husband."

"And you came back because I'm such a charming, good-looking guy, or because the Blue Lady is so seductive, you want to hear more about her?"

I grinned. "Maybe both."

He stepped back and ran his hand over his head and tugged on the nub of a ponytail. "Huh. So do you want to hear about the second time I saw her?"

The woman next to me leaned forward. She had long black hair and wore a black cocktail dress. "You saw a ghost?"

JD looked at me. "Madison's call. Do you want to hear about the same incident you heard this afternoon or a new one?"

"Go ahead and tell that story first. I'll concentrate on my taco," I said.

He smiled at me as if he was pleased that I was so easy-going, that he could entertain all his customers without having one cranky customer who tried to dictate what he did and acted put out because they were only thinking of themselves. He went through the whole story while the woman on my left sipped her martini, the second one since I'd been there. She gazed at JD as if she wanted to jump over the bar and climb on top of him. He didn't acknowledge that he was aware of this, but he'd have to be brain-dead not to notice.

The story was longer and more dramatic this time. I imagine this was because he had a more attentive audience. Cindee's blatant disbelief, bordering on disgust, as if he was a spokesman on an infomercial, must have made him hold back some of the details that afternoon. This time he mentioned that the temperature in the main dining room dropped just before the Blue Lady appeared. He said it was a cliché to mention that, but it was true. Even though she hadn't drowned, the chill had the same sensation of icy cold that you get when you wade into the ocean and that sixty-degree water bites you like you've stepped into a steel trap. He said the chilled feeling started at his feet as if he *had* waded into the ocean. First his toes and the tops of his feet, and then his ankles. It spread up through his body. He didn't shiver like you would in a cold wind but experienced more of a numbness.

He said the ghost seemed to be trying to speak. Although he didn't hear anything physically, he had a feeling, as if he knew what she wanted to say, that she was asking where her lover was. I could imagine Cindee's scornful expression if he'd mentioned this earlier. I did wonder about his "feeling" that the Blue Lady was trying to speak, so maybe I was skeptical too, since I'd read on the sheet of paper that the legend says she's looking for her lover. A cynical person would say JD was parroting the story off the paper, but to me, he seemed sincere. He said her lips moved slightly and he knew inside what she was asking, despite the lack of words, of any sound whatsoever. It wasn't as if she spoke by telepathy, it was more of a feeling of just knowing. It was difficult to describe.

The martini-drinking woman sucked the last olive off the stir stick that leaned against the side of her nearly empty glass. She chewed the olive then swallowed the rest of the liquid while she was chewing.

"Do you want something to eat?" said JD.

She shook her head and pushed her glass to his side of the bar. "Olives fill me up just fine," she said.

"Are you asking for another?"

It was clear he didn't want to offer her a third martini in such a short span of time, but also didn't want to offend his customer or disrupt the story-telling.

The woman ran her fingers through her hair. It was draped over her arm, and her fingers glided through the strands all the way down to her forearm. Her hair was so black, it almost looked green. It might have been green, because it appeared to be dyed, and the color could have shifted slightly from solid black. When she moved, her dress glistened as if it was wet. It was so tight that the shiny stuff looked like fish scales, giving the impression of a mermaid with a black tail.

"Yes, I'd like another. And a glass of water," she said.

The request for water seemed to make JD relax. Maybe he thought she'd have to pee soon and once she slid off that chair and tried to make her way to the restroom in shoes with heels that were taller than the stem of her martini glass, she'd realize she had no more capacity for gin. Olives aside.

My tacos had come with a pile of tortilla chips and I'd only eaten one. I pushed my plate toward her and said, "Do you want any chips? I can't eat another bite."

She wrinkled her nose.

I suppose she thought it was creepy to eat off a stranger's plate that was littered with bits of fish that had fallen out of the tacos. However, when JD set her martini in front of her, she reached over and grabbed three chips, like she was famished and had to snatch food on the sly.

I was curious about her story, dressed up like that, so much makeup – smoky black shadow and thick eyeliner – sitting here alone, drinking too much and refusing food. It didn't seem as if she was waiting for anyone, because she never looked at the door or glanced anywhere around the restaurant. She kept her gaze solidly glued to JD.

"Tell us about the other time you saw her," I said.

"It was on the beach. Early in the morning, before sunrise."

"Why were you on the beach that early?"

"I went down to dig clams. I set the bucket and shovel on the sand right at the water line and was stopping for a quick smoke."

I don't know what JD saw on my face or the martini drinker's face, but he smiled and looked past us. "I'm trying to quit, but you know how it is. Or I suppose you don't know how it is, but anyone who smokes and wants to stop knows it's hard to let go. Mentally as much as physically."

"Actually, I do know," I said. "I've been trying to quit for three years."

He grinned, then glanced behind him. "I need to take care of some folks. I'll tell you the next story in a minute."

When he was finished making two frothy things with pulverized ice and something thick and pink, pouring wine, filling beer mugs, and taking an order for appetizers and closing out two tabs for the guy waiting on the tables, he pushed the register drawer shut and poured himself a glass of water. He filled my glass. The martini woman hadn't taken more than one or two sips of her water, but I noticed that when I hadn't really been watching, she'd managed to eat half the chips on my plate because only the broken pieces were left.

JD leaned his elbows on the bar. The way he moved made his shirt sleeves pull up a bit, revealing more of his biceps, nicely developed from an activity that required more effort than mixing drinks. It could be from digging clams, but I thought that would use your shoulders and back more than your biceps. Maybe the whole apparatus gets worked in an activity like that. He tugged on his ponytail, then pinched his ear slightly, as if he was trying to turn on a switch in his brain.

The woman leaned over the bar. Her hair cascaded across the wood and she lifted it back over her shoulder with a wide sweep of her arm.

It was clear JD saw something else in his mind, was trying to recall every detail of what he'd seen on the beach before dawn. "It was early fall," he said. "Right around this time of year. The sky was clear already even though the sun wasn't up. I was really enjoying my cigarette. I guess you do know how that is. Sometimes you smoke in a hurry because you need your nicotine fix and you hardly notice what you're doing. Other times, it's so completely blissful, like some kind of Zen state of mind, that you know you'll never be able to quit."

"I used to smoke too," said the green-black-haired woman. "You make me want to take it up again."

JD smiled, but his eyes didn't focus on her. She looked annoyed.

"I'd been looking out over the water – it's amazing what you can see, how the water glows, even when it's dark and you think there's no light at all. When my cigarette got near the end, I turned to face the bluff and I saw something moving. At first, I thought it was the smoke getting caught on a gust of air and pulling up into a coil. Then she was there, standing on the cliff and looking down at the beach. I felt as if ..." He paused. He lifted his elbows off the bar and straightened. He took a step back. "This is the weird part. I thought she could see me. I thought she was looking at me and that she either thought she knew me, or had a question for me. The feeling was so intense, it's still there, even now."

A man three seats away held up his empty beer mug.

JD walked over and took the mug, chatted and laughed with the group of guys, then filled their mugs. He moved on down the bar, checking on the status of each drink, wiping up moisture where it had pooled on the glossy wood.

The woman turned to me. "Thanks for the chips."

"No problem."

"Do you believe all this shit? The ghost?"

I put my hands on the bar and pressed my fingertips on the wood until they turned white, not really wanting to talk to her. To be honest, I wished I had the stories to myself, I wished I had JD to myself. If Cindee hadn't been so anti-ghost that afternoon, I wouldn't have come back. Now that I was here, I wanted to listen without the interference of someone trying to persuade JD that what he'd seen wasn't real. "I think it's absolutely possible."

"But you don't really believe it."

"I said it was possible."

"That's not the same as believing it. Like he does." She jerked her head toward the other end of the bar. "He's a little nutty."

"If you don't believe it, why are you listening?"

"Are you kidding? Look at him."

Well, yes, there was that. But if she thought he was nuts, did she really want him to ask her out? At least I assumed, after that last comment, that she wanted him to ask her out. Did she troll through ocean-front bars, searching for good-looking guys, appearing on Friday or Saturday nights in her shimmery dress? "Have you been here before?" I said.

"A couple of times. Last weekend was the first time I noticed him." She shivered and it turned into a little shimmy.

"And you never heard the stories before?"

"I read the leaflet. It's just their shtick. Gets a crowd in, maybe. Or at least gives people a way to remember the place. But I didn't sit at the bar, I didn't hear this line."

"There are lots of things we can't see. It makes sense there are beings that we aren't aware of, and if the circumstances are right, they make themselves known."

She rolled her eyes.

She was worse than Cindee. I almost didn't want JD to come back and talk about it, if that was what she was thinking. It sounded like he'd had an amazing experience and I wanted to know more about it. I sort of wanted to tell him about my encounter with the recently deceased couple at Central Avenue Church just a few weeks after I started working there. Except for the day the police had questioned us about the murder of the church gardener, I'd never talked about the apparitions I'd seen. Pastor Joe discouraged me from bringing it up, and my friends tended to change the subject. It wasn't that I *wanted* to talk to JD about what I'd seen, I *needed* to talk to him.

JD returned. "Coffee? Iced?" He picked up my plate.

From the corner of my eye, I saw the woman look at the plate with such longing I think she was ready to start eating the bits of fallen fish and picking out tomato chunks from the leftover pico de gallo. She was nearly finished with her martini, but seemed satisfied not to start in on another drink, at least for now.

JD filled the glass mug with ice, added coffee, and set the miniature pitcher of cream on the bar in front of me. He topped off my water and then handed me a long-handled spoon. "Can I close out your tab?" he said to the woman.

She glared at him. "I think I'll have another."

"Are you driving?" said JD.

"Maybe you can drive me." She winked.

I turned so my shoulder was toward her. Even though I didn't know her, didn't like her much at all, I felt embarrassed for her. How strange is that? I almost wanted to pay my bill, but the desire to tell JD about my experience was stronger than my misplaced embarrassment. There was another tiny desire creeping up my spine – I wanted to see the Blue Lady.

"I'm on duty until closing," said JD. "I won't be out of here until three."

"I can wait."

He entered a few things on his computer screen. A receipt printed on the machine beside the computer. "That's not a good idea." He ripped out the receipt, stuck it in a plastic folder and placed it on the bar in front of her. "I can't serve you any more alcohol."

The woman reached into her purse, pulled out a hundred dollar bill, and slapped it on top of the folder. She slid off the chair. The way she'd been acting, I thought she couldn't afford any food, so now I was confused, but I guessed I'd never know the explanation for that.

She took a step back. Despite the heels and the martinis, she didn't wobble at all. JD handed her the change. She walked to the foyer, pushed open the door, and walked out.

I couldn't have been happier. I decided to cut to the chase. "Do you think it's true that everyone who dies a violent death comes back to finish up their business or to get some kind of closure on their life?"

He shrugged. "I don't know. I never thought a ghost would have a question for me. I always assumed they knew it all, having crossed over. But after giving it some thought, I've decided that since they're not all the way over to the other side, it's possible they have as many questions as we do."

"Maybe they have more," I said.

"Could be."

"I wonder if the spirit of the woman who drowned last night will linger. The sheriffs are leaning in the direction of murder. Maybe she'll let us know who killed her."

"It's not that clear cut," said JD. "The Blue Lady is around all the time, and although people are fairly certain it was her estranged husband because he was a violent guy, known for abusing her, she hasn't let anyone know for sure."

"I'd like to see her," I said.

He laughed. "That's not how it works. She reveals herself on her terms."

"I know, but don't you think there's a way to increase the chances?"

He laughed harder. "Everyone is interested in the Blue Lady, but I've never met anyone who wanted to stalk her."

"I don't want to stalk her." All this time I'd wanted to tell him about the ghostly couple I'd seen at the church, but now that the conversation had given me a perfect opening, I couldn't speak. If I talked about those ghosts, it would sound like I had an agenda and I didn't. So I didn't want to say anything, and it's not often I censor my words. Usually, if it's in my head, it comes out my mouth.

"All I know is what I've heard and what I've seen. If you want, we could meet on the beach before dawn. I'm going fishing with my buddy tomorrow, but Sunday, we could meet down there, about 3:30 or 4. Maybe she'll show up. I'll bring coffee and some breakfast."

Right up to that last part, I thought he was offering me increased odds to see the Blue Lady, but then when he added that bit about breakfast, I wondered if he was asking me out. Not many people go on dates at three-thirty in the morning, but why not? If it *was* a date. I was free all Sunday morning because the members of Central Avenue Church would be conducting their worship service and religious classes.

JD made it clear there was nothing I could do to encourage the Blue Lady to appear, but since she felt comfortable around him, I figured that might help. I think the reason I was suddenly hesitant about mentioning my own experience with ghosts is that I did have some doubts after all. The whole thing had started to feel like a dream, something that Fred and I imagined. If I saw the Blue Lady, and if I saw her at the same time JD did, maybe I would know for sure that there are spirits lingering around us and I'd no longer doubt my earlier experience. Besides, if this was a place welcoming to the spirits of murdered women, Lorraine's spirit might show up. That sounds absurd, I know, but I couldn't help wondering, because of the similarity between the two women – both trying to escape from cruel men.

CHAPTER 4

ON SATURDAY MORNING I went downstairs to get a chocolate croissant and coffee. The croissants not only had chocolate in the center but also drizzled on top. They were huge, as big as both of my fists pressed together. I went early to make sure I got one because they only had a few. Most of the tray was occupied by sweet rolls, and I'd noticed the first morning that the croissants were snatched up very early.

The sheriffs who had questioned all of us the day before were waiting in the lobby, their slacks and ties announcing their profession to other hotel guests. No one else within twenty miles was dressed like that. They stood near the buffet table drinking coffee. The younger one was spooning yogurt and granola into his mouth. They re-introduced themselves as Detective Phillips and Detective Wagner. I guess they thought I hadn't kept the business cards they handed me when we were standing on the shore while Lorraine's body was removed.

"We'd like to ask you some more questions, Ms. Keith," said Detective Wagner.

"I don't know anything else. I already told you how I found her body, but I didn't really know her."

"But you know the rest of the church folks," said Detective Wagner, "You've been more frank with us than the others have, and we thought you might be able to provide some additional help."

Wasn't it their job to make sure everyone was *frank*?

They must have noticed my surprise. "We're still questioning the members of the church, but Reverend Kenyon mentioned that you're not a member and we thought you might have a detached perspective."

"I'd like to eat my breakfast first." I really wanted to take my food to my room, sit on my balcony, and look at the water while I let that chocolate melt around the inside of my mouth. Talking to them would take all the sweetness out of it.

"You can eat while we talk."

How was it they were able to say that without thinking of what I wanted? How were they able to say it in a way that made me feel I couldn't say no? I'm sure if I had said no, they might have grudgingly agreed, but I suppose detectives aren't used to people saying no, and most people aren't inclined to. There's some ingrained instinct that it's not in your best interest to resist, even if you've done nothing wrong. And yet, it sounded as if the sheriffs hadn't successfully persuaded the members of Central Avenue Church to be *frank*.

They led me to a corner area that had a bench and some chairs arranged in a U-shape with a round glass-topped table. On the table was a large clear vase, wide enough to hold a flamboyant arrangement of flowers, but instead it contained several cups of sand with seashells and a miniature starfish nestled on top to give the illusion of the shore. I took a bite of the croissant while they drizzled the same questions as they had the day before, in a crisscross pattern similar to how the chocolate was laced across the top of the croissant. Somehow, the chocolate wasn't as soothing as I'd anticipated.

Detective Wagner looked old enough to be a grandpa, so I assumed he was in charge. He had gray hair that needed a bit of a trim and very blue eyes and pale skin that was probably his natural coloring with those light eyes, but made him look like he hadn't seen the sun in a long time. His fingers were narrow, and he held a smartphone like he wasn't quite sure what to do with it. He kept moving his hand toward the table as if he planned to set the phone down, but he didn't.

"The church members are so shocked that one of them was murdered, they can't seem to provide much useful information about her background," said Detective Wagner.

I took a sip of coffee followed by a big bite of my croissant. It seemed he was going to explain the background for awhile, so I had plenty of time to chew and enjoy the flakiness and the puddle of chocolate.

"Ms. Kenyon knew the victim the best. In fact, they'd been classmates in high school. When Reverend Kenyon was transferred back to California, they became reacquainted."

Hearing that gave me a stab of guilt that I hadn't been more attentive to her the day before, instead of letting my attention get lured away by a very good-looking JD and a very sociable blue ghost. I'd thought for awhile that Cindee is someone I could be friends with. Sure, she's married, she's seventeen or eighteen years older than me, and she has four daughters. What could we possibly have in common? But there's something intriguing about her. She keeps to herself and you can tell she's always thinking, and that she probably sees a lot of things other people miss. She can be funny, too. I hoped I hadn't lost my chance to be a friend to a live person because of all my enthusiasm over dead people who refuse to depart.

"Ms. Kenyon tells us that the victim was planning to leave her husband. Although he never hit her, he was emotionally abusive. In the extreme."

"How so?"

Detective Wagner looked into the vase full of sand and shells. He picked up the little starfish and looked at the underneath side. He probably thought he shouldn't give me that kind of confidential information.

"If you're asking me questions, don't I get to ask a few?"

A flicker of a smile crossed his face. He put the starfish back in the vase and wiggled it slightly to burrow it into the sand. "You remind me of my daughter, Ms. Keith. You're very blunt. And your eyes are almost the same shade of green."

I wasn't sure what to say to that random comment. He looked a little sad, which made responding even more dicey. In fact, I was almost positive his eyes were tearing up. But I didn't have to say anything, he rushed back to the topic at hand.

"Ms. Kenyon went on about it for quite some time. Even though we explained that we've already checked on the husband's location and gotten solid confirmation he's in Chicago. She's absolutely convinced he found a way to fly back here secretly, kill his wife, and return to Chicago in time to attend a business dinner."

I took a tiny bite of my croissant and held it on my tongue for a moment, waiting for him to answer my question. Or maybe this was how he planned to dodge it.

"He wouldn't allow his wife to make any decisions on her own. He bought her clothes, dictated what she would cook, disallowed certain types of food in the house. He forced her to play act humiliating sexual scenarios. He made her prepare his dinners naked while he stood behind her and traced the point of a knife across her skin."

I swallowed and thought about Lorraine, how her hand sometimes trembled and how she never made eye contact. I pushed my croissant toward the vase of sand. I couldn't look directly at the sheriff because my eyes were filled with tears.

"I'm sorry," said Detective Wagner. "You asked."

No wonder Cindee was certain he'd found a way to be in two places at once. No wonder she was fixated on how he could have managed to get here. "So what do you want from me?"

"Yesterday you said you'd met the victim, but didn't know her very well and that you hadn't spoken to her during your stay in Half Moon Bay."

"Can you call her by her name? It makes it seem like she didn't exist when you call her *the victim*."

Detective Wagner nodded. "I'm sorry. I, of all people, should understand that. My daughter was the victim of a crime."

I looked down at my fingers. Flakes of croissant had glued themselves to the tips. I waited for him to say more.

He set his phone on the table. "How did you meet Ms. Jarvis?"

"She came into the church office a few times to give me prayer requests to include in the monthly newsletter."

"What were those about?"

"Oh, nothing personal. Prayer requests for the bulletin rarely are, in my experience so far. They're mostly for people in the hospital or out of work."

"So she never mentioned anything about her life to you?"

"I don't think she would. It sounds pretty horrible. Not the sort of thing you tell a stranger."

"Reverend Kenyon said he's met with her several times for counseling, but he refused to disclose what they talked about."

I shrugged. I wasn't sure why the sheriff told me that. Maybe he was hoping I knew what they talked about, but it was news to me that she'd come in to see him.

Detective Phillips flipped open his notepad and wrote something on it. Even though he was younger than Detective Wagner, he was the low-tech guy. There wasn't a smartphone in sight. Not that I'm judging, but his buzz cut and his jacket that was too tight for his beefy arms made him look like he wasn't a very hip guy from any angle.

"What did she talk about when she came into the office?"

"Small talk, mostly. Churchy small talk. She would tell me the prayer requests in great detail, try to impress on me how urgent it was that they not be left out of the newsletter. She was a very praying woman."

Detective Phillips scribbled on the notepad. He slid the pen cap on and off a few times and didn't look at me. I was dying to know what he was writing. I might have misjudged him. Maybe he wasn't the beefcake he looked like. Perhaps he was struck by the irony of a woman needing prayers far more than most, obsessed with praying for those who were temporarily unemployed, while her own life destroyed her soul.

They continued to ask me questions, trying to find out whether I knew of anyone who hated her. They were fairly certain the contusion on the side of her head had happened prior to her death, although they wouldn't know for sure until after the autopsy. It was baffling that the one person in the church who had significant odds of getting killed by her husband had been killed by someone else. But they were quite sure Cindee's alternate suggestion, that Lorraine's husband had hired someone to murder his wife, didn't fit the evidence. They wouldn't discard it entirely, but the signs of a struggle didn't seem like the results of a professional killer.

They thanked me for my time and said they might want to talk to me again. They stood and turned sideways to maneuver themselves out from the space between the bench and the table. Detective Phillips gushed his appreciation that I was so open. That made me think the members of the church had dodged their questions. I hadn't provided any worthwhile information.

"Ms. Kenyon knew her better than anyone. And if she would stop fixating on the husband, she might be able to offer more insight," said Detective Phillips.

I thought his tone was somewhat snarky. He stared at me for several seconds.

"Do you think Ms. Kenyon would withhold information if she thought it might create a scandal in her husband's church?" said Detective Phillips.

"I can see why it's hard for her to consider any other possibilities," I said.

"Yes, but when you talk to her again, we hope you'll let us know if she says anything that might be useful," said Detective Phillips. "Try to encourage her to look at the whole picture of Ms. Jarvis' life."

WTF? He was asking me to do his job for him. To pry information out of Cindee. I'm sure my mouth fell open, because Detective Wagner's face turned redder than I thought was possible on his pale skin.

"You don't have any reason to think she'd keep something important to herself. But I'm not going to try to get her to spill her guts and pass it on to you," I said.

"We're not asking for that," said Detective Wagner. "That's not what we meant."

"It sure sounded like it," I said.

"There might be a third party involved," said Detective Wagner. "Even though Ms. Kenyon said there wasn't, she might know something seemingly insignificant that would indicate there was."

"This is a homicide investigation," said Detective Phillips. "It would be appreciated if you could help us out."

Sure. Pump my friend for information about something that sounded painful beyond what most people want to even think about. "If anything related to Lorraine's death comes up, I'll let you know." I'm sure they took that at face value. Of course, anything Cindee said about Lorraine's marriage would have nothing to do with her death, so I was off the hook.

CHAPTER 5

$\mathcal{A}$ FTER THE CONVERSATION with the detectives, I threw the rest of my croissant away. Between their not-so-subtle hint that I help them do their jobs and pump my soon-to-be-friend for information, and the things they'd told me about Lorraine's marriage, I didn't even want to finish my coffee. I took a few quick slurps of it, tepid by now, to ensure I didn't get a caffeine-craving headache, and left the cup on the tray where they collected dirty plates and cups.

I went to my room and sat on the balcony. I watched the water turn from a gray-green to deep blue as the sun rose higher in the sky. It wasn't as pleasant as it could have been, with my mind flipping between imagining my date with JD and the memory of Lorraine's face in the bay. There were quite a few clouds over the inland hills and they were predicting a chance of late afternoon rain. I decided on an early lunch due to my lack of breakfast, and I wanted to walk the coast-side path before it rained.

By one-thirty I'd done all of that, eating clam chowder in an old place right on the docks, with heavy plank floors and wooden tables. The chowder was nice and thick, filled with firm potatoes and fresh clams. If you think you can't tell fresh clams from canned when they're buried in thickened milk and butter, you haven't tasted good clam chowder. I walked the path, past the boats that sat alone in the harbor, waiting for their owners to find a free afternoon. I mingled with bicyclists and dog-walkers, as well as gulls who had taken to the path looking for picnic leftovers.

The church members were done with their morning activities when I got back, so I worked for an hour, straightening the room, putting out the agenda pages and background reading material for their discussion of community projects. I checked with the hotel events person to make sure everything was on track for the afternoon snack being brought in by a local coffee shop, then I went to my room and took a nap.

At three I woke craving a cigarette. I'm trying so hard to quit smoking. I've smoked since I was seventeen. I know it's inexplicable and a little depressing that someone my age, who grew up being force-fed facts about the dangers of smoking, would take it up, but what can I say? Some things are inexplicable. For me, the allure wasn't the age-old desire to look sophisticated. It was pure enjoyment of smoke. That, and having something to do with my hands. Especially when you're a teenager, you feel awkward standing around, stuffing your hands in your pockets or fiddling with your hair or your earrings. No one knows what to do. I don't know why arms are so difficult to manage, why they feel like they're in the way, why we tend to feel awkward with them simply dangling at our sides, but that's how it is. For me anyway, and for a few others. I know because I've asked.

Besides having one hand occupied, something to fiddle with, a reason to move your arm from time to time so you're not standing like a concrete statue, there's the smoke. It contains a soothing, captivating, almost mysterious quality. Maybe because a puff of smoke looks similar to reported sightings of ghosts, we have the two things all wrapped up as one image in the reptilian part of our brains. Not only is smoke seductive to watch as it floats in the air, smoke flowing out from your lips in a thin stream is even more entrancing.

There is the whole death angle. It will kill you, in most cases. But when you're young, even when you're not so young, you tend to think death is going to happen to the other person, not you. So even when I'm coughing like I'm going to puke up a lung, I don't necessarily focus on the reality of my own death. Especially at age twenty-seven. It's easy to think I have lots of years to quit. I'm working on a plan for the slow withdrawal from my addiction. I smoke one cigarette with my morning coffee, one after lunch, and one in the evening. The next one to go will most likely be the lunchtime smoke, but I'm not quite ready for that yet.

The clouds had started to cover the sky, so I changed into a long-sleeved pale green shirt that didn't look that great with my jeans, but it was soft and warm. I brushed my hair and left it loose and put on my navy blue hoodie. Outside the hotel, I walked across the side patio. I went down the steps to the path and walked a few hundred yards north then cut across toward the sand dunes. Once I hit soft sand, I kicked off my sandals and walked up the slight incline and down toward the boat-launching ramp. Out of the way of the dog walkers and families digging in the sand and the windsurfers, I figured there was less chance of someone complaining that I wasn't supposed to be smoking on the beach. Smoking wasn't allowed on hotel property, so my choices were limited.

The air was warmer than I'd expected, the sun still peeked through the clouds, glittering on the water. I lit my cigarette and leaned against the rail on the side of the ramp. I was only about three puffs into it when I saw a woman from the church walking across the dunes. She moved quite purposefully, headed in my direction. She wore a tee shirt and cardigan sweater, jeans that had a crease ironed down the center of each leg and bright white tennis shoes. It always strikes me as uncomfortable when I see someone walking in shoes on the beach. Why would you do that? Sand feels so good, whether it's soft and dry like warm powder on the soles of your feet, or hard packed and cold, when it's close enough to the water line that a wave can slide up and lap at your toes. Wearing shoes puts distance between you and the earth in the one place where you can really feel you're part of the whole planet. Not to mention the practical side, stopping to dump sand out of your shoes when you leave the beach, and you can never rid them of every grain.

I'd met this woman once or twice before, but we'd never said more than a few words to each other, and it seemed odd that she looked so determined to hunt me down that she was willing to trudge across the sand in her athletic shoes.

"Hi Karen."

"Hi." She waved her hand in front of her face.

If the smoke was bothering her, why had she marched all the way over to the boat launch area?

"You're always lurking around smoking, aren't you."

It sounded like an accusation. As if I was putting her out by finding a place where the smoke wouldn't bother anyone.

"That's the whole point. Most people don't like the smoke, so I have to find areas where I can be alone." I put the cigarette to my lips and drew in a bit of smoke and blew it out quickly. I didn't bother to turn away, after all, she'd sought me out.

"It makes you seem a little sneaky. I bet you see all kinds of things."

"Maybe."

She smiled, but it looked more like she was leering at me. "We've never really talked much," she said.

"Nope." I wondered if she wanted to be friends. If so, it seemed rather sudden, to come running at me across the beach, seemingly out of nowhere. Karen's about six or seven years older than I am. She wears a silver wedding band and a silver ring with a very large diamond, seeming to balance the metal and stone with silver and gold bangles covering her right wrist. Not that I judge every friendship by whether a woman is married, look at Cindee. We'll be great friends over time, I can feel it. But marriage does make a difference in what kind of friendship you have, and with Cindee there's a hint of a connection that goes beyond our life situations.

Karen took a step back, closer to the dunes so she wasn't directly downwind from my smoke.

"I'll be finished in a minute," I said. "I was going to walk down and wade for a while. Why don't you take off your shoes and come with me."

"I can't swim," said Karen.

"Well, I didn't mean let's go dive in head first. It's pretty cold, you have to be in the mood for a full-on swim."

"I'm afraid of the water." She looked down at her feet. She turned her left food sideways and dragged the side of her shoe along the sand, pressing hard, creating a ridge.

"I meant we could walk at the water line, where it's just a few inches."

She shivered, even though the breeze was too mild to cause an involuntary shaking. "I couldn't. I'd be afraid of getting washed out to sea."

"Really?" I knew that sounded rude, but I couldn't believe what I was hearing. "We're in a cove within a bay, with waves that were six inches, max. How could you possibly get swept out to sea?"

"Look at Lorraine."

"She didn't get dragged out by a rip tide, she hit her head."

Karen nodded. "But she drowned."

I took a long drag on my cigarette and thought about putting it out, but maybe one more. "But they aren't sure it was an accident."

"Did the police talk to you?" said Karen.

"Yes. They talked to all of us, didn't they?"

"I guess so. What did they ask you?"

"Mostly questions about how well I knew her. How about you?"

"They wanted to know where I was Thursday evening. Why would they think I would know anything about her drowning? I told them I was terrified of the water. I'd never go within even ten feet it."

Right then I abandoned any idea of being friends. She was too neurotic for me. Maybe we could be acquaintances, talk from time to time, but there was no way I wanted to hang out with her. It was a little disappointing, it's not like it's easy to make friends if you don't meet people where you work. I suppose if I were involved in some kind of activity it would be good, but I'm not. I have considered taking pottery classes, but I don't play a sport which is where a lot of people find like-minded friends to hang out with. I might take yoga classes. I took yoga a few years ago. That's where I met my friend Renee. We're still pretty close, but she moved to Oregon after she got married, so obviously our friendship is mostly on Facebook and texting.

Karen stared at me, waiting for me to speak. It seemed like she wanted reassurance but I had no idea for what. Surely she didn't expect me to be supportive of her absurd fear. I can see how wading out past your knees would be scary if you can't swim, but not even touching the water's edge was way over the top. It's not as if the sea is a giant squid that will lash out a tentacle, press its suction cups onto your back and drag you kicking and screaming to the bottom of the ocean. Finally, I said, "They asked where I was too."

"What did you say?"

Another slightly off-balance question. A more normal, accurate question would be – *where were you?* "I told them where I was, at the office supply store making photocopies about one of the service projects – finding a thousand homes for the homeless by 2015."

"Of course someone saw you there, and you have the receipt," said Karen.

I shrugged. I bent down and put out my cigarette in the sand. When the tip was good and cold, I put it inside a small plastic bag I try to remember to carry with me, so I'm not leaving litter wherever I stop for a smoke.

"That's nice of you to not leave your butts all over the beach."

I smiled. "Are you sure you don't want to go wading? Where the water's only a few inches deep?"

She shook her head. Her hair, straight and a little like straw in color and texture, whipped across her face. She looked as if she was dramatizing a woman shaking her head. The movement was so violent, her hair slapping her face, that it made me suddenly aware of the breeze blowing my own hair, a strand sticking to my lip gloss and a small chunk clinging to my forehead. I pulled a hair tie out of my pocket and ran my fingers through to separate it into three sections, pulled it over my shoulder and wound it into a loose braid. Karen was still shaking her head.

"I was in my room," she said. "I can't prove that I was there all evening."

"I'm sure you won't have to prove anything. It's not like they think you killed her." I started laughing.

She stared at me. I guess it wasn't that funny.

"I would never go down to the edge of the water. Especially in the dark. I told you, I can't swim," said Karen.

"Are they sure she died during the night?" I said.

"I think so. They said she'd been in the water between ten and fifteen hours when you found her, so if it was early afternoon, it makes sense that she died during the night."

I didn't really want to think about finding her body, seeing her pale face, bloated with sea water flashing before my eyes. Since thoughts of the Blue Lady kept passing through my mind, it was easy to change the subject. "Have you ever seen a ghost?"

"What does that have to do with anything?" said Karen.

"I was at this restaurant up the coast." I waved my arm in the direction of the far side of the bay. "The Distillery. It's known for ghost sightings – there's a woman dressed in blue who makes appearances along the coast and inside the restaurant. She died on the beach up there."

"Ghosts are only real to people who fool around with the occult," said Karen. "That's what Central Avenue Church teaches."

"Does that mean they don't exist, or only people in the occult see them?"

"I don't know. I never thought about it. I just know that Godly people wouldn't be seeing ghosts."

It made me understand why Pastor Joe and Pastor Kate didn't discuss my experience, they pretended it hadn't happened, tried to overlook it as a personality defect of mine, maybe. "That makes no sense," I said. "If ghosts are real, wouldn't anyone they chose to reveal themselves to be able to see them? Are you saying they would go around selectively avoiding people who are members of Central Avenue Church and other similar churches?"

"If I'd seen one, or if someone I trusted had seen one, I might think differently," said Karen. "But no one I know has."

"Almost one-third of Americans believe in ghosts or have seen them," I said. "I *Googled* it."

"They must be the one third who don't go to a church that makes it clear that you die and go to heaven. You don't roam the earth looking to complete unfinished business, or whatever it is they supposedly do."

"It sounds like you do know a bit about ghosts."

She laughed. "Everyone knows that's the theory."

"Then it makes sense that someone who died violently would still be around."

"Only if you believe that."

"Pretend for a minute it's true," I said.

"Are you saying Lorraine will come back and help find her killer? If there is a killer? If she didn't just trip and smack her head and drown, which I'm sure is how it happened. Why would anyone want to kill her?"

It was a statement, not a question, so I stayed focused on the ghost rather than Lorraine's death. "I think it's more mysterious, more vague than that. I've never heard of a ghost solving a crime. I don't think they communicate that clearly."

"You seem to have put a lot of thought into it," said Karen. "Have you seen one?"

"Yes."

I told her about my experience at the church, seeing the girl and her lover who used to smoke pot in the church prayer garden, and how the girl had been murdered by their drug dealer, and the guy later died and they returned to meet in the garden, loving each other beyond death. As I told her, my eyes watered, but she didn't seem to notice.

"That's a wonderful story," said Karen.

Her tone sounded condescending or maybe mocking, I'm not sure which. Suddenly I regretted telling her. She didn't really believe me, or her mind was somewhere else, maybe still thinking the dead only linger to solve their crimes. I don't believe that at all. There are so many better reasons to return, and love seems like a much better reason than delivering justice. It was the same with the Blue Lady. She came back looking for her lover, not to get revenge on her ex-husband, if he was the one who killed her. "I heard Lorraine was going to leave her husband, and if he hadn't been traveling they'd be checking him out in detail," I said.

"People aren't supposed to get divorced," said Karen.

"Well, it's not the ideal. But …."

"It's against God's law," said Karen.

I didn't know what to say to that. "You seem to feel strongly about the subject."

"It's not how I feel, it's what I know. I don't care what complaints Lorraine thought she had, it was her duty, her obligation to make it work. She took a vow."

"Her husband sounds like he's pretty sick." I worried that I was gossiping and wished I hadn't said that, but it kind of popped out because I was thinking about Karen's self-righteous attitude and not about watching what I said.

"What goes on between a husband and wife is no one's business. She should never have told that story to Cindee. Or me."

It sounded as if she knew everything, so I stopped worrying I'd said something I shouldn't have.

Karen took a few steps away. She glanced at the water. "I don't want to keep you from your wading. I'm sure the police will figure things out. It will probably turn out to be an accident after all, or else they won't know who did it because there aren't fingerprints and fibers and all that kind of stuff."

"You're sure you don't want to come with me? I'm a good swimmer. I wouldn't let anything happen to you."

She shook her head once. "I need to run to the store."

I couldn't imagine why she would need to run to the store when she was spending the weekend at a retreat, supposedly thinking about less earthly things. "Okay. See you later."

"Bye." She grabbed her right wrist as if she was afraid her hand would start waving goodbye when she didn't want it to. She had on one of those sweaters with the too-long, sagging sleeves, and she pulled at the edges, stretching it further as if she intended to pull it all the way over her fingertips.

I left my sandals where they were. I could feel Karen watching me as I walked to the shore. Sometimes the chill of the water feels as if your skin is burning off. I rolled my jeans up a few inches. The water was very cold, but soothing after standing on dry sand that sucked the moisture out of my feet. Tiny waves spread around my ankles as if they were welcoming me into the water.

When I turned to look back, Karen was crossing the dunes. Her arms were folded tightly around her middle, and she was hunched forward as if she was fighting a hard, cold wind.

CHAPTER 6

$\mathcal{W}$ HILE I WAS WADING, it started to rain. I went back to my room and took a shower. Pastor Joe wanted me to attend the late afternoon session to take notes on their discussion about community projects. That evening I joined the church members for dinner at Sam's Chowder House where we ate cracked crab and fries and coleslaw. The rain had stopped an hour or so earlier, and although it was cold, we sat outside near the fire pits, wrapped in sweatshirts and scarves, and drank coffee.

Some people had wine or beer, some had liqueur in their coffee. It's a strange phenomenon to me that these people are so opposed to the concept of lingering spirits after death, yet most of them have no issue with drinking alcohol. Yet, other church groups forbid drinking even wine. It's endlessly amazing to me that churches can have such a difference of opinion as to what's "okay" and what's not considered conducive to spirituality, when they're all, more or less, going off the same book, or set of books to get their direction on how to live in the world. Some drink alcohol, some don't, some give precise percentages of their income to the church, some don't, some want to help the homeless, some are only interested in converting people to their brand of god. It's not only the variation in rules that's confusing, it's how rabid they are about their points of view. As if it was spelled out, chapter and verse, that *thou shalt or shalt not do this or that or wind up cast out of paradise.* I wondered if there was any brand that believed in ghosts. As if ghosts need us to "believe" in them in order to exist. It's funny when you think about it.

During dinner, their lips glistening with butter, they talked about the meetings they'd had that day, marveled over the moon shining on the surface of the ocean, now that the rain had moved on. They speculated a bit about Lorraine's death. One or two of them voiced concern over her husband's grief, but no one mentioned what he was really like because they didn't know. Cindee was quiet, staring out at the water the entire time.

Once a few people got up to leave, I said good-night and walked back along the path with them. When they turned at the stairs that led to the Beach House, I kept going. They were a little worried about me walking alone in the dark, but I said I'd be fine, I'd stay on the path. That was a total lie, but I knew I'd be okay.

I wanted to walk out on the breakwater in the dark. I thought it would be exciting and a little scary, in a good way, to see the waves crashing up on the rocks in the moonlight, to be out there by myself, alone with the ocean.

I walked over the fine ground gravel that led to the rocks. It was hard to tell if the rocks were held together by concrete, or if they were just piled and stayed that way under their own force. No concrete or other material was visible, and they were arranged so that it was fairly easy to walk along without making huge leaps, each rock offering a choice of footholds, so it was possible to feel safe stepping from boulder to boulder. Still, with the waves crashing against them night and day, I didn't understand why they never moved, never had one roll off leaving a gaping hole. It was fun, like a puzzle, trying to figure out the best spot for the next move forward, trying to look ahead a step or two to make sure I didn't put myself into a position where it would be difficult to keep going forward. My plan was to walk all the way out to the fog horn. I loved looking at the water splashing on my left, and the gentle lapping at my right in the protected area. When the tide was out, as it was then, the right side of the rocks was sandy beach quite a ways out, so there was the extra sense of safety that I could hop to firm ground at any time.

A few clouds slid over the moon making the water look darker, giving it almost a thick quality as the waves calmed slightly and moved with swells that broke softly rather than giant crashes of power.

One man stood at the left side of the breakwater, his fishing line moving with the swaying of the water. I whispered hello, surprised that my voice came out so quietly, but I hadn't spoken for nearly fifteen minutes, so I suppose that's why. He seemed to appreciate my quietness, knowing I wouldn't disturb his thoughts or his fish. He nodded and said, "'Evening." He turned back and then spoke as if it wasn't even directed at me, but I was the only one there, "Watch your step."

"I am," I said, and then leaped to the next boulder which was more to the right side of the breakwater.

I walked across two more rocks. The next one was larger than some of the others and had a flat area that would be perfect for sitting down and looking at the water for a few minutes. I settled down, and looked out past the foghorn and the endless expanse of dark water and dark sky, meeting each other at some undefined spot that was difficult to pinpoint, even with the moonlight.

The waves moved with a rhythmic sound that made me feel calm. I hoped I was getting into the mood of the place and maybe that would increase my likelihood that I'd see the Blue Lady before dawn the next day. Of course, do ghosts really need us to be in a particular mood to see them? Do they need anything from us at all? They must need something, or they wouldn't be hanging around, right?

I thought about the church and their strong anti-ghost views. I thought about Karen and her strong anti-everything views – ghosts, smoking, divorce. It's always easy to say something is wrong if you aren't in the situation. No one *plans* to get divorced, but look what the guy was doing to her. It was sick. Who knew where it might lead. That's not marriage, that's sexual slavery. Good for Lorraine that she was going to leave him, and like Cindee said, good for her if she had found a man who loved her. Of course, Karen knew how much Lorraine was suffering and still judged her. That's some kind of arrogance, to be happily married, flashing around her diamond ring, and telling someone who was supposedly her friend that she had no right to happiness. That she had to keep a promise that, if you ask me, was made under false pretenses. I wondered why Karen was so adamant about it. She sounded as if she had some kind of major investment in Lorraine's decision, like it was a personal affront that Lorraine would "break her vow".

I looked down onto the damp sand where the water had been sucked away and saw something glittering under the moonlight. I stood and blinked, trying to help my eyes see more clearly. I reached into my messenger bag and pulled out my keys which have a small plastic disk from some trade show I worked at in my previous job. When you squeeze the disk, there's a tiny light that's extremely bright. The object on the sand looked like one of those cuff bracelets. The light made the bracelet glitter because it was silver with a large cut stone at the center.

I slipped off my sandals so my toes could get a better grip on the boulder. I glanced out into the cove, then realized it wasn't as if I would be able to tell just by looking whether the tide was coming back in. Climbing down to the sand would only take a few minutes, and the tide wouldn't move in that quickly. I picked up my sandals and made my way down to the beach. The wet sand wasn't as cold as I'd expected. I picked up the bracelet and wiped it on my jeans. I don't know anything about gems, so I couldn't tell if it was valuable. I folded it around my wrist. It looked silly on my arm. I rotated my hand and the bracelet didn't move. I imagined the grip of the metal was similar to how handcuffs might feel. I wondered why you would ever wear something so uncomfortable. As I pulled it off, it scraped the skin along my wrist bone.

I climbed back up the rocks and walked fairly quickly out to the foghorn, holding my sandals in one hand and the bracelet in the other, trying to think whether I should turn it in at the hotel desk. What were the odds that it belonged to someone who was staying at the Beach House, or had stayed there recently? It could have washed over from anywhere, from the trailer park near the Beach House, from one of the larger sailboats in the harbor. If that was a real gem, maybe it had washed all the way over from the Ritz Carlton. It could also have belonged to Lorraine, so perhaps I should show the sheriffs before I took it to the front desk.

Back in the light of my room, I saw the stone was red. I put the bracelet in the drawer. It was getting late, and I would be waking in four or five hours for my ghost stalking date with JD. The bracelet could wait.

CHAPTER 7

$\mathcal{M}$AKING A LEFT TURN from The Beach House onto Highway One is usually tricky, with the constant flow of traffic along the coast. At three-thirty in the morning, it was a breeze. I raced up the highway, the moon behind me now and the sky moderately pale because the fog had come in during the night and the whiteness made it look lighter than it was. I turned down the street that led to The Distillery. I was a little jittery, thinking about meeting JD outside the bar where we had clear roles – bartender and customer. Now, what were we? It didn't seem like a date. And yet, we were meeting alone, eating breakfast together. At the same time, our purpose was getting to know the Blue Lady a little better, not getting to know each other. That would be a side effect.

When I reached the parking lot, there were two cars. One sat under the lights, a white Toyota streaked with dirt and rusting around the wheel wells. A few slots over was a dark blue Explorer. JD leaned against it with his hands in his pockets. He was looking directly at me, as if he'd been watching the whole time, waiting for me to show up. Maybe he wasn't sure I would.

I pulled my Beetle in next to his SUV, and before I turned off the engine, he was walking around to his tailgate. He lifted the top half open at the same time I opened my car door. I grabbed my jacket off the passenger seat, put my purse in the trunk, and the car key in my pocket. It wasn't as cold as I'd expected. It was quiet, not even the sound of gulls marred the silence. The sky looked even whiter as if it was closed off from us because the parking lot lights reflected off the fog.

JD took out two of those metal coffee containers and walked to where I stood. He held out one of the coffees. "I made you a latte. I hope that's okay. I figured if you like coffee with cream, you probably like lattes."

"You have an espresso maker?"

He shrugged. "You know this is a total crapshoot, right?"

I nodded. I put my tongue to the tiny hole on the lid of the cup and tipped it slightly to test the temperature. It was still too hot.

He went back to the truck, pulled out a blanket, a paper bag with handles, and closed the hatch. "Then let's hike down. At least we'll have some muffins and if the fog moves out, a nice sunrise."

Now it definitely felt like a date. Suddenly I realized he didn't expect to see the Blue Lady at all. And how naïve and hopeful had I been, thinking I could just show up and a ghost would humor me? She'd only been seen intermittently over the years. It wasn't as if she made a daily, or even monthly, appearance. I guess that's how much I wanted to see her. I thought simply showing up would be enough. Or maybe I didn't. Maybe I thought this was a date all along. A very strange date, but a chance to get to know a very good looking guy and talk about something we had in common. Maybe there would be other things in common.

Lots of very non-beach-like vegetation covered the hillside and a path had been worn through, winding down to the beach below *The Distillery*. JD went first, following the steep twists and curves fairly quickly. When we reached the bottom, he stopped and peeled off his shoes — those rubbery sock-like things with individual pockets for each toe. When I first noticed he was wearing beach shoes, I figured he was a walk-in-the-sand-barefoot kind of guy. Something else in common, although a very small thing. I unbuckled my sandals and kicked them off. We left our shoes at the base of the trail and I followed him across the sand.

That strip of beach is narrow and short, only a few hundred yards from the ends where the cliffs sloped down into piles of rock. The surf was calm. We walked across the dry sand that was covered with a thin crust that showed each footprint. JD stopped just before the line of kelp that marked the water edge from high tide. He handed me his coffee and set the bag on the sand. He spread out the blanket, took back his coffee, and waited while I sat down.

"After I suggested we do this, I realized I mis-led you by even suggesting we should meet to see what happens. The possibility that we'll see her is almost non-existent."

"I know," I said.

He looked at me, but I couldn't read his expression at all.

He settled on the blanket. "Are you hungry?"

"No, my stomach thinks it's still asleep."

He laughed softly. "Let me know when you are." He sipped his coffee.

For a few minutes, we listened to the waves.

"The other day you said that seeing the ghost changed your perspective," I said. "What happened?"

"It's hard to describe." He was quiet for a minute or two, but he didn't sip his coffee and he looked like he'd drifted off somewhere and the mug might slide out of his hand. Finally, he spoke. "I realized that the only perspective that really matters is my own. That sounds arrogant, but the reaction when I mention the ghost is what you'd expect. Some people laugh, some people are curious, quite a few think I'm certifiable. But I know what I saw."

"Exactly," I said.

"And on top of that, I realized there might be a lot more going on around us that we don't notice."

"Ghosts and things?"

"Not only people who've died, a whole other realm."

He talked about it for quite a while longer, until I had a glimmer of realizing why some people might think he's certifiable. I didn't think that, but I could see it. He was really into it. Then we stopped talking, or rather, he stopped talking and I stopped asking questions. We sipped our coffees and watched the waves, much larger here, outside the bay. Despite the caffeine, my eyelids started to droop, weighed down by the quiet, interrupted only by the swooshing and splashing of the waves slapping the beach. Every few minutes I wanted to crawl back into bed to finish sleeping. I took the lid off my cup and took a long swallow now that it was cool enough. That helped. Not the caffeine, but just doing something and the warm liquid.

The sky had grown lighter. I'd hardly noticed it changing. The fog didn't move at all, in fact as the sky lightened, the fog became thicker and sank down until it was the type that prevented you from seeing very far. Even the rocks forty or fifty yards from shore were shrouded in white. The water was pale gray. The waves seemed to get bigger and more insistent.

I felt the warmth radiating off JD's body. The whiteness of his knuckles and the bones at the top of his feet appeared more prominent, which of course made me think of skeletons. And corpses. And Lorraine. I pushed that out of my head, that image. It was nice sitting next to him, not talking. I was glad he didn't feel the need to ask me questions or tell me more stories. We could do that later. I imagined we could do it pretty soon because everything was light enough now that I was sure we wouldn't be seeing the Blue Lady. Although he had said the first time he saw her was mid-morning, so you never know.

He opened the bag and pulled out two muffins. He handed one to me. He pulled out some grapes, flattened the bag, and set the grapes on top. We peeled the paper down the sides of the muffins and ate them so fast the gulls didn't even notice we had food. Usually, the minute you put something in your mouth, even make a move to peel off a wrapper or open a bag, they're right in front of you, standing a few yards from the blanket, staring you down, supremely confident you'll eventually share a bit with them. If you don't, they start hopping closer, or taking off in flight and swooping back down as if they're sure you just hadn't noticed them and a dramatic landing will get your attention.

"It was worth a shot," said JD.

"It was."

We sat nibbling grapes until all that was left was the stem structure. After a while, he stuffed the grape stems and muffin papers in the bag and folded it over. Until then, I'd been sitting cross-legged. I straightened my legs to let the blood flow better and stretched up so my back wasn't hunched over.

"Why are you so intent on seeing the Blue Lady?" said JD. "Or was it me you were interested in seeing?" He winked.

Those two questions were much too close to each other. I didn't know which to answer, so I opted for the easy one. "It's such a strange feeling to see someone who is no longer living, who can appear and disappear. Even if they still have questions, they must know things I don't, that none of us will know until we get wherever it is we're going."

A gull screamed and dropped out of the sky landing a few feet from JD's toes. "A lot of people don't believe in them," he said.

"A lot of people do."

"Fair enough. But most people read the restaurant's blurb about her and lose interest after a few minutes."

"The woman sitting next to me last night thought the Blue Lady was a hoax."

"The restaurant blew it a couple of years ago," he said. "They'd had a fair amount of publicity around the haunting, and a few staff people played it up. They hid a speaker with some ghostly laughter, and a two-way mirror with a flashing blue image of a head, stuff like that. When a ghost story research group came to investigate, they found all the fake stuff."

"Why would anyone want to fake it when they had the real thing?"

"They liked the uniqueness of it all. How many restaurants have their own ghost? And especially one as glamorous and mysterious as the Blue Lady, but she's unpredictable. She hadn't been seen in a while, so they wanted to keep the mystique going. Still, it made some people think she was finished with her time on earth and wouldn't be around anymore. It reinforced others' views that it had been a hoax all along."

"That's too bad."

He shifted on the blanket so he was facing me more than the ocean. His toes were only a few inches from my ankle and I hoped they would touch my leg. Although then I'd be left wondering whether or not it was deliberate, so maybe it was best that it didn't. "The other reason I'm interested is because I saw some ghosts a few months ago. For my whole life before that, I'd never given much thought to ghosts, or anything supernatural." That wasn't really what I'd planned to say, I'd wanted to say I had also come to see him, but that moment had passed. It had been several minutes since he'd tossed that hint out there like he was throwing fish pieces at the gulls.

"Your whole life?" He laughed. "You make it sound like you're fifty. And I'm sure you're not a day over forty."

"My whole life is still my whole life, even if it's not that long yet."

"How old are you? Twenty?"

I smiled. "Twenty-seven."

"Oh. You seem younger."

"So I've heard."

"I assumed you didn't order a drink yesterday because you were underage."

"How old are you?"

"Thirty-three."

That made me feel weird. I'm so used to thinking of myself in my twenties, noticing guys in their twenties. I guess thirty is closer than I'd realized, but honestly, until that minute, I hadn't thought about it much and hadn't realized how fast it was coming at me. I feel like a kid most of the time, thinking I'm not completely an adult yet, thirty sounds old. It just does. "How old was the Blue Lady when she died?"

"In her early thirties."

"Oh, that's sad."

"You've seen ghosts more than once?" said JD.

"No, I saw two at the same time. One was a girl who was shot and killed in the church garden. Her boyfriend was there when she was shot, but he ran away. He died not long after her, also murdered. They returned to find each other."

JD shifted into a cross-legged position, and I felt more disappointed than I should have that it was no longer in the realm of possibility that his foot would lean against my ankle. "Did anyone else see them?"

"Don't you believe me?"

"How do you translate that into not believing you? It was a simple question."

"I guess I'm sensitive about it. The ministers of the church where I work, Joe and Kate, aren't big on ghosts. You heard what Cindee said – that they're wishful thinking on the part of people who are grieving. But someone else did see them. The father of the boy was the church gardener. He saw them. Several times. And I saw them twice."

The fog had started to lift as a stiff breeze whipped across the beach. I was sure it was the wind making me shiver, not thoughts of ghosts and not disappointment over not seeing the Blue Lady, and not from wanting JD to touch me. I wondered about this feeling because I hardly knew the guy. Although we had had several conversations, twice at the bar and now. And there's something about the beach, the gulls, the utter lack of human presence, that makes you feel you are more connected to the other person. The only two people for as far as the eye can see or the ear can hear.

My hair blew across my face, and a long strand laced itself through my eyelashes. JD reached over and ran his finger along my hairline. The piece of hair was caught on one of my earrings, and he lifted it free, tucking it behind my ear. His finger was so warm, the shivering kept itself going. I so badly wanted him to keep his finger on my cheek, just in front of my earlobe, where he'd paused to make sure it was secure, but he moved it away.

"You look cold. Should we head back up?"

He stood and reached out his hand. I took it and he tugged, making the rise to my feet so effortless I felt like a ballerina being swept across a stage. Not that I've ever been on a stage, or even taken ballet classes, for that matter. When I was standing, he kept hold of my hand for a few seconds, squeezed it gently, and then let go. He stepped off the blanket and bent to lift up the edges. We each held a side, but didn't have to flap it to be rid of the sand, the wind took care of that while we both turned our heads, squinting as sand flew off like tiny nails pricking at our hands and cheeks.

He folded the blanket, and I walked over to the bag of muffin wrappers that had danced a few yards away from us.

I led the way up the trail and he followed. When we reached the top, he put the blanket in his truck, and I walked over to the area behind the restaurant and tossed the trash in the dumpster.

We met in the center of the parking lot.

"I'm going to run inside and check the liquor status real quick. I forgot to do it last night. I need to let the owner know if anything is unexpectedly low before our mid-week delivery."

I nodded. I wasn't sure what to do. I needed to get back to the hotel in an hour or so. I guessed it was about five-thirty now, so I didn't feel rushed, but I wasn't sure how all this was going to end. To be honest, it felt awkward. It's not like we could go to breakfast since we'd already eaten, and it's not like there were a lot of other things to do at daybreak on a Sunday.

JD went to the front door, unlocked it, and went inside. I walked back to the edge of the parking lot toward the area between the front of the restaurant and the cliff. On a lower level, there's a second bar and an outdoor sitting area with Adirondack chairs. They keep blankets stacked inside so people can sit out and enjoy the ocean and the sky even when it's cold.

The chairs were damp from the fog. I gazed past the restaurant, turning slightly to face the opposite cliff. Then I saw her. A faint blue against the white. At first, I thought it was wishful thinking on my part. I had it pressed so hard into my brain that I wanted to see her that my eyes were playing tricks on me. That, plus she's dressed in blue, against a blue and white sky. As Cindee said, it's not hard to imagine seeing a pale blue figure.

It was getting light fast even though the sun wasn't actually up yet, and the sky was mostly white with fog. I wrapped my arms around me anyway. I closed my eyes and hoped that she wouldn't disappear, but I had to clear my head for a minute to make sure I was really seeing her. I opened my eyes. She was even sharper than she'd been a few minutes earlier. She stood on the far cliff, looking down at the beach where we'd been sitting. Her hat was tipped forward, and she had her hand on the brim as if she was trying to keep it from getting caught by the breeze.

For a moment I had the feeling she was looking at the beach to see if JD and I were still down there. Then I realized we never would have seen her from where we were sitting, and it was possible she had been trying to hide from us, but then she realized she didn't know where we'd gone. Her skirt clung to her legs making it appear as if she was experiencing the same breeze I was.

I didn't want to blink, didn't want to move, desperately hoping JD wouldn't come out and make a sound, causing her to disappear. I wanted to observe her for as long as I could although I had absolutely no idea why. Part of me still wondered if I was imagining her, but another part of me knew without a doubt that I was seeing her. I couldn't make out the features of her face, just the distinctive hat and her dress, touching the grass around her feet. She took a step closer to the edge of the cliff. As I watched her stare at the ocean, a coolness filled my throat and spread to my lungs. With it, there was a deep longing. It was so intense and so different from anything I'd felt in my normal life that I knew it came from her. It was a longing that made the coolness inside my throat turn to ice as if there was something that I would never have in this world or the next. A longing that made me feel as if I'd never been loved and never would be. I almost collapsed from the weight of it, but managed to lean over and press my hands on my knees to catch my breath. I straightened myself as quickly as I could because I didn't want to lose sight of her. It seemed as if the longing was hers, but more than hers, that she was expressing something that went beyond her search for her lover.

It seemed as if I'd been frozen there forever. Then she slowly moved her hand, the one that had been limp at her side, up to her throat. She tipped her head up, still holding the hat with her other hand and moved violently as if she was gasping for air. She lowered her hands and tugged the tight-fitting sleeves of her dress toward her wrist bones. Then she faded. Very quickly. One moment she was there and then she wasn't.

I couldn't move. I could hardly feel my feet or my legs. I knew, I just knew that she was trying to tell me something about Lorraine. Some people might think this was all in my own mind, the desire of wanting to see her and having just discovered a drowned woman two days earlier, that all those things stirred up my imagination. But that's not the case. Besides, it wasn't as if I received some definitive message. I had no idea what she was trying to say. I already knew Lorraine drowned, so it wasn't as if that was some big news flash.

"Enjoying the view?"

I turned at the sound of JD's voice.

"I saw her."

He raised his eyebrows.

"You don't believe me?"

"Why is that your first reaction?"

"Maybe I'm accustomed to having people disbelieve me."

"Where was she?"

I pointed at the cliff across the gorge. "This sounds bizarre, but I think she was telling me something about Lorraine. The woman who drowned."

"What do you think she was saying?"

"I don't know. She didn't speak. It was just a feeling. Still is a feeling. Nothing really, she acted as if she was drowning."

"Huh."

"But I already know that."

"Maybe she wants to let you know that Lorraine died the same way. Killed by a violent husband."

"That's what Cindee thinks. But Lorraine's husband was in Chicago."

"People can fly back and forth easily."

"The police already checked into that."

JD tugged on his ponytail. "Maybe you'll see her again and it'll be more clear."

"I'm leaving later this afternoon." I started walking toward my car.

"You live just over the hill, right?"

I laughed. "No. That's where the church is located, and most of the members live there, but I can't afford even a studio apartment in that area. I'm in downtown San Jose."

"Still, it's nearby."

I waited.

"Can I get your number? I could head over your way and take you to dinner some time. If you want."

"Sure," I said.

He pulled his cell phone out of his jacket pocket. I gave him my number and he tapped it in. We walked side by side to our cars. We stopped near the back of his SUV. I got my cell out of my trunk and plugged in his number. He put his hand on my shoulder, bent down and kissed the tip of my nose.

I laughed, and so did he.

I walked around to the driver's side of my car. "Thanks for introducing me to the Blue Lady."

"I'm glad she turned up. I hope you figure out what she wanted to tell you."

He could be sure of that, I wouldn't be able to think about much else.

He lifted his hand. "I'll call you."

"Okay."

On the drive back to the highway and all the way to the Beach House, I thought about JD and his black hair and blue eyes. I was supposed to be thinking about what the Blue Lady might have wanted me to know, but my mind drifted back to him every time I tried to recall her image. There was a thrill of excitement, as if my blood vessels were jumping around, twitching inside my neck and stomach, and I wasn't sure if it was from JD putting my hair behind my ear and kissing my nose and asking me out to dinner, or the essence of the Blue Lady riding beside me in the car.

CHAPTER 8

HEN I RETURNED to the Beach House, the staff was setting up breakfast in the lobby. They had all the bakery items, fruit, and yogurt on one table. A guy about my age with shaggy blonde hair was carrying pitchers of orange juice and tomato juice from the room behind the front desk area. He set them on a second table and went back for more. When he came out with the first coffee pot, I said, "I know it's early, but can I grab one of those chocolate croissants?"

"Sure," he said. "Do you want coffee?"

"I can get it." Breakfast didn't technically start until seven, but the food was there, so why not? It's interesting how if you ask for a favor or an exception to the rules, nine times out of ten, you'll get it. Although my friend Renee said I'm always getting special attention because I'm cute. That sounds like I'm stuck on myself, but that's what she said. And not just once, but many times. She was always commenting when we were out together that my dark red hair and green eyes, not to mention my tattoos, are attention-getting in themselves. Add on that I'm petite and have a great smile, well, of course doors always opened up for me. I don't think her view is entirely true. I think you get back what you put out. If you smile, most people will smile back. If you ask without being combative or demanding or acting entitled, people want to be nice.

The guy set the pot of coffee on the table near the juice.

After he left, I picked up a mug, pressed the pump to squirt coffee into it and then carried it and the croissant on a small plate to the sitting area in the far corner where I'd talked to the sheriffs the day before. I was still sleepy and I thought if I went to my room to eat, I'd be too tempted to take a nap. And napping at 6:30 in the morning makes no sense.

There was nothing but flakes of dough on the plate, and I was on my second cup of coffee when Detective Wagner walked into the lobby carrying an enormous white and blue plastic mug that said *San Jose Sharks* on the side. A blast of damp air came with him. It looked as though he was making it a habit to hang out in the lobby at breakfast time every day. I suppose that was the easiest way to bump into the hotel guests, but you'd think he would march up and down the halls knocking on doors instead of lurking around the breakfast buffet. He walked to where I was sitting and stopped a few feet away. "Madison. Uh ... Ms. Keith. Good morning."

"Hi," I said. "Have you found out anything more about Lorraine?"

"Some. We know she definitely hit her head *before* she drowned. And there are scrapes on her sides that most likely came from sliding down the rocks. Of course, it's impossible to find the spot where she entered the water."

That didn't sound like much new information to me, but he looked quite confident that it was a huge step forward. I stood and picked up my dirty dishes.

"Here, let me help you."

I didn't need help, but he pulled the plate out of my hand and carried it to the still-uncluttered dirty dish tray.

I squirted more coffee into my cup and added cream. "Can I ask you a question?"

"Sure." He stepped away from the table, and we walked to the front doors and outside where a large concrete fountain with water lilies and papyrus growing in it splashed and gurgled as background music.

"It's hard not to think it was her husband, especially after what you told me about him. Even though it seems impossible, doesn't that bother you?"

"Yes."

I thought of the Blue Lady, the feeling I had that she and Lorraine suffered similar fates. I pushed her image out of my head. "I mean, who else would want to kill her?"

"That's what I'm trying to figure out."

"How do you do that?"

"In most cases, homicide victims are killed by a person they know. From what we've seen of the body, there was obviously a struggle, and she wasn't sexually assaulted, so it's less likely to be an attack by a stranger. There weren't any prints we could get off the wine glass. And we don't even know if it was hers."

"Or the killer's," I said.

"We checked the wine glasses in all the guest rooms, but since the condos are privately owned and rented out, the inventory isn't as precise as it could be, so that was a dead end."

"I can't stop thinking about her husband," I said. "How cruel he is."

"One-third of the women that are murdered are killed by their partners," said Detective Wagner. He turned and faced the highway. He put his hand on the top of his head like he was trying to hold it in place.

"That's so sad."

He turned back. He pressed his lips together.

"The person who's supposed to love you more than anyone in the world, kills you." As I spoke, my eyes got teary. I looked down and pressed my finger gently on one of the water lilies. I remembered what he said about his daughter being the victim of a crime.

"There are lots of sick relationships out there," he said.

I leaned against the fountain. The bowl of it was right at hip height. I pressed the lily again. The water was warmer than I'd expected, I suppose because the fountain was close to the building, or maybe because I expected it to be as cold as the ocean and it wasn't. What a horrible way to die, breathing in salty, dark, cold water until your lungs are filled.

"So if it's not her husband, then what do you do?"

"Ask questions. Lots of questions."

Neither of us spoke for a minute or more.

"I guess I'll be going up to my room for awhile if you don't have any questions."

"I don't. Not right now."

As I walked to the stairs, I was glad to escape. There was nothing else to tell him, and I was sure he wouldn't want to hear some flakey idea about a woman who had been dead for ninety years giving me information about a woman who hadn't even been dead for ninety hours. Not that she'd given me any information beyond hinting at the obvious.

On the second floor, I walked down the hall, still tasting chocolate. My room was cold because I'd left the balcony door cracked open when I left at 3am. Already that time on the beach, in the dark, being with JD, then seeing the Blue Lady was fading into something as thin and transparent and hard to hold onto as the wisps of fog that still hung over the bay. I kept my hoodie on and went out on the balcony and sat down. I jiggled the chair closer to the front edge so I could stretch out my legs and prop my feet on the rail. Maybe because I'd been so focused on JD and then on the Blue Lady, and then on JD again, it finally sunk in that there was a good chance someone from Central Avenue Church had killed Lorraine. I was so startled by the reality of that idea, my feet slipped off the rail and thudded on the balcony floor. I put them back up on the rail, crossing my ankles.

I suppose thinking it was Lorraine's husband would be the easy answer. If there's a husband who is already known for cruelty, it's neatly tied up before you even start working on finding the killer.

But a whole church full of people? Where would the investigators start with a project like that? And no wonder they wanted to talk to me. They thought I might know enough secrets to narrow things down for them, when in fact, I didn't know much at all.

I closed my eyes and imagined the Blue Lady as I'd seen her. It would have been awesome if she could help point out the killer. But really, how would she know anything? After all, she's dead too. She might know the mysteries of death and life, but that didn't mean she knew specifics or had some kind of omniscient awareness. Unless Lorraine was still wandering about and had passed along the identity of her killer. I'm sure the Blue Lady didn't deliberately try to mislead me, maybe she wasn't trying to say anything to me at all. Maybe she hadn't even noticed me. When I'd seen the ghosts of that young couple at Central Avenue Church, I'd had the impression they weren't at all aware of my presence.

As the light changed the color of the water to a darker blue, the sun moved higher in the sky, and the rest of the fog dissolved, I realized I'd been so enraptured with the Blue Lady that I assumed just because she was in a realm beyond mine, she knew more, that she had some special insight into Lorraine's death. That, and the fact that she pantomimed drowning, so I thought she was trying to tell me she knew all about it. And that made me think that Lorraine had died the same way the Blue Lady had. But of course, the sheriffs had ruled that out before I even got the supposed "message".

Maybe the Blue Lady was simply fixated on her own death, devastated by the outrage of it after nearly a century, and she could only think of two things – the lover she'd been torn away from, and her brutal death. After all, isn't that why spirits linger? Because they're stuck on one point? It's really the same as it is in this realm, when we fixate on one part of our lives, one hurt or injustice from the past that we can't let go of and it comes to rule our lives, consuming our thoughts, influencing everything we do. Even the sheriffs could get fixated. They're human. And if they know that nine times out of ten a woman is murdered by her husband or boyfriend, then that's the first place they look. And what do they miss when they're chasing that thread to see whether the assumption will unravel? With their eyes solidly focused on their own hypothesis, it would be easy to miss something small, to ask the wrong questions.

I was so taken with the Blue Lady, so longing to see her, so wanting a message that I got pulled into her aura, or whatever you want to call it. She probably had nothing whatsoever to say about Lorraine. She most likely wasn't even aware of Lorraine's death.

It wasn't until I was out of the shower and drying my hair that I remembered the bracelet sitting in the drawer near my bed. With JD and my hopes for seeing the Blue Lady weaving through my dreams, and then waking early, going to meet them both, the bracelet had completely evaporated from my mind. I wondered if I should rush downstairs and look for the detectives. It wasn't as if it belonged to Lorraine. She was not a jewelry-wearing woman. I'd seen her those few times in the church office, and she didn't wear a diamond ring, just a thin gold wedding band. Her ears weren't even pierced. I dropped it into my bag anyway.

I put on a little mascara, which is the only makeup I wear, and many days I don't even bother with that. But the black inky stuff makes my eyes look greener, so when I'm not feeling lazy, I use it. I brushed my hair and left it down across my shoulders and back. It was still damp at the ends, but it would dry on its own. Blowing hot air at long hair can take a lot of time and I get bored. Or maybe I'm lazy there, too.

It was nine-thirty when I left my room. The church members were nearing the end of their worship service. I needed to sit down with the hotel event manager and go over the bill before the hotel started preparing for check-out of the thirty members of Central Avenue Church. By the time I was done with that, the service would be over and I was supposed to touch base with Joe so he could tell me if he needed any administrative work done for their afternoon meetings.

The lobby was full of bright morning light, clean and inviting, now that the tables from the breakfast buffet had been cleared away. A man wearing a pink shirt and pink and green plaid shorts stood at the front desk, checking out. I walked down the hall toward the meeting room. I heard the church members singing. I paused a few feet past the door and listened. It wasn't that I was forbidden to attend their worship services, it just isn't my thing. I prefer to encounter spiritual things in nature, or when I'm meditating. Alone. In fact, I don't really understand the notion of approaching god as a group activity. I can understand forming groups for bowling or quilt-making, but isn't being with god something you do alone? Just your soul and the mind of the universe? Even if you die at the exact same moment as someone else, you're still crossing over all by yourself. It's a solitary event.

After I listened to their voices, beautifully harmonized, although surely they couldn't all have gifted voices, I guess the good ones drowned out the flat and toneless ones, I went back to the front desk and met with the manager to review the bill. When it was all signed off, I walked past the conference room again, where the church members were now silent, most likely praying, and out the side door to the patio area. The bracelet was on my mind, consuming my thoughts, actually, as if that cut red stone in the center of the wide, silver band was glowing at the center of my brain, radiating out through all the nooks and crannies. There was part of me that thought I should hand it over to the sheriff, and another part of me that wondered why I even thought it was related to Lorraine's death. I could have found anything on that beach when the tide was out. Did that mean it was related to murder? What if I found a tube of lipstick, pock-marked by sand and water? Or an earring or a hair tie or a scarf or a button?

It puzzled me that I had this strong impression I was withholding something, a guilty feeling almost, as if I was trying to disrupt their investigation, or wanting to figure something out on my own first. At the exact same time, I had this feeling of being ridiculous, giving them some lost item I found on the beach, acting as if I was helping them solve a crime by gathering flotsam from the ocean floor.

I took one of the wood patio chairs and turned it to face the bay. I slipped off my flip-flops and propped my feet on the planter box. The surfers sat on their boards in the water to my left. The water undulated beneath them, making them look like they were riding gently moving camels, loping across a desert. Every so often a wave would break, but the crests weren't more than a few feet high, so half the time the surfers didn't even bother to stand. You had to wonder why they'd chosen this area. Maybe they were newbies, not wanting anything too wild so they could get the feel of their boards and an occasional ride to the shore.

The bracelet continued to shimmer in my mind, as if the red glow was pulsing larger, filling my whole head. I finally decided that if Detective Wagner were hanging around, if he approached me again, I would mention the bracelet, but I wasn't going to make a big thing out of it. Since I was confident it wasn't something Lorraine would have worn, I had no reason to believe it was related, except for the nagging feeling inside that it was strange to have something so large and possibly valuable go missing in the ocean. Most of the stuff you find on a beach is either garbage, or something people wouldn't bother looking for if it went missing, like a rubber flip-flop or a tee shirt.

Sitting in the sun made me sleepy. Despite the caffeine, my three a.m. date with JD was catching up. I let my thoughts wander to him. I was disappointed that the weekend was already over. I could really get used to living near the beach. Then, just as I was imagining peaceful days of watching the waves, Lorraine's swollen, pale face appeared in my imagination, and I wanted to drive inland and never see the ocean again. I hoped the image of her face and her floating hair, like kelp, wouldn't haunt me forever.

CHAPTER 9

I WAS STILL SITTING on the patio with my feet up when the church members emerged from the conference room. Most of them turned left down the hall, heading back to their rooms to finish, or start, packing up. We'd arranged a deal where they could stay past the regular checkout until the meetings were over at four. On a Sunday afternoon, there wasn't a huge influx of people, so the hotel had worked out a reasonable rate for the five extra hours.

After a few minutes, Cindee and Joe came out. Cindee had her camera. She said *hi*, then walked over to the garden area that was situated between the swimming pool and the trees and shrubs that blocked the parking lot. She sat on one of the benches and balanced her camera on her knees, watching a hummingbird drinking from the tiny purple blooms of a Mexican sage.

Joe dragged a chair over next to mine, sat down, and put his feet up on the planter. Out in the bright sun, I could see a few strands of gray in his goatee.

"I'm jealous of you sitting out here rather than cooped up in a conference room," he said.

I thought it was best not to respond to that. After all, they could have gone one Sunday without a service, couldn't they? Staying cooped up had been his call. Well, maybe not his, but the expectation of most of the members and I suppose he felt obligated to "do his job" which included leading weekly services, supplying the thoughts and insights that he'd accumulated all week.

After a few minutes of silence, I said, "The bill's all settled."

He nodded. "Did you have a good weekend?"

"My room was amazing. Thanks for hiring me for an awesome job that requires four days at the beach."

He smiled. He didn't say "you're welcome" which is what I like about Joe. Even though I felt like I should let him know I appreciated it, he didn't make me feel beholden.

"What have you been up to when you weren't working? Besides finding Lorraine." He looked toward the harbor. "She had a sad life, with a terrible end."

"It's hard not to see her face every time I close my eyes."

"That will fade. I remember my first funeral with an open casket. I thought that guy's plastic-looking face would stay with me forever, but eventually, it goes away."

I nodded. He seemed to be forgetting this was the second time in less than six months that I'd found a corpse. What was it with me? Was I somehow attracting them? Or was I just in the wrong place at the wrong time? Would their inanimate faces stay with me forever? I hoped not. And then I thought of Fred and realized it had already changed. When I'd found him with a pair of sewing sheers pierced through his neck I thought I'd remember his face like that forever, but lately, I remembered him with a cigarette in his lips, staring across the garden at the roses, talking to me about his son and ghosts.

"Cindee said you went to The Distillery for a glass of wine," said Pastor Joe.

"Except I had iced coffee."

"She mentioned you got pretty caught up with their PR campaign around a supposed haunting."

He couldn't have figured out a more negative combination of words to describe the Blue Lady if he'd sat there and planned it for several minutes. Maybe he had. I turned to look at him, but he was still staring at the boats, and I'm not sure he noticed I was studying his beard, seeing every tiny little hair, trying to look past his side-burns and into his brain to figure out why he was so negative on anything in the spirit world. For a guy who made his living talking about and studying things you can't see or touch or taste or hear, he was pretty set on dismissing the existence of ghosts.

"A lot of people who work there, and who have had dinner or drinks there, have seen the ghost," I said.

He laughed. "It's not surprising that people sitting in a bar drinking a few too many would think they'd seen a ghost." He laughed harder at his own joke.

"Why are you making fun of it?" I said.

He stood and moved in front of the planter circling the patio. He turned and folded his arms across his chest, so all I could see on his sweatshirt was the dark blue logo for his seminary. His arms covered the motto –Where God and Man meet. "Rational people don't believe in ghosts, Madison."

"Some people might say that about god."

"Good point."

This is why I can't help but respect the guy. A lot of people that have a strong opinion will immediately argue with you if you point out flaws in their logic, but Joe doesn't do that. He listens. That's why I couldn't understand his antagonism toward ghosts. When I'd mentioned to the police investigating Fred's death that I'd seen the murdered couple in the church garden, the detective shut me off. Later, Joe said he preferred I didn't go spreading stories like that when it was most likely a combination of my *active* imagination and sympathy for Fred's grief over the loss of his son that made me think I'd seen ghosts.

"So how do you explain rational people believing in god?" I said.

"Recognizing the Creator is a matter of faith," he said. His tone was so deep, his preacher voice, I suppose, that I almost expected him to stroke his goatee like he was sitting down with Socrates or something. "But most so-called sightings of spirits are people who are grief-stricken, or slightly off-balance, people prone to fantasy and for some reason unable to deal effectively with reality."

"I saw the Blue Lady," I said.

"What?"

"The ghost who haunts The Distillery. She's called the Blue Lady. I saw her."

I thought he'd at least ask when, ask me how I knew, give some kind of credence to what I said. He knows I'm not grief-stricken, at least not anymore. And he's talked to me enough to know I'm not off-balance. After all, I manage the church office, I'm responsible for the petty cash fund. It wouldn't say much about his judgment if he thought I was *off-balance*. He shook his head and looked at his feet. He walked back over and sat in the chair next to me. "I'd really prefer you not be talking about ghosts. Like that incident at the church a few months ago."

"Are you going to fire me because I've seen ghosts?"

"No. Because I don't believe you've seen them."

"That's a little insulting."

"I think you're a very spiritual person. You're searching for what you believe in, and you're sensitive, so you pick up on what other people are imagining."

I stood. "I know what I saw. In fact, I think she was trying to tell me something about Lorraine's death."

Joe looked like he was going to puke on my sandals. I stepped back, just in case.

"Did you mention that to the detectives?" said Joe.

"Not yet."

"Madison, please."

"You can't tell me what I did and didn't see."

He nodded. "Can I ask you not to talk about it?"

"Why? What is the big deal, and why are you so opposed to the possibility?"

"It's contrary to what we know about life and death and how God operates in the world."

"How do you know how god operates in the world?"

"Let me put it this way. If you think it's relevant to the investigation, you can tell them whatever you want and see how they deal with that kind of thing."

"You bet I can tell them whatever I want."

He held up his hand. "Don't get upset, I'm not finished."

"You're patronizing me."

"I'm sorry, I didn't mean to." He smiled. "Because it's not the kind of view we want to encourage at Central Avenue Church, I'd like to ask you not to talk about things like that when you're at work."

I shrugged. "I thought you wanted someone in the office who wasn't a member. So isn't it natural that person isn't going to have the same beliefs as all of you?"

He laughed.

"Why are you laughing?"

"Because you out-smarted me."

I smiled. How can you not, when someone gives you a compliment like that? He managed to wash the irritation right out of me as if he'd poured a bucket of warm water over me after I emerged from the Pacific Ocean, with salt and sand caked on my skin.

I don't mean to make Pastor Joe sound like a patronizing jerk, although he was kind of acting that way. For some reason, he has a huge bias against any unexplained phenomenon that doesn't fit with his view of unexplained phenomenon. There must be something behind that rigid view. Maybe I'd figure it out someday. He and Cindee were certainly of the same mind on that, and I wondered whether it was for the same reason.

"What do you think about Lorraine's death? From your ... experience."

"Do you mean my experience with the Blue Lady?"

He didn't nod or respond in any way. I guess he was curious but wasn't going to admit that there was any validity. I suppose he was planning to categorize it as intuition.

"It was actually kind of misleading. I had the impression she was telling me Lorraine's death was the same as her own. Although they never proved it, they're pretty certain the Blue Lady was murdered by her husband when he caught her with her lover."

"Pete's in Chicago," said Joe. "Or he was. Now he's on his way back to California."

"I don't know why the Blue Lady would mislead me. Of course, maybe she only wanted to tell me about her own death."

He sighed.

I suppose I told him more than he wanted to hear about the ghost and now he regretted asking me about it. "We want it to be Lorraine's husband," I said. "Because it's easier to understand than knowing someone else in the church is capable of murder."

"Maybe. He's always seemed like a good guy to me, I don't understand why anyone would jump to that conclusion."

I stared at him, but he was looking out at the surfers, so he didn't notice my expression. *A good guy?* It sounded as if Cindee hadn't told him anything about the situation. I decided it was best not to let him know his wife was keeping secrets. I admired her for that. I'd thought it was common knowledge she was leaving him, the way Karen talked about it. "People knew she was going to leave him."

"What people?" He sat down on the bench near the planter so he was looking more directly at me.

"Karen, for example."

He sighed, almost as if he wanted to sound dramatic. "That's another sad situation."

"Why?" The question slipped out before I thought about the fact that I wasn't supposed to be caught up in their secrets, but Joe seemed to have forgotten about his concerns over gossip.

"Her husband disappeared three or four years ago."

"Was he killed?"

"No, abandoned her. He left her a note, but that was it. She was never able to locate him."

"She wears her wedding rings."

"She believes against all evidence and reason that he'll come back. She can't seem to move forward with her life."

I thought back over my conversation with Karen the day before. Everything she said made it sound like she was married, but maybe I read that into it because of her rings and all the things she didn't say. I suppose that might explain why she was so upset, almost angry that Lorraine planned to leave her husband. It really wasn't any of her business, yet she'd acted like it was her job to enforce whatever opinion she believed god had in the matter. It also made me wonder what she was really like, and what other secrets she had. Not that her husband wouldn't disappear because of his own inclinations, but disappearing completely seemed a bit extreme.

"It's almost 12:30."

I looked up. Cindee was standing behind me. I hadn't heard her walk across the patio and Joe's face hadn't given any hint she was standing there.

"I saw them deliver the sandwiches to the conference room," said Cindee. "I'll bring you a sandwich, or do you want to come pick out your own, Madison?" She settled her camera in its case and clipped the buckle to secure it.

"I'll come pick my own."

I already had a plan. I was going to take my sandwich and drive back to The Distillery. The afternoon meeting would last two hours, so I had plenty of time to walk around the cliffs and see if the Blue Lady appeared again. Even if I didn't see her, I might get a glimpse of JD, and that would be equally satisfying.

* * *

WHILE I DROVE, I ate half the turkey and cheddar cheese sandwich on sliced sourdough bread. I kept it on my lap, so I only had to take one hand off the wheel for a few seconds at a time for each bite. On the road out to The Distillery, the sandwich bounced around on my legs, leaving a sprinkling of breadcrumbs across my thighs. Usually, I don't eat in my car, but I didn't think munching on a sandwich and expecting a ghost to make an appearance went hand in hand. Plus, I was hungry.

The parking lot was packed. It was a beautiful Sunday afternoon and except for the members of Central Avenue Church, eating sandwiches and chips in a conference room, most people along the coast preferred brunch and a view of the Pacific Ocean. Not to mention Mimosas and Bloody Marys. I figured JD was busy.

I found one of the last two spots, parked, and got out of my Beetle. I walked to the edge of the cliff where I'd seen her earlier that morning, which seemed like ages ago now. The experience had been similar to when I'd seen the ghosts in the church garden, the slippery sense of time shifting position so you weren't sure how long they were there, if it was a moment or an hour.

I made my way down the trail and then across to a small hill that stood apart from the rest of the cliff area, covered with vines and wildflowers. There were quite a few people on the beach below. I wondered if it was too crowded for the Blue Lady to consider making an appearance. Then I started to feel ridiculous. What was I expecting? To invite her to a police line-up with all the members of the church and the Blue Lady would lift a skeletal finger and point to the killer?

The ocean was deep blue without any whitecaps. The only foam was at the far side of the strip of sand below The Distillery. Waves crashed over an outcropping of rocks at the base of the cliff where I'd seen the Blue Lady that morning. It was difficult to believe it had only been seven hours. I felt as if I'd been pursuing her, longing to see more of her for days, months even. That's what constant thinking on a single topic can do to you. The thing grows until it worms its way into every twist of your brain.

I really had no idea what I was expecting. It's just that I couldn't

escape that insistent pressure inside my chest that she had something she wanted to say to me.

It was getting cool, and clouds were moving in by the time I
decided I had to give up. A number of people had come and gone
from the restaurant, some of them staring at me from the overlook
point as if they weren't sure whether I was some kind of jeans-
pink-hoodie-and-coffee-colored-flip-flops-clad security guard, or if
perhaps I was mourning my own lover, looking moodily over the
sea, or possibly considering a dive from the cliffs.

When I first drove over, I had planned to head into the bar and
say *hi* to JD, but now I wasn't in the mood. We'd said goodbye, he
said he'd call, what else was there to discuss at this point? Maybe I
planned to go into the bar because I'd been confident I would see
the Blue Lady and then I'd have a second encounter to discuss with
him, but now I had nothing. The only thing left was a strong thread
of irritation at myself for thinking I could conjure up a ghost at will.
I'd glimpsed two ghosts, late at night, and now the Blue Lady, and
suddenly I was an expert who could invite them to sit down for a
chat whenever I had a question or felt they might have something
useful to tell me?

This line of thought stimulated a burning urge for a cigarette. I
realized that with my unusual schedule that morning, and talking to
the detective at breakfast, and eating my lunch in the car, I hadn't
had one all day. This should have prompted me to realize I didn't
need one right then, but that's not how it works. I truly am trying
very hard to quit, and I think my plan is a good one, to cut back one
cigarette break, then stick with that for a significant amount of
time, then drop another. The trouble was, I'd been at my currently
allotted three a day for almost two years now. I'd say that's a consid-
erable amount of time to adjust my body's nicotine cravings, but I
don't seem to have the will to go lower. I enjoy smoking, the quietness of it, the way it forces you to go off to spend some time alone,
or the way you can meet people you'd never talk to otherwise,
because you have that deadly, anti-social habit, that addiction, in

common. That's how I got to know Fred so well, and even though he's dead, I still consider him a very good friend. It's also how I met my one and only boyfriend to-date.

When I was nineteen, I was enjoying a cigarette outside a bookstore-slash-coffee- house. It's one of the few places in my area that allows smoking, on the side patio only. I was reading a short story in *The New Yorker* which this bookstore, The *Book Brook*, named for the small creek running below the non-smoking patio, keeps in stacks that you can read for free once they're a few weeks old. This guy said I looked very high brow, reading *The New Yorker* and smoking, wearing a red tunic and red pants and red sandals. Of course, once I started talking, he realized I'm anything but. We hit it off. We were together for three years after that. When I told him one day that I liked to meditate because it helped me empty my mind, he called me an air-head. I know he was teasing, sort of, but after that, I said it wasn't going to work out. There are some things you tease about and some things you do not.

Anyway, smoking is a great way to meet people, at least the ten percent of Californians who still smoke. We are a dying breed, so to speak.

I wasn't sure where smoking was allowed around The Distillery. At the opposite side of the parking lot was an empty grass area, so I went over there. I hoped no one would be upset about me smoking around all the vegetation, but I'm very careful, and I never throw cigarette butts on the ground. Even if I step on them to extinguish them, I still pick them up. I try to always have a sandwich bag with me, similar to responsible pet owners who carry blue plastic bags when they walk their dogs.

I lit my cigarette, dampened my fingers to make sure the match was out good and tucked it into the front pocket of my jeans. A few people walked past and gave me disapproving looks, but no one was too aggressive about it. One woman in a bikini top and a denim skirt waved her hand in front of her face as if my smoke was going right up her nose. I smiled, but she didn't smile back.

Clearly, the Blue Lady wasn't going to be making an appearance. There were too many people around, for one thing. Although the stories indicate she can be quite the entertainer, playing tricks and wanting to join in when people conduct ghostly manifestation events, she wasn't likely to come out for a Sunday afternoon stroll with the weekend crowd. I knew I should stop thinking about her, but what if there was something I was missing that she wanted me to know about Lorraine? It didn't sound like the detectives were getting anywhere. Cindee's idea that her husband could have hired someone to kill his wife never felt right. He sounded like the kind of guy who would prefer to do it with his bare hands.

The Blue Lady had pantomimed drowning. Why would she bother with that, telling me something I already knew? I wondered how many other women had drowned along this part of the coast. Maybe it was a metaphor. Lorraine's husband was suffocating her in that cruel marriage, and it really was the same as if he'd killed her. It could be she was simply telling me her story was not that different from Lorraine's.

I squatted and stabbed my cigarette into the sand. When it was good and dead, I carried it in my palm to my car, found an empty water bottle under the back seat, and put the cigarette butt and match into the bottle and tossed it in the trashcan behind The Distillery.

I got in my car and drove back to the Beach House. It looked like I was going to be going home without seeing the Blue Lady again and without knowing who had killed Lorraine, not that it was my job to figure that out. There were detectives to take care of that, and I needed to get a grip on my curiosity and focus on something more productive. I could spend time thinking about a restaurant to suggest so I'd be ready when JD called to ask me to dinner.

CHAPTER 10

*T*HE PARKING LOT at the Beach House was nearly empty, most of the weekend guests long gone. A few church members were loading duffel bags and small suitcases into their trunks. I parked near the pool end of the lot and walked along the path to the patio. It would have been nice to go for a swim. It didn't even cross my mind until that minute. I suppose finding a drowned woman had made all association between water and pleasure disappear from my thoughts for awhile.

I walked over to the pool and opened the gate, went inside, kicked off my flip-flops, and stuck my left foot in the water. I yanked it out faster than I'd dipped it in. The water was colder than the ocean. I picked up my flip flops and walked to the steps and down to the path. I crossed the dunes to the beach and went to the water line. I curled my toes into the wet sand and waited for a wave to slide up the beach and meet me with just a gentle touch of water.

The beach was deserted. There were people fishing off the breakwater, as always, but no one on the sand. Usually, there were families with kids playing in the water and people tossing balls to their dogs. Maybe word of a body floating in the harbor had traveled around the beach like the stench of a dead seal rotting on the sand, and people were avoiding it for a few days. I was happy I could have the beach to myself and figured it was safe to have a cigarette, even though smoking another so soon was not moving me in the right direction in terms of breaking the habit. I should not be eager to have makeup smokes just because I'd missed the one with my morning coffee.

When I tucked the cigarette pack into my purse, I felt the cool surface of the bracelet. I still hadn't decided if I should give it to the detectives. Part of me wanted to keep it. I don't think that's stealing. I found it, and even though it's not really my style, there was something about that dark red stone that gripped me. I suppose I could have left it at the hotel desk to see if anyone asked about it, but if I lost something at the beach, I'd never in a million years think that someone might find it. I needed to make up my mind soon since I'd be leaving for home in an hour or so.

I held my cigarette between my lips and pulled out the bracelet. The gem wasn't as shiny as when it was wet. I supposed it needed cleaning. Or maybe it wasn't real, and the salt and sand had been enough to dull it like a piece of glass. Maybe it had been in the ocean awhile. Here I was thinking someone might ask about it, assuming it had been lost in the past few days, when it was possible it had been months, maybe years.

After a quick drag on my cigarette, I left it between my lips again, spread the sides of the bracelet, and wrapped it around my wrist. I squeezed it a bit so it would stay in place. When I stretched out my arm and turned it slightly, the bracelet it remained immobile, making my inner wrist bone ache as the metal resisted its movement. I didn't see how anyone could wear something that uncomfortable on a regular basis. It was impossible to make even the slightest movement without it biting into my skin or pressing against my bones.

The first time I tried it on, I thought it looked silly on me. But now I realized it made me feel different. It was the same as when I put on a pair of high heels. They have the ability to transform me into someone else, someone who walks more slowly, whose hips move differently, whose legs look longer and sleeker until I'm not sure who I am. I wonder what it would be like to be this other person all the time. The bracelet was having the same effect. I was wearing it on my left wrist, so I shifted my cigarette to that hand, even though it was uncomfortable to go through the motions of smoking with the constant pressure of the bracelet. If I wore it all the time, maybe the bracelet could help me stop smoking. The discomfort would make me think differently, remind me that I really did want to quit. Although, I also looked more exotic smoking with that big silver band wrapped around my wrist. Maybe it wouldn't work at all. And if I'm honest, the problem isn't that I need a reminder that I should cut back further on the smoking, work harder to reach the end game of being a non-smoker, I first had to want that more than I wanted to keep it up.

"You sure smoke a lot."

I jumped at the sound of the voice barging into my thoughts. I turned. Karen was a few feet behind me. Goosebumps ran all over my back and arms at the thought of her watching me. She might have been observing me the whole time, even as I walked out onto the beach. Usually, I'm aware of what's around me, but the sound of the waves, even though they were low and gentle, and my wandering thoughts of smoking and the bracelet must have carried me too far inside my own head.

"Where did you get that bracelet?" She waved her hand in the air to brush away the smoke, even though it wasn't really lingering due to the breeze sweeping along the beach. It's always such a senseless movement anyway. It's not like you can wipe the air clean with your hand.

"I found it."

"Where?" She waved her hand in the space between us again.

I took the hint, bent down, and snuffed out my cigarette. I pried the bracelet off my wrist.

"Are you just going to leave that there?" She pointed at the cigarette butt. Her eyes were glassy, which I assumed was from the smoke she found so irritating.

"I'll pick it up when I leave." I dropped the bracelet into my bag.

"Where did you find it?"

"Why? Do you know who it belongs to?"

"It doesn't look like something you'd normally wear. I was surprised, that's all. So, where did you find it?"

"Out there." I pointed at the curve in the breakwater.

"Were you swimming? That close to the rocks?"

"The tide was out. I was climbing on the rocks."

"Are you keeping it?" Her eyes were still glassy, but maybe it was her hair. She had it yanked back into a ponytail, pulled so tight it made her look like she was experimenting with a facelift because it stretched and tightened the skin at the sides of her eyes. Her hair was hard and shiny as if she'd used a lot of gel to get it to stay in that style. Still, a few wisps stood up from her head, lifted by the wind, and looking more out of place because there were so few of them.

"No. It's really uncomfortable," I said.

"What are you doing with it?"

"I haven't decided. I'm either going to leave it at the front desk or give it to one of the detectives who's investigating Lorraine's drowning."

"Why would they be interested in it?"

A wave rushed up right then, stronger than the gentle waves that had been lapping at the shore for the past few minutes. It grabbed the rolled up fabric of my jeans. Karen jumped away from the water and managed to avoid it touching the toes of her tennis shoes. When I'd seen her before she said she was terrified of the water, and yet now, she didn't seem that fazed. I suppose she'd exaggerated when we'd spoken the day before, to make the point that she didn't want to go swimming.

When the wave receded, Karen stepped back closer to where I was. "If you found it way out there, it's unlikely it was dropped recently."

"I thought of that."

"It's a very unusual piece. If you don't want it, can I have it?" She smiled and it made her face appear even more pinched, as if smiling was a strain that her skin couldn't manage, that hairdo working hard to keep everything tightly in place.

"I have a feeling I should at least show it to the detectives, since it was more or less in the same area where I saw Lorraine's body."

"I'm sure her body drifted. The bracelet could have come from anywhere."

"I still think I should show it to them. It doesn't look like the kind of thing that normally washes up on the beach."

"I never saw her wearing that bracelet," said Karen. "Or anything like it." She rubbed her arms, even though she wore a long, flowing sweater and the breeze was still calm. "Are you leaving soon?"

"Yes," I said. "How about you?"

"This is such a healing place, I extended my stay another night."

"Nice." It seemed strange to call a hotel healing, although maybe not. Maybe it was the word, in that context, that was strange, not the idea. Karen's face looked anything but peaceful, with her hair yanked back like that, making a vein on her temple more visible, lifting her eyebrows so she looked shocked.

"I could take the bracelet and ask the detectives if they think it will provide any help," said Karen. "Since you're leaving."

"I can stop by the sheriffs' office in San Mateo on my way home. I have their business cards."

"They'll be back here later this evening. To talk to Pete," said Karen.

Her voice sounded quieter when she said Pete's name. As if she felt sorry for him. She would be the first person to sound that way. Cindee thought he was a monster, and so did the sheriffs. He sure sounded like one from the little bit I'd been told. I couldn't imagine any redeeming qualities canceling out that kind of horror.

"Were you good friends with Lorraine? And Pete?"

"I suppose. Lorraine and I used to be closer, but when she started saying she might leave Pete, we drifted apart."

"How come?"

"I didn't agree with her decision. Divorce is unacceptable."

"You said that before, but what if someone treats you badly and you can't love them anymore?"

"Not loving the person who loves you is the worst thing you can do."

I wasn't sure what to say. She was right, but somehow it was twisted inside out.

"Telling someone they're unlovable destroys their soul," said Karen.

"It sounds to me like he didn't love her at all."

"Of course he did. He married her."

"Yes, but he …."

"She promised to love him until death. It's more painful than death when someone's spouse stops loving them."

I so badly wanted to ask if that's what happened to her. I sort of wished Joe hadn't mentioned it, and now that I was looking at her, seeing the spasm of pain on her face, I wondered why he'd told me. Wasn't that supposed to be confidential?

She stared at me, her eyes round, filling with tears, waiting. I assumed she hoped I would agree with that one thing, even if I disagreed on all other points.

"Yes," I said, "But sometimes there's a reason."

"The only way a marriage should end is with death," said Karen.

A huge wave crashed against the far side of the breakwater. It sent spray up into the air, splashing over the rocks, as if it wanted to object to what Karen had said. The fishermen scrambled away from the edge. Even so, they were drenched. I suppose Karen would interpret that as the ocean agreeing with and punctuating her outrageous comments, but somehow, it felt like the earth itself was shouting, *no way*.

"I hate it when waves do that. It's scary. That's why I'd never walk out on those rocks, it's why I hate standing even this close. Doesn't it seem like the ocean wants to wipe us off the earth?"

"It's unpredictable," I said. "But I don't know about it wanting to kill us. It's not a conscious being. You just have to respect it."

Karen folded her arms across her ribs and turned to face me. Clearly, she knew nothing about what the ocean is truly like because the first rule of happily coexisting with it is to never turn your back on it. Sure, we were in a protected area, but I found her wild swings between extreme terror of the water and a near-lack of concern unnerving.

"So why don't you let me take it for you. The bracelet."

"I don't know." I pinched my messenger bag closer to my side. I wasn't sure why I did that. What did I think, that she was going to lunge at my bag and grab the bracelet? She seemed awfully interested in it. I really didn't care. I'd never wear it, and maybe she was hoping the detectives would shrug it off, and she could acquire a new piece of jewelry for herself.

"It's no problem for me to stop by the sheriffs' station. I'm the one who found it, so it makes sense for me to turn it in."

"It doesn't matter," said Karen. "It's not like you'd be able to point out the precise rock and patch of sand where it was."

She made total sense. I didn't know why I was being so stubborn. Although maybe I did know. She was pushing too hard. She wanted the bracelet, and that struck me as pathetic, or greedy. Maybe she wanted to look important, bringing the sheriffs something interesting. Trying to help.

I turned and glanced at the Beach House behind us. It's an imposing structure, three stories, with a peaked roof. It has bright white balconies and trim against mauve siding. It looks very Cape Cod, not that I've ever been to Cape Cod, but it's what I would imagine the houses of the families that carried lots of cash from generation to generation looked like. Very simple, yet still imposing in the sheer size of the thing. Since it's the only large building for half a mile in either direction, it definitely stands out. The sky behind and above it was darkening, fat clouds moving in that stretched for miles, so they looked more like an enormous charcoal gray wave instead of simple clouds. "Thanks for offering to give the bracelet to them," I said. "But it's not like I have to get home to cook dinner for my family. I have plenty of time to stop by there."

She nodded. She kept nodding. Her ponytail, like a whiskbroom behind her, swept up and down with a stiff jerking motion rather than swaying like a normal ponytail. She bit her lip and stared past me at the harbor like she was still trying to figure out how to either assault me and grab my bag, or say something that would make me change my mind. For several minutes, she kept chewing her lip and staring. I worried her lip was going to start bleeding. Finally, she said, "I'll walk back with you."

"Sure."

Neither one of us spoke as we walked across the sand and up the slight incline to the dunes. As we made our way down the other side to the path, Karen started going on about Lorraine, how she had no right to leave her husband, how she should have been grateful for what she had, how many women would be thrilled, would do anything to have a man like Pete, a church-going man with a good job, who provided a home for his wife. Karen made it sound like a woman should be grateful to have a roof over her head. She was only about thirty-five, if that, but her belief system made it sound as if she'd recently hatched from a cryogenic tube from the 19th century or a cult at odds with society, creating its own obscure rules.

"The more I think about it," said Karen, "I don't think the detectives will be interested in the bracelet."

I stopped and looked at her. "Why do you want it so badly?"

"I don't. It's just that you don't want it, so why not. Besides, that's a ruby."

"How do you know?"

"They're the gem from the month I was married."

I put my hand inside my purse. The silver filigree, almost sharp at the edges, felt like a knife blade, ready to slice my skin. I ran my finger over the flat part, feeling the red stone. I wasn't sure if she was being deliberately obtuse. "How do you know the stone on *this* bracelet is a ruby?"

"Don't make such a big deal about it," said Karen. "You found a piece of jewelry on the beach, you leap to the conclusion it's related to a woman who slipped off the rocks and drowned, and now you're acting so territorial, like it belongs to you."

"Really?"

She stared at me, eyes bugging out. As I walked faster, she slowed her pace, which was fine with me. The space between us expanded and pretty soon I couldn't even see her shadow chasing mine on the path.

I lengthened my stride, not caring if she thought I was being rude, ditching her. Her convoluted interpretation of my intention for the bracelet twisted around in my brain. I wasn't sure if she really thought I wanted the bracelet or if she thought I was acting as if it belonged to me because I found it. Actually, it was the opposite. She kept fishing as if she hoped I'd say it wasn't important, that I thought it was ugly and she could have it.

When I reached the stairs, she scurried to catch up with me.

"I didn't mean to insult you," she said.

"Why are you so interested in the bracelet?" I stopped and waited until she was near my side. In front of me were plants growing up the side of the incline where the Beach House sat, large leafy things with enormous torpedo-like pieces covered with tiny purple flowers.

Karen saw that I was looking past her shoulder and turned. She faced me again, squinting. "What are you looking at?"

"Just those flowers. They're unusual." I looked back at her. "You can't have the bracelet until the sheriffs decide whether it could be related to Lorraine's drowning."

"That would be a huge coincidence."

"I need to at least let them know I found it. Maybe if they decide it's not important, you can have it."

"I think you're wasting their time." She followed me into the hotel, and we walked along the back corridor to the lobby.

Detective Wagner stood in the center of the lobby as if he'd been waiting for us.

CHAPTER 11

*W*HEN KAREN SAW Detective Wagner, she made an about-face and scuttled up the main stairs to the second floor. I wasn't sure where she was going or why she didn't want to see him. Maybe since I wouldn't let her be in charge of the bracelet, she didn't want to be involved anymore. I'd already met a few women like her at the church – women who want to be in charge and really don't know what to do with themselves if they aren't running the show. That shouldn't sound as if I'm saying only women have this issue, plenty of men want to be in charge as well, it's just that some women seem to be okay with being in charge of petty, insignificant things, while men with that issue want to really Be. In. Charge.

Detective Wagner greeted me, then said, rather abruptly, "I have a question for you. Do you think Ms. Kenyon is protecting anyone?"

"What do you mean?"

"Do you think she knows Lorraine had an enemy, of sorts, and she's hiding that person's identity because she doesn't want a scandal to touch her husband's career? A bad name for the church?"

"No," I said. "It's the opposite. She's devastated and would tell you anything she knew, if it would help."

"But she's fixated on the husband when we know his involvement isn't possible. I'm starting to wonder if that's a diversion tactic."

"I'm sure it was awful for Cindee to hear about how Lorraine was suffering and not be able to help. Maybe she thought he was a threat for so long, worried about it happening for so long, she can't think of any alternative."

He leaned against the shelf above the fireplace. He put his foot up on the ledge in front of it and slapped his notebook against his knee. "Okay, then. There's nothing else you can think of?"

"Well, there is something, but I don't know if it's related." I pushed my hair behind my ears, suddenly warm because my thoughts had shifted to feeling as if I'd withheld something important. I wiggled my fingers into the open top of my bag and pulled out the bracelet. "I found this."

He looked at it but didn't make any move to touch it.

"It was on the beach at low tide. Out by the breakwater, not far from where I saw Lorraine's body."

"Hunh."

"I suppose it's unlikely it has anything to do with her. She didn't wear much jewelry, from what I've heard."

He reached into his pocket, pulled out a rubber glove, popped it over his hand, and took the bracelet. It seemed odd that he felt it important to wear a glove when I'd already had my hand on the bracelet, not to mention that it had been rattling around in my drawer for a day or so. Although I hadn't told him that part. He pulled out a plastic bag and dropped the bracelet inside. "Thanks."

"Even though it sounds like it couldn't have been hers, it did seem odd to find it so close to where her body was, right after she drowned. It's not like you find exotic jewelry lying around on the shore under regular circumstances."

He nodded. "Anything else?"

"No."

He looked frustrated. I think he was puzzling over the same

thing we all were – he just didn't want to admit it because he was a cop and wasn't supposed to be thinking along the same lines as everyone else – we couldn't get past the fact that her husband had the potential to kill her, possibly a reason to kill her, and yet he hadn't been anywhere around, and it seemed too strange that someone else popped up and killed her. Maybe it was just a terrible accident. They found that wine glass, maybe she was tipsy and had an unlucky fall off the breakwater and gashed her head. If that was the case, how would they ever really know? But if that were true, wouldn't the glass have shattered when she fell? I wondered if the detective felt like giving up. He still held the plastic bag, gripped between his thumb and forefinger, as if it stank and he didn't want it too close to him, or the smell might find its way onto his white shirt and dark gray slacks. It dangled from his fingertips like a piece of paper, swaying just a bit from the weight of it.

"I guess I should be heading home." I said this, but I didn't move.

His eyes were helpless as if now this woman's death was on him. Maybe I'm over-dramatizing that, he probably thought no such thing. It seemed as if he had more questions but wasn't even sure what they were.

"Nothing else, then?" I said.

He shook his head. "There's still her husband coming into town, but I doubt we'll learn much from him."

"What will you do then?"

"Sometimes, you never find out. Sometimes, a witness comes forward later, so we can hope for that."

I thought of the Blue Lady, but I suppose that was not at all the kind of witness he was hoping for. Besides, it was silly to think she'd wandered down the coast, away from the place where she left the earth in time to witness a murder.

We stood silently for several minutes. It wasn't an awkward silence, but a longing to know the truth, to have some hint of an idea that there was a way to find answers, when we both knew there wasn't, but that didn't stop us from hoping.

I heard a sound behind me, like a quick intake of breath. I turned.

"Hi," said Karen. "I thought you were gone."

"Nope, still here."

She glanced at the bag in Detective Wagner's hand, then moved closer until she was standing almost touching my right side, squeezed between me and the armchair. Her gaze turned to the detective then darted back to the bracelet in the plastic bag. I couldn't read her expression. She didn't seem disappointed that she couldn't keep it for herself, she seemed like she was thinking about something completely unrelated to wanting a new, free piece of fine jewelry.

"I gave him the bracelet," I said. "Since you never know." This was a stupid thing to say. She could clearly see I'd given him the bracelet, I have no idea why I felt compelled to point out the obvious.

"It's probably unrelated," said Detective Wagner, "But we'll check it out."

"That's what I told her," said Karen. "Everyone knows Lorraine didn't wear anything but her wedding ring and that teeny gold cross." She laughed but didn't look at me. "I'm sure you don't need people turning in random things they find that will just create paperwork."

I didn't understand why she was making it sound as if I was complicating things by turning over the bracelet. It seemed like she wanted to discredit me. But why? I moved to the side so I was standing apart, watching how Karen stared at the detective, as if the force of her eyes would make him hand the plastic bag to her. It was bugging me that she wanted it so badly. It wasn't that she couldn't afford nice jewelry. She wore some obviously expensive things, a necklace that was the style that reminds me of a dog collar. Not that it was up around her neck, but a solid piece of silver molded into a heart-shape that laid flat against her collarbone, an oval turquoise stone attached at the tip. Every time I'd seen her, she was wearing those gold and silver bangle bracelets halfway up her right arm, circling the outside of her sleeve. There had to be about twenty of them, clinking and moving against each other. And there were her meaningless wedding rings.

The detective held up the plastic bag. "Like I said, we'll check it out."

"What's there to check out?" said Karen. "You can't get fingerprints or anything after it's been tossed around the Pacific Ocean, can you?"

"It depends," said Detective Wagner.

"On what?"

"A lot of things."

He didn't seem to want to continue the conversation. It sounded as if he didn't really think anything would come of it, but he didn't want to discuss it with her.

He shook my hand. "Have a good trip back."

I kept hold of his hand, not wanting to walk away with no resolution.

"Is there something else?" said Detective Wagner.

I wanted to tell him that maybe the bracelet was important. Possibly, when the Blue Lady was tugging on her sleeves, rubbing her wrists, she was trying to indicate something about a bracelet like that. Because the bracelet looked very uncomfortable, so I could see why you would tug at it. But there's just no smooth way to tell a detective, or nearly anyone, for that matter, that you're getting hints from a ghost about the circumstances of a murder. No one would believe that. No one except me. You would think they would. After all, everyone wonders if the dead have universal knowledge, if they're watching us, observing even the things we do when we think no one can see us. If people believe in heaven or even in hell, they still don't seem to give a lot of thought as to where those two places are actually located. Their occupants could be right here beside us, unseen and un-felt, walking on the same pathways, staying in the same rooms. How do we *know*?

I just couldn't start babbling about some local legend that half the people around here think of as a fun story to add color to a restaurant's theme.

Detective Wagner extended his hand to Karen.

Her bangles rattled as she pumped his hand. She opened her mouth as if she wanted to say something. Then she closed it. She opened it again and closed it again and I thought if she did that one more time she'd look like a fish, swimming close to the glass in her bowl, trying to find a speck of food, or gasping for oxygen, I was never sure what fish were doing when they opened and closed their mouths like that.

After she let go of his hand, Karen clasped her hands together, then released them and tugged on her left sleeve. That's when I knew the Blue Lady had helped me after all, by making that same gesture. And I remembered how Karen had gripped her hand that weird way the first time she talked to me on the beach, and I realized she was constantly tugging at her left sleeve. All those bangles were on her right hand, perhaps she was used to wearing a cuff bracelet with her anniversary stone on her left hand.

"Is that bracelet yours?" I pointed at the plastic bag swinging from Detective Wagner's fingers.

"I said I'd love to have it, since it's probably not related to Lorraine."

"It already belongs to you," I said.

"I wish it did."

"No," I said. "It's yours already. You lost it on the breakwater."

"I wouldn't walk on those rocks, I told you I'm afraid of the water."

She tugged on her sleeve.

I reached over and grabbed her hand. She twisted her arm. "What are you doing? Let go of me."

I pushed her sleeve up and there was a bruise on her wrist bones, scrapes all over the back of her wrist, and welts on the underside.

"How did you lose your bracelet. Did Lorraine rip it off your arm?"

She yanked her arm away from me and tugged her sleeve over the damaged skin.

"All he has to do is show the bracelet to Cindee. She'll know it's yours. If you'd lost it on the beach, you would have said that the first time I showed it to you."

Karen sat down in the chair facing the fireplace. She put her hands over her face as if she was crying, but her shoulders didn't move and she didn't make a sound.

Detective Wagner sat across from her, and I sat on the ledge of the fireplace.

"What happened?" he said.

"We were walking on the breakwater," she whispered.

"I thought you were afraid," I said.

Detective Wagner held up a finger. I was kind of insulted he was silencing me, but I suppose it was his job, not mine. It's just that questions were flooding my mind and it's hard for me to keep my curiosity inside.

"I am. I can't swim. But Lorraine and I took our wine out on the beach. She walked down to the edge of the water and dropped her wine glass in the water. She turned around and said dropping her glass in the water was her declaration of freedom. She said she wanted to walk out on the rocks, that she wanted to start doing things she'd never done before."

Karen uncovered her face, but kept her head down, looking at her lap, still tugging on her sleeve, twisting it around her wrist. "She insisted we had to walk out there. That is was good to defeat your fears, to come face to face with the earth, that it was the only real thing there is. I went because I didn't think she should go alone. It was after midnight and no one was out there. I was scared to death. When we got out near the foghorn, she told me she was leaving her husband, that she had friends who were helping her move out of the state, he would never find her."

I bit my tongue, reminding myself not to break Joe's confidence, but it was difficult not to blurt out the obvious parallel. I bit harder.

"I … that's the worst thing you can do to a person. You promise to love them forever, to stay with them until you're dead! And then to turn around and say you never loved them." She stopped and folded her arms across her chest.

Now I understood that desolate feeling I had when I was observing the Blue Lady tugging at her sleeves, clutching her throat. That terrible weight that I'd known was far more than just the Blue Lady's longing for her lover. Those were Karen's feelings, maybe even feelings from other people, that deep, endless pain of not being loved.

"Can I have the bracelet? It's mine," said Karen.

Detective Wagner stuffed the plastic bag containing the bracelet in his jacket pocket. "How did you lose it?"

Karen's eyes looked blank as if she wasn't seeing the fireplace or the sheriff or me. "When she told me she was leaving him, I said she was cruel. She said I had it backwards. I told her my husband ripped my heart out when he said he didn't love me anymore, that he couldn't stand the sight of me. The pain never stops. Lorraine said I must have done something to make him not love me. I smacked her. She stepped back and started to slip. She grabbed me by my bracelet and tore it off as she slid down the rocks."

Karen wasn't even crying. She was suddenly matter of fact as if she was explaining a sporting event or a sightseeing trip.

"You didn't try to hang onto her?" said Detective Wagner.

"She would have pulled me down. I can't swim."

"Why didn't you call for help?"

She shrugged. "Only death should end a marriage. So if she wanted to end her marriage, she only had one way out."

After that, Detective Wagner had nothing else to say. Neither did I.

* * *

AS MY BEETLE CLIMBED the curves of Highway 92 toward the 280 freeway, my phone chimed. I don't like things inside my ears, so I don't use a hands-free connector, so I couldn't talk. If I was driving around town, I might pick up, but not on the curving two-lane highway. Too bad I hadn't left earlier, because I definitely would have picked up this one. Since I was heading into the incline with no place to pull over, I had to watch JD's name winking at me. Maybe I would suggest that instead of him coming my way, I'd drive back to Half Moon Bay for dinner or whatever he proposed for a date. I might get a chance to see the Blue Lady and somehow let her know she'd helped point my thoughts in the right direction so that Lorraine's death could be explained, even if nothing is ever *really* explained.

SHALLOW WATER is inspired by the Blue Lady who is said to haunt the Moss Beach Distillery Restaurant near Half Moon Bay, California.

UNHOLY CHILD

A Suburban Noir Ghost Story

By
Cathryn Grant

Published by D2C Perspectives

CHAPTER 1

I FOUND THE STRANGLED WOMAN on the church altar behind the nativity scene. A nativity scene that was empty of the holy infant because the church has a tradition of setting the ceramic figurine out of sight near the back of the sanctuary, letting the children take turns moving him closer to the barn each day leading up to Christmas. So there was just Mary, Joseph, two shepherds, a few smug-faced sheep, a donkey, and Linda Birmingham.

Linda's face was purple, which scared me, and her eyes bulged. I won't say any more because it was too awful and I had to look away. I hoped that she would like her original beautiful self in her new realm. She was seventy-three years old, so it was fairly easy to overpower her with a string of lights that had been removed from one of two fir trees standing on each side of the altar. Linda Birmingham was wealthy. Very wealthy. She'd been widowed for over twelve years and was childless. Someone wasn't thinking when they thought killing her would stop her from giving all that cash to the church.

* * *

THINGS HAD HEATED UP QUICKLY after the early December meeting when the congregation was asked to vote on whether the church should open a childcare center. The daycare facility and pre-school was Pastor Kate's baby, so to speak. She'd been talking about it since I first started working in the church office, and over the past six months, she'd put together a complete plan, including information about the required permits, construction costs to modify some of the classrooms for small children — like the addition of restrooms with tiny sink and toilets — as well as other expenses including the purchase of small tables and chairs, and educational toys.

People had been allowed to submit their votes by mail, which Kate wasn't very happy about, since she felt that simply reading about her proposal, rather than sitting in a room and hearing the passion in her voice, wouldn't allow people to see the beauty of her vision, to truly grasp the need and get enthused about the service they would be providing to the community. The church is in a community where the typical household income is well into the six-figure range, so you don't think of them needing "services". But a lot of people have all that money because the moms and dads both work in high-powered jobs. They want high-quality early education to go along with that, and Kate was eager to offer it.

Pastor Joe was solidly behind her, but Kate was the one driving it. She was the one who could see it in her mind as if it already existed, the one who had the fire in her bones. She's the youth minister, so of course she took the lead. There had been some resistance already, worries about liability and setting up a governing board, whether there would be enough people enthusiastic enough to volunteer all those hours needed for hiring, for managing the teaching staff, for overseeing thousands of details for what basically amounted to running a business.

The meeting went well, at first. The agenda was dedicated to the discussion and vote for the childcare center. Kate wanted to run an operation equipped to care for twenty children. That meant a director and three teachers and lots of remodeled space. But like I said, this church sits in a wealthy community, so it wasn't as if that was a huge problem, and tuition costs would take care of most of it. Although that's where the trouble started.

Kate had presented her sketches of the classroom layout, her curriculum plans, her structure for the governing board, and most importantly, her explanation of the importance of early childhood education. She was so excited, her eyes looked like she'd fallen in love and was singing the praises of the object of her affection. Kate wears a lot of make-up, a *lot*, and I don't know if it was the foundation and blush and eyeliner and shadow and whatnot, but her face glistened while she talked for nearly two hours, fielding questions in a calm, clear voice, enjoying center stage, a spot usually reserved for Pastor Joe. The meeting was held in the sanctuary since so many people showed up, and she stood on the altar steps, the spotlights making her pale blonde, almost white, hair cast off such a glow it almost seemed as if there was a halo circling her scalp.

I was there taking notes and recording any questions that Kate couldn't answer on the spot, requiring further research.

The budget was the last thing she covered. When she explained that five of the twenty slots would be reserved for children on scholarship, Ben Chambers stood and asked who was funding these *scholarships*. And he said it in that tone of voice. He might as well have used his fingers to create air quotes. It sounded the same.

"The church will cover those," said Kate. "Anyone who has a strong affinity for the mission of this program can contribute earmarked funds. We were thinking they could even sponsor a specific child, providing access to the adjunct teachers who will offer further enrichment programs like learning a musical instrument or a foreign language."

"These kids are babies," said Ben. "Why do they need to learn a foreign language?"

"Most early childhood education experts will tell you that if children are exposed to language or music or even sports in a play environment, at a young age, they learn more quickly, and since it's fun, they retain it longer."

"Now I have two concerns," said Ben. "Why are we opening this up to kids who can't afford it? We don't want to be attracting people who can't afford to live around here. That's just asking for trouble. And what kind of languages?"

I wanted to know what kind of trouble he was asking for, but Kate didn't seem concerned with that, and since I was the note-taker, I couldn't very well poke my hand in the air and start acting like any of this was my business. Although I supposed it could become my business when children were buzzing around the property and I was managing the office. That made me suddenly wonder what would become of my pleasant mid-day cigarette breaks near the garden. If they didn't like me smoking when teenagers were around, I was pretty sure they would absolutely hate impressionable little kids seeing me blowing out a thin, sexy stream of smoke.

"I'll address the foreign language question first," said Kate. "And actually, it will depend on what the parents want to pay. If there's a unique language and they want to cover the price of a tutor dedicated to their child, we'll facilitate that."

Ben coughed.

Kate paused. I think she expected him to interrupt her, but he didn't. "In some cases, the foreign language might actually be English. If we have children who speak other languages at home, we could provide that as well. Help prepare them to be fully bi-lingual when they reach school age."

Ben's neck turned red, made more obvious by his white shirt, and because he wore a tie, it looked as if he was suddenly choking to death. The strange thing was, his face stayed a normal color. "A childcare center is one thing," he said, and his voice also sounded like he was choking. He coughed. "But nowhere in this two-hour presentation did you mention funding low-income people. Until now. Or teaching English to kids whose parents refuse to do that."

"Ben," said Joe. "Let's not get ugly."

Kate glared at Joe, not happy that he was undermining her authority. She folded her arms across her chest, which was no small feat for a woman built like her.

From time to time, this competition arises between Kate and Joe. Although it isn't really between them because it's all on Kate's side. In fact, Joe seems to be completely oblivious to it. He didn't so much as glance at Kate, keeping his attention glued to Ben as if not blinking would make Ben retract his words, or at least keep him from heading any further down the route he seemed to be taking.

"Thanks, Joe. But we should let Ben express his concerns," said Kate.

Was she really going to encourage Ben to say something racist, which is what it sounded like, just so she could make sure everyone knew this was her meeting, that she could handle it, that she didn't need Joe's help, and wanted him to keep his mouth shut and stay out of it? I suppose that's a lot to infer from one *thanks* and an invitation to Ben to keep talking, but that was my impression. I stared at my notepad, trying to figure out what I should write down. What I wanted more than a pen and pad was a laptop so I could type fast and capture their words, or better yet, a video camera. All I wrote was, *Ben Chambers doesn't want language classes.* I'd think of a way to make it sound more official, more "minutes-like" later.

The room was silent. Finally, Kate said, "Do you object to offering scholarships?"

"Yes, I do."

"Will that affect your vote?"

"Yes."

"Isn't it part of our mission to care for people less fortunate?"

"Not people who are law-breakers. I don't want this church involved in providing assistance to people who are in this country illegally, consuming our resources, destroying our infrastructure, getting free handouts."

Joe stood.

Kate held up her hand as if her tiny, pale palm would keep the words in Joe's head. She kept her hand there while she spoke. "I don't think we're here to check immigration status. At the end of the day, though, these are children. They're innocent."

"The parents aren't. It's a risk issue. I don't want this church to get involved in immigration issues. Teaching English is an invitation to people who are highly likely to be illegal."

The sanctuary was quiet. The lights on the trees glittered. One tree was decorated with red lights and one with white. The tree with red lights represented sin and the white lights represented goodness, or something like that. It bothered me that they had to assign labels to tree lights. I love red. And in December, isn't everything red and green, silver and white? Why did they have to take a beautiful noble fir tree, put sparkling little dots of light all over it and then call it something bad? I didn't get it. I'd asked Joe and Kate, but their answers had been unsatisfactory. Something about using symbols to teach. They didn't seem to get my concern that they were making it seem as if a color was something bad. Yes, blood is red, and for those who believe in hell-fire, that would obviously be red, but the sunset is red and so are gift-wrapped packages, and my hair, for that matter.

Still no one spoke. I could hear little coughs and sniffles. The longer it went on, the more likely it was that Joe would speak up again, so I wasn't sure why Kate was letting the silence swell as if thick wads of cotton had been stuffed in our ears.

"I think we're getting off track," said Kate.

"You told me to express my concerns. I'm not supporting this if we have an open door for illegals."

Kate's skin was smooth and she didn't look sweaty, but her slow responses told me she was very nervous. Usually, she's sharp and quick and doesn't ever seem like she's considering her words.

She'd told me that morning she thought the vote would be close. She'd told me many times for the past few weeks. She was almost angry about it, not understanding why people couldn't see the need, why they would not be in favor of it when it would be almost completely self-supporting. The church buildings stood vacant all day on weekdays, except for a women's book club, a senior citizen's lunch, and evening activities for kids and adults, and various business meetings a few nights a month. The property included the sanctuary, a social hall, the big basement under the sanctuary, and ten classrooms. All empty every day and many evenings. During the summer they had a kids' camp for two weeks that filled up the classrooms for half a day, but that was it. Such a waste. Kate had been pretty vocal, with me at least, that it was downright selfish to have all this property and all these buildings and not offer them to the community. It disgusted her that some of the church leaders worried more about insurance and liability than they did about being a force for good in the world; even if it was a very wealthy part of the world, a self-satisfied part of the world that didn't think it needed much in the way of good forces.

"Is your major concern the concept of teaching English as a second language? Because if that's the case, those details will be something for the governing board to iron out. If your concern is the offer of scholarships, we should discuss that, but the two aren't related."

"They sure are related," said Ben. "And we're not going to hand off fundamental issues of the school's charter to a handful of people. The results affect all of us." As he spoke, he waved his arm in the air, which made him look a little silly. He reminded me of a coach at a basketball game, his tie swinging wildly, his neck still red, and now his face had joined in, shouting at the team to get control of the ball.

Joe walked to the front of the sanctuary and climbed the steps until he was on the same level as Kate, which of course he was not at all level because Joe is over six feet tall, and Kate is about five feet, five inches. Not about, that's what she is, because she's the exact same height as me.

"Tonight we're voting on whether the church wants to open a childcare center," said Joe. "The curriculum and all of that will be decided later. If we want to write into the charter that some issues need to come to the church for a vote, that's fine. But we can't vote on every single aspect. The scholarships will be voluntary contributions. They won't be funded out of the church budget. So I think we're ready to vote."

If such things were visible to the human eye, we would have seen steam rising off Kate's hair. She took several steps away from Joe, until she was standing directly in front of the goodness tree, white light behind her, reflecting off her pale hair and white sweater, making her look like she was an angel, except a very pissed off and very voluptuous angel. Maybe voluptuous is the wrong word. Kate has large breasts and narrow hips and thin legs. That doesn't mean she looks disproportionate. The only thing out of proportion is her head because it's a bit on the small side for her shoulders and breasts. I don't mean to make her sound like a freak, she's very attractive, but in an unusual way. Which is a good thing.

I looked down at my pad and realized I hadn't taken any notes since I wrote that Ben had an objection to languages. I scribbled a few abbreviated words from Joe's summary and figured I'd fill in the rest later. But I knew that typing up the notes had better be the first thing on my to-do list the next day, otherwise I might forget the details. It was a little unclear to me who ever went back and read all these notes that needed to be taken at every meeting. The notes were distributed in email, and I wondered how many people even read them then. If they were interested in what happened, they would have been at the particular meeting, and if they'd been there, did they really need notes three days later to tell them what happened? The notes were supposed to be documentation in case there was disagreement at some future point about what had been said, but so far, in my almost ten months working there, that situation hadn't occurred.

Kate managed to get a grip on her animosity toward Joe and walked back to the center of the altar. "John?" She nodded at the deacon who was responsible for handling the ballot collection. "We're ready to vote." Her voice was a little weak when she hit that last word. I think she was really scared that Ben's fears would influence those who were on the fence. People who agreed with him, but were too ashamed to voice those kinds of opinions, might be lurking in every row. I'm sure she didn't like ending on a sour note, but she couldn't very well argue with Joe. That would make it worse. She decided to recoup by giving her own summary, as if she was a defense attorney in a criminal courtroom, wrapping it all up for the jury. She talked about children and how this was a chance to influence lives at the point in time when the potential for impact would be at the maximum. She talked about how cute kids are, how they would infuse the church with a spirit of life, how their parents might start attending the church, and bring their children for religious classes on Sundays. She talked about how children needed to socialize and that parents needed to feel secure that their kids were well-cared for, thriving when they were at work.

All in all, it was a very inspirational summary, and I was sure the image of Ben's red skin and waving arms, and the intensity behind his harsh words faded for most people.

The youth band performed three songs while people voted, the ballots were collected, and the deacons went off to tally the results.

The childcare center was defeated. By two votes.

CHAPTER 2

$\mathcal{K}$ATE CAME TO WORK very late the next day. It was almost lunchtime when she opened the office door and let it fall closed behind her. Joe was out at the hospital, making his usual visits and he was heading to the convalescent home after that, so I didn't expect to see him until late in the day, if at all.

The first thing I noticed was that her face looked perfect. Her cheeks were creamy rose, technically artificial, but she'd managed to make the color appear natural nonetheless. Her eyes were outlined in charcoal and her shadow a pale silver, the shade varying as it spread from her lashes to her brow with a hint of blue. Her lips were painted a paler color than usual, almost a flesh tone. She glowed, and I wondered how much she spent on makeup. I wondered if I would glow like that if I spent money and time and took classes on how to design my face as if I were a painter with a canvas and access to every shade of color in the world.

"You have at least twenty messages," I said. I handed her the stack of pink slips. It's a very old-fashioned way to take phone messages, but the church is behind the times in several areas, and this is one. Although it's deliberately behind because Joe and Kate, they agree a hundred percent on this point, want to present a different image than what people are used to in the world these days. They want a live human being answering the phone most hours during the day, even if I have to give directions fifteen times a week, or spell the church's email address or website url forty-seven times a week. They also want the human voice for those who call in distress. If someone you love just died, or lost their job, or their baby, they don't want to listen to a machine ramble on. If they can't reach the Pastor immediately, at least I know where he is and when he's coming back. I can listen and tell them I'm sorry. That goes a long way, even if they don't know me. It's just the real-time voice, the knowing someone else knows your pain exists.

Kate stared at the messages, but she didn't take them. I stood, so I could reach a bit closer. I thought her eyes might tear up, but they didn't.

After a minute, I put the messages on the corner of my desk and sat down.

Kate walked across the room to the coffee stand. She lifted the pot, peered at the steaming liquid, then put it back on the warmer.

"I'm really sorry about the childcare center," I said. "Joe said you're going to have some small groups to study it more and then vote again in January."

She nodded.

"It was only two votes. It shouldn't require much effort to over-come that. If you get ten more people to vote, you'll take care of it by more than enough."

She picked up the coffee pot again, pulled a mug off the tray, and filled it. She set it on the counter next to the coffee stand. It's a long counter that runs around two sides of the room that I use for folding and putting address labels on the monthly newsletter. This is another area where the church is outdated — sending newsletters printed on paper. They figure the cost of paper and postage is worth it to avoid that *one click delete* problem that comes with an emailed newsletter. Lots of people get the newsletter who haven't shown up at church for years, sometimes decades, and Pastor Joe and others see the newsletter as a small thread, keeping them in the fold.

I hoped Kate's hot mug didn't wreck the white Formica surface, but then, if you can't set a hot cup of coffee on it, what good is a counter, even if it's in a church office?

"It's not that it only lost by two votes," said Kate. "It's that the feeling is so evenly split. I was worried it might not pass. But in the middle of the night, it hit me that it's not only about not having the center get rolling right away, it's that so many people don't want it. For whatever reasons." She picked up the mug and blew on the surface of the coffee. Her breath was loud, like she was whispering or hissing. "It makes me look at this church in a whole new light. I can't comprehend how you can sit in that building every Sunday," she lifted her head toward the ceiling, indicating the sanctuary sitting above us, "and not want to help people. Especially children."

"No one besides Ben said anything overly negative," I said. "Do you think they all object for the same reasons?" I felt sad for her. She wanted this so badly. And not just because she wanted to extend her influence, or make her job more important or anything like that. She really loves kids. She wants the church swarming with kids. Not just cute little kids either, bratty kids, and awkward pre-teens, and sulking, swaggering teenagers.

"You took the notes," said Kate. "For a lot of them, it's all about money and liability. And there's an underlying, or maybe not so underlying, tone of racism. Faith doesn't enter into it. We might as well be a risk analysis company." She laughed.

It actually sounded like she was amused, so I was glad she was shaking off her funk. She walked to my desk and picked up the messages. "What do they say?"

"Most of them wanted you to call them back, so they didn't leave anything specific. But a few of them said to have you call so they can help you figure out how to get this rolling."

She smiled and tucked the stack into the outside pocket of her bag.

"No threats? Nothing from Ben?"

I shook my head and before I could shake it back the other way, the office door opened and Ben stepped inside. He wore his usual white shirt and necktie. The guy's been retired for several years, since he's about seventy, but he still wears that ridiculous get-up every single day, at least every time I've seen him. I shouldn't judge him for that, but I can't help thinking it explains a lot. How can you think clearly when you have a thick silk cord around your neck all the time?

It's not that Ben is a bad person, or heartless, or a creep or any of those things. He's really nice. He gives ten percent of his income to the church. I know, because on Mondays I double-check the offerings that are counted on Sundays. I get the cash and checks ready for the deposit and take them to the bank. Of course, I don't know that he's giving ten percent, but his checks are large, so I'm guessing if it's not, it's quite close. He's always been super nice to me, calling me by my name, asking what I'm up to. He helps serve the senior citizen lunch, even though he qualifies, age-wise, to be eating lunch with the older folks that come for that. He sings in the choir and Joe told me that his kids and grandkids visit the church every Easter and Christmas. In fact, until the night before, I didn't think he had a mean streak in him. He's just proper and conservative, I knew that. And he's very business-minded, retired from being a real estate developer, which I guess partially explains all the focus on infrastructure and availability of resources.

"Good morning, Ben." Kate spoke in a very even-toned, extremely fake sounding voice. She turned and walked to the door that leads to the basement area. Her office is on the adjacent side of that vast, empty, underground room.

"I'm here to see you," said Ben.

She paused. "I have a lot of calls to make, let's set an appointment for later this week."

"I know you're not going to let this go, but neither am I."

"Okay."

"So maybe you should focus your energy on something that has a better chance of succeeding."

"I really believe in this, Ben. If we can't use this space to meet the needs of children in the area, then what are we doing here?"

"The members of this church paid for these buildings and we pay a lot of money to maintain them. We have a right to control their use."

"No one said you don't," said Kate.

"I'm not opposed to a childcare center," said Ben. "My grandkids go to a church daycare center. But that's the point of private schools. You don't let in people who will drag it down, people who don't respect property, people who …"

"I already know what you think. I don't want to listen to that poison," said Kate.

"It's not poison. It's reality. Truth isn't always pretty and dressed up in cute little Santa hats and angel wings."

I tried to picture that. An angel in a Santa hat? Or Santa with wings? I wasn't sure why he threw those two bizarre images out there, but I didn't have time to consider it further because suddenly he was talking quite loudly and his neck was red again.

"It's fine to have a school or daycare for kids whose families step up and pay for their own. But I'm sick and tired of paying the bill for freeloaders. And you know that adding all these other languages will be like honey for flies, pulling in all these characters who refuse to speak English, who clog up the hospital emergency rooms, and send our insurance rates skyrocketing. They cause discipline problems in the public schools, fill up the jails, and spray paint all over every public building and freeway overpass we have. We need to get rid of them, not offer them an incentive to have more kids and bring their family members here!"

"They're children!" Kate dropped her bag on the floor.

For a minute, I thought she was going to curl her hands into fists and land one on his jaw, but she shoved her hands into her pockets.

"Children who should go back where they came from. Close the school access and the parents will be forced to leave."

Kate's face was as red as Ben's, the glow-y look replaced with a moist sheen that made her skin look spongy. She stared at her toes and kicked at her bag that was still sitting near her feet, successfully avoiding meeting Ben's eyes. I still had the feeling she might punch him. Heck, I wanted to punch him. You can worry all you want to about problems in society or with government or whatever. There are lots of hot feelings around illegal immigration, but I wondered if Ben ever stopped and listened to what he was saying. Was he suggesting we let people die in the gutters? What if his kids were starving? His precious grandchildren in their church daycare, wearing brand new designer shoes, with their hair trimmed and their lunches packed in cute, colorful containers and their juice in a box and their little outfits that made them look like tiny replicas of the entertainment industry. Would he break the law if those kids were crying? Or sick? Or had no money?

"What do you want to do, Ben?" Kate was still looking down at her bag, studying it as if she expected a child to emerge, having smuggled itself into the office with her. "Should we let people die in the gutters?"

"I didn't say that." Ben's voice was quiet.

"Do you want kids sitting home alone in crowded apartments? Babies cared for by ten-year-olds? The parents aren't just going to *go back* because they don't have subsidized childcare."

"Eventually they will." Ben crossed his arms.

I shivered. It felt as if a spider web had draped itself across my arms. It was usually a little on the warm side in the church office because once you cranked up the heat, the whole building turned into a nice sauna. I'd learned to wear short-sleeved shirts, even in December. Now the webby stuff drifted across my lower arms. I rubbed them. The tickling, goose bump feeling continued. I looked down at my arms because the sensation was so vivid and so uncomfortable, I was sure a cobweb had fallen down from the ceiling.

Nothing was there. It must be in my head. Hearing Kate talk, it was as if my thoughts had gone to her and come out of her mouth. I suppose that's ridiculous. If two people think along the same lines, it makes sense that they'd say similar things, but her words were so close to my thoughts, I felt as if I was speaking. I shivered again. The threads draped across my arms persisted. Soon I was rubbing them so vigorously, that Kate frowned at me.

Ben turned to see what she was staring at. After a moment, he rubbed his own arm even though he was really just crinkling his sleeve. That really freaked me out because I felt like my thoughts and feelings were transferring themselves to someone else's body. I forced myself to stop rubbing my arms, and folded them across my ribs, wrapping my hands around the muscle part of each forearm, hoping that tickling, shivering feeling would stop.

Ben continued rubbing his arm, but he turned back to Kate. "It doesn't matter what you think. I stopped by to tell you that I'll organize a group to look into legal issues, our responsibility to the state of California, whatever it takes to make sure we don't have any access in this program for illegals. If you want this center, you need to get rid of that part of the plan. It's very simple."

"Why are you so hateful? All we're doing is opening a childcare center. You didn't answer me. Do you want kids wandering the streets without adult supervision?"

"That's not our problem," said Ben. "You can't save the world. People have to take some responsibility for themselves."

"But that's how crime starts," said Kate. "Can't you see how it's related? And it's not like we're going to have twenty kids with questionable status. We probably won't have any. We're talking four or five scholarship slots. That's all."

"One is too many."

Ben backed toward my desk. He rubbed his arm again and glanced at me. It seemed that he didn't realize what he was doing, that his hand was acting outside his control. He looked down and stopped, pulled his hand away from his sleeve, and shoved it in his pocket.

"So you'd sabotage the whole program out of fear that one child might be undocumented?"

"Illegal," said Ben.

"Undocumented," said Kate.

Would this disintegrate into a one-word fight, where they spit their chosen phrases back and forth at each other? Maybe it would unravel further until they spoke single letters, and then finally just emitted sounds, like dogs barking at each other.

Ben turned slowly and walked to the door. He opened it gently as if he was over-compensating for his cruel opinions. As if he wanted to prove to someone (to me?) that he was a nice guy and that keeping the school focused on kids who already had privilege and money was really a very godly thing to do. When he stepped outside, he continued his gentle movements, easing the door closed until there was a soft click.

Kate kicked her bag with the toe of her cowboy boot. She kicked it again and it moved closer to the door to the basement area. It appeared as if she planned to kick her bag all the way across that empty room to her office door.

"Well," she said. "I guess we have a battle on our hands."

I nodded. I wasn't supposed to get too involved in the church politics, but how could I not when they were arguing right in front of my desk? It was like I had front row seats to a holiday pageant where Ben was determined to close the door in the face of any children he deemed unworthy. A bit of a mockery of the whole Christmas story, no room at the inn and all of that, if you ask me.

CHAPTER 3

$\mathcal{A}$FTER THAT SCENE in front of my desk, Kate picked up her bag and went to her office. I heard the door close, and a minute later the light for her line turned red on my phone, so I figured she'd be busy for a while. She probably needed a lot of shoring up after that. It's amazing how one angry voice can derail something. I was starting to learn that the members of Central Avenue Church feel very strongly about their property, the decisions of the church, everything that goes on there, as if it's their own home, their family – which I suppose it is. I wondered whether Ben would be able to find enough people that were as determined as he was to dictate what children would be invited into the program. Would they be willing to keep fighting to prevent the church from ever opening a childcare center?

I grabbed my bag, forwarded the main line to my mobile phone, and went outside for a cigarette break. Normally, I smoke my mid-day cigarette at lunch, but I felt like I needed to clear my head and smoking is one of my favorite ways to do that.

The tip of the cigarette barely had time to develop a small nubbin of ash when I turned and saw Jim Gilchrest walking up the stairs from the parking strip. I was standing at the end of the classroom wing. I'd been looking at the grove of trees, wanting to sit on the concrete bench, but that isn't a good place for smoking because there are dead pine needles all over the ground. Besides, that bench would be like a block of ice at this time of the year. Even though the daytime winter temperature in the Bay Area usually hovers in the fifties, a concrete bench can bite through your clothes pretty fast, and the coat I wear to work is only hip length. It wasn't as if I had a thick piece of wool to sit on.

Jim carried a large red shopping bag. Several packages wrapped in paper that featured white angels on a blue background poked out the top. I assumed he was bringing them to set under one of the Christmas trees in the sanctuary where packages for the holiday toy program were being collected. I wondered if Ben had a problem with that activity as well, if he wanted to personally meet every child that received a wrapped toy and check their social security cards. Maybe he hadn't thought of that yet. Or maybe it was okay with him, as long as the unwanted kids weren't on church property.

The shopping bag banged against Jim's lower leg as he walked along the path and started up the steps to the sanctuary. He paused on the second step and sniffed the air. His nose twitched. For a moment, I thought he would sneeze. He backed down the steps and turned to look at me.

I waved. Big mistake. He walked toward me, but it was more of a marching cadence than a casual stroll to say *hi, how ya' doin'?*

"Smoking will kill you," said Jim.

Nice greeting. I'd met the guy once, never said more than seven or eight words to him, maybe fourteen or fifteen, but that was it.

"That's what they say."

"It's proven."

I smiled.

"It makes the garden stink, and it doesn't give a very good impression of the church if people drive past and see you smoking," said Jim.

"Pastor Joe is okay with it," I said. I pointed my cigarette at his shopping bag. "What toys did you bring?"

"A set of math workbooks, colored pencils, and a dictionary."

The colored pencils sounded okay.

"Suzie is bringing more gifts this weekend. This is just my contribution."

"Who's Suzie?"

"My fiancé."

I'd never seen him with a woman, but then, I don't attend the Sunday morning services, so what do I know? "Is she bringing *toys*?" I made the emphasis as light as I could. After all, I hardly knew the guy, and it wasn't my business to criticize his selection, but math books? I had to force myself not to picture the face of the poor little kid who opened that gift.

"Suzie didn't like my selections either."

"What did she buy?"

He shrugged. He shifted the bag to his left hand and flexed his fingers. Red lines ran across the creases behind his knuckles. Those must be some heavy-duty math books. Or maybe it was the dictionary.

I couldn't keep my mouth shut. I had to point out his mistake, even though Suzie had apparently failed to steer him away from math. "The idea of the program is to give them some Christmas morning excitement. Kids like to open toys."

"Have you ever watched kids unwrap a toy?" said Jim. "They play with it for ten minutes and then they're bored."

"I don't think that's true. They might get distracted, but they're thrilled when they open it, and then they play with it later. Plus, these kids might only get one or two toys, so it won't be the same as it is with kids who have a lot."

"Are you arguing with me?"

"I'm just saying that the purpose of the program is to know that parents who can't afford gifts will get to see that thrill in their child's eyes. To give them an experience that parents with a good income take for granted."

"If their parents don't have money, the kids should be thankful for my gifts." He lifted the bag. "Maybe these will help them get out of the poverty cycle." He took a step back and shifted the shopping bag back to his right hand.

Jim is a good-looking guy, one of those chiseled types, with dark blonde hair, perfectly trimmed, and posture like he'd been in the military, but I knew he hadn't because he's an Ivy League college, business school graduate kind of guy. He wore an overcoat, which you don't see much in California, even when the temperature drops to the forties, so that made me think the Ivy league thing had wound itself around his brain and followed him to the west coast. His genuine smile was contradictory to his peevish attitude about kids needing educational gifts. Although, I guess if he was that excited about his own education, maybe he thought school was the greatest thing in life. And I suppose he did, since he'd obviously mentioned the details of his education since I seemed to know all about it. So maybe we had spoken more than fifteen words, maybe it was more like three hundred and fifteen.

"Will a kid be thinking about her education on Christmas morning?"

"My mother was a single mom. She didn't have anything. The best gift I ever got was when an old guy in our apartment complex helped me with math. I had bad allergies, and our apartment had a lot of mildew in the walls. That guy told me to study as much as I could and I'd get a scholarship to college and I'd never live in a mildewed apartment again."

"Aren't there other programs to help kids with their education? It's Christmas. They should get toys."

"Christmas is not about toys."

I didn't want to get into that conversation. And really, I was kind of badgering the guy. He was being generous, and he'd already bought and wrapped the gifts, and maybe that angel paper would give the kids a clue that there wasn't a truck or a game inside, so they wouldn't be that disappointed. Kids pick up on those little clues. They would know that a fun gift would come wrapped in paper with Santa or snowmen, even reindeer, not the shadows of angels that looked as if they'd been cut out of the dark blue, leaving blank spaces in an evening sky.

"People think they can buy happiness for their children," said Jim. "Christmas is not about kids being happy and getting whatever they want. It just sets them up for disappointment in life."

"I suppose."

"Eventually you reach a point where your parents can't make you scream over some piece of crap toy that you outgrow in three months. And then you realize Santa leaves nicer toys at other kids' houses."

"But can't you enjoy that when you're little? It doesn't last long. Just a few years, and then you know how it really is."

"You've already been set up," he said.

Wow. I took one last hit on my cigarette and dropped it on the ground. I stepped on the tip and pressed hard. I bent down to pick it up and dropped it into my nearly empty coffee mug. "You sound pretty cynical for a guy delivering Christmas presents, looking forward to getting married and all that."

"I just know how reality is. When you're trying to buy a house, and you're stuck at the bottom of the corporate food chain, you know how it is."

I do know how it is, but I'm not so bitter about it. When I was a kid, there were presents under my family tree that made me squeal. Once there was a puppy. How great is that? How many kids want a puppy under the tree and how many actually get one? He was a Golden Lab with silky fur on his head, and his ears were like soft pieces of suede, and he had big clunky paws and round eyes that looked at you like he owed you his life. I named him Sherlock, and he was the greatest playmate a kid could ever have, especially one like me who lacked siblings and was short on neighborhood kids and was home-schooled until she was twelve. Does that mean I expected a life full of awesomeness and puppies? "It's very generous that both you and your fiancé are bringing gifts. When are you getting married?"

"July 23rd."

"There must be lots of planning going on."

"Suzie handles all that. I'm focused on trying to buy a house."

I nodded. Now that my cigarette was gone, I wanted to get back inside. I was wearing a silky skirt, and even though I had on tights and boots, plus my coat, my legs were cold.

He set the bag on the ground. Obviously, the weight was getting to be too much for the tender skin inside his fingers, but I wanted to wrap things up, and he seemed to be hunkering down for a long chat about house-hunting. From hating my smoking to hating Christmas, to suggesting he also hated wedding planning, judging by the way his lips got all stiff when he said *Suzie handles all that*, I had no idea why he wanted to spend another minute talking to me.

"It's tough to find a house around here with a down payment and a mortgage we can manage."

Now I was not only cold, I was annoyed. Did he really think I was going to feel sorry for him because he couldn't afford one of the million dollar homes that surround the church? And the million-dollar ones are average ranch-style homes. You spread out a few blocks from where the church is located, ooze up into the foothills between the Santa Clara Valley and the ocean, and you can pay considerably more than one million dollars. And I say *you* rather loosely. Sometimes when I drive to the area from my condo in downtown San Jose, where nothing costs a million dollars, where there are some blocks in which you could buy four houses for a million dollars, I'm amazed that there are so many people that can afford to spend that much on a house. But maybe it just seems like there are a lot of people with a lot of money because they're so spread out. If you compare the area to street after street of apartment complexes, you realize there aren't that many after all.

"Most of my friends got help from their parents, but clearly that's not an option for me."

I wished I had my cigarette back. Apparently, he planned to keep explaining his situation to me. I looked into my mug and longed for the soggy remains. I had a pack in my bag, but I really, really did not want to break my rule of one mid-day cigarette. I'm trying to stop, not expand, my bad habit.

"And of course, none of the government programs are offered to someone like me," he said. "I give up everything normal kids have to study hard, get a good education, and now I make too much money to qualify for any assistance. People who took on loans they didn't understand get help — bailouts and restructuring — and I get shit."

That was not a word I heard often, if at all, from the members of Central Avenue Church, but Jim didn't blink. In fact, his eyes got wider and he kept talking, the words rushing out at a faster pace. "Everyone talks about justice. The biggest injustice of all is that people like me put in sixty or seventy hours a week, but don't get any assistance, and some guy who's too lazy to work more than forty hours gets all kinds of handouts. People come here illegally or overstay their visas, and it comes out of my pocket when they go to the emergency room with the flu or end up in prison. And the guys who come from money pass it back forth inside the family."

I nodded. It was becoming less and less clear why he was telling me this. "I'm sure you'll find a house eventually," I said. There are lots of condos in my area, but I didn't mention those. There are also lots of homeless people and even the occasional hooker and drug dealer. That was not what Jim had in mind.

"All I want is to buy a home for my bride, like I promised." He sounded as if he might cry.

I folded my arms, trying not to shiver.

"I'm hoping for a foreclosure so we can get a good deal."

"Isn't that sort of hoping someone else will suffer so you can do better?" I know that was a snarky thing to say, but he didn't seem offended. Maybe that's why I said it, trying to get a reaction, trying to make him hear how he sounded. Not that it's ever possible to help someone see their flawed thinking, but that doesn't stop me from trying. It doesn't stop anyone from trying. It's possible we spend our whole lives trying to convert people to our points of view.

"Eat or be eaten," said Jim.

"Well, if I'm going to have time for a lunch break, I should get back to work now," I said. "And I'm sure you have things to do after you leave your gifts under the tree."

He pulled his smartphone out of his pocket. "I do. But it's been nice talking to you."

"Same here." I moved my mug, swirling the dregs of the coffee, watching my cigarette butt bob like a tiny canoe. I'd have to take the mug to the kitchen during lunch and give it a good scrubbing.

We walked back to the stairs, one set leading down to the offices, and the wide steps that led up to the fifteen-foot double doors of the sanctuary. The sanctuary doors were kept unlocked during the day in case people wanted to come by and think or chat with god, but in the eight months I'd been working there, I wasn't aware of anyone who had ever done that. Of course, I'm down underneath most of the time, so if someone slipped in and slipped out and didn't stop by the office to chat with Pastor Joe, or even if they did, how would I really know whether they'd been inside praying?

I said good-bye and hurried down the stairs, hoping the quick movement would warm my frozen legs. When I reached the bottom, I heard the door of the sanctuary fall closed with a loud clank. Maybe Jim would linger in there and do some thinking and re-consider his gifts, but I doubted it.

I walked along the path that runs past the window near my desk. Before I reached the office door, something brushed across my face. I stepped back and waved my hand, and it was not lost on me that I looked exactly like the people who wave their arms to dispel cigarette smoke. Of course, this was something tangible, so it was justified. I thought at first it was a cobweb, just as I'd felt earlier when Kate and Ben were arguing in front of my desk. Nothing stuck to my skin, at least I didn't feel anything. I looked at the side of my hand and spread my fingers but there was nothing. Yet, I was sure I'd felt something. I stepped back and looked at the overhang. It was free of cobwebs. I took a few steps back trying to get the sun at a different angle to see if there was something dangling further up, from the branch of a tree at the top of the steep slope that surrounded the lower floor. Nothing.

Everything was suddenly quiet. Presumably, Jim was still in the sanctuary since I hadn't heard his footsteps along the path back to the front parking strip. The birds were silent. That's the funny thing about birds in suburbia. You hardly notice them much of the time, but when they're silent, you wonder where they all went. Or why they suddenly have nothing to say. Even the swoosh of traffic on the main thoroughfare had stopped, and of course, there wasn't any sound coming from the offices. Kate's office is way around the side, and she probably wasn't even aware that I'd left the building, probably still on the phone lamenting the delay or possible loss of the childcare center, talking to her fans and supporters. I don't mean to make that sound critical, I was glad she had people behind her. Ben was being a jerk, or worse, and I hoped they figured out a way to silence him, and people like him. It really would be a shame to watch the building continue to sit empty 80% of the time. Such a waste, when there is so much need for space in other places. The world really is quite unbalanced at times.

Since I didn't see any cobwebs or anything else that might have brushed across my face, I stepped forward again and wrapped my fingers around the doorknob. The sensation occurred again. Now I wondered if I was imagining something. I thought I'd felt a cobweb and now there was some kind of cycle going on in my brain where it kept repeating the impression. I ran my fingers across my cheeks and my nose, feeling ridiculous, but absolutely certain that something was touching my face.

I told myself to put it out of my head, to stop thinking about it and then I would stop feeling it. I turned the knob and pulled the door more slowly, more thoughtfully than I usually would, and that's why I noticed the edge of the doorframe. All down the wood piece where the door fits into the wall were feathery carcasses of moths. There were ten of them, smashed between the door and the frame, interred there for quite some time since their bodies were turning to dust. I shivered and jumped into the office and let the door close on its own. It doesn't close very fast, and I had an irrational fear that the moths were going to swarm into the office.

Once the door was closed, I sort of wanted to go back and look. My first instinct was that they'd all been smashed there with a single slam of the door, but that made no sense. There was no way all those moths would have flown up to the doorframe and sat waiting for death as a door came at them. But they'd all looked like they were in the same state of decay, so it seemed as if they died at the same time. It was bugging me so much, I pushed away the wiggly feeling in my knees and stomach, and opened the door again. I stepped outside, well away from the threshold, and held the door open, studying the moths.

Despite the obvious powdery consistency of their bodies, I continued to worry that they were going to fly at me, or into the office. Then it occurred to me that the cobwebby sensation could have been the brush of a moth's wing. I stepped closer and looked up at the eaves to see if there were other, living moths hanging out. I saw one moth, but it also looked dead. I can't say why, it just seemed a little not fresh. I wasn't a hundred percent sure, but what did it really matter? I was disgusted by all the dead ones, and I don't know why I thought checking for more would matter one way or the other. I suppose I wanted to know where they'd come from. I'd never seen that many moths, living or dead, in one place before.

I reached into my pocket and pulled out my mobile phone. I

have no idea why. Maybe I thought I was imagining this. Or maybe I wanted to brood about it later, to remind myself of this strange sight even after they were cleaned up. I had no idea who was going to clean them up, it certainly wouldn't be me. It also seemed odd that no one had noticed them before. They'd clearly been there for a while, and with all the traffic through that door, multiple times a day, no one had ever noticed them.

I held up the phone and snapped a picture. Several pictures, moving closer. At least as close as I dared because I still was afraid they'd come to life and fly at me, or maybe I thought they were playing dead. Moths kind of do that – they look dead when they plaster themselves on a wall, not moving, hugging it as if they want to crawl inside. I dropped the phone back in my pocket.

The church had finally hired a new groundskeeper. It had taken them over a month after Fred was murdered to have the stomach to look for someone new, and this guy had started last May. Even though he'd been around three times longer than I'd known Fred, we hadn't really connected. This new guy had a son and daughter who sometimes came to help him do weeding around the church. It's not that the church hires out everything. They have clean-up days three times a year when the members come and pull weeds, paint, and do other maintenance. But I was pretty sure the moth removal would be the groundskeeper's job, since the moths needed to be disposed of now, not remain stuck to the doorframe like some kind of grotesque Halloween garland.

I yanked open the door and hurried into the office. I could have gone and looked for Carlo, the groundskeeper, but it was simpler to call his mobile phone. It was almost lunchtime, but after seeing those moths, I wasn't very hungry, so I went to work on typing and formatting the agenda for Sunday's church service. It wasn't until I was halfway through typing out the prayer requests that had come in over the past few days, that I remembered that cobwebby feeling. I lifted my fingers off the keyboard and closed my eyes. If I'd imagined that stuff brushing against my skin, you'd think I would feel it when the thought came back through my mind, but I didn't. It seemed like the sensation outside the church door was related to the moths because that's what made me go more slowly and notice them to begin with, but that really made no sense. I wasn't even sure why I connected the two, the thought popped in out of nowhere. Anyway, I hoped I didn't feel it again, because it gave me the creeps. I shivered, just thinking about it.

CHAPTER 4

*J*D, THE BARTENDER I'D MET at The Distillery restaurant in Half Moon Bay a few months ago, had called to make good on his suggestion that we go out sometime. We'd made plans to go to dinner at an Italian place call Paolo's in downtown San Jose, but then everything went sideways. His twin brother, who had been living in Australia for two years, crashed his motorcycle. The accident was pretty bad, and JD took time off work to fly to Sydney and take care of him when he got out of the hospital. Apparently, JD has quite the savings account, so it was no problem for him to take a two-month vacation, although I'm sure it wasn't really much of a vacation.

He stayed in Sydney until the first week of November. We kept in touch on *Facebook*, and even though he was providing transportation and housekeeping help and cooking for his brother, he managed to find time to see a fair number of kangaroos and koalas, and seemed quite taken with them because he posted various pictures of them on *Facebook* every four or five days. That made me even more excited that we had something in common besides our experiences with ghosts. I love animals, and although I only have a parakeet right now, I plan to expand the animal population in my home in the near future.

While JD was on the other side of the world, I'd signed up for a yoga class on Monday nights and a sculpture class at the Junior College on Tuesday nights. It wasn't until he was back and we tried to make plans for dinner that I realized he worked most nights, I worked most days, and the nights he had off were now consumed by my classes. In mid-December, my sculpture class ended, so here we were, three months after we'd met, going on our first date. Well, the first date if you don't count our muffins and coffee on the beach at four a.m., hoping to catch a glimpse of the ghost that haunts the Moss Beach Distillery.

He came to my condo to pick me up. It's always startling when you see someone again after a purely virtual relationship. The 3D presence of their actual body, their voice, their smell — every tangible thing about them — is more intense when you've been limited to words on a screen, and a thumbnail of a picture, and in this case, that picture often depicting a kangaroo rather than the cute guy with dark hair pulled into a ponytail and slicing blue eyes.

When I opened the door, I felt my face smile all on its own before I had a chance to put on a more aloof demeanor. After all, do you want a guy to know he's making your stomach flip flop when you're first getting to know each other? Even for someone like me who is a *what-you-see-is-what-you-get* type of person, I don't want to completely rip open my chest and show my heart.

He wore crisp but faded blue jeans and a navy blue raw silk shirt that flowed around his body like water. A crinkled brown leather coat dangled over his left arm. He had dark brown oxford-type shoes, which I really like because, for some reason, they make guys look like little boys. And that is what they all are inside, little boys, so it's nice when that's visible. His eyes were even bluer than I remembered. I think it's partly his black hair that makes his eyes look as blue as a glacial lake.

To calm myself down, and to stop from staring, I opened the

door wider and stepped back. "Why don't I show you around my condo?"

I don't know if he thought that was a strange suggestion, an unconventional way to start a date. He didn't act as if it was. It seemed awkward, but on the other hand, it's a good way to get to know someone, to see where they live, what kinds of photographs and artwork they like to look at, the style of furniture they've chosen, and whether they have houseplants or not. I have a lot. Of houseplants.

I showed him my kitchen first, which is all white and beige and very minimalist in terms of what's on the counters. The kitchen opens to a deck and a small patch of yard where I've planted an itty bitty lemon tree which usually has two or three lemons on it, and a peach tree that I hope will grow large enough to bear fruit while I'm living here, and if it doesn't, then someone else will benefit from my watering and fertilizing with all my coffee grounds and food scraps. The deck extends past the living room, and I showed him that next, with my pale blue couch and matching armchair, a coffee table that cost twenty bucks at Ikea but is very nice looking with a shelf underneath for magazines and my iPad and the speaker station for my iPod. Yes, I'm an i-addict, but if you live in Silicon Valley, it's hard not to be.

JD especially liked the Ficus in the corner of the living room and the white orchid on a stand in the opposite corner. He paused and studied all of my photographs, of my parents, my friends from high school, pictures of Lake Tahoe, and the ocean, and my trip with my friend Renee to New York City for my 25th birthday.

I didn't bother to show him the laundry room or the bathroom, but took him upstairs quickly to show him my bedroom where my blue parakeet, Simon, lives. JD made chirping sounds at him. Simon tilted his head and looked at JD, but said nothing. Don't worry that Simon is all alone in the bedroom. He only stays there at night so I can hear him tweet when the sun comes up. Usually, I keep him in whatever room I'm in, whether I'm watching TV or reading, and in the kitchen when I'm baking oatmeal cookies or eating.

JD didn't seem bored at all, which encouraged me to show him every little detail, and when we wound up back in the entryway, I wondered if I'd shown him a bit too many details, but when someone is interested, it's hard to restrain yourself from telling or showing them everything.

* * *

PAOLO'S HAS BEEN AROUND downtown San Jose forever — since the late 50s. It's a more traditional place, right near the Guadalupe River. While we were looking at our menus, JD asked if I wanted to order a bottle of wine. I reminded him I don't drink alcohol.

"Not even wine?"

"Does wine have alcohol?" I smiled in case that sounded too harsh.

"Yes, but people enjoy it for the taste, to enhance their food."

"It makes me thirsty and it's too sour."

"Maybe you haven't had good wine." He picked up the wine list and turned the page. "But if you don't want any, I can just order a glass."

"I don't want any."

He closed the leather folder. "Maybe another time." He smiled.

How can something so sweet be so sharp on the other side? He implied there would be another time, and yet he also seemed to think I was going to give in and drink something I don't like. Something I told him quite clearly I don't like.

We ordered our food – veal rolls for him and Italian sausage with olives and potatoes for me. He ordered a glass of Chardonnay, mentioning the name, but it really meant nothing to me. I ordered water with a slice of lime.

"How was your week?" he said.

I relaxed and forgot about the wine. It was nice that he wasn't going to start in on some *let's-get-acquainted* first date exchange of our histories. That always seems fake, and then it seems like you're repeating yourself ever after because you already gave the overview of your whole life, so any memory that pops up is just more detail around something you already said.

For a few minutes I debated whether I should start with the squashed moths in the doorframe, the creepy cobweb experience, fighting the silky, cool strands which turned out not to be there, something that was right in line with our previous conversations about ghosts, or to tell him about the conflict over the childcare center. Or maybe I should ignore all of that and tell him about my yoga class. I opted for the moths. The cobwebs might make me sound a little nuts right off the bat, as if that was the highlight of my week, and the childcare center wasn't a quick, casual story, even though it was eating away at me. "I should tell you the most disgusting part of my week before our food comes."

"You had a disgusting part?"

"Yesterday I opened the door to the church office and there were ten moths squished along the doorframe."

He wrinkled his nose. It looked very cute, if a guy can look cute.

"They were all powdery, as if they'd been there for a long time."

"How would a whole bunch get trapped at one time?"

"That's what I was wondering. And why didn't anyone notice them before? They were almost turning to paper, so they must have been there for months."

"You're an unobservant group. Maybe your minds are all on unearthly things."

I laughed. "I don't think so. Wait until you hear about the fight over the childcare center. But tell me all about Australia first."

"I didn't see hordes of dead insects. I didn't see any of the weird creatures they're known for either."

"But you saw kangaroos and koalas."

"I did."

The server delivered JD's wine and my water. I took several sips, enjoying the coolness slipping down my throat. He didn't touch his wine at first, which made me strangely glad, that he wasn't so in love with alcohol that he had to grab it right away. I don't mean to sound like I'm anti good times. It just struck me. That's all. "How was it seeing the real thing after seeing them in photographs all your life?"

"Pretty amazing. But in the end, the kangaroos, except for their pockets and their size, were a lot like rabbits. They made me think of that invisible giant rabbit."

"Harvey?"

"Yes. The koalas are unreal. Even up close, touching them, watching them move around, it seemed like I was looking at a video clip."

"What weird creatures are they known for?"

"The box jellyfish, for one. It's an incredible blue color, but can be deadly."

I shivered. "Jellyfish are beautiful, but I'd rather they stay in the water. I hate it when I'm walking on the beach and there's this big glob of goo. How can something so gorgeous underwater look so revolting on the beach?"

"Maybe because it's dead? Or out of its environment." He winked.

I wasn't sure how to take that wink. It seemed as if he was hinting that his words had a double meaning. Saying it was dead seemed obvious. But adding that bit about being out of its environment made me wonder if he was referring to me. I have no idea why that thought came to me. It sounds a little paranoid, reading too much into a simple comment, and a wink, but there it was. It popped up and it wouldn't go away. Of course, if he *was* talking about me, how would he know when I'm out of my element? I don't even know what kind of environment I fit into, so he surely wouldn't. I took a piece of bread and spread the butter across in a thin layer. I took a bite. It was soft and the crust was easy to chew, which was nice. "How is your brother doing?"

He told me about the damage to his brother's knee and hip, all the scrapes and burns, even though he'd been wearing a helmet and a long-sleeved shirt. Coming into contact with pavement at forty-five miles an hour rips right through your clothes. But his brother was doing okay now, back at work and going out with his nurse from the hospital.

"What's it like having a twin? Is it true that you know each other's thoughts, that you know when something unusual has happened to him?"

He laughed. "I sure didn't know he was being flung off his motorcycle while I was sleeping. I didn't even have a dream."

"Have you ever? Had a dream about him that was true?"

"No. But he's had them about me."

Our food came and we started eating and talking about the sauce on the veal rolls and how much he liked the grilled zucchini and how he didn't like cauliflower and why did so many restaurants feel compelled to steam up white stuff that looks like it belongs on the ocean floor. I finished my bread and cut off a slice of sausage. I cut the disk in half. It melted in my mouth but had a definite kick. I ate some potatoes to calm the spiciness.

"So what was it?"

He looked at me. He tipped his head to the side and squinted.

"Your twin. You said he's had dreams about you. What did he dream?"

"I shouldn't have mentioned that."

"Why not?"

"My brother's a weird dude."

"Aren't we all?"

"No. Not like him."

"What's wrong with him?"

"He doesn't have any self-restraint. He drinks too much, drives too fast. He's too much all the way around. He eats too much, although it doesn't seem to show up anywhere. He'll sit down and eat eight boiled eggs and three bowls of oatmeal. Sometimes he stays awake for over 48 hours. He has sex with too many women. And it's easy for him to attract women, so I mean a *lot* of women. It's out of control."

I could see that. If they were identical twins, attracting females seemed like the easiest thing in the world.

"Are you identical?"

He laughed. He took a bite of veal and chewed it for a few seconds then took a sip of wine. It wasn't a difficult question, I couldn't figure out why he didn't just nod, if he was so hungry and had to put food in his mouth right that minute.

"Yes."

"Why did you take so long to answer?"

"We're nothing alike in who we are. We look the same. That's all."

"It sounds like you're a little disconnected from him, but you took off all that time to go help him out?"

He shrugged. He looked out the window. It was dark, and all that was visible were shadows of people walking along the plaza near the Guadalupe River. He drank some more wine. "Were the dead moths the highlight of your week? Or do you have other news to report?"

"Why won't you tell me about your brother's dream?" Although this was not the flirty, fun approach one should take on a first date, I don't believe in all that stuff. Being coy and too nice just wastes time. I figure you might as well get to know each other in a more realistic way immediately. Which explains why I haven't had more than the one boyfriend. I think it's better that way, though. Why spend time going out and being superficial only to find out you don't like each other at all? I suppose you could go out as friends, but then why not just be friends?

"It was … unsettling. I don't like to talk about it."

"You brought it up."

He sighed. He put down his fork and picked up the wine. The noise in the room suddenly seemed louder. Everyone was talking, and talking at an accelerated pace as if they couldn't get their thoughts out fast enough. JD was the opposite, he couldn't contain his thoughts tightly enough.

"What's your brother's name?"

"Luke."

Ah. Luke and Larry. JD's real name is Larry, but his buddies gave him the nickname. It stands for *Jack Daniels* whiskey. And now that we'd had that little hiccup over him thinking I would eventually *change my mind* and start drinking wine, I wondered if alcohol played a somewhat bigger part in his life than it did in mine. Obviously, it played no part in mine. I hadn't thought of that when he first told me he was called JD, but now it kind of stuck in my throat. "So what did he dream? You can't mention it and not tell me the story."

"You're a very curious person," he said.

I nodded. I ate half a piece of sausage and waited. He wasn't going to divert me, no matter how many times he nudged the subject to the left.

He looked at me for a moment or two. "I really wish I hadn't mentioned it. And now I've made it seem more ominous than it is, but he won't shut up about it, he couldn't just tell me and let it slip out of my memory because it was insignificant. In fact, he brought it up every single day I was there."

A woman at the table next to us shrieked. I looked over. JD looked too. She was laughing so hard she had to lean over the table. The ends of her hair fell onto her plate of spaghetti, painting the tips red. Soon, everyone at the tables around her and her two girlfriends were staring. Her friends' faces turned as red as the spaghetti sauce. After a minute, a few people around them chuckled, then a few more. I felt myself kind of laughing. It was the type of laughter that's like a virus, spreading on moist breath from one person to another.

It was quite a few more minutes before she wound down. Her

friends leaned toward the center of the table and whispered. Everyone went back to eating and drinking and talking, a few of them laughing in normal voices.

"How's your dinner?" said JD.

"Delicious. You were going to tell me about the dream."

He raised his eyebrows and set down his fork. I think he'd hoped the laughing women had diverted me. I suppose he didn't know yet that nothing diverts me.

"He had a very specific, vivid dream that I formed a cult," he said. "I shaved a strip down the center of my head that cut off my pony-tail, but left the remaining hair long on the sides. I dressed in black shorts and a black t-shirt all the time and never wore shoes. I set up a commune in a warehouse in San Francisco."

I shrugged. "You're right, those are very specific details, but it doesn't seem that upsetting. It's not like he dreamt you died, or that you did something violent."

His eyes glittered, like small lakes in bright sunlight, the shimmering blue inviting you in for a swim, not letting on whether the temperature was pleasant or as cold as snow melt. "It was upsetting to me."

"Why? It's just a dream."

"Like I said, he won't let go of it. He acts as if it's prophetic, or some bullshit like that."

I laughed. "Can't you just ignore it?"

"Our parents are into a lot of fundamentalist religious stuff. They're Catholic, so you wouldn't think of them as fanatical, but they're obsessed. They were gone nearly every other weekend when we were kids, off at one retreat or another, always trying to drag us along, get us involved in things. They shoved their wacko ideas down everyone's throats until most of their friends got sick of it. No one wanted to be around them unless they were members of the same group."

I could see why he'd be sensitive about it, but still, who cared what his brother dreamt? Or was that a twin thing, where you put extra weight on the thoughts of your womb-mate?

"If you don't let it bother you, I'm sure he'll stop talking about it."

"It's not just the dream, it's that even when I ask him to stop, he won't. He talks about it constantly and you start to feel like maybe he knows something you don't."

"Then you should stop believing it means anything." He looked like I betrayed him when I said that. But I couldn't see why it was so upsetting, even with what he said about his parents. If you don't want to start a cult, don't start a cult. Who cares what someone dreamt? Of course, I never had siblings, so maybe I don't understand a single thing about how they might be able to irritate you. Especially a twin.

"After I saw the ghost of the Blue Lady at The Distillery, he got worse. I wish I'd never told him."

I smiled. "You would make a terrible cult leader. You're too easy going."

He laughed. "I know I shouldn't get so irritated. It's partly the way he is, so insistent. Too intense. He fixates on an idea and it takes over. Like when he decides he has to eat eggs."

That made me think there might be a bit more to it than just the dream and the teasing, but I decided not to push it. "Are you close?"

"Closer than we would be if he lived nearby."

I sliced my last piece of sausage in half. I didn't want it to be gone already. I put the first half in my mouth and chewed super slow. When I was finished, I stabbed a few olives and filled the rest of my fork with potatoes — a nice tart and creamy combination. "I don't have any brothers or sisters."

"I can't imagine being the only kid," said JD.

"It's fine. I don't have anything to compare it with."

While we finished eating, I switched to the subject of the child-care center and told him about all the drama regarding scholarships and letting kids outside of the community into the program. He was disgusted by Ben's attitude, and that fueled my energy to talk about how hard Kate had worked planning the program and how sad it was to watch the whole thing come to a screeching halt. He said if Ben didn't want kids that lived outside his cozy, elite suburban neighborhood, how did he reconcile that with the baby they were supposedly celebrating despite, or maybe because of, his birth in a barn. I said, "My thoughts, exactly."

We didn't finish dinner on that dark and philosophical note. We ordered dessert – cheesecake for JD and chocolate cake with blood orange caramel sauce for me. That chocolate was like cream, melting around the insides of my mouth, and when I was finished, I was afraid to smile because I was sure I had lines of dark brown cake filling all the places where my teeth cozied up to each other.

"Do you like chocolate?" he said.

"Mmm."

"You look like you want to take a bath in it."

I laughed, and I didn't worry about chocolate between my teeth.

We walked outside. The air was cold and smelled clean, even though there was a steady stream of cars going past, their lights on and their exhaust visible. I stuck my hands in my pockets. The rest of me was warm, chocolate cake and coffee on the inside, my boots and leggings and long wool coat on the outside. I was glad JD didn't put his arm around me, using the cold air as an excuse. Instead, we walked to the corner, side by side with our shoulders pressed against each other. We waited for the light to turn green, then crossed, and went up half a block to the parking lot. Even though we walked quickly to keep warm, I didn't want to get to his car too fast, didn't want to get home to my condo, and then have to say goodnight.

"What do you think that woman was laughing about during dinner?" I said. "Her friends seemed like they wanted to shut her up."

"Maybe they told her it was her turn to buy dinner." He pressed the remote to unlock the doors of his SUV and walked to the passenger side to open the door for me. I climbed inside. Part of my coat dangled out, and he pushed it up and tucked it under my leg, which made me feel meltier than the chocolate cake.

It was only eight or nine blocks to my condo. If it had been spring, we could have walked to dinner. I wasn't sure whether I should invite him in to watch a movie, but I don't have a great movie collection and I don't have streaming, so I decided to wait to see what he did. It turned out he did nothing.

At the door, he didn't say anything about coming inside or calling or getting together again. He just put his arms around my waist, pulled me close, and kissed me. Long and slow. I tried to keep my mind focused on his mouth and not on phone calls or second dates, or third, depending on how you're counting. For the most part, I was successful.

"Good night," he said. He kissed my nose and walked back to his car.

Part of me was frustrated and sad that he didn't say a word, but another part of me was warm from his kiss and thought it was absolutely perfect because why spoil it with planning and talking and all of that?

I went inside and straight upstairs to talk to Simon about it. He seemed annoyed that I hadn't covered his cage, and wasn't in the mood for chirping and chattering.

CHAPTER 5

MY DATE WITH JD was on December twelfth. On December thirteenth, he called while I was finishing my lunch and asked if I'd like to come to his place a few days before Christmas. He'd make game hens, and we'd have a holiday meal. Of course I said yes. I asked what I could bring for the meal, and he said, nothing, except maybe my voracious desire for chocolate. I agreed.

The same day, Linda Birmingham had an appointment with Pastor Kate and Pastor Joe. Her appointment was at one, and I'd just hung up from JD when she came in the office door. She had hair the color of walnuts swept into a bun that was loose at the nape of her neck. Her hair was streaked with gray strands that sparkled under the fluorescent lights. She wore a camel coat and a longish dark brown skirt and camel colored UGG boots, which I thought was a great touch for a lady her age. Not that you don't want comfy boots at any age, but it was fun to see her looking half like a teenager and half like a grandmother. She smiled and looked right at me, which I'm sad to say, is a bit unusual for most of the people who come into the office. They aren't that interested in the person answering the phones and typing newsletters, they have their minds on church things or their problems, whichever it is that brought them in.

"You could be a Christmas elf with those red cheeks," said Linda.

I smiled, and I'm sure my cheeks got redder, at least my skin felt warmer. The redness was the lingering effect of talking to JD and wondering whether I should get him a gift for this *holiday dinner*. Why did things have to be so complicated? Couldn't we have gone out in October or November when I wouldn't have to consider that? I hardly knew him, but he said it was a *holiday* dinner, so I had to think of something.

Linda sat in one of the armchairs that face my desk. She didn't remove her coat, but she crossed her legs and the coat fell open, revealing more of her dark skirt and a turquoise sweater that I wouldn't have minded owning.

"I love your sweater. It looks great with your hair," I said.

"Thank you." She smiled.

Linda lived in the foothills in a house that could honestly be called an estate. I'd never been there, but I knew from the address label I stuck on her copy of the monthly newsletter that her house was at the end of a very exclusive road that wound up to a hillside that looked over the Santa Clara Valley. I probably couldn't afford that sweater.

Instead of meeting in Joe's office, Linda and the two pastors went into the conference room adjacent to Kate's office. It's a ho-hum room with inexpensive green carpet, walls painted a strange beige that's almost yellow, and sliding glass doors that look out on the ivy-covered slope. Everything about the room is pale and insti-tutional-looking, except the cherry wood conference table that could be proudly featured in an executive boardroom. Someone that died left earmarked funds for a nice conference table. Of course, they probably hoped the rest of the room would be remod-eled to fit the glamour of the table, but that still hasn't happened and, of course, the person who had such hopes is no longer available to see they're carried out.

People often leave funds to the church, and as if they're trying to control the place from beyond the grave, they specify how that money should be used. That can make for a collection of buildings and gardens that don't always look like they fit together. For example, there's the ornate concrete bench in the grove of pine trees that was supposed to be the start of a prayer garden, but after three years there's no garden, and the aroma all comes from dead pine needles that cover the ground. There's also a series of rose trees lining the path leading to the grove. They were donated in memory of a girl who was shot right in front of the concrete bench. None of it quite fits together.

Since Joe, Kate, and Linda were tucked away in the back, I got busy entering events into the calendar tool so I could print the next two months' calendars for the newsletter. I let my mind wander to my next date with JD and what I would wear, and what perfect gift I would choose that showed we were more than friends but wouldn't imply we'd had more than two dates, and would make him smile and wouldn't make him feel obligated to force a thank you but would make him amazed that I'd figured out exactly what he'd like. No pressure there. I love buying gifts, but I want them to be the right gifts. I hate the whole idea of gift cards that are so easy, and you can choose your price down to the dollar, and you don't have to go beyond thinking, *Does she prefer Mexican food or Chinese, clothes or music?* Nothing came to mind, but I had a week. It was too soon to get tense over-thinking it.

They weren't in the conference room for very long. I hadn't even finished the calendar when Joe appeared in the doorway. He looked worried. He was followed by Kate who looked confident and pleased and calm, almost grinning. Linda brought up the rear, looking the same as she had when she came in and I didn't know her at all, so I couldn't read her expression. Joe gave Linda a light hug, said, *See you Sunday,* and went into his office.

I noticed again how the fluorescent lights made the gray threads in Linda's hair sparkle. She was really a beautiful woman, and I hoped I looked as sleek and happy in my own skin when I was her age.

Kate put her hand on Linda's shoulder.

Linda looked a bit startled like she didn't want to be touched, but she didn't move away.

"Thank you for being so supportive," said Kate.

Linda made a move to get out from under Kate's hand. "You know what they say, all it takes for evil to prevail is for good men to do nothing." Her voice was soft and clear. The way she said the words sounded sweet, not critical, but she didn't smile. "It's so easy for fear and selfishness, even hatred, to take over. Especially when you have a group that thinks so much alike, they keep handing the same ideas back and forth like a holiday fruitcake."

Kate nodded.

"I saw that in Ben the other night. And the other things he said to you ..."

I agreed with her, but since I wasn't in their meeting, I figured it was best to keep my mouth shut. That's the hard part about working in any office, in a clerical position. There are times when people treat you like a piece of furniture. They have in-depth conversations right in front of your desk. They act like you aren't there, going on about their interests, even gossiping. It's kind of strange because it's insulting, and yet it's also entertaining because they're so oblivious, it doesn't seem to occur to them that they're giving you all kinds of information they might not want you to have. Not that I can always do anything with that information, but still. When I worked at TDP, I heard about people who screwed up projects and were going to lose their jobs, people who had stabbed others in the back, taking credit for something they hadn't done. One time I heard about a woman who had been laid off and was suing the company because her co-worker in the same group wasn't laid off, and the second woman was sleeping with their boss. I never heard the outcome, and I still wonder if she was able to stand up to a billion dollar company and all their lawyers and win. I hope she did.

I ran my fingers along the seven earrings in my left ear, trying to find something to keep me from feeling like I was just sitting there eavesdropping at my own desk. If I turned and started typing, I'd call attention to myself, and ditto for getting up and moving around. It was kind of awkward, and yet I had no reason to feel awkward, I wasn't the one having a private conversation in a somewhat public place.

"I've always said this church took a bad turn from the day they dug up the first shovel of dirt. They should have ..." said Linda.

Kate glanced at me. "Let's not dwell on something that happened sixty years ago." She started in for the shoulder patting again. She was so vigorous, I wondered if Linda felt patronized. A somewhat frightened look crossed Linda's face, her eyebrows raised slightly, and her head pulled back as if she wondered why Kate was treating her like a child.

"Well something was disturbed and we can't keep pretending ..."

"Thank you so much for your generosity. It's wonderful that you're in a position to do something that has a lot of impact."

Kate was really bent on not letting Linda finish her thoughts, but Linda didn't seem inclined to fight it. I could see she'd decided to give up on whatever it was she was trying to say.

After a moment, Kate walked to the door and opened it for Linda. She followed Linda out and closed the door behind them. That made me think of the moths, and I could see how the door slamming shut, even though it wasn't hard enough to shake the walls, fell with a fair amount of force and a moth taking a break at the wrong time would be smashed. That still didn't explain how so many had ended up there at one time. The groundskeeper had cleaned them up the day I first saw them, but I continued to think about them and found myself looking at the doorframe every time I came into the office. A couple times a day, I pulled out my smartphone and looked at the photo I'd taken. It was as if I had to remind myself I hadn't imagined the whole thing.

It was about fifteen minutes before Pastor Kate returned to the office. She settled herself in one of the armchairs and grinned again. She picked up the wood carving of a sea lion whose back she was fond of stroking while she talked to me. "Did Joe tell you what happened?"

I shook my head. Although his door stood half open, I hadn't heard a sound from his office since he went inside, not even the clack of his fingers on the keyboard.

"Linda is giving an endowment to the childcare center. Three million dollars." Kate's lips stretched so thin they were all but invisible except for a thin line of pink lipstick.

I think my mouth opened slightly and although I was aware of it and knew I should close it, my brain wouldn't focus on that because I was too busy thinking about having three million dollars to toss around. I knew Linda, and quite a few other members of Central Avenue Church, had a lot of money, far more than the already upper-middle-class incomes of the bulk of the congregation, but hearing it in a naked number like that was hard to get my head around.

"Isn't that great? The church doesn't have to approve the financial part of the plan. We can get the center running, and offer scholarships out of the endowment."

"Does that work?" I said.

Kate was nearly bouncing in the chair. "Does what work?"

"I don't want to sound negative…"

"But you do already. You sound like Joe." Her mouth was smiling, but her eyes had given up on it. She stared at me, waiting for me to argue, to prove I was undermining her excitement. "Why wouldn't it work?"

I wheeled my chair away from the desk and stood. I went to the counter near the photocopy machine and opened the bottom door. I pulled out a box of bulletin covers for the next Sunday's service. They were printed with a posed photograph of some very fierce looking angels on one side. The agenda for the service got printed on the opposite side, with additional pages inserted. Central Avenue

Church orders them from an outfit that provides covers to lots of churches, so presumably, if you attend services at any like-minded church, you'd see the same cover on any given Sunday. I loaded the stack into the copy machine and went back to my desk to print the information that would get copied on the decorative paper. I might as well photocopy and fold them while Kate talked. "They could still vote against it. The objections weren't about the money itself," I said.

"It's a private gift to the childcare center. No one will know she's made that donation. I won't ask for funding for scholarships, and the vote will pass."

"But you're deceiving them."

"I'm not. Linda asked that we keep her contribution private. People do that all the time. Some people don't need to get public attention or a pat on the head for donating a lot of money. They feel good just doing it. It's actually quite spiritual."

"But Ben …"

"Ben is one bigoted guy who swayed people into focusing on the worst side of human nature."

"How do you know what effect he had? What does Joe think?" I was surprised he hadn't come out to join the conversation. Surely he heard us talking. We weren't whispering and he wasn't making any noise that would drown our voices. Unless he was reading, he does seem to be able to lose himself in a page of words and not hear anything that's happening nearby.

"Joe doesn't like it." Kate stood. She put the sea lion back on the table between the armchairs, with more force than she should have. The table vibrated slightly.

"What doesn't he like?"

"Are you his echo chamber?" said Kate.

"No. It's just that Ben made it clear he's not objecting about the money, and I wonder if other people see it that way. Maybe it's better to start the childcare center without offering scholarships and ask them to vote on that idea again in six months or a year."

Kate folded her arms. She looks like one of those Russian stacking dolls when she does that. "Aren't you supposed to stay uninvolved in church matters?"

"I'm not getting involved. I'm just asking. I think a childcare center would be a great thing to have. All this space is wasted. When you gave that speech about how hard it is to find good childcare I could tell people paid attention. But don't they have to know what they're voting for? Otherwise, you're lying to them."

She moved closer to my desk. "Sorry. I shouldn't take it out on you. It's frustrating. This needs to move forward, and I'm not going to let a bunch of Scrooges and bigots and whatever else get in the way." She put her hands on my desk and pressed down as if she was trying to stretch her wrists. Her nails were cut like mine, with no white showing. They were smooth and clean, her fingers ringless and delicate as a child's.

I looked at Joe's half open office door and wondered if he was ever going to come out or if this was going to turn into something where Kate went plowing ahead, and he remained on the sidelines. After all, it isn't like he's necessarily her boss. Yes, he's the main pastor, but they cover different areas, and they're supposed to be a team.

"Linda is totally on the same wavelength that I am. A church is supposed to influence the community for good, to help change the world. The world is not going to change if all we do is show up every Sunday and sit in the pews, sing and listen to a sermon and drop ten bucks in the offering plate. Then we go home and watch the football game or work in the yard, eat dinner, and make sure the laundry is folded? If that's it, then why are we even here?"

Hearing her describe it made me want to cry. Is that what she thought most people's Sundays were like? Is that what hers was like? It sure didn't describe mine, except maybe the laundry folding part, although I try to do that on Saturdays so that on Sunday I can take the whole day to play and rest and totally enjoy life and the world. I suppose it doesn't always work out that way, and I suppose when you have a house and kids it's not quite that simple, but maybe it could be. "I'm not arguing with you. Or Linda," I said.

As if she hadn't even heard me, as if she was preaching to a congregation of one, Kate stepped away from my desk. Her voice got louder. "Unless we start doing something dramatic, even shocking, nothing will change. People will keep starving and dying and killing."

I wasn't sure how all of that tied into a childcare center in any specific way, but I could see the point she was trying to make. I felt the air get more dense, or maybe I felt the temperature change. I glanced at Joe's office door. He stood a few feet from the threshold and I wondered, suddenly, how long he'd been there. I thought I'd looked up a few moments earlier and he wasn't there, but now I wasn't sure. Or maybe he'd been standing near the doorway but out of my line of sight for quite some time, for the entire time.

Kate noticed me staring past her and turned toward Joe. "Are you really going to tell Linda she can't donate money to whatever project she wants?"

Joe rubbed his forefinger across the bottom of his goatee. He flicked at it as if it was itching him, or he wanted it off his face. Because his hand was there, I couldn't see the set of his mouth, so I wasn't sure if he was angry or just worried about how all this might blow up. A school for small children. It was amazing it had turned into something where you had one guy trying to get a following to make sure they kept out people he didn't approve of, and another woman who, if you looked at it from one angle, thought she could buy her way into getting what she thought was the right thing to do. There are some things you can't buy, like changing people's points of view.

"Well?" said Kate.

"There will have to be another vote."

"I want it before Christmas," said Kate.

Joe shrugged. "You can try talking to Ken Miller about setting it up, but I don't think people are going to be favorable toward what you want if they have to stuff something else into their holiday schedule. It's unlikely anyone has a free evening right before Christmas."

Kate looked like she was going to cry, her eyes shiny and her lip curled in a loose way that wasn't a smile or a frown. Or maybe she wasn't going to cry, maybe she was going to open the childcare center without getting anyone's permission. After all, she'd been working on this for over six months, and here she was, not even close to getting approval for the project. "It's so unfair. It's outrageous that all I want to do is provide a nurturing environment for twenty children and you'd think I want to level the buildings on this property and construct a strip club."

Joe laughed. I laughed, but softly, because Kate did not look amused at her own joke. She turned and walked to the door leading to the basement area.

"What are you going to do?" said Joe.

"I'm calling Ken. I'm sending an email to everyone to point out that you don't refuse to care for children when you're supposedly celebrating the birth of the most important child in the world. Someone who said we should care for children, by the way."

Joe was still picking at his beard. He looked at me, dropped his hand to his side, and went back into his office. I hoped they didn't plan the new meeting for the same night as my holiday dinner with JD. If they did, I was telling Joe I thought they could manage without a note taker. After all, it wasn't as if there were a lot of details to cover. There was only one question, and really, not much to debate.

CHAPTER 6

$\mathcal{T}$HE REST OF THE MORNING was the quietest I'd ever experienced with Joe and Kate both in their offices. Of course, it was quiet when I was there alone. But this was eerie. There were no footsteps, no sounds from Kate's office. Joe left his door open, but it was like it had been earlier, I didn't hear his fingers on the keyboard or even a soft clearing of his throat. It was as if they weren't really there.

At quarter to twelve, Joe left for lunch, saying he was going to visit a woman who just delivered twins and he'd be going home after that. He and Cindee had a few more gifts to pick up for their kids. He said he hoped the mall wasn't a zoo. I laughed. The mall is always a zoo, from the day after Thanksgiving until the weekend after the new year. Clearly, he didn't spend much time at the mall during the holiday season if he thought that just because it was a Tuesday afternoon, mall traffic would be light.

Kate left at twelve-fifteen and didn't say anything except goodbye. I wondered if she'd already sent her email. It would have been nice to know in case I got phone calls asking about it. But she didn't look like she was in the mood for questions, so I let it go. No matter what happened, I'd be able to handle it. I'm pretty good at talking my way through most situations, even if someone called and complained, or even if Ben dropped by to give a piece of his mind to Kate or Joe and got stuck with no one to hand his mind to except me.

I had a container of soup stored in the fridge in the church kitchen. Since it was drizzling outside, I would have to forego my noontime cigarette, which was fine. It was a good nudge toward quitting. Maybe I wouldn't miss it.

When I stood to go outside and up the stairs to the kitchen at the rear of the multi-purpose hall, I realized I needed to go to the restroom. I should have thought of that before Kate left. With the weather like this, it was darker than usual, even with all the fluorescent lights. And I hated having to walk through that enormous, hollow underground hall that has lots of shadowy corners, no windows, and unless the door to the other, unused office and the conference room had been left open, only a small amount of light filtered out from Kate's office into that center basement area.

The design of the ground floor is poor, not only is it oddly shaped, with these three somewhat random rooms off of the five sides, but the light switch is at the opposite side, inside the alcove that houses the restrooms. I'd asked Kate and Joe why it was such a strange layout, but neither of them knew. Neither did they really seem to know why the room was never used. I'd been planning to ask one of the long-time members these questions, but I never seemed to think of it when one of them dropped by the office. Usually, they had some kind of business, and their questions and conversation kept me from thinking about the basement floor plan.

I picked up my bag. It somehow made me feel safer, having my bag with me when I trekked across the dark, unfurnished hall. My heels echoed on the linoleum, a blackish green that added to the impression that the basement was a cave in disguise. The low ceiling made the echo sharper, closer. I hated myself for succumbing to jittery thoughts, but I turned and glanced back, even though I knew I was alone.

When I reached the far side, I stuck my arm into the alcove, felt for the switch, and flicked it on. The alcove has the women's and men's restrooms and a door to the outside that no one ever uses, but I assume that's why the light switch was at that end of the basement — it must have been used at one time.

Inside the women's restroom, it was pitch black because there aren't any windows. Carrying on the theme of poorly placed light switches, the lights inside the restrooms were operated from the same panel as the light in the alcove itself, and I'd forgotten to flick the switch for the women's. For a moment, I found myself enjoying the total lack of light. I'm not scared of the dark. Or maybe I'm not being honest. Encountering absolute darkness doesn't happen very often for a woman in the twenty-first century living in an industrialized country. There's always light bleeding from somewhere – the moon, the streetlights, cars, another room in your home. It's not scary, but it is unnerving when you actually encounter total darkness because it's so rare. Even the basement I complain about isn't solid darkness.

I went out to the alcove and turned on the light. Back inside, I opened the stall door and saw there was no toilet paper. I checked the other stall – same thing. By this time, and maybe because of all those thoughts about darkness, which had plucked at my nerves, I really had to pee. I didn't want to walk all the way to the supply cabinet, so I thought I'd check to see if the men's room had a roll to spare. I went out of the women's restroom and pushed open the door to the men's room. I thought I could grab a roll off the shelf by the sink, but of course, the men's room is laid out differently, and the sink was behind the door, and before I knew it, the door swung closed behind me, and I was in total darkness again.

I reached behind me for the handle, in a hurry to get out and turn on the light. Something brushed across my wrist. Immediately I knew it was the exact same experience I'd had in the office when Ben was there, and again right before I saw the dead moths. I wiped my hand across my wrist, trying to find the door handle at the same time. Something like strands of thread brushed across my face and down my neck. I cried out and let go of the door handle. I wiped at my neck, unsure how this cobwebby thing even got that close since my hair was down. It was almost as if something was *trying* to touch me. I'd lost my sense of where the handle was, so I batted my hand around again, trying to find it quickly, still feeling the webbing across every part of exposed skin – my hands, my wrists, my face. Then I felt it on the backs of my knees, even though I was wearing tights.

I found the handle and yanked hard, wrenching my arm socket, but I didn't care. I leaped into the alcove, blinked in the brightness, and went to the switch panel to turn on the lights in the men's room. By now, I wasn't even sure I had to pee, there were so many ripples running across my skin and through my muscles, down to my bones.

Worse than the physical torment was a darkness creeping through my head. I don't know how else to describe it. I felt sad and angry and alone all at the same time. There was an unreasonable disgust or disrespect, I guess, for all the people in the church. They all seemed selfish and ugly and self-important. I had a flashing thought that the childcare center was stupid and who needed a bunch of undisciplined kids running all over the property. I'd probably end up being forced to babysit them, eat lunch while they screamed down the hallways. I'd never felt like this before, and there was a prick of guilt, but those other thoughts lodged themselves in my brain with the same clinging stickiness of the stuff draped across my skin.

I stood for a few more seconds, wiping at my arms as if I could remove the substance plaguing me, but really, all I had now was the memory of it, and rubbing my arms wasn't going to remove the memory. Very slowly all the bad feelings and thoughts dissolved as if someone had come into my head with a whiskbroom and done a thorough sweeping.

Once my breathing slowed to a normal rate, all I heard was the silence. No footsteps, no phones ringing, no human voices.

At this point, I wondered if it would be more pleasant to get the key to the education wing and use the restroom in that building, or walk through the sanctuary sitting over my head to the restroom off the little study at the back where the pastor prepared for the worship services. But then I was embarrassed. A few cobwebs brushed across me, and now I was afraid to grab a roll of toilet paper? I could go back to the supply cupboard. All the ideas of what I could do made me feel even more ridiculous, and I decided the best thing to do was turn on the light, go into the men's room and get the freaking toilet paper like I'd planned. I wasn't going to have my mind twisting itself into a tangle of excuses. I yanked open the door of the men's room, walked inside, and grabbed two cellophane-wrapped rolls of toilet paper.

The incident nagged at me all the way back across the basement and up the outside stairs. I wished I wasn't eating by myself, that there was someone to talk to about any subject on earth besides what had just happened, even if it meant listening to Ben spout his opinions about who should be allowed in the childcare center, even if I had to listen to one of the older women in the church who has nothing to talk about except what the doctor did or did not do on her last visit and what's wrong with her ears and her stomach and nearly every other organ residing inside her body.

I poured my soup into a bowl, heated it in the microwave, and pulled my iPad out of my bag. Right then, I would have preferred something mindless, a *Cosmo* magazine shouting *Food vs. Sex, the results are in!* Or some other completely unimportant thing that they make sound critical to a woman's ability to survive in society. I wasn't sure I could get into reading a novel right now because those thread-like feelings and sensations on my skin weren't completely gone.

I'd put two spoonfuls of ham and pea soup into my mouth and

taken a sip of water when the door to the kitchen opened. It was Carlo.

"Hi," he said, but rushed on so fast, I knew the *hi* was more to get my attention than any actual greeting. "Did you cover that soup before you heated it?" he said.

I nodded.

"Someone doesn't cover their food. I'm tired of scrubbing stuff off the microwave." He frowned, pulling his chin closer to his neck so he looked like he didn't have a neck at all. "I don't like cooking my food in a dirty microwave."

"I don't think I splattered more than a drop or two."

"Pea soup looks like snot even when it's in the bowl," he said. "Stuck to the walls of the microwave, it's like someone sneezed out every ounce of mucous in their head."

I hadn't realized he was such a descriptive guy. I also wasn't sure why he was being so hostile to me. I guess he really couldn't deal with a dirty microwave.

"I'm not the janitor," he said.

I pushed my chair away from the long table, designed to seat eight, but it was the only place to eat. "I'll wipe it down," I said.

"Thank you."

"I don't expect you to clean up," I said.

"Except for dead moths."

Now I got it. "You were here, and I thought …" What had I thought? Maybe that wasn't really his job. Maybe it seemed like I thought I was too good for picking up insect carcasses. I walked to the microwave, popped open the door, and looked inside. There were a few green puddles on the turntable and a couple of green bubbles on the back wall, one with a sliver of ham stuck in the center, so it looked like an infected pimple ready to pop. Carlo's description of snot had turned my thoughts in the direction of bodily emissions. I tore a piece of paper towel off the roll hanging under the cupboard. I reached inside to wipe up the spots of soup. My sleeve pulled back on my arm, and I felt him shift his gaze to the vine tattoo running around my wrist. "There you go," I said.

"Thank you."

"And thanks for cleaning up the moths. I suppose I could have done it myself."

"It's not your job either."

He was very focused on roles and responsibilities. It would be interesting to see how he reacted to a childcare center that would surely bring extra debris to the gardens. It might be that there were all kinds of slender threads running through this establishment that made people less than excited about opening a school, depending on their particular areas of concern. The school might have their own microwave for the kids' lunches, but the teachers might use this one. Then he wouldn't know so easily where to point the finger if he found it riddled with dried food.

"That's quite an elaborate tattoo," he said.

"Thank you."

"What does it stand for?"

"It doesn't stand for anything. I like plants."

"Oh."

"None of my kids better ink up their skin, deface what God created. It's like graffiti."

Clearly, his first comment had not been a compliment. "I don't think tattoos deface my body."

"They're not necessary. And you shouldn't mess with what is."

"Of course they're not necessary. But neither are rings." I pointed at his wedding ring.

"That's not permanent," he said. He unwrapped the plastic covering his bowl of rice and chicken and pale green broccoli florets. He stuck the bowl in the microwave and laid the plastic over the top like he was spreading a tablecloth. He closed the door and pushed the button for auto-cook.

"Do you ever take it off?"

"No."

I smiled. "Anyway, I should have left a note for the janitor to remove the moths, but you were there and they gave me the creeps, so I wanted them out of there as fast as I could, and you were the first person I thought of. Gardens, weeds, moths – in my mind, I thought they went together."

The microwave hummed. He pulled a fork out of his lunch bag.

"I still can't figure out how so many of them were caught in that spot, or why no one noticed."

"No one would slam the door on ten moths and not notice," he said.

"Do you see a lot of moths in the gardens?"

"Quite a few. Leaving the lights on in the corridors and at the front of the sanctuary all night attracts a lot of moths. Mosquito-eaters too."

The microwave bell chimed. He popped open the door. He lifted the limp plastic off the top and carried it to the sink. Moisture dripped on the floor as he walked, but he didn't seem to notice. He opened the door under the sink and dropped the plastic into the trash. He returned to the opposite counter, pulled off a paper towel to hold his bowl, and carried it to the doorway. He paused. "Do you mind if I join you?"

"Of course not." I thought it was funny that he asked. He might have realized he was rude, first with the soup stuck to the walls of the microwave and then with his comments about my tattoo. Of course, while I ate, my sleeve would naturally ride up my arm and he'd have to look at the shades of green and gray ink that formed my tattoo. He wouldn't see the ladybugs on the back of my neck until it was summer and I wore my hair in a ponytail again.

"How do you think all those moths got in there?" I said. I scooped up a spoon full of soup. It was still nice and warm.

He shrugged and stabbed a piece of chicken and a piece of broccoli with a stem long enough to make it look like a miniature tree. The broccoli split in half and fell off the stack he was trying to build on the tines of his fork. I had to look away. It looked so limp, like a tree falling apart because worms were consuming the wood.

"Some people think moths are dead relatives returning to visit," said Carlo.

"Like ghosts?"

He made another stab at the broccoli. "I don't believe in ghosts, except for the Holy Ghost." He set his fork against the edge of the bowl and put the first two fingers of his right hand on the center of his forehead. He tapped his breastbone and each shoulder, crossing himself.

His attitude made no sense at all. Could you call something a holy *ghost* and then say in the same sentence you didn't believe in ghosts? I didn't want to point out the flaw in his logic because we were getting along just fine after his initial growling about my lack of cleanliness and implying my tattoos had wrecked my body.

"Whether they're dead relatives of someone here, or not, how did they all land in the doorframe and get smashed?"

He had picked up his fork, then set it down again. He put his elbows on either side of his bowl and leaned forward, his fingers spread across the table around the front of the bowl. "I don't know how they got there or how they all died at once or why no one noticed them since they were dead a long time. But I know it means something bad."

"How do you know?"

"Moths are ugly creatures. They fly at you and beat their wings too fast, and they hide in houses where things aren't properly cleaned and aired out."

"Why does that mean something bad?"

Carlo shoveled the rest of the rice and chicken into his mouth as fast as he could chew and swallow. He'd given up on the broccoli, and a pile grew at the side of his bowl, limp and sagging over each other like a pile of weeds, decaying on a humid summer day. "They're creatures associated with death. I don't know what they mean in this case, but what you found in that doorway isn't normal."

261

"You're scaring me."

"Why is that?"

"Because there are other things that don't seem normal. When I first saw the moths, I felt like I ran into a cobweb, that the strands were sticking to my arms and face. But when I tried to brush it off, nothing was there."

"You're confusing spiders and moths."

I slurped up the soup on my spoon. "No I'm not. I said it *felt* like cobwebs, not that it *was* cobwebs. And this sticky stuff grabbed onto me two other times. Once when I was at my desk and then right before I came up for lunch today. In the men's restroom in the basement."

"Why were you in the men's restroom?"

"I had to get an extra roll of toilet paper."

He stared at me. He looked into his bowl as if he hoped there was more to eat, but the chicken and rice were gone. The smell of the broccoli seemed to rise up into his face because he pulled back slightly and wrinkled his nose. When it gets overcooked like that, it smells funny, more pungent. He stood and carried the bowl to the kitchen. I heard the water running and then he turned on the garbage disposal.

He came back and stood in the doorway. Since I was facing away from the kitchen, I couldn't see him. "I need to get back to work. Thanks for eating lunch with me."

"Any time." I didn't turn to look.

"If you find any more moths, call the janitor."

"Okay."

It seemed that Carlo thought there was something ominous here, but I wasn't sure if he knew what that might be, or if he had a thing with moths, so he was assuming something ominous. Maybe I was on edge because of all my encounters with delicate yet surprisingly strong threads wrapping themselves around my body, creeping into my brain.

CHAPTER 7

I DIDN'T SEE KATE or Joe the rest of that day. The next morning, Kate's champagne-colored Camry was in the gravel parking strip in front of the sanctuary when I arrived at work. Downstairs, the office door was locked. I opened it, checked the frame for moths, half expecting to see a hundred of them lining the doorway, their wings crumbling, heads and torsos turned to fur, but it was wiped clean, just as Carlo had left it when he used bleach to wipe off all the stuck-on bits of broken wings and smashed bodies and tiny threads of legs.

I put my bag in the bottom desk drawer, filled a mug with coffee, and walked through the basement area to Kate's office. Her door was partially open. It usually is. I think she likes to hear what's going on and doesn't feel safe with it closed and that cavernous room between her and everyone else. In some ways, it could be viewed as a little insulting that Joe has this nice office right off the main office and she's stuck in the back of this basement, clearly not as important as the main pastor. But there was no other choice.

Her office was filled with sunlight. It was one of those winter days that makes you glad to live in California because looking out the window, you can't even tell it's cold, everything is so bright and full of life, ivy covering the slope. If you stand close to the glass doors and look up, you can still see a few stubborn rose blooms.

I knocked on the partially open door and she looked up, not at all startled because the tap of my boots across the linoleum floor had announced my arrival. Then I wondered why her head was down as if she didn't know I was coming. Did she want me to know I was interrupting her? The entire surface of her desk was covered by a large piece of poster board, and she'd stacked her stapler and cup of pens and calendar on one of the bookshelves, shoving the jar of paintbrushes and bottles of paint to one side to make room.

"What are you working on?" I said.

She stuck the cap on a red felt pen and shoved it in her pocket. She lifted the sheet of paper and turned it so I could see. In large red block letters, carefully filled in with strokes of felt pen, it said, *Bring the little children to me.* Below it, she'd glued a photograph, clipped from a catalog, of a little girl's tennis shoes.

"What's that for?"

"To announce the special meeting for a final vote. I convinced Joe to have it four days before Christmas. I think people will be in a more charitable mood."

Or more stressed out, adding one more thing to their schedules, but I didn't point that out.

As if she read my thoughts, Kate said, "The meeting will only be twenty minutes. I'll give a brief overview, lay on the guilt, and then we'll vote."

I sipped my coffee and leaned against the doorframe. She laid the poster board back on the desk, uncapped a light brown felt pen, and began filling in the outline of a teddy bear she'd drawn near the top edge.

"You think they'll vote for it if you make them feel guilty?" I said.

"Not in an obvious way, not being harsh." She waved her arm toward the ceiling as if she was pointing at the sanctuary overhead. "We can't let one or two people with icy hearts dictate our mission."

"It's not just one or two people."

She shrugged and pressed harder so the broad tip of the pen squeaked on the poster board, sending chills along my arms and up the back of my neck. It felt as if the ladybugs tattooed there were skittering along the knobs of my spine where it entered the base of my skull. I set my mug on the shelf near the door and rubbed my neck.

"Do you have a headache?"

"No, the felt pen gives me the shivers when it squeaks like that."

"Oh, sorry."

"I've been getting the shivers a lot lately."

"Why's that?" She capped the brown pen and picked up a dark blue one.

"Have you noticed a lot of cobwebs around here?"

"No."

"I don't mean cobwebs, exactly. Something that feels like cobwebs. I keep running into these sticky string-like things, but when I try to brush them off, nothing's there." I realized the minute I said this that I sounded deranged.

She didn't break the pace of her pen strokes and didn't indicate with even a glance that she thought I was crazy. "I have no idea what you're talking about," she said.

"It happened first when Ben was here the day after the vote failed. And another time when I was walking up to the office door, right before I found all those moths. Then yesterday, I was in the men's restroom and ..."

"Why were you in the men's restroom?"

"I had to get a roll of toilet paper."

Kate kept her pen moving in steady, even strokes. "So if it wasn't cobwebs, what do you think it was?"

"I don't know. I keep getting these creepy sensations, bad feelings, stuff sticking to me, tickling my skin."

She set the felt pen on the desk without replacing the cap. She sat back in her chair and folded her arms. "Don't start going on about ghosts again. Please."

"Did I mention ghosts?"

"I can tell that's where you're headed. And just because they found the bones in that area doesn't mean anything."

"They found a body?"

She glanced at the window. "Two bodies — an adult holding the bones of an infant. They found them when they started digging the foundation for this building. But there's no ghost."

"Does anyone know why they were buried there?"

"How would anyone know that for sure?" said Kate.

"So who do people say they were?"

"It was a long time ago. It's just stories," she said.

"Why don't you want to tell me?" I said.

"It's just a story. And Linda, to be honest, twists it into something it's not. I don't want to talk about it."

I picked up my coffee mug. Part of me wanted to walk out right then and think over what she'd just said. In her effort to divert me from thinking my experience was supernatural, she'd explained quite clearly that it was. I smiled and felt a small laugh poking me in the ribs, but I suppressed it. Kate didn't tend to see the humor in the same situations I did. In fact, she's quite serious, which makes her not as popular with the kids she's supposed to be serving, but does make her very passionate and determined to accomplish her goals, which is good. But it would be great if she lightened up a bit.

"Has anyone else felt weird things down here?

"It has nothing to do with any lingering spirits. Did Linda put that idea in your head?"

I really wanted to laugh. That's what happens when you're so determined to force things in your own direction, sometimes, you end up doing the opposite. Now I knew that whatever Linda was trying to say when Kate kept interrupting her, must have been about a lingering spirit. "I definitely felt some strange things back there," I said. "And it wasn't just that stuff, like cobwebs on my skin. It was something else. Something, a mood, terrible thoughts that made me feel very bad for a few minutes."

Kate actually looked sympathetic. She looked a little surprised too, her mouth opened as if she was going to say something, but she paused before a sound made its way out. I had the distinct feeling she realized for the first time that I had complicated feelings. That I wasn't just a dumb kid with tattoos and too many earrings, smoking cigarettes, folding newsletters into packets, answering the phones, and spending far too much time thinking and talking about ghosts. That I had a brain.

"Obviously, you're a very sensitive person," she said. "And you think you see things, and you think you know things or pick up on things that others don't."

Okay, maybe she didn't dismiss me as much as I'd assumed, maybe she just acted that way to try to assert her authority.

"But there's no evil spirit and the opposition to the childcare center is nothing but pure human selfishness. There's no spirit from the past, or ghost, or whatever, influencing people."

"Is that what Linda was trying to say yesterday?"

"Forget about all that. Remember, you're not supposed to get involved in church business."

"That's kind of difficult when it happens right in front of my desk, and I'm required to attend meetings and take notes."

"Then just take notes. You don't have to provide editorial comments."

"I felt something very disturbing, and I'm trying to figure out what it was."

"It's your imagination."

"No, it wasn't."

She lifted the poster to study it from a different angle. Without bothering to look at me, she said, "I should get back to work."

If she thought she was going to shut me up and make me stop thinking about the things I'd experienced, she didn't know me and my intrusive behavior very well at all.

I went back to the front office, reached under my desk for my bag, slung it over my shoulder, and went outside. I wanted a cigarette, and I wanted to think about whether it would be too bold, too nosey, too upsetting to Pastor Joe, or jeopardize my job if I called Linda and asked her a bit about the bones of people buried on the property and the *bad start* to this church. Clearly, Linda thought about it enough that she'd mentioned it to Kate in the past. I didn't blame Kate for wanting to ignore it. She's a very practical woman, and that's good. If you're going to start a childcare program, work out all those details to get something like that up and running, not to mention keeping it going, it's important to be focused on down to earth things. But for a woman teaching children and teenagers about the supernatural, she sure had a tremendous amount of disdain for it. I guess it's not the kind of supernatural that fits her belief system — the same avoidance I'd observed with Joe.

The sky was that crystalline blue that makes you feel like crying because it heightens all the colors until they're sharp and so beautiful that you chastise yourself for how often you ignore the earth and all the amazing things about it — blue skies and trees and birds, and even the weather. It was so cold I wished I had my mittens, but it's nearly impossible to smoke a cigarette with mittens on. And probably quite dangerous to be working with a flame and fluffy wool.

I jogged up the stairs. My messenger bag flapped against my hip in a way that hurt, but I really wanted to get away from that basement with its sticky threads and dead moths and unearthed skeletons. It felt good to be moving, to feel my heartbeat pick up the pace, and to breathe in the burning pain of all that cold air. By the time I reached the top of the steps and started along the path, lined with roses, toward the education building and out to the parking lot, my fingertips were white and my nose was numb.

When the flame hit the end of my cigarette, I took a long, slow drag. Non-smokers are probably disgusted by the pleasure of that, inhaling the smoke, feeling it wind its way through your brain, instantly calming you and pulling you into every facet of the moment, the taste, the smoke, the breath moving in your lungs, but it's one of those things in life that's quite enjoyable, even if it's deadly – like eating a super-sized order of fries from McDonald's.

Carlo was working at the front of the property, pruning dead pods off the rose bushes. It's hard to believe there would be roses in December, but in California, they last most of the year if you keep them pruned so new blooms are produced. He hadn't seemed to notice me pass by, and that was fine. I wasn't in the mood for conversation. Although I also wasn't in the mood to be alone. It was one of those times I really missed Fred, the former groundskeeper. We hadn't known each other very long when he was murdered, but we used to take smoking breaks nearly every day during the six or seven weeks I did know him, and even though he was nearly eighty and I'm only twenty-seven, we had a great connection. What I loved about Fred was we could stand and smoke and enjoy our companionship. We didn't need to talk nonstop. He was an easy guy to know, and the empty spot he left was much larger than I would have expected. I wondered if he'd known about the bodies buried beneath the basement. Somehow, I think he would have mentioned them if he had.

It only took me three puffs to decide I was definitely calling Linda. I didn't care if I was supposed to mind my own business, or if I was stirring up some kind of trouble. It was malicious of Kate to tempt me like that and not tell me any details. Of course, she'd assumed Linda had already told me about it, so why not follow that through? I had the definite impression that Linda would know immediately what I'd experienced. Maybe she could even explain the moths. Or maybe that was a huge leap of wishful thinking because I wanted them explained and no one could.

By the time I was back at my desk, it was nearly eleven, which seemed a perfect time of day for calling an older woman. She would be long past completing whatever it was she did to get herself going in the morning, she wouldn't be eating lunch, and she certainly wouldn't be napping. I looked up her number and punched it into the phone. She didn't answer until the third ring and I was almost ready to give up, debating whether or not I should leave a message because what would I say? *I'm calling to find out if there's an angry spirit throwing around sticky fibers and making me feel hateful and killing moths, and I heard you might know something about skeletons underneath the church basement, and I'm wondering if all these things are related?* I was leaning toward not leaving a message when she picked up the phone.

When she said *hello*, her voice was clear and strong and didn't sound at all like she was seventy, not that the voice of a seventy-year-old woman is supposed to tremble, it's just that she sounded young. Vibrant. Maybe I'm being a total bigot in even thinking these things, falling prey to ageism.

"Hi Linda. Do you mind if I call you by your first name? This is Madison Keith, the administrative assistant at the church."

"Hi, Madison. I know who you are, and of course you can call me Linda. Everyone does except my doctor, and who wants to think about doctors on a gorgeous day like this?"

I smiled even though she couldn't see me. It happened naturally, without thinking, and I knew instantly that we were kindred spirits. I couldn't wait to ask her my questions. "It's a little strange that I'm calling when I don't know you that well, but I'll jump right in. Pastor Kate mentioned they found some bones, or skeletons, when they were building the church. She said you knew all about it. Not that she suggested I call you. She assumed I'd heard about it from you and I haven't, so I was wondering ..."

"Do you have plans for lunch? Why don't I come over to the church, and we can eat together in the fellowship hall, and I'll tell you all about it."

"Sure. That would be terrific," I said.

"What time do you take your lunch break?"

"Any time, really."

"I was just fixing mine. I'll pack it up and be there in twenty minutes. Does that sound okay?"

I said yes, and we hung up. So much for calling at eleven not disturbing her lunch. If you have all day and no employer dictating your schedule, I guess you have a lot more freedom to eat when you're hungry, and eleven seemed as good a time as any.

* * *

LINDA WALKED INTO the main office at eleven twenty-nine. A picnic basket hung over her arm. A blue checkered cloth poked out from under the wicker flaps. She wore a pale pink cape with a hood falling down the back, and even though it was the wrong color, my first thought was of Little Red Riding Hood.

We walked up the stairs together. As we made our way along the path, I thought even more of Red Riding Hood because Linda bounced on the balls of her feet as she walked, which gave the impression of skipping along the path. She told me she'd brought chocolate chip cookies for our dessert and then I stopped thinking about Red Riding Hood.

Once we were settled at one of the long tables in the fellowship hall, I pulled out my cheese and tomato sandwich. Linda's avocado and bacon sandwich with lots of sprouts looked very good. The fellowship hall is a strange place for one or two people to eat lunch, rattling around in a room built to accommodate 150 people, but there's no table in the kitchen since it's designed strictly to prepare food for serving meals to a crowd.

"Why are you interested in the bones?" she said without skipping a beat after spreading the contents of her basket on the table — sandwich, juice-in-a-box, red grapes, and a tin with reindeer on it that presumably contained the cookies. It was a good-sized tin. I was looking forward to dessert already.

I told her about my experiences. She nibbled her sandwich and listened to me ramble on without interrupting. By the time I described each strange event in detail, she had finished her sandwich and I'd eaten only three bites of mine. I figured I'd catch up while she told her story.

"When I told Kate what happened in the restrooms, she didn't want to discuss it, and right away she asked me if I'd been talking to you. Which of course made me want to talk to you."

Linda laughed. "There are some strange things about this church."

"How long have you been a member?"

"Sixty years. I started coming here when I was a teenager."

"How did they find the bones?"

"It happened when they started digging the foundation for the new sanctuary. Originally we had services in this building. In 1953 they decided to build a real sanctuary. I remember that day like it was last week. I can still see those skeletons lying there."

"You actually saw them?"

"It was during the summer, so some of us kids hung out here every day watching the construction. The equipment was roaring, and then suddenly it was deathly quiet. One of the workers yelled, and we all went running over. They tried to keep us away, but we wanted to see. It was so sad. Seeing that skeleton cradling the newborn. It was so tiny, the baby's bones so small, like a bird."

"What did they do?"

"The police came and got them, but the conclusion was that they were so old, it wasn't worth investigating."

I took a bite of my sandwich and chewed slowly. The tomato was cool and refreshing.

"I've always thought their spirits won't let go of this place," said Linda.

"No wonder Kate didn't want me to talk to you. She hates thinking about the idea of people's spirits hanging around. So does Joe. I don't understand why they're so opposed to even talking about it."

"It doesn't fit what they believe," said Linda. "It could be that it frightens them."

"If you don't believe the same things, why do you keep going to church here?"

"There aren't two people on the entire planet that believe exactly the same thing," she said. "Every single person in this church has different views in one way or another. All you can do is find people that think like you in the ways that are the most important and try to ignore the rest." She laughed. "Try."

"Except restless spirits are hard to ignore," I said.

"They're impossible to ignore."

"Why are Joe and Kate so opposed to even talking about it?"

"Maybe they think talking about it proves it's real."

I finished the first half of my sandwich and tried to digest it and what she was saying at the same time. It just made me feel full. I wrapped the plastic around the second half of my sandwich to save for later.

"Aren't you going to finish?" said Linda.

"Do I not get a cookie if I don't finish my sandwich?"

She laughed. "No. I was worried I said something that upset you." Your eyes looked tired for a minute.

"Not at all," I said. "So you think they're haunting the church? For all these years?"

"It hasn't been constant. It's as if something stirs them up from time to time."

"What stirred them up?"

"Ben. His hateful attitude."

"Really?"

"Not just Ben. In fact maybe not Ben at all. I think it's the people who think the same way that Ben does, but they hide it. I've noticed over the years that when people want to build walls, isolate themselves, shut out other people, unusual things seem to happen."

"What unusual things?"

"The cobwebby feeling you described. Insect infestations. Most people dismiss it because you could explain them all as natural phenomena."

I put my sandwich back in my bag. Now I really wasn't hungry. I wasn't sure whether I wanted a cookie. My skin felt crawly just thinking about the cobwebs, swarms of insects. "Do you mean moths?"

"Have you seen an extraordinary number of moths?"

I told her about the bodies in the doorframe. She nodded but didn't say anything.

"What does it all mean?"

"It's hard to say for sure."

"Why is it happening to me?"

Linda picked up her napkin and patted her forehead. She put it down and lifted the cape off her shoulders. "It's warm in here."

I didn't think it was that warm, but I didn't want to get off track, so I didn't say anything. I sipped my water and waited. She didn't speak. She looked past me into the kitchen.

"Why doesn't anyone else notice?" I said.

"No one else saw the moths?"

"Carlo did. So did Joe and Kate, but it didn't bother them that so many died at once. They didn't think there was anything odd about it."

"It's easy to put something out of your mind and not let it trouble you if you think you won't like where your questions might lead," said Linda.

"It makes my head hurt. The cobwebs, the moths, the skeletons. A baby."

"Like I said, the police didn't investigate. They didn't have all the technical stuff we have now, and they figured it was so long ago."

"I nodded."

"But I was a curious girl."

"Like me."

She smiled. "Exactly like you." Her smile slid away. "I talked to some older people who had lived in this area all their lives. One woman told me about the family that used to own a lot of land around here. About fifty acres. She gave me some old journals. They were written by a woman — a girl really — she was seventeen. She fell in love with a Native American man who worked in her family's orchard. She got pregnant. The day she gave birth, her brother went to her room to visit her before anyone else in the family. He asked to hold the child. He smothered the baby — a little girl — right in front of his sister. Her journals were filled with gruesome poetry about the child's death."

I'm sure my mouth was hanging open because Linda paused.

"Are you okay?" she said after a minute.

I nodded.

"Her brother buried her child on their land, he decreed the baby couldn't have a proper burial because she didn't have a proper father. He told everyone the baby was born dead. The midwife didn't contradict him."

"Why would she go along with that?"

"Things were different then, people were different. They didn't usually challenge authority, especially women. When his sister screamed and cried, he told everyone she was ranting because of her grief. She was so close to her brother, they assumed he was telling the truth. Or maybe they didn't want to know any different. They didn't want an illegitimate child, a mixed-race child, any more than he did."

"Who did the other bones belong to? The ones holding the baby?"

"A few months after he killed the child, the brother got a bad case of the flu. He had a fever, with delirium."

"He died?"

"His sister smothered him when he was too weak to fight back."

I folded my hands and rested my arms against the table. I squeezed my fingers until I could feel the bones, then quickly unfolded them. "How did they get buried together?"

Linda shrugged. "No one seemed to know. She had some poems in her book that were quite dark, and very difficult to interpret. But they could make you think her lover helped her dig up her brother's body and put it in the grave with her child."

"And you think the brother is haunting the church?"

"Haunting is a strong word. But he was a cruel man. A man with a lot of hatred."

"If he's not haunting, what do you think it is?"

"There are so many things we don't see or aren't aware of. If solid things aren't really solid, made of atoms and all that, how do we know un-solid things, like hate or murder, or injustice don't have a tangible form? I think that man's hatred, his racism, lingered after he was gone."

I really could not believe I was hearing all of this from a member of Central Avenue Church. She was the complete opposite of Joe, with his repeated suggestion that only the gullible believe in the possibility of ghosts, that visiting spirits aren't to be talked about, that considering supernatural beings was anti-god. Linda had clearly thought a lot about this, and I suddenly realized she was enjoying talking to me. There probably weren't many people in the church who shared her beliefs, and I could imagine the reaction she usually got to speculating about the source of bad feelings. "Something else happened when I felt those cobweb-like strings in the men's room," I said.

"What's that?" She pulled the tin toward her and popped off the lid.

I looked at the cookies, layered over each other, large, pale brown with dark spots of chocolate. The edges folded down slightly, which meant they were soft. Instantly, the full feeling disappeared.

She pushed the tin to the space between us. I took a cookie. "Right after those cobwebs attacked me."

"Attacked you?"

"Yes. It felt like they plunged out of the ceiling and grabbed at my skin."

Linda ran her fingertips through her hair, lifting off a piece that had fallen across her forehead.

I wondered if talking about threads adhering themselves to my arms made her skin tingle because she ran her fingertips across her forehead again, like she thought the piece of hair was still there.

"Right after that, I had these terrible feelings, not like anything I've ever had before," I said.

"What do you mean?"

"Bad thoughts flooded into me at once, uncontrollable sadness, thinking about how horrible death is, feeling like I hated everyone and everything." Tears came into my eyes. I felt a little bit ashamed telling her those things, although it wasn't as if those were my normal feelings. That's one reason why they'd been so disturbing.

The door from the corridor into the kitchen opened. Linda reached out and grabbed a cookie as if it was her last chance to get one. She took a big bite and chewed.

"Are you filling her head with ghost stories?" Kate's voice was loud. She laughed, but the tone was high pitched and sharp. Kate was in an awkward spot. Linda had given all that money to the childcare program, was almost as excited about the project as Kate was, but she harbored ideas that Kate considered fairy tales at best, delusional at worst.

The room was silent while I ate my cookie. I drank a few sips of water, wishing I had a cup of coffee. Somehow water takes away some of the sugary, soft comfort that cookies offer. I'm not sure why that is. I don't know if it's programming or habit that makes things go together, or if they really have some kind of connection. Although what the connection might be with cookies and coffee, I have no idea. And quite a few people don't like coffee at all, so it's not as if there's some chemical combination that makes them fit together. Still, I wanted coffee. I wondered if Linda would offer a few cookies for me to take with me so I could have one with an afternoon cup of coffee. Surely she couldn't eat everything in that tin herself.

Kate pulled out a chair and sat down. She reached for a cookie, took several bites, chewed very slowly, almost as if she was moving in slow motion, and said, "What did I miss?"

Linda smiled, but her eyes looked sad. "Nothing you haven't heard before."

Kate nodded. "Why don't we focus on the next vote for the childcare center instead of horror stories from the past."

I thought that was a very clever way for her to dismiss it without offending Linda. She acknowledged that a crime had been committed. At the same time, she skipped right over Linda's suggestion that any spirits from that horrendous murder lingered on the church's property. More than anything, I wanted Kate to go away so Linda and I could continue talking about what happened all those years ago, and more importantly, what was happening now. But she wasn't going anywhere. She took another cookie. "Don't you agree? Whatever happened then is terrible, but all we can do is move forward in life. Nothing gets accomplished by dwelling on the past."

"Sometimes the past explains the present," said Linda.

Kate nodded. "Good point."

I felt queasy, and it wasn't the rush of sugar. You always hear how money affects people, but I didn't expect Kate to turn into someone who was so desperately and obviously trying to placate someone with a lot of money. It was kind of depressing and embarrassing to watch, although depressing in a more casual way, not in the way of that dark mood that wrapped itself around me in the basement, trying to suffocate me. It was so bad, and I could still remember it so clearly, I didn't want to use that restroom again.

I pushed back my chair and stood. I took another cookie.

"Don't go," said Linda.

"I need to get back to work. My lunch break is half an hour."

Kate didn't disagree, although she could have dismissed the idea that my schedule had to be so rigid. There had been days when I ate my sandwich or a cup of noodles at my desk.

"Would you like to meet for coffee after you get off work?" said Linda. She pressed the lid back on the tin. "We could finish our conversation."

So we weren't finished. "Sure."

She handed the tin to me. "These are for you."

"The whole thing? I can't eat all those."

"I bet you can. You're young, you're thin."

I still didn't take it from her.

"I have lots more at home."

I took the tin. "Thank you."

She stood and wrapped her cape around her shoulders. Kate was still nibbling her cookie, looking smug, I thought, at having blown up the conversation, ended our lunch, and gotten a cookie out of the deal. But she had to know she hadn't put a stop to our discussion of ghosts and long-forgotten crimes.

CHAPTER 8

KATE'S FACE WAS AS RED as her holiday sweater. It made her look like a light bulb because her scalp shone slightly through her extremely pale blonde hair. "How did he find out?" she said. She stared at Joe, her eyes glassy.

Pastor Joe stood in the doorway to his office. The color of his face was the exact opposite of Kate's, white enough that he looked as though he wanted to be sick to his stomach. "I told you keeping Linda's contribution a secret was the wrong thing to do."

"It was the right thing to do," said Kate. "That's how she wanted it, and it was very gracious of her, not to want to strut around, crowing about how generous she is."

Joe shrugged. His black hair, sprinkled with gray in his sideburns and goatee, softening the hardness of the black, and his black turtleneck and black slacks, made him seem like anything but the pastor of a suburban church – a film director, a painter, maybe even a hitman, not that I know what kind of outfits hitmen wear, but I could argue it would be black slacks and a black shirt. Although a hitman, or hitwoman, would probably wear jeans so she could crawl around inside abandoned buildings or seedy hotels or wherever it is they ply their trade.

"So how did he find out?" Kate took a step closer to Joe, tilting her head up in an attempt to look him in the eye.

"Linda made the first installment on her gift, and she told Michelle the funds were earmarked."

"Why would she do that? She wanted it kept quiet."

"Not as much as you did. There wouldn't be a problem if you weren't trying to circumvent the process," said Joe. "The treasurer has to know what account the money goes to. I told you it wasn't right."

"Don't be so self-righteous. You've never been inclined to keep a secret from an antagonistic person?"

"I don't think I have," said Joe.

Kate raised her eyebrows.

I knew she wanted to say something, but it was clear her mind was not providing an example to throw in his face, so she just kept her eyebrows lifted for an extraordinarily long time, hoping he would remember a slip-up on his own and admit she was right without her having to come up with a solid fact to stick into his ribs like a shiv.

After a moment, she walked to the armchair closest to the door to the basement area and flopped down. "Why did Michelle tell Ben? Why would she tell anyone? That shows a complete lack of discretion."

"You're putting blame on everyone but yourself," said Joe. "If you weren't trying to pull a fast one, there wouldn't be a problem."

"I'm not trying to pull a fast one." Kate's voice was a whisper, hoarse and quivering slightly. "I'm trying to meet a need in this community, and all I wanted was to offer an opportunity for kids whose families don't have money. Is that so wrong?"

"Of course not," said Joe. "But you have to work with the individuals who are part of this church. You have to compromise. I've told you from the beginning, change comes slowly, and when you try to force it down people's throats, they choke."

I laughed. Both of them turned and looked at me. I had the

distinct impression they'd completely forgotten I was sitting there. Like I said, I'm a fixture. It didn't stop their conversation for more than half a second. Neither one laughed, or smiled, they went right on as if I was a light that had blinked on the verge of going out or an unexpected hiss from the heater.

"So you think only rich kids should get to have quality child-care?" said Kate.

"He didn't say that at all," I said.

They both looked at me again. Joe smiled and I imagined Kate's pouty lips were her way of reminding me that she thought I was his *echo chamber*. I'm not anyone's *echo chamber*, I just don't like it when people aren't accurate in their repetition of what someone has said, putting words in their mouths that suit their own agenda, twisting things into something that wasn't intended. Since neither of them spoke, shocked, I suppose, that I'd burst in where I didn't belong, I forged ahead. "He's saying you have to be patient."

"I have been patient," said Kate. "I've worked on this project, gotten support, spent six months helping people understand the goals. We've had multiple meetings, and one cold-hearted man is able to sabotage the whole thing. It shouldn't be like that."

"The problem is," I said, "It's not just one guy. If Ben were alone in his views, they would have voted to open the childcare center."

"Madison's right," said Joe. He walked over and sat in the chair next to Kate. He leaned forward so he was looking right into her eyes. "Why don't you take a step back. Get a list of things people object to and start looking at how to address those."

Kate closed her eyes. She wore pale beige eyeshadow. The coffee color contour shadow in the crease of her lid had congealed into a dark line that made her look tired and a little frightening as if her eyes were still open, but missing the iris and pupil. I had to close my own eyes because it creeped me out so badly. No one spoke for several minutes, and I didn't want to break the silence because I'd already intruded more than I should have.

After a minute or two, I opened my eyes.

"You know Madison, you are right," said Kate. "Half this church doesn't want to open the childcare center, for one reason or another. Ben is so vocal and so obnoxious, so ... I lost sight of that. There are a lot of people who don't support it, whether they agree with him or have other reasons. It could be pure laziness for all I know. Maybe I should give up. It would be better to put my energy somewhere else. Find a small group of people who have a vision for helping the community and see what other organizations we can join with who do want to do something worthwhile. Instead of banging my head against a brick wall."

I felt bad for Kate. She was the one doing the right thing, trying so hard to help people do what their beliefs told them to do – reach out beyond their own lives to make someone else's life a little better. All she wanted was to offer care for a few children who might not have other resources. It was actually a little frightening that such a large group of them was opposed to doing that. And it wasn't right how she was ending up looking like the bad guy. Sure, she shouldn't have tried to keep secrets, but it wasn't as if she was hiding some-thing evil. And Linda had wanted her gift to be private. What a mess. I felt a little bit bad about jumping all over Kate for being inaccurate.

Joe was staring past my desk at the picture window. A figure passed by, shadowy behind the blinds. The office door opened and Ben stepped inside.

Kate's eyes popped open. She stood as if the opening of her eyes had pulled a mechanism that drew her to her feet.

"You're out of line," said Ben. "Nothing good can be built on a deceitful foundation."

Kate opened her mouth, but before she could do more than grunt, Ben interrupted. "I didn't come here to debate. I'm dropping off gifts for the toy program and I saw your car. I wanted you to know I'm very disappointed. I thought this was a place where we discussed our views honestly and let the majority decision prevail. No matter how right you think you are, the program is not pleasing to God if you lie about it."

"I'm not lying," said Kate. "You …"

Ben opened the door. "I said I'm not going to debate. I think you should search your heart and think about whether your desire to hide what's going on, to open the door to people who are breaking the laws of this country, is a Godly attitude. If you and Linda Birmingham think you can buy and deceive your way to getting what you want, if you think that money has the final vote, we have a much bigger problem than any disagreement over a childcare program." He slipped out the door and let it fall closed behind him.

Kate turned and walked out the other door, thumping through the basement. I heard her office door close.

Joe looked at me with a tired half-smile and went into his office and closed the door. That was a lot of door closing in less than two minutes.

I picked up the stack of bulletins for the coming Sunday service. I was eager to do something mindless, to put all their arguing out of my head, and think more about what Linda had told me when I met her for coffee the evening before. Her story had kept me awake half the night.

* * *

OVER COFFEE, SHE'D TOLD ME THAT the story of the man buried with the infant he'd killed wasn't the complete picture of what had happened. She said despite the restrooms being the approximate location of where the bones were discovered, she didn't think the brother was the only spirit visiting the church basement.

When the brother was found dead in his room, everyone assumed that the girl's lover was the killer. Within a day, her lover was found dead, hanging from a beam in one of the buildings on the property. It wasn't considered a big deal that a Native American had been murdered, much less unjustly executed. No one was ever prosecuted for the crime.

Linda went on to explain that she believed the unrest from those incidents, the history of murder, the cold-blooded killing of a newborn baby, the hard-heartedness to outsiders, lurked in the roots of the church. She'd had experiences similar to mine, something that came upon her from the outside, a mood so dark and heavy that she knew it wasn't the normal ups and downs of her emotions. It was so dark and so foreign, she felt like she didn't know her own mind.

The refusal to open their arms, or even their doors, to children that might come from outside their community, had stirred up that darkness — the side of the human heart that can so easily fill with hatred. The same thing that made a man kill a child because her father was from a different ethnic group, that hatred and racism were stirred up by Ben, as well as the church members who agreed with him but remained silent. From there, it grabbed tighter, wrapping them up in their own concerns, feeding on itself.

Linda told me all this with round, staring eyes, her lips pulled into a look of sadness. She had no doubt that no matter how mystical and far-fetched it sounded, it was true. She said it scared her. Sometimes she thought of changing her membership to another church, but she'd been here so long, she couldn't bring herself to make the break. She hoped that someday, even if it wasn't in her lifetime, that the grip these beings had on the church would be undone.

The evening before, I hadn't been sure what to make of her theories. I'd experienced other ghosts firsthand, and I didn't doubt their existence. It was easy to see how someone's spirit might linger, especially if a person died suddenly and brutally. The spirit might linger, might not leave the body in a calm and orderly exit, but get caught in some mid realm — an interim place, a rest stop along the highway to the next world — where it wandered aimlessly. All of that's believable to me, especially since I'd observed some of those beings first-hand. But this was too much, despite all those ugly feelings, despite the constant sense that something was touching my skin, wrapping itself around me, trying to pull me into its cocoon, it was difficult to believe there was a group of spirits with a stranglehold on Central Avenue Church.

* * *

THE OFFICE WAS QUIET except for the hum of the lights. It was that kind of quiet that eats at your brain, making the buzz of electricity seem louder, more insistent, like another presence in the room because of the way it demands attention. I picked up the first bulletin, lined up the top right corner of the cover with the inside upper right corner and pressed my finger down the length to make a crisp fold. It was something a child could do as a volunteer project, yet I enjoyed assembling the bulletins because it left my thoughts free to continue wandering.

While these stories and events were running through my head, half of them still not making sense, and my finger was pressing down the crease of sheet after sheet, stacking them and getting them laid in the box for the Sunday service, I made a decision. I wasn't going to know if Linda was crazy, starting to lose her mind, making up stories, putting together things that didn't add up, if I didn't test it out more for myself. There was one sure way I could check into this. I could use the restroom at the back of the basement and see what happened this time. I hadn't wanted to use it since my earlier experience. But now was a good time. Kate and Joe were closed behind their office doors, and I could easily go back there without being disturbed by them. If something really terrifying did happen, they were just a shout away.

I folded the last twenty bulletins, put the box on the counter behind my desk, ready to be carried up to the sanctuary on Sunday morning, and took a deep breath. That's a cliché, I know, but I was anxious. Half of me was scared and half of me felt foolish.

When I stepped onto the hard linoleum floor, the heels of my boots clunked so loudly I thought for sure Kate would pop out of her office to see who had entered the underground hall. My heels clacked in an uneven rhythm across the wide expanse, about fifty feet, all underground, in the near-darkness of that large, never-used room. My left heel thunked like my foot was more solid, and my right heel tapped as if that leg wasn't moving with as much force. The sounds pounded against my head, echoing through the basement, surely letting Kate know someone was passing by.

At the doorway to the alcove that housed the bathrooms, I reached inside and flicked the switch to turn on the light in the women's restroom. I pushed open the women's door. It made a soft whoosh as it settled closed behind me as if it was a vacuum seal and I was shut inside. I wasn't sure what to do. I didn't actually have to use the restroom, I was too keyed up thinking about troubling spirits.

For a good five minutes, I stood there staring into the sink. Then I closed my eyes. Once they were closed, I was afraid of who might burst in on me, but I felt nothing abnormal, just that low-level disquiet that comes from having your eyes closed in a place where you aren't completely comfortable and don't like not having access to all your senses. There was no unpleasant mood, no sensation of anything touching my skin. Nothing but the chilly air of an unused room, the echo of my breath that came from too much tile and porcelain and metal. I thought about turning out the lights and standing in the dark, but that just seemed silly. What was I doing, trying to scare myself? Trying to create some atmosphere that existed only in my imagination?

After a few more seconds, I turned on the faucet and washed my hands, if only to convince myself I hadn't completely wasted my time. I dried them on a paper towel and went back out to the alcove. I thought about entering the men's room, which was where I'd actually had the experience, but the possibility of Joe or Carlo coming upon me made me decide against that. You can't manufacture something that was a unique experience. I turned out the light and thunk-tapped back across the basement.

* * *

I COULDN'T LET IT GO. The next morning I arrived at six-thirty to be a hundred and ten percent sure I beat everyone else into the office. I was ready to try again. Feeling even more foolish at this notion that the darkness wouldn't manifest itself when there were other warm bodies around, but determined to find out if it had all been my own over-reaction to a bad mood and heightened nerves, that I'd fabricated the whole thing, possibly wanting to add drama to my life.

I checked the doorframe for dead moths – there were none. I turned on the lights, locked the main door behind me, dropped my bag on my desk, and headed into the basement area. The sound of my footsteps was louder and more insistent than the day before. The echo stretched further so the tapping and thunking swelled around me, making it sound as if there were three of me marching across the hall. I moved quickly to avoid thinking about how silly and anxious I felt. The hall smelled like modeling clay. From the center of the basement, the alcove was a lightless cave. With each step, I reminded myself that I would not turn on the lights. This vow is what created the assurance that I was stupid, inviting malevolent spirits to brush up against me, if that's what it was.

Why would a person go into an empty building when it was still dark out, hoping to repeat the experience of one of the worst feelings she'd encountered in her life? I suppose I have a bit of craziness in me or at least a compulsion. I'd heard enough strange stories and experienced enough odd things over the past week, I had to try to understand some of what was going on.

Once I was well inside the alcove, I stood in the dark for several minutes feeling more scared and more ridiculous by the moment. It occurred to me that if I did experience another presence or something brushing my skin, I wouldn't know if I was conjuring it up in my own head, a sensation fed by Linda's stories and fierce insistence that something terrible dwelled in this basement.

The darkness in the alcove wasn't the pure blackness where you can't even see the outline of a figure, but pretty close. I could make out the silver handles of the doors and a faint pale square that housed the fluorescent lights overhead.

I was there as the result of the same stubborn and somewhat arrogant attitude I'd demonstrated a few months ago when I was so eager to see the ghost that haunts the Half Moon Bay restaurant. That attitude sent me to the beach early in the morning to meet JD, hoping to see a ghost, and it did the same the previous spring when I had a vigil outside the church waiting to see the ghosts of the young couple that occasionally appeared in the would-be prayer garden. Where had I gotten the idea that I could make ghosts appear on command? It's not that I think I have some special power or some authority over the spirit world. I think it's that I'm so curious I can't stand to let anything just be, and I'm open enough that I guess I can see and know things that other people don't always recognize. It's probably mostly the curiosity. It drives me mad when I don't know what's going on around me. It makes me nosey, and it makes me do things most people wouldn't even think about, much less bother with.

I stood in the darkness and felt nothing but a chill that had settled in through the soles of my boots. My kneecaps were cold and the tips of my fingers had no feeling at all. I put my hands in my coat pockets and waited. I don't know how long I stood like that, feeling stupid and cold and a little bit bored. My kneecaps grew colder and colder until all I could think about was my knees. That, and the hardness of the linoleum-covered concrete floor under my feet. The ache from standing on that rock-solid floor ran all the way up my bones. Soon, my feet hurt so badly I didn't think I could stand there much longer, and I was wondering what the point was anyway, and what I would say if Joe came into the office and wondered why I was standing in the dark. Then my mind kind of settled in and went blank, as if the cold had worked its way up my spine and spread across my skull, hardening it into a block of ice.

Suddenly I started crying, overcome with a sudden realization that the world was a horrible place, and we all hated each other, that the grave was just eating away at us like moths eat their way through a wool blanket until it's full of holes and falls apart in a pile of dust. You would think a girl like me, growing up in a suburban home in the late twentieth century, wouldn't know much about moths eating through wool. How many things do we have that are pure wool anymore? And we have chests lined with cedar and cedar balls and disks and even cedar hangers. We spray everything to death, which is why we hardly see any insects. Or spiders, for that matter. We're busy eradicating crawly things from our lives. That thought made me even more depressed, that we hate the very earth itself.

The tears felt like that sticky stuff, clinging to my face, instead of running down my cheeks like normal tears would. I felt the threads brushing my knuckles, and despite my brain telling me it wasn't possible, I felt them around my legs, through my tights, and even across the back of my neck. I grabbed at my neck, lifting my hair away from my skin, which made no sense because that wasn't the only place I felt it. I hopped from one foot to the other, scratching, trying to get whatever it was to stop creeping across my skin. Then I was sobbing.

A huge part of my mind still thought I was overreacting to normal itchiness, yet at the same time, I was shaking. The room grew colder if that was possible. The feeling of strands of thread snaking along my skin became more intense, almost as if the threads had found their way inside of me, winding through my blood vessels. Tears poured out of my eyes, and finally, it occurred to me that my curiosity was tormenting me and I didn't need to just stand there like a fence post and take it. I turned toward the light switch, swinging my arm blindly, trying to make contact with the wall, but all I touched was air. The wall seemed much further away than I remembered. I lunged, but instead of my shoulder crashing against plaster, I felt nothing. I fell, and my whole left side smacked the floor.

It hurt so badly, I started to cry harder. And still, the crawling continued, winding its way through every part of my body until I thought I would scream. I had an inexplicable desire to pull my hair, anything physical to stop the thoughts seeping through my mind. I didn't understand why I'd misjudged the distance of the wall. I desperately wanted Joe or Kate to arrive, but I knew it was too early.

I writhed on the floor, scratching at myself, rubbing my legs and arms as hard as I could, wanting it to stop more than I'd wanted anything in my life. I wriggled my way toward the wall. Finally, my fingers touched it, and I pulled myself into a sitting position, grabbed my hair and yanked it back and twisted it into a knot, hoping the tugging of my roots would distract me from the other snaking sensations. I stood and felt around for the light switch. At this point, I was so disoriented, I wasn't even sure which wall I was touching.

The tremors in my fingers were impossible to control as I pressed my hands to the wall, rose to a kneeling position, and then stood. I spread my arms along the wall, rubbing plaster, picking up grit on my hands, knowing the dust covered the front of my light green t-shirt and the sleeves of my coat. After what seemed like an hour, but was probably a minute and a half, I found the plastic plate and flipped the switch. The light came on with a buzzing sound, and I saw there were three moths caught between the cover and the bulbs. Each time they fluttered their wings, there was a sizzling sound, and I knew they were burning themselves to death. Despite my earlier squeamishness about them, I felt like crying all over again, not wanting to hear, or see, their violent deaths.

One by one their bodies fell from the bulb to the plastic cover with a soft tap.

Gradually the crawling underneath my skin and feeling of sticky threads across the backs of my hands and neck subsided. I still felt this sense of hatred, not as if it was me feeling that way, but something gripping my heart. It seemed as if whatever had been brushing across me and crawling inside me had found its way to my heart and stuck there. It wasn't really hatred, more of a sense of not wanting anyone to get in my way, to take what belonged to me. Is that hatred? I don't know.

I left the light on in the alcove and walked back across the basement to the main office. It looked absurdly bright. The white metal mini blinds were down, and the overhead lights reflected off them as if it was the backdrop for a film set. I had no idea what to make of the things that had just happened. Part of me wanted to lock up and leave a note for Joe that I'd gone home sick.

I collapsed on my chair, glad of the stiff webbing that supported my back and eased the trembling that had spread from my fingers throughout my whole body. The computer stared at me with its blank screen. I picked up the handset to call Linda. Not that she was some kind of expert, someone who had vast experience with anything like what I'd just gone through, but she would surely be more helpful than Kate or Joe. It crossed my mind to call JD, but I wasn't sure how he'd react, and I didn't need him thinking I was crazy. I wasn't even sure myself if I was losing my mind. Although I was analyzing every thought, so that gave me some comfort that I remained sane.

It was seven-thirty. Too early to call most people. Most people aren't still sleeping at that time, but it's an odd time, when no one wants an intrusion from the phone, when they're still preparing to start the day and don't want an outsider barging into their thoughts.

Then I decided, what the heck. I was scared and alone, still shaky, and I needed help — now. I'd written Linda's number on the desk pad, covered with doodles and phone numbers. I'd drawn a box around her number and shaded it for a 3D effect. She answered on the first ring. When I explained what had happened, making an effort not to include too much overblown, gory detail, she invited me over for coffee and muffins. Since my regular start time was eight-thirty, I left a note on the outer door, just in case the visit took longer than expected.

CHAPTER 9

*L*INDA'S HOUSE AT Fourteen Hundred Bellevue Road was like nothing I'd ever seen in real life. After I passed through iron gates, the driveway curved around a small hill. I wondered if she'd come down and opened the gates or if they always stood ajar like that. The front yard, which was more like a city park than a yard, was filled with flowering shrubs and lots of grass that looked like velvet, even up close. There were two enormous oak trees, some smaller trees, and a fountain with a bench facing it. A latticed arch laced with wisteria shaded the bench.

The bell was a normal button next to a normal door. After that yard, I expected chimes and fifteen-foot doors, but all the drama was behind the door. The entryway was larger than the ground floor of my condo. There was a staircase that swept up and then split into two and reached a landing that ran all along the second floor.

Linda hugged me the minute I stepped inside. As if her hands pressed liquid out of my back, tears rushed into my eyes. She took my hand and walked me into a breakfast room that featured glass walls on two sides. We sat in wicker chairs with flowery cushions and she poured coffee into teacups. Next to the cups was a bright blue ceramic plate with six muffins. Surely she didn't think I was going to eat three muffins, or more. We sat down. I took a muffin and peeled the wrapper off half of it. I took a big bite. It was banana, and for the first time since my terrifying experience in the alcove at the back of the church basement, my fingers stopped shaking.

She didn't sip coffee or take a bite of her muffin the entire time I was telling her what had happened. She didn't even nod. She sat perfectly still, her lips slightly parted, and managed to make me feel as if her whole being was listening to me.

"What do you think is going on?" I said.

"I told you the history. It sounds nutty, but I think the intensity of Ben's beliefs, has stirred up the spirit of that poor girl's brother, and maybe others — the men who killed her lover."

"It feels terrible, but it's hard to believe," I said.

"People are afraid of things that are unfamiliar," said Linda. "We want to protect ourselves or stay away from anyone who isn't like us. A lot of people are uncomfortable with different cultures, different views of the world, of languages and religions they don't understand."

"But Ben isn't a racist or anything like that, he's upset about people breaking the law and putting a strain on our infrastructure."

"That's what he says."

I pushed back my chair and walked to the floor to ceiling windows. They looked out over a backyard more magnificent than the front. There was a huge patio of light brown tile streaked with a creamy beige color. Past the patio was a swimming pool and a wide stretch of grass surrounded by trees. Beyond that, the property looked out over the Santa Clara Valley. Without turning to face Linda, because I couldn't take my eyes off that beautiful yard and the view, I said, "How do you know what he's concerned about? Shouldn't you take what he says at face value? He said it's about enabling people to break the law, and I don't see how that would stir up some spirit of a guy who was so upset about his sister's relation-ship, he killed her child."

"It's the same at the root," said Linda. "The first thing that got Ben riled up was people who don't speak English. He assumes they refuse to learn, but what he doesn't like is the influence of a different culture. Everyone wants to be around people who are similar to them. For some people, for a lot of people, the greater the difference, the more afraid they are."

"Ben doesn't seem like he's afraid of anything."

"Look at it this way – what do you like to do in your free time?"

"Lots of things. Right now I'm taking a pottery class. And Yoga."

"Why not a computer programming class?"

"It doesn't seem interesting."

"So would you rather have coffee with someone who was interested in pottery or computers?"

I laughed. "It's obvious, I'm sure. But I don't see how that's even remotely the same."

Linda was quiet. She folded her hands in her lap and looked down at them. She was obviously waiting for me to draw a connection, but it was too absurd. Of course I'd rather hang out with people who are interested in the same things I am. But that was quite a long ways from hating people who have a different culture.

"What if some people in your pottery class were interested in computers? What if they started talking about computers during class? What if they invited their friends and soon the conversation was more about computers than pottery?"

"That would be upsetting," I said. I could see how I would be afraid the computer geeks were going to take over. I could imagine not wanting any more of them in the class, or suggesting to my friends that we sign up for a different class where they weren't around. I turned and walked back to the table but didn't sit down. I picked up another muffin and nibbled at the top. "I get it," I said. "Still, it's so hard to believe — a haunted basement."

"Lots of things are hard to believe," said Linda. "But look what happened to you."

"If I didn't imagine it."

"You know you didn't imagine it, or you wouldn't have called me."

I laughed softly. I picked up the cup. It was empty. I put it down again and filled it with coffee. "Why am I encountering this ... whatever it is, and Ben isn't? Or Kate? Or Joe?"

Linda shrugged. "Maybe you see it for what it is and the others don't. Ben is blind to any point of view other than his own, and Kate is mostly concerned with starting the childcare program, not specifically with Ben's attitude. She's only interested in how it affects her goal."

"I guess that makes sense. How do you know all this?"

"Like we said before, you and I are sensitive people. You feel things, and you think about it, you try to understand it. When hateful attitudes flare up, I think that spirit, or whatever you want to call it, is aroused."

"So what should I do?"

"You can't *do* anything."

"Why not?"

"What are you going to do? Change how people think?"

"Other places don't have spirits or whatever hanging around."

"How do you know?"

She had a point. I didn't know.

"You know how they say we only use a small part of our brains?"

"I nodded."

Linda sipped her coffee. The muffin still sat on the plate in front of her, only one bite missing. She pushed her fingers through her hair, fiddling with the back of it. She was quiet for so long, I thought she'd forgotten what she was going to say. She seemed to be looking past me, her gray eyes shimmering like polished metal. "I think there are a whole lot of things we aren't aware of. Just like some people who are really smart probably use more of their brains, people like you and I sense more of what's in the atmosphere around us."

"So I'm doomed to have all these creepy feelings? I can't ever use that restroom again? What if it follows me to other places?"

"I don't know. Maybe after the issue with the childcare center is resolved, it will recede."

"I don't see that happening any time soon."

"Things can change suddenly," said Linda.

* * *

I MADE IT BACK to the church office by nine. The parking strip was empty and my sticky note was still on the door. I pulled it off and checked voice mail. I worked through lunch to make up for the lost time, then went outside for a smoke break. The weather had changed since the morning, and it wasn't as cold because the sky was covered with those nice spongy clouds that keep the chill down, rather than that blank white fog that makes you feel like you're inside a deep freeze compartment.

Carlo's truck was in the back parking lot, so after I finished my cigarette, I walked out there and told him about the dead moths trapped in the light fixture in the basement. "I know I shouldn't be asking you again, but I can't stop thinking about them. I'll help get rid of them if you can pop open the cover."

"No problem." He followed me along the path and down the stairs to the church office. "I wish I could figure out where all these damn moths are coming from all of a sudden. They give me the creeps."

"Me too. I wonder why that is? If there were dead butterflies, we'd be sad. Moths are practically the same, but I don't like them. I don't know if it's because they aren't pretty, or their wings are thicker, or they don't fly gracefully like a butterfly."

Carlo opened the door and held it for me. I walked inside but not without glancing first at the doorframe. I wondered how long it would be before I stopped checking it out every time I walked into the office. I noticed he glanced at it too and I smiled to myself.

"They're pests. They eat your clothes. That's why they have a bad reputation," he said.

"So I'm brainwashed not to like them? It's nothing about them physically?"

"There's a legend about moths." He walked through the door into the basement.

He wasn't going to leave me with that lure dangling in front of my curious brain. I followed him into the basement and across to a closet where maintenance supplies were stored. He opened the door and pulled out a stepladder.

"What's the legend?"

"It's Native American. Navajo."

"What's the story?"

"There was a mythological god who was the leader of what were called the butterfly people. This god met the sexual needs of all the butterflies." He looked at me. "I forget the god's name, but that's what the legend says. This god decided to leave for whatever reason, looking for better food, I think."

"Then what?"

Carlo walked across the hall to the alcove. The atmosphere of the room was completely different with him there, almost welcoming.

"Someone left the light on." He set up the ladder and looked at the light fixture.

"That was me. I forgot."

He climbed the ladder and used a screwdriver to pop the cover off the lights. He tipped the cover toward the ground and the dead moths fell out, landing on the linoleum without making a sound. "What's the rest of the legend?"

"Without the god to meet their needs, the people committed incest rather than marry outsiders. That made them "go wild" — you know how they say incest breeds madness after a few generations. They rushed into fires, the same way moths rush at lights or into flames."

"Interesting."

"Why do you say that?" Carlo climbed up another step as he fitted the cover back into the metal bracket.

"It's a strange coincidence. Linda Birmingham ... do you know her?"

"Older lady? Regal looking?"

I laughed. "Yes, she does look regal. That's her. She was also talking to me about people not liking outsiders. She told me about the bones of a man who was found here when they built the church. That he killed his sister's baby."

"I told you I don't believe in ghosts." He crossed himself the same as he had the last time I brought up ghosts.

"I know. It was more about the outsiders, how most of us want to exclude people who are too different from us."

"True enough," said Carlo. He snapped the cover in place and climbed down the ladder. He carried it back to the supply closet.

I stared at the bodies of the moths. I wasn't sure how they'd gotten inside the plastic cover, they must have been very determined, compelled to rush at the light.

Carlo walked back into the alcove carrying a dustpan and a small broom. He swept up the moths, turned out the light, and walked into the basement. I followed him across the room. "Thanks for cleaning them up," I said.

"No worries," said Carlo.

"Where did you hear that story?"

"My wife is part Navajo. She has all kinds of stories. The kids love them."

I could tell by the grin on his face, that he loved them too.

After he left, I decided to allow myself another cigarette break because I wanted to think about all this stuff — outsiders and haunted basements. Usually, I only smoke three cigarettes a day, one in the morning, one mid-day, and one after dinner. I'm going to cut that down to twice a day. Soon.

I finished my cigarette and walked along the path to the sanctuary. I went up the steps and opened one of the doors. I was curious to see how many gifts had been left under the trees. Christmas was eight days away, but the packages would be picked up on the twentieth. The sanctuary was fairly bright because it has a large window behind the altar area. This made the red and white lights on the trees look dim. A woman stood near the white tree where all the gifts had been piled. She was arranging packages that were wrapped in blue paper covered with white angels. Judging by the paper, I guessed she was Jim's fiancé, hopefully leaving gifts that were more interesting than math books. Stickers of Santa faces with glossy red noses were stuck on the paper, which made me think she had a better sense of the recipients. Thinking about gifts made me remember I hadn't come up with a single idea for a gift for JD and our date was on Sunday. I pushed the worry about a gift out of my mind. I walked down the center aisle. "Hi," I said.

She stepped down and turned to look at me. She had thick blonde hair, cut straight along her jawline. Her eyes, nose, and mouth were all small, so despite the sophisticated haircut, she looked young enough to be in high school. She wore black slacks, high heels, and a black jacket with a pink sweater underneath.

"I'm Madison Keith, the church administrative assistant."

"Oh, right. Jim mentioned you. I'm Suzie, Jim Gilchrest's fiancé." She stuck out her hand and I shook it. "I'm just adding to the gifts Jim left. A remote control truck with big tires, so it climbs over small objects. And a bucket and shovel."

I smiled.

She laughed. "Jim told me you didn't think much of his gifts. He said you thought the kids wouldn't like them."

"I don't think I said that."

"Words to that effect."

"Would you be excited to open a math book on Christmas morning?"

She shook her head and her hair swung across her cheeks. "I tied them together with ribbon so the math workbooks go with the truck."

"Good idea," I said.

"Jim's a very serious guy," she said.

I wasn't sure why she thought she had to explain that to me. Maybe she was afraid I thought she was marrying a creep. I wondered what he'd said about me. I didn't think I'd been that negative, but maybe I had.

"He didn't have a great experience with Christmas. In fact, that's kind of why I bought the remote control truck."

"Why's that?"

"Oh, he asked Santa for something like that when he was a kid, but he got socks and shirts instead. It soured him on the whole magic of Christmas idea."

I could see that.

"I'm hoping the truck I bought makes it different for some other little boy."

I nodded. I wondered how Jim felt about that, if it was such a bad memory. Maybe he didn't know what Suzie had wrapped up. "How are your wedding plans coming along?" I said.

Her nose exploded bright red, and her eyes got so watery I wasn't sure she could see my face. She blinked a few times, but it didn't help. She ran the tip of each ring finger under her eyes and managed to keep the tears where they belonged. Her diamond ring sparkled, and for a moment, when she moved her hand away, the diamond blended with the white lights of the tree behind her.

"What's wrong?"

"Jim wants to be conservative with what we spend on the wedding." She rubbed her thumb across the top of her diamond, then lowered her hands. "I don't know why I'm crying. Or talking about him. I don't even know you."

"It's okay. I won't say anything."

She smiled, and a tear slipped out and ran across her cheekbone. "He's got very strict ideas about how life should be."

"I noticed."

"I'm not complaining. I love him. It's just that he decided we won't have wine at our wedding."

"I'm sure it can still be a great party without wine," I said.

"I know. I mentioned the wine, but that's not really the problem. The worst part is too hard to talk about."

I waited. I knew she wanted to tell me.

"He doesn't want my best friend to be one of my attendants."

"Why not?"

"My friend thought not having wine was about the money. Which it is. Her parents have a lot of money. She offered to pay for the wine. Jim got angry because he doesn't like people who think they can control things by throwing money around. He felt like she was trying to take over our wedding. He said it was insulting and now she'll put a negative mood over everything if she's part of it."

"Maybe he'll come around since you aren't getting married until next summer."

"It doesn't matter. It's too late. Now it won't be perfect. Even if he does change his mind, I'll feel uncomfortable and always be worrying what he's thinking. We were going to go shopping for bridesmaid dresses, and now I can't do that until I figure out what to do. I already asked her to be in the wedding."

Tears poured out of her eyes. She coughed and pulled a tissue out of her pocket and blew her nose. "Thanks for listening and letting me cry." She smiled. "I don't know why, but it helps."

Usually, I'm quite aggressive about telling people what I think. At least I've been told I'm aggressive, but that's not really it. Things just bubble out of me, and it seems aggressive because words and opinions and thoughts don't erupt quite so easily from most people, although I have no idea why they're so muzzled. For some reason, words weren't rushing out of me into Suzie's face. I think it's because I wasn't sure what I thought so there was nothing flowing from my brain to my lips. I felt sorry for her, that she was planning to marry someone who appeared to want to control her as much as he thought her friend, or anyone with money for that matter, wanted to control other people. I was surprised that she didn't appear to recognize that. I also was a little surprised she told me. She'd just met me, and less than two minutes later she was crying and telling me what appeared to be the most painful thing in her life right now. People do tend to tell me their secrets, but not always quite so fast after shaking hands. That surprised feeling and the sadness twisted around each other, but there was no definite thought that could leap out of my mouth. And maybe it's just as well.

Then she surprised me even more. She walked closer and wrapped her arms around me. She thanked me for listening, let go of my shoulders, and walked down the aisle and out the door. After she was gone, the door stood open for a moment, then closed slowly until the last few inches when it slammed shut. The sound echoed through the sanctuary, up along the exposed beams, filling the entire space.

* * *

THINGS CAN CHANGE SUDDENLY, Linda had said to me when we were drinking coffee in her breakfast room. What she didn't tell me was her plan to make things change.

I was assembling the newsletters, getting ready to fold them in half, staple the sides together, and stick on the address labels so they'd be ready to take to the post office by noon.

The office door opened and Linda walked in carrying a cardboard box. She set it on my desk, removed the lid, and lifted out a stack of thick white paper. It had that linen texture, very expensive. A color print of a very pregnant Virgin Mary on a donkey, Joseph walking beside her, consumed the top section of the page, followed by two short paragraphs of text.

"I'd like to mail these out with the newsletter," she said.

It wasn't an unusual request. As long as people weren't

promoting things not related to the church – like their children's fundraising or sports events or their local business, they were allowed to include notices for mailing with the newsletter. I was supposed to review the insert, and if I wasn't sure whether it belonged, I had to run it past Joe or Kate.

I picked up the top sheet and read.

About two thousand years ago, a pregnant woman was told there were no vacancies at any of the roadside inns, no place for her to rest, and later, give birth. She and her husband were tired, strangers, a long way from home. Perhaps the inns were full. Perhaps the couple looked too poor and bedraggled and "no room" was simply an excuse.

Does a church have any place in this community if it invites privileged children into its rooms for care and education, but sets policies designed to exclude children who are strangers, a long way from their homeland, too poor? Something to think about this holiday season. – Have a blessed Christmas, Linda Birmingham.

I wasn't sure if Joe was going to like this at all. Kate would be thrilled. I stared at the paper and thought about the directive that I was not supposed to get overly involved in church business. More than anything, I did not want to be standing there holding that piece of paper, trying to decide whether it was *okay*, and worse, decide who I would give it to for the final call. As long as I got them to the post office by noon, the newsletters would arrive in most mailboxes the following day, Monday at the latest. Five days before Christmas. I shivered. The chill was so deep, I looked up to see whether Linda had left the door open. It was closed.

"I know it's controversial," said Linda. "But sometimes you have to be bold, or nothing will ever change."

"It's kind of a guilt trip," I said.

Linda was silent. I looked up and met her eyes. They were the same color as a stormy winter sky. "It's supposed to be."

"Oh."

"Sometimes guilt is a good thing," she said. "The children of illegal immigrants have no choice in the matter. Many of them were born in this country. And we don't know that any undocumented parents would even want to send their children here. All of this is over what *might* happen."

Lots of people create guilt trips, but Linda and Kate were the only people I'd ever heard admit that was their intention. Most people, when pressed, would say, *oh no, I don't want to make anyone feel obligated or bad about it.* Guilt and religious institutions tend to go hand in hand, but Joe usually steered clear of that kind of thing.

The paper was soft in my hands. The weave was so silky it almost felt like a piece of fabric, and it made me want to keep holding it, to admire the sheer beauty of the paper and the rich colors of the shelter-less couple, letting the words blur into the background. I felt Linda watching me, waiting for me to make a decision. The thing was, I already knew my decision. Choosing whether Joe or Kate should give final approval was a decision itself. So I wouldn't ask either one. Why not put it in the newsletter? It was related to the church. Nothing that I could think of fit the criteria more than Linda's very short guilt trip. "No problem," I said.

She didn't smile. It seemed she'd had no doubt what I would do.

I carried the box to the counter where the newsletters were stacked. I opened one and slid a copy of Linda's letter inside.

She put her purse on the chair near Joe's office, lifted the pink hooded cape over her head, and walked to where I stood. She picked up a copy of the notice and placed it inside one of the newsletters.

"I can do it," I said.

"I added more work and you have a deadline. Let me help."

By eleven-thirty, everything was folded, stapled, labeled, and stamped. I put them in a metal box I use for transporting them to the post office. Linda and I walked out together. We said goodbye and got into our cars. It was possible Joe, or even Kate, would throw a few fiery darts my way, but Linda was the one who would catch the real flames.

When I saw Pastor Joe later that day, I didn't mention the insert. There was no point.

CHAPTER 10

*T*HE SUNDAY AFTER the newsletters were mailed, I
drove over to Half Moon Bay at three. That allowed me
to refresh my memory of the highway during daylight. I also
planned to do some shopping. There are lots of unique stores in
Half Moon Bay, and I figured I had a better shot at finding a gift for
JD there than I did at the mall, wandering through an endless array
of chain stores.

I wore a black skirt and black top with spaghetti straps, black
tights, and black high-heeled shoes. It had been at least six months
since I'd worn high heels, so I was a bit wobbly, but I figured by the
time I walked around downtown, I'd be back in stride. Quite a few
females might wear red to a holiday dinner, but I don't like things to
be obvious. Besides, with my dark red hair, most shades of red don't
look that great on me.

By four-thirty, I'd found a hand-thrown pitcher with very
striking red and white glaze. JD knew I was taking a pottery class,
but I'd told him what a battle it was to keep a lump of clay centered
on a wildly spinning wheel and it would be many classes before I'd
have something larger than a three-inch bowl. I made so many
mistakes that my bowls had to be constantly trimmed, and so far, all

of them were about three inches in diameter and very shallow. I was sure he wouldn't mistake the pitcher for something I'd made. Although I knew nothing about his taste or the design of his condo, or much about him, for that matter, I figured it was beautiful enough on its own. You could think of the red as similar to my hair color. He might get that connection or he might not.

I wasn't due at his place until five, so I spent the next twenty minutes walking along Main Street. It was cold, but not unbearable.

The condo was in a complex that had been converted from apartments, but when you're a few blocks from the beach, you aren't as picky about how much space and superficial building design you're getting for your money. I walked slowly along the path to his building, carrying the gift tucked against my side, and a plate of cookies I'd made, all cut into stars and reindeer, sprinkled with green and red sugar crystals.

JD's place was on the second floor. Despite my walking around, I was still somewhat wobbly on my three and a half inch heels when I got to his door. I hadn't thought through the combination of high heels, gift, cookies, and a small splash of hyped of nerves. When he opened the door, all I wanted to do was unload my packages, so I shoved the cookies at him fairly quickly. At the same time, I smelled an amazing aroma of something roasting with sage.

He kissed my lips with a soft, quick movement, which turned the splash of nerves into a deluge. I handed him the gift, relieved to have empty hands so I could focus on looking at him and, of course, his condo. I was very curious.

He wore a charcoal gray shirt and black slacks. The slacks surprised me because he seemed like a beachy, jeans-and-shorts-all-the-time kind of guy. His ponytail was slightly longer than I remembered, but it had only been two weeks, so I wondered if I hadn't noticed when we went out to dinner that it now went past his collar. When I first met him, it barely fit into an elastic band.

The living room had a black leather couch and a matching armchair, a small coffee table with a top made of wine corks, and a large TV with an even larger framed photograph of the Half Moon Bay harbor hung over it. There was a small tree in the corner, decorated with nothing but multi-colored lights. There were three gifts underneath. A wood rocking chair looked as if it had been pushed out of the way to make room for the tree. The dining room was part of the living room, and there was a small table with a fat white candle in the center. The flame reflected of the white plates. The tablecloth and napkins were also white. He didn't offer to show me the rest of the place, which was disappointing, but I decided a guy probably doesn't think of giving house tours.

He took my coat and asked what I wanted to drink.

"What are the choices?"

"Soda, iced tea, or water. Or I could make coffee."

I was cold enough the coffee sounded good, but it wasn't made. There were glasses on the table but no coffee cups, so I felt pointed toward a chilled beverage.

He went into the kitchen and I followed. It was the neatest kitchen I'd ever seen, except maybe mine. There wasn't a single utensil, crumb, or droplet of liquid anywhere on the counter. There was a wooden spoon lying on a ceramic spoon rest and another with its handle poking out of one of the pots on the stove. The sink glistened white.

"Did you order the food from takeout and put it in pots?" I said.

He looked at me, not smiling.

"That was a joke," I said.

"Oh."

I waved my hand at his countertop. "It looks so clean, it's hard to believe someone was cooking in here."

"You don't believe I made dinner for you?"

"There's no mess, no dirty dishes. It's just an expression that it's hard to believe."

"I don't want you to think I'm the kind of person who'd pretend I'm someone I'm not."

Thinking back over what I'd said, I wasn't sure how this had gotten off course so quickly. I wanted him to know I liked him, not think I was accusing him of being a phony. I didn't think that's what I'd said, but he looked so disappointed, I felt like I'd spit the meal out on my plate and told him it disgusted me. If I knew him better, I might squeeze his arm and tell him that wasn't what I'd meant. But all we'd had were those few little kisses, I didn't really want to grab his arm. I'm not a touchy person, and the fact that I thought about it made it the wrong thing to do. Instead, I stood there staring, a little worried that anything I said might make it worse instead of better. Which of course, made it worse. He looked even more upset because I didn't rush to say he wasn't a poser. "I was teasing."

"Oh. Okay." He lifted one of the pot lids and peered inside so I couldn't tell if he was still upset.

After he poked around inside the pots, he went into the living room and clicked on his MP3 player to some jazz. But not the slow, moody type of jazz, something peppier. I was glad he didn't put on holiday music because that would have been too contrived, even though this was a holiday dinner. The jazz was perfect. And it was instrumental, no woman moaning like she'd lost her best friend. Or told the guy she liked he was being fake.

For dinner he served game hens, crispy on the outside, with juicy meat and a stuffing made of cranberries and cornbread. There was wild rice, fresh green beans, fresh carrots with butter and brown sugar, and a green salad. I hadn't eaten a meal this large since our dinner out, but I figured I'd better polish it off to make up for insulting him. He seemed to be over the insult, and during dinner we talked and laughed about our jobs, and lame stuff we did when we were kids, like me collecting loose screws and bent nails and those metal disks you see lying on sidewalks all the time. I always wonder where they come from, and why they seem to be the most prevalent bits of construction material dropped all over the place. When he was a kid, JD collected candy bars. Even though they got stale and decayed, he wouldn't eat them. His mom tried to make him throw them away, but he pitched a fit. Although the topic of ghosts is endlessly fascinating to me, especially now that I've had several experiences with them, I was glad we talked about normal things.

It was hard to concentrate on eating. The table was small, and he was so close to my right elbow, that every time I lifted my water glass, I thought I was going to brush his arm. I wanted to brush against his arm, but I didn't want to do it deliberately and then bump him and spill food on his lap or the white tablecloth. Each time he moved, it seemed as if the air around me changed consistency, my body following every gesture. He chewed slowly but never seemed to be caught with a mouth full of food when he wanted to speak. Watching his jaw work, his lips touch each other, made me forget to chew my own food. I'm surprised I made it through the meal. Although it was really good, so at least I was paying enough attention to taste it.

For dessert, we had chocolate truffles and coffee. They were divine. He wouldn't let me help wash dishes, so we stacked them on the counter.

We sat on the couch, and he gave me a small box wrapped in white paper with red and white satin ribbons. I made him open his gift first, and he seemed to like it. He got up and set it on a table near the armchair.

"That table was waiting for something," he said.

"Why was it empty?"

"The right object hadn't come along yet. Open yours." He sat down, a little closer than before, unless I was imagining it, but I don't think I was. His knee bumped mine and he didn't move it, just left it so close it looked as if we were touching, but there was a very small gap. My fingers wouldn't cooperate when I picked at the ribbons to untie the bow. It took me several tries before I pulled it apart. The ribbons fell across my legs. I tore the paper away and lifted the cover off the white box. Inside was a nest of shredded brown paper and in the center was a rock shaped like an egg, polished and covered with swirls in various shades of blue. It was so beautiful and so unusual I think I let out a small sigh.

"It's not very useful," he said. "But for some reason it made me think of you."

"It's gorgeous. Sometimes things that aren't useful are the best."

"I agree."

I lifted it out and held it in the palm of my hand. It was cold, even though it had all that shredded paper around it, and it was heavy, weighing my hand down until I rested it on my leg. I lifted it up and held it against my cheek. The cool hardness took away the heat in my face that had built up from all that good food and the nearness of JD's legs and hips and his shoulder, much higher than mine, begging me to lean against him.

The paper and ribbons were still on my lap. I cradled the egg and he watched me. After a few minutes, I placed it back in the box and put the lid on it. I set it on the cork-topped table. JD picked up the paper off my lap and crunched it into a white ball. He tossed it in the air and caught it and then set it on the table. He pulled the ribbons, letting them trail across my legs. When the very tips were the last part on my leg, he reversed direction and dragged them back across the other way. I was wearing tights, so I couldn't really feel it, but the red and white against my black tights was mesmerizing. Not to mention the warm pulsing rushing up and down my legs as I watched the slow movement of his hand.

After a few minutes, he lifted the ribbons and dropped them on the coffee table. He moved closer, put both of his arms around me and pulled me against his chest. "This is when I wish I had a fireplace," he said.

"That would be nice."

"But you're warm enough."

His hands felt wonderful on the skin of my shoulders. We sat cuddled up like that, listening to the music and not talking for a while. There was no clock, so I don't know how long we sat there. Eventually, he started kissing me and we stayed busy with that for quite some time, maybe longer than the cuddling part. He didn't do anything more than kiss me and run his hands up and down my arms and back. I was glad. We really didn't know each other that well yet, and I didn't want to get into a big hassle over what we would and wouldn't do. When it happens too soon, it is a hassle and turns into a conversation. Not that I'm all that experienced, with only one boyfriend and all, but I know from other guys I've gone out with. If the timing is off, it's a hassle.

The candle on the table had the flame sinking deep inside by the time I pulled away and told him I should get going home. He didn't argue. We kissed again at the door and then he got my coat and walked me to my car. We kissed again with the car door open, but after a few minutes his arms were like ice since he hadn't brought his coat and we laughed and said *goodnight* and *happy holidays* and *Merry Christmas* and *I'll call you.* JD said that last part.

CHAPTER 11

*O*N MONDAY MORNING, when I was the only one working because Joe and Kate take Mondays off, I arrived to find someone had dropped a box of wrapped gifts near the office door with a note they were for the gift program. I went into the office and made coffee, got the key to the sanctuary, and hoisted the box onto my hip. Considering it was a box full of packages, it was somewhat light, which made it easy to carry up the stairs.

I unlocked and opened the sanctuary doors and stepped into the narthex, a room similar to a lobby but it's called a narthex for some obscure religious reason. It has several doors, one leads to a hallway that runs along the side of the building to the front of the sanctuary, and one leads to a room with a window where parents can take fussy children during the worship services. The music and talking get piped into the room, but the crying children don't get piped out, so everyone is happy. A double set of doors open into the sanctuary itself. I pushed open one of the swinging doors.

Inside, the air was colder than it had been outside. The tree lights were out, of course. The tree with red lights leaned a bit to one side. As I walked down the aisle, my eyes adjusted to the dim

314

light and I saw that the string of red lights was partially pulled off the tree, tugging it to the left.

I took a few more steps, then turned and set the box of gifts on the third pew from the front on the left side. There was a funny feeling running through my legs, a fluttery sensation that made me think first, of course, about moths, since they'd been on my mind. It was like cottony wings brushing against my legs, even though I was wearing jeans and there was no way any type of bug, except maybe a mosquito or a wasp, could make itself felt through denim. There was a hint of that darkness creeping across my heart, although not as strong as it had been in the basement. It drifted away after a moment.

Something was so wrong with that tree. When I took a few steps closer, I saw the lights were pulled taut, down behind the wood stable that housed Mary, Joseph, and the sheep. The stable was about two feet high, so I couldn't see what the lights were caught on. I took a few steps closer. A woman's feet and lower legs were visible under the tree. I hadn't noticed them immediately because the shoes and pants were dark green and blended with the lower branches of the tree. It sounds horrible to say this, but the first thing I thought of was that they were set there like gifts because the shoes were forest green flats with bows made of wide, gold-edged ribbon. I knew those shoes belonged to Linda Birmingham. She'd worn them the day she dropped off the letters.

I took one step up and saw the rest of Linda's body behind the stable. Her face was purple, her eyes bulged, and the string of lights was wrapped around her neck like a vine clinging to a trellis. Then I looked away. When you observe a dead person's face, you want to see peace. You want to know they're resting and they left the earth satisfied. It's not like that when someone is murdered. Or maybe the face says nothing. If the eyes are the windows to the soul, and the soul is gone, maybe the expression has nothing at all to do with their state of mind when they passed.

To the left of the stable was one of the packages for the toy program, separated from the growing mound under the tree with white lights. It was one of the ones Suzie had given. Or at least that's what I noticed first, since it had the blue paper with the white angel cutouts, the wrapping enhanced with Santa stickers. The package had been stabbed, leaving big gouges in the paper. The cellophane that covered the front part of the box containing the toy itself was torn, and the paint on the remote-control truck was scratched.

Even though Linda wasn't stabbed, it was obvious that her murder and the Christmas gift that was the victim of assault were related. I didn't have to be a detective or a psychic to have figured that out. It makes you wonder if the perpetrator even cared whether or not he, or she, might be identified. When you're in a rage, you probably don't think about those things — getting caught, making your feelings obvious. In fact, I suppose you *want* to make your feelings obvious. It might be the first time in your life that you're expressing your unvarnished viewpoint on a particular subject.

I was out the doors of the sanctuary, halfway down the stairs to the office, before I remembered the box of gifts I'd left sitting on the pew, but I figured they could wait. I hoped the police wouldn't take all the gifts for use in some kind of expanded evidence gathering, which would mean lots of kids without a happy Christmas morning. I called 9-1-1, Joe, and Kate, then went back up the stairs to stand in front of the sanctuary. I wanted a cigarette in the worst way but figured I'd better wait.

* * *

THE COPS WERE THE SAME TWO who came when Fred was murdered. This time, Detective Palmer gave the younger cop, Brad Holcomb, more leeway in asking questions. When they talked to us after Fred's death, she'd basically told Officer Holcomb to shut up.

Kate arrived before Joe. She was crying. She immediately informed the detectives that they should direct their investigation at

Ben. She went on about how he thought she and Linda were trying to subvert the democratic process.

It's so easy to assume the person who is the most vocal, who stands out in the group as behaving badly, is the first one who went over the edge and committed murder. But I didn't think it was Ben. He's the kind of guy who says what he thinks. He had no problem telling Kate what he thought, and he wasn't worried about standing in front of a hundred people and expressing a viewpoint that revealed his ugly and cold-hearted thoughts. But he wasn't someone to explode because he was trying to hold all that anger inside.

Officer Holcomb asked me questions about what time I found Linda, whether I moved anything, if I'd heard anything before I went into the sanctuary. At first, I thought he wasn't going to ask me any interesting questions, and I wouldn't get to give my opinion at all. Finally, he circled around to whether there was anyone who didn't like Linda, whether there was anyone who would gain financially from her death.

At least this time I was able to tell the detectives what I thought without bringing any ghosts into it. Of course, Jim wouldn't have known that Suzie told me about the truck he never got. The truck that poisoned him against Christmas. A lot of rage came from spending his whole life letting that disappointment fester inside. I didn't like myself for revealing a story Suzie had mentioned in confidence when she couldn't stop herself from crying to a stranger, but I couldn't hide the truth. And I also knew it was more than that. Linda had done something that upset him even more than that truck. Giving so much money to help people who couldn't afford childcare — another handout that skirted around people like him. Outsiders were getting assistance when she could have helped someone like Jim, a member of the church.

* * *

TWO DAYS LATER I was in the sanctuary. There hadn't been much of an investigation because Jim Gilchrest confessed right away. It was a few days before Christmas, and the day after the second vote for the childcare center. I was boxing up the wrapped gifts under the tree. The organization collecting the toys was making the rounds with a truck, and they had a tight schedule, so consolidating everything made it easier for them. I heard one of the outer doors to the sanctuary open. My hands shook and I almost dropped a heavy box that I imagined was filled with building blocks. Working in that room with a ceiling that goes on forever, and all those rows of empty pews and the altar draped with a white cloth made me feel small and a little bit alone. When Pastor Joe walked through the second set of doors, my hands shook even harder, and I realized I'd been terrified, not knowing who was out there.

Joe walked down the aisle and up the steps before he spoke. "Need some help?"

"Sure. I'm leaving the large ones separate, like this." I put the package of probable building blocks near the steps. I picked up an empty cardboard box and handed it to Joe.

He grabbed several packages all wrapped in candy cane paper and tucked them inside. "Are you okay being here? It's not too soon after finding Linda?"

"No problem at all," I said. What I didn't say was that I'd sort of hoped her spirit would return and let me know she was okay. I kept glancing at the tree with the red lights. Someone had bought a new string and woven it through the branches to fill the place where the police had taken the other string — the murder weapon. I shivered.

"I just got back from visiting Jim Gilchrest."

"How was that?"

"He's very contrite."

Big deal. I couldn't believe Joe would say that, like it mattered. It was too late for Jim to be regretting what he'd done. He could be contrite all he wanted, but it might as well be a puff of smoke.

Joe didn't seem to recognize how pointless Jim's feelings were, because he kept on. "He was really upset about that truck. Not the truck itself, but the pain of realizing the childhood view of Christmas was a myth. It was one of those relatively insignificant events that can eat away at you for a lifetime. He came by the church to get the truck Suzie had given. When he ran into Linda, he yelled at her, demanding to know why she was giving all that money to something that wouldn't make any difference in the long run. He told her it wasn't fair that low-income people got all the help. People with less money qualified for programs to help them buy homes, and someone like him was left to struggle on his own. I guess she told him what she thought of that attitude. He told her to stop talking. She didn't. She told him his thoughts were ugly. He grabbed the lights and wrapped them around her neck and ... he couldn't stop ...pulling ..." Joe straightened and dropped a small package into the box. He closed his eyes. "I never imagined I'd have to listen to a man tell me things like that."

I was supposed to be sympathetic. I tried to think about what Joe was feeling, but there was nothing there. I'm sure it was hard listening to gruesome details like that, but why did he even listen? My eyes teared up, thinking of Linda.

"Jim said he couldn't stop himself. He said he felt a hatred he'd never experienced. It was irrational, he looked at Linda and all he could think of was that she wanted to help children and families who didn't even attend the church."

As Joe talked, I couldn't help wondering whether Jim experienced the same dark feelings that had come over me. Could that really happen? I didn't know and I didn't want to know. All that mattered was that Linda was dead. For half a minute I wanted to smack Joe's face, but then the feeling went away, and all I wanted was for him to stop telling me about Jim.

I grabbed one of the cardboard boxes. "I'm going to set these in the narthex so they don't have to make a bunch of trips back and forth." I walked down the steps and along the aisle as fast as I could, glad that my arms ached under the weight of the box. I hoped lots of kids grinned and squealed when they opened their packages. I hoped their parents forgot to be afraid for a few minutes while they watched their children's faces.

* * *

THE MEMBERS OF CENTRAL AVENUE CHURCH voted 267 to zero, with one abstention, to open a childcare center.

The day before Christmas, I found four dead moths. I scooped them up and buried them in the church garden. You never know. I didn't use the restroom in the basement, and I didn't have any more frightening experiences, but in some ways that was more unnerving, because I felt the possibility hanging out there.

* * *

I ATE CHRISTMAS DINNER with Joe and Cindee and their daughters. JD went to visit his parents in Sacramento, but he called me early that morning and we talked for an hour. We made plans for New Year's Day. A bartender pretty much has to work on New Year's Eve, and I thought New Year's Day sounded more fun anyway. It was something different than what everyone else does — partying to say goodbye to the old year. We'd be saying hello to a new year rather than going crazy over what was already finished. We decided to walk across the Golden Gate Bridge, no matter what the weather was like. It turned out to be perfect.

CATHRYN'S BIO

Cathryn is the author of sixteen psychological thrillers and the ALEXANDRA MALLORY series, featuring a sociopath you can't help but love. Readers have called the series "addictive".

The things that torment us in real life—obsession and revenge, guilt and envy and longing—are endlessly fascinating in fiction and she never grows tired of writing stories about characters struggling to overcome the worst.

Cathryn also writes ghost stories because who knows what lies beyond our senses—The Haunted Ship Trilogy and the Madison Keith series of novellas.

When she's not writing, she's usually reading, walking on the beach, or playing golf, going way out of her way to avoid hitting her ball in the sand or the water. She lives on the Central California Coast with her husband and her cat, Cleopatra.

You can get in touch with her by email, find her social media links, or sign up for her monthly newsletter at cathryngrant.-com/ contact. As a thank you for signing up, you'll receive a free short story about Alexandra Mallory.